Rogue Target

Mark Sennen was born in Surrey, but spent his formative years in rural Shropshire where he learnt to drive tractors and worm sheep. He has been a reluctant farmer, an average drummer, a failed Ph.D. student and a pretty good programmer. He lives with his wife, two children and a rather large dog, beside a muddy creek in deepest South Devon. He is the author of the DI Charlotte Savage series, plus the standalone thriller *The Sum Of All Sins*.

Also by Mark Sennen

Holm & da Silva Thrillers

The Sanction
Rogue Target

ROGUE TARGET

MARK SENNEN

CANELO

First published in the the United Kingdom in 2020 by Canelo

This edition published in the United Kingdom in 2021 by

Canelo
31 Helen Road
Oxford OX2 0DF
United Kingdom

A CIP catalogue record for this book is available from the British Library.

Print ISBN 978 1 80032 221 9
Ebook ISBN 978 1 78863 990 3

Look for more great books at www.canelo.co

Printed and bound in Great Britain by Clays Ltd, Elcograf S.p.A.

Part One

Prologue

The flight is the 8.25 service from London Heathrow to New York Newark Liberty International. The aircraft is a Boeing 787-9. It has a length of 62.8 metres, and a wingspan of 60 metres. The maximum take-off weight is 247 tonnes. The range is 15,400 kilometres, and this particular plane is configured for four classes and seats two hundred and sixteen passengers. The call sign of the aircraft is Speedbird 117 and the flight is due to arrive at Newark at 11.05 local time.

Today's pilot is Captain Brian Hammond. The co-pilot is Senior Flight Officer Jermain Phillips. There are ten other crew and two hundred and five passengers. Hammond has fifteen years' experience commercial flying, all of which has been with British Airways. Before that he was a military transport pilot for the RAF and saw action in the Iraq War. His passion is flying and he owns a Pitts Special aerobatic biplane, regularly entertaining crowds at air displays. He's married with two children – a boy and a girl – and lives in a small village near the town of Guildford.

Pushback has been delayed by fifteen minutes, but now the ground crew are moving the plane away from the gate.

Hammond keys the radio and speaks.

'Heathrow Tower, Speedbird one one seven heavy, ready for departure.'

A moment later the tower responds.

'Speedbird one one seven heavy, hello, line up and wait runway two seven left.'

'Line up and wait runway two seven left, Speedbird one one seven.'

After the pushback has been completed, they move down the taxiway, Hammond running through the checklist, Phillips responding to each item. When that's complete, Hammond leans back in his seat and turns to Phillips. 'Do much at the weekend?'

The question is chit-chat to pass the few minutes it will take to get to the wait position. Nothing complicated or distracting. Phillips had a barbecue, it turns out. A dozen guests. A bouncy castle hired for the kids. Alcohol-free lager for Phillips. Hammond listens as the aircraft rolls forward. He turns on to two seven left, and eases off the power. The chit-chat stops. Time to focus. They wait in silence for a few seconds until the tower comes back to them.

'Speedbird one one seven, cleared for take-off two seven left, wind two four one degrees fifteen knots.'

'Speedbird one one seven, cleared for take-off, runway two seven left.' Hammond flicks a couple of switches on the dash and pushes the throttles forward. Phillips casts a glance at the instruments and then smiles as Hammond utters the catchphrase he is known for across the fleet: 'New York, ready or not, here we come.'

Aside from the destination, the words never vary, and if they did it would be bad luck. An omen such as seafarers used to fear: a woman on board, mention of rabbits, or setting sail on a Friday.

As the plane gathers speed, Phillips scans the array of screens in front of him. 'One hundred knots,' he says.

'Check.'

The aircraft judders as the huge mass of aluminium and aviation fuel rolls down the runway.

Phillips glances at the screens again. The airspeed indicates 135 knots and half a second later he speaks.

'Rotate,' he says.

Hammond pulls back on the wheel. The nose lifts and the juddering stops as the aircraft becomes airborne. The ground drops away.

'Positive climb,' calls Phillips and a few seconds later they pass the end of the runway, fields and villages below, the gleam of the sun on the surface of a huge reservoir ahead.

Unbeknown to Hammond or Phillips or any of the other two hundred and fifteen people on board, the seven hours forty minutes flight time they were expecting is about to be cut drastically short. A shoulder-launched surface-to-air missile has just been fired from the garden of a small dilapidated bungalow a couple of miles to the west of the airport. The aircraft's speed is now 153 knots. If Hammond and Phillips were aware of the missile, they could try to take evading action, but they can't see the laser cross hatch painted on the underside of the aircraft, and even if they could it's unlikely they could do much to avoid it.

'Gear up,' Hammond says and Phillips flicks a switch. Hammond opens his mouth to say something else, but before he can speak the whole aircraft rocks violently as the missile hits the rear of the fuselage and explodes.

'What the fuck!' Phillips' reaction is to heave himself round and peer through the side window. 'Engine?'

The possibility of a catastrophic turbine blade failure has occurred to Hammond but he can see the displays for both engines. In a microsecond he can tell they're functioning correctly.

'No rudder,' he says. His years of experience as a display pilot have given him a sixth sense of what an aircraft is doing, even when that aircraft is two hundred tonnes of lumbering Boeing. 'Nothing.'

The aircraft is slewing sideways, like a bicycle with the rear brake jammed on. Lateral control is non-existent.

'Christ, Brian!' It's Kelly Peterson, the chief steward. She's opened the cockpit door and now stands braced in the doorway. She makes a gesture to the back of the plane. 'It's gone.'

She doesn't need to say anything else. Hammond knows that somehow part of the tail is missing. In half a second he considers the possibilities. An airframe failure? Unlikely. The impact of a large commercial drone or a light aircraft? Possible. An altitude-dependent timer on a bomb? Could well be. A scenario involving a man-portable air-defence system – a MANPADS – doesn't cross his mind, because – even though he's served in the military – why should it? Who the hell could get hold of a surface-to-air missile?

The aircraft feels skittish now and although they're gaining altitude, they're losing directional stability. The plane has adopted a left-wing-down attitude and is banking round to the south in a huge graceful curve. Hammond lets the aircraft go, not wanting to disturb the airflow. Something flashes silver through the port window, the sun reflecting off water, and Hammond knows he has an awful decision to make.

'We're going down there,' he shouts as he gestures out through the cockpit window. 'Queen Mary.'

Queen Mary Reservoir lies three miles south of Heathrow. In the few moments he's had, it's the only option Hammond can think of, the only option worth considering. Without the tail, a return to the airport will be next to impossible and that's without further structural damage. To try and crash-land anywhere else would be catastrophic.

'My God!' Phillips's voice betrays a mixture of terror, shock and realisation.

'Yes.' Hammond eases the throttles forward. The last thing they want now is any more height. He makes a quip, as much for his benefit as anyone else's. 'We ain't going to New York but we need to find our very own Hudson.'

He says no more. Doesn't need to. Every airline pilot on the planet knows about US Airways flight 1549 and its captain, Chesley Sullenberger. Every pilot has studied what happened. Every pilot has prayed that they never need to execute such a landing.

'Mayday, mayday, mayday.' Phillips is on the radio. 'This is Speedbird one one seven.'

Hammond blocks out the distress call. In his head he tries to visualise the curving arc which will take the aircraft to the reservoir, tries to sense the glide path. He has an advantage over flight 1549 in that he has functioning engines, but that has to be countered by the fact he has little or no rudder control. He pushes the throttles forward and now the engines are doing no more than spinning over. As the engine noise subsides, Hammond becomes aware of another sound: screaming from the passengers. He shuts the screams from his mind. He needs to focus.

'Call the altitude,' he says and Phillips begins to recite the numbers.

'Seven hundred. Six fifty. Six hundred.'

The aircraft is still banking left, but it's slicing lower too. Hammond's fingertips are barely touching the controls. He wants the plane to continue turning until the reservoir is lined up. He glances through the side window to check his positioning and sees houses below. There's a garden with a trampoline. A girl on a swing. She's wearing pink trousers and a red jumper and Hammond reckons she can't be more than three or four years old. He remembers his own daughter at that age, a memory that now seems a lifetime ago. In the next-door driveway a man lies beneath a classic car. It's a green TR4 and is identical to the one his father used to own. Everything is so close, so detailed, the colours vivid.

The glance takes half a second, no more, and now Heathrow itself is to the left. They're parallel to the airport and Queen Mary Reservoir is ahead. Hammond needs to stop the turn. The rudder is useless so he needs to execute the manoeuvre using the ailerons alone. As he lowers the right wing the plane begins to yaw to the left. Without the rudder there's no way to compensate using the flight surfaces, but Hammond pushes the throttles on the left engine forward. Immediately the attitude corrects and they're lined up.

'Two hundred. One fifty.'

They're coming down too fast, but all Hammond can do is feed in a little more power and raise the nose. The plane yaws once more and he makes another micro adjustment to the throttle.

'One hundred. Fifty.'

The reservoir is a sheet of glass ahead and below. A mirror reflecting Hammond's life back at him. Lovers and friends and his wife and children. Things he's done. Things he wishes he had done. Mostly a jumble of words flashing before him, words he wishes he'd said to his wife and kids before he left home this morning. But it's too late for regrets now. Too late for anything much beyond a prayer. A wing and a prayer.

'Twenty—'

And then the aircraft slams into the water.

Chapter 1

Four weeks earlier

Rebecca da Silva woke in the dark to the smell of an exotic fragrance carried on stifling, humid air. She flinched, alert for the sound of gunfire or a shout from her commanding officer, but there was nothing. Her mind raced along with her heart. Perhaps the insurgents were already inside the compound, the sentries killed before they'd had the chance to raise the alarm, the rest of her squad murdered as they slept. She reached for the pistol she always kept close to hand, groping by the side of the bed and trying to find the comfort of cold metal. With the pistol in her hand she'd feel a lot safer and at least they wouldn't be able to take her alive.

The soft bed yielded as she rolled over and spilled the light sheet from her body, but instead of touching the gun, her fingertips brushed thick carpet.

Not Afghanistan, she thought.

Her heartbeat slowed. For a moment she'd been unsure where she was, and it was as if she'd been transported back in time and space. She'd served two tours in Afghanistan as a sniper, part of a specialist team helping mop up insurgents long after the war had supposedly finished. Whether out in the wilds or in the relative safety of the base, sleep had rarely been restful, and being woken in the night always signalled trouble.

She relaxed, stretched and turned on the bed. There was an expanse of glass, a door left open to allow access to a balcony. Through the opening, neon signs flashed and a blaze of lights cast a soft glow on the underside of low rain clouds. Now fully awake, she remembered.

Bangkok.

She groped to the side of the bed where her phone sat on a low table. Blinked at the glare. Noted the time. Three a.m.

She sat up, groggy and a little disoriented. She tried to run the times in her head. She'd taken off from Heathrow at a little after noon and, after a twelve-hour flight, landed at Suvarnabhumi International at six in the morning local time. Disembarkation and the journey from the airport to the hotel had taken the best part of two hours. A freshen-up and then a trip downtown, before finally returning to the hotel and crashing at a little after four in the afternoon.

Now there was the best part of eleven hours to kill before a connecting flight onwards to Manila. Her companion on the trip, Richard Smith, better known to friends and colleagues as Itchy on account of his inability to keep still, was in a room next door. Itchy had been Silva's spotter when she'd been in Afghanistan. He was older than her by five years and had a level head on his shoulders. Nothing seemed to fluster him, the only manifestation that he was under pressure his constant movement. Still, he'd never had a problem sleeping, even when they'd been deep in enemy territory. While Silva kept watch, he'd grab the Zs, but when he was on guard duty, she could never settle for more than a handful of snatched minutes. 'You think too much,' he'd say, and Silva knew he was right. Thinking was a curse, especially at three in the morning.

Knowing she wouldn't get back to sleep, she swung her legs over the edge of the bed and padded across to the balcony doors. The view across the night-time cityscape of Bangkok was awesome. A myriad of lights sparkled on wet streets, tower blocks pushing into low cloud. It was a pity they were only here for a few more hours.

Her East Asian adventure had kicked off three weeks earlier. She'd been staying at her father's place west of London, a big rambling manse set in a couple of acres of grounds. Increasingly he needed help with its upkeep, but accepted her assistance begrudgingly, almost as if he was doing her a favour. Once there she stripped and painted woodwork, replaced broken roof slates and tidied the garden. Order was important to her father, decay a sign of social breakdown. He was ex-military himself and had seen action back in the nineties in the Gulf War. Discipline, he explained to her, was what had kept him alive back then, and leaving the military didn't mean abandoning order. Maintaining a regimented life was his attempt to hold back the tide, and keeping the house and garden looking good was a proxy for the gradual decline of his ageing body.

It had all been too much for her mother. She'd left him back when Silva had been a kid, taking her only child with her. Her mother was of Portuguese extraction, evidenced in Silva's dark hair and light tan, and Silva often wondered if it had been a clash of cultures that caused the acrimonious split. That or her father's stubborn nature. She'd grown up with him as a distant authoritarian figure she'd visited on occasional weekends, never quite under-standing how or why her parents had got together. Her father had mellowed recently, especially in the months since her mother had died, his own mortality increasingly on his mind. Helping him out was Silva's way of compensating for the absence of her mother.

She'd been up to her thighs in mud at the shallow silted-up end of the small lake when a shout from her father alerted her to the arrival of a couple of guests. She looked up to see one of her father's friends – Matthew Fairchild – along with an attractive Chinese woman, standing on the terrace. Her father was fussing them into chairs at a table, and beckoning Silva over.

'Rebecca, look who's dropped by!' Her father moved to the French windows, about to disappear inside. 'Come over and say hello while I make some tea.'

Silva shook her head in disbelief. Fairchild lived a good fifty miles away and wouldn't have simply 'dropped by'. This was likely another one of her father's regular attempts to find her some legitimate employment. Only Fairchild wasn't exactly legitimate. He ran a global security consultancy – a euphemism for the hiring out of mercenaries – and had tricked Silva into working for MI5 on a kill mission. Silva, not realising what she'd been getting into, had taken the job because it had meant a chance to avenge her mother's death. The botched operation had involved the attempted assassination of a US presidential candidate, a run-in with arms smugglers, and an encounter with an arch terrorist. It had led to an arson attack on her father's house and Silva being captured and interrogated by rogue CIA agents. She'd survived, narrowly, and afterwards received glowing praise from the head of MI5. She'd also been offered a job with MI5's highly secretive Special Accounts division, a black ops unit that worked far outside what was legal. Had she been treated differently, she might have accepted, but the head of the unit – Simeon Weiss – had played her at every turn. She decided working for someone for whom deception was a way of life wasn't for her, so she turned down the offer. Since Fairchild was intimately connected with the security services and with Weiss, she was highly suspicious of the reason for his visit.

She heaved herself out of the lake and stood on the bankside. She was plastered with mud and made a vain attempt to splash some lake water on her legs and arms to wash some of the muck away. That done, she strode up towards the house.

'Rebecca!' Fairchild stood. 'It's been a long time.'

Not long enough, Silva thought as Fairchild offered his hand.

Fairchild was rich, but you wouldn't have guessed from the way he dressed. Today he wore his usual off-white suit with a white shirt and no tie. He was in his mid-sixties and looked and acted like some colonial relic from a bygone era. That he was one of her father's closest friends was thus no surprise.

The woman also rose. She was in her late twenties and wore business attire consisting of a sharp black jacket, matching short skirt and an ice-white blouse. She wasn't Chinese as Silva had first thought, more likely Korean; in fact she could have doubled as a member of a K-pop group.

'This is Park Chin-Sun, Rebecca,' Fairchild said.

'Pleased to meet you,' Chin-Sun said. She made a small bow and held out her hand. If there was an accent it was American if anything. 'Mr Fairchild has told me a lot about you.'

'Has he?' As Silva shook hands she was aware of her dishevelled appearance in contrast to Chin-Sun's. The mud on her body, pondweed in her hair, her wet and filthy clothes. Chin-Sun was immaculate. Silva wondered whether she was a new girlfriend Fairchild had acquired on his travels, but then dismissed the thought. The woman was way out of Fairchild's league.

'Yes. Your reputation precedes you and I have heard you are passionate and honourable. That's why I am here today.'

So, this was either one of Fairchild's mad schemes or some devious attempt by her father to find her a job.

'Right.' Silva pulled out a chair and, aware of the fact that the pieces of glutinous mud stuck to her body had a pungent odour, she positioned the chair a few strides from the table. She sat down. 'We should wait for my father, I'm sure he'll be out with the tea in a minute.'

'This has nothing to do with Kenneth,' Fairchild said. 'Ms Park came to see you. She flew into the UK this morning especially.'

'From where?' Silva said, trying not to appear rude but wanting some background.

'The Philippines,' Chin-Sun said. 'Fourteen hours non-stop.'

Silva felt a smidgen of panic rise. Nobody flew fourteen hours to make a social visit.

'You should have warned me.' Silva stared at Fairchild for a moment. 'At least then I'd have had a chance to clean myself up.'

'I'm sorry,' Chin-Sun said. 'Matthew told me—'

'The truth is,' Fairchild butted in, 'if I had warned you, you'd have told me where to get off. But, as you'll see shortly, Ms Park has a very lucrative offer for you. Why don't you hear her out?'

At that point, if Chin-Sun hadn't been so formal and polite, Silva would have told her and Fairchild to fuck off. Then she'd have gone inside and berated her father, before getting on her motorbike and leaving him to do his own pond clearing. Instead, faced with Chin-Sun's innocent smile, she caved in.

'OK then,' she said, thinking this was going to end in trouble. 'Tell me.'

–

Over the past few months he has been cursed with a recurring dream involving the destruction of a large civilian aircraft. A Boeing or an Airbus. Stuffed with passengers. Two hundred or more. The dream always starts with the plane floating above the clouds, everything peaceful and serene. A rising sun paints the sky gold, the aircraft moving silently towards an empty horizon. But then there's a vapour trail from something curving in the air, a missile banking hard to intercept the plane. He wills the pilot to take some sort of evasive action, but the aircraft carries on in a straight line. He counts down the seconds to impact. Three. Two. One.

The missile hits the fuselage and an orange fireball bursts out. Just like a special effect in a movie, he thinks. CGI. Not real. Except now he can see the body of the plane breaking in half, the tail falling away while the rest of it continues to glide on. Until it doesn't. The nose begins to tilt up and the plane stalls. Little dots of something tumble from the broken fuselage. Spinning and spiralling in the air. Passengers. All of a sudden he's no longer a distant observer but is one of them, up there in the sky, his arms flailing in a futile attempt to fly as the ground rushes up to meet him.

'No!'

Stephen Holm lunged in the darkness, a sense of vertigo deep in his stomach as he sat up with a start. He blinked, seeing the pre-dawn halo flare round the curtains at the window. For a second he waved his hands in front of him, grasping for something to hold on to. Then he took a breath and let the tension in his body subside.

'Christ.' He lowered his hands and felt the softness of the duvet. He pushed it away and swung his legs over the edge of the bed. No way he was going to get back to sleep now. He got up and went to the window. Drew back the curtains and stared at the blank sky that hung above the houses on the other side of the street. It wasn't blank like a canvas awaiting brush strokes, rather it was blank like a broken TV screen. Lifeless. Beyond repair. He refused to expand the metaphor to encompass his own life. Things weren't that bad. Not yet.

In the kitchen he scooped some instant coffee from a jar into a cup. Boiled the kettle. His heart rate slowed until it almost matched the ticking of the clock above the sink. He noted the time. Five thirty. This wasn't the first occasion the nightmare had woken him. Not by a long way. The dream had been plaguing him for six months. The details sometimes differed in that the aircraft and airline varied, as did the impact point of the missile. What never changed was the end result. The plane fracturing in two and the passengers raining from the sky. Waking in a jolt with a cold sweat. Knowing that someday soon the dream was going to come true.

–

Stephen Holm was a senior analyst with the Security Service, the intelligence organisation better known as

MI5, even though it hadn't officially been called that since 1931. He'd been with the Security Service for ten years or so, and before that was a police officer on the Met, beginning as a beat bobby and then serving in various counter-terrorism roles. His whole life had been spent trying to stop evil people doing evil things. At the start of his career that had been the IRA and the UDA or the occasional left-wing or right-wing nutter. Later, post 9/11, the enemy had been Islamist extremists. Some people tried to equate terrorism with a war, but Holm always thought that sort of analysis was wrong. A war, at some point, ended. There were winners and losers, the spoils were divided, and history was written. There was no end to the struggle against terrorism, and as for winners, well, there weren't any, only losers.

The losers in his dream were the passengers falling from the sky, the people the burning wreckage crashed down on. The fact the event hadn't happened yet didn't provide any comfort though. It was only a matter of time, and whichever way he played the premonition through in his mind the end result was the same. When it *did* occur it would be his fault.

For a number of years Holm had been after a terrorist known only by the alias Taher. Holm had pursued the man with a dogged determination that had led to him being sidelined within the MI5 hierarchy. However, in the aftermath of an atrocity in Tunisia that had targeted foreign tourists, Holm had nearly caught Taher. During his investigations into the attack he'd uncovered a smuggling operation that had involved a Saudi prince and members of a wealthy American family who ran a huge American armaments company. In return for a lucrative arms contract with the Saudis, a consignment of surface-to-air missiles had been shipped from the UK down to Italy and across the Mediterranean to Tunisia. There they'd been distributed to various terrorist groups in North Africa. Holm had deliberately let the missiles slip through his fingers so he might have a chance to capture Taher. Unfortunately the plan had failed and Taher had got away.

Coffee made, Holm lowered himself into a chair, feeling every bit of his sixty years. The milestone birthday had arrived unexpectedly a couple of weeks ago. Sneaked up from behind and then slapped him in the face, laughing.

There you go, mate. Nearly over. All done.

Christ. Was that *it*?

He played the words back. Wherever he put the inflection didn't seem to make a whole lot of difference. *Was* that it? Was *that* it? Three score years and ten didn't leave a whole lot of time left. He rubbed his eyes, thinking on something his young colleague, Farakh Javed, had said on his birthday as he'd handed over a card.

'You got a bucket list?' Javed had asked as Holm had stared down at the card. The picture showed three naked men with well-oiled bodies. They were intertwined in a way Holm would have thought impossible. The caption was 'Try anything once twice'. Holm had winced as Javed had continued to press. 'Well?'

'No,' Holm said. He nodded at the card. 'And if I did, that wouldn't be on it.'

'Spoilsport.' Javed grinned. Paused for a moment. 'Have you heard of a spit roast?'

'Only in the context of a pub barbecue. Beyond that I don't think I want to know.'

'Your loss.'

Javed was Asian, Muslim and gay, three characteristics the young man had explained to Holm didn't always sit easily alongside each other. Since the Asian part was unalterable, and the gay bit non-negotiable, it was on the religious side where compromises had to be made.

'Part time,' Javed had said. 'Which I guess is about the same as most Christians, right?'

Holm hadn't answered. He'd long ago given up believing in anything. As for a bucket list, well that would have to wait until his retirement.

He sipped the coffee, the caffeine banishing any tiredness and pushing the dream about the aircraft to the back of his mind. A piece of toast and a shower and a shave later, and his body felt a little better too. Not fighting fit, but certainly not ready for a Zimmer frame just yet.

By the time he was ready to leave his flat for work his thoughts had moved on to the day's business. Fiona Huxtable, the director general of MI5, was conducting a six-month review into the hunt for Taher. After Holm's near success in Tunisia, she'd been more than willing to throw everything at the operation, but recently her patience had shown signs of being depleted. Other issues were beginning to take priority and Holm feared that trying to catch Taher would once again be put on the back burner.

He picked up the newspaper from the mat and opened the front door. *The Times* was leading on a spate of stabbings in a northern city. He wondered if the metropolitan elite would be much interested. Not on their list of priorities. As he folded the paper and headed down the street towards the station he wondered if his own priorities were mixed up too. He'd focused on his job to the exclusion of everything else. He'd split with his wife, rarely saw his daughters, and had few friends. When he retired, what would he have to show for all the effort he'd put in?

If I don't catch Taher, he thought, I'll have bugger all, that's what.

Chapter 2

Getting into trouble was, as her on-and-off boyfriend, Sean, often told her, something Silva excelled at. Sean worked for the CIA and was currently deployed in the Sahel region of West Africa where warring jihadist groups were causing havoc in Mali, Niger and Burkina Faso. When they'd last met up a month ago in London, Sean on a flying visit to the US embassy, he'd asked her what she'd been up to. Her response of 'not a lot' was met with a smile and a wink.

'That's good, Becs. Try and keep it that way, huh?'

'Sure,' Silva said. 'Dull is my new middle name. I just hope that's good enough for you.'

'Beats me worrying and it's perfectly fine for now.'

'On the other hand I'm supposed to put up with you risking your neck in the world's trouble spots, right?'

'Most of the time I sit behind a desk and write reports. If the air con breaks down it can be a little unpleasant but that's about as bad as it gets.'

Silva knew the situation in West Africa was highly volatile, but Sean always underplayed what he did out in the field. When they parted she made him promise to be extra careful.

'You too,' he'd said.

Back then dull and careful was the full extent of her life. She was living on her tiny boat moored in Plymouth, trying to survive with little to no income, and occasionally visiting her dad. He'd offered to help her out, but she knew the money would have been conditional in some way. She preferred to scrape by, finding the odd piece of work here and there. At Christmas she'd temporarily returned to her old job with the Post Office, but delivering letters again soon became boring. She found other jobs cleaning yachts, gardening or helping Itchy with whatever mad scheme he'd launched himself into.

Now, as she stood at the window and looked across Bangkok, she wondered what Sean would say if he knew what she was up to. Luckily, when he was on station, they didn't have much in the way of contact so she wouldn't have to lie. Not that there was anything dodgy to lie about anyway.

She thought back to the meeting at her father's place with Fairchild and Chin-Sun. As Chin-Sun had made another gracious half-bow, a picture of integrity and virtue, Silva had decided she may as well listen to what the young woman had to say.

'I work for Mr Jun Tan,' Chin-Sun said. 'Mr Tan is a businessman with a residence in the Philippines and he wishes to avail himself of your services. I have been given permission to authorise whatever payment it takes to secure you.'

'Hold on.' Silva raised her hands. 'I'm sure Matthew's told you I'm not for hire as a mercenary.'

'Oh yes. Mr Tan understands that and respects you very much. You were a top sniper in the army, right?'

Silva winced. Her last tour in Afghanistan had ended in ignominy after she'd shot a young boy she'd thought was an insurgent. She'd been court-martialled, found guilty of manslaughter and sentenced to twelve months in a military prison. Until then, yes, she'd been one of the army's best snipers, allowed time off for competitive shooting and even winning a medal at the Olympics. The death of the boy had ended all that.

Over and over she'd told herself it had been a tragic mistake, but no matter how many times she repeated the mantra, she was left with the feeling that she alone was to blame. Whatever the mitigating circumstances – and there were many – she was the one who'd pulled the trigger and ended the boy's life. If she hadn't taken the shot he wouldn't be dead, she'd still be in the army, still be the poster girl, and still have a career and prospects. Instead she was a disgrace.

'I was a sniper,' Silva said. 'But Matthew should have made it clear that the military part of my life is history now.'

'Of course, but while Mr Tan would like to use your skills with a rifle, he doesn't expect you to shoot anybody. He wants to hire you as part of the security detail for a party he's holding on his island home.'

'You're contradicting yourself.' Silva tried to be as polite as possible, but was rapidly losing patience. 'You say I don't have to shoot anybody, but then say he wants my sniping skills.'

'Don't worry, Mr Tan wants to use your specialised skills in a rather innovative way. He is very concerned about privacy, do you see? As he is a high-profile businessman there will be a lot of media interest in the party. Pictures of Mr Tan and his family or of the various guests will be at a premium.'

'I can't go around shooting reporters,' Silva said. 'Even if I wanted to.'

'Of course not,' Chin-Sun said. 'And you won't be asked to, but these days there are ways of taking pictures which don't require a photographer to be present.'

For a moment Silva didn't understand, but then she had it. 'Drones.'

'Yes!' Chin-Sun clapped her hands together in a gesture Silva thought more appropriate for a five-year-old. 'The celebrity magazines will do anything to get pictures of the party and that includes piloting drones to overfly Mr Tan's property. Your job will be to shoot them down.'

'Is that legal? Is it even safe?'

'In this case, yes. The party will take place on Mr Tan's private island. He has obtained special dispensation from the local chief of police to take action against any drone approaching within one kilometre. In addition, the police have said he may sink or disable any boat that comes within a similar distance. Don't worry, that won't be your job. Mr Tan has hired a world champion power boat racer to scare off any intruders who come via the water.'

'But why me?'

'Mr Tan always wants the best. He's an Olympic medallist himself. He says that once you've won a medal you become a member of a special club. He feels an affiliation with you and that's why he would like you to come to the Philippines. He is also aware you have other talents.'

'But I'm not necessarily the best and I've certainly never had to shoot drones out of the sky.'

'You'll be able to practise first. And who knows, perhaps your mere presence will keep the locusts away?'

'Locusts?'

'The journalists. That's what Mr Tan calls them.' Chin-Sun smiled. 'To be candid, Mr Tan likes to have what he calls "talking points" at his party. There'll be a handful of celebrities, of course, but there'll also be people like you. People who have achieved in the real world through hard work and dedication. There's the aforementioned power-boat racer, and an America's Cup skipper will be taking all the guests on a sailing trip. There'll be a world-famous magician teaching magic tricks, a martial arts demonstration, and more. You get the picture.'

'I'm to be on display like some kind of curio?'

'I expect some of the guests might want to talk to you, yes.' Chin-Sun paused. 'But Mr Tan would never want you to feel you were a curio.'

Chin-Sun went on to detail the arrangements. Silva would be flown business class to Bangkok and overnight there before a shot hop to the Philippines. There'd be a transfer from the airport to a marina where she would be ferried to Mr Tan's private island. She'd have a week to settle in before the party. On the day she would liaise with Mr Tan's head of security and they'd find and destroy any drones. She'd mingle with the guests, chat, and, if there was time the next day, give some personal instruction on Mr Tan's private range. Afterwards she was welcome to stay on the island for a few days before the trip home, once again business class. All expenses would be paid separately from the fee which was to be twenty thousand pounds. Was that acceptable?

Was it acceptable? Chin-Sun was offering Silva a couple of weeks' work at a luxury retreat, paying more than she earned in a whole year in her previous job as a postal worker. Of course it was. Still, Silva didn't answer 'yes' immediately.

'I'll need to think it over,' she said. 'But if I accept then I'll want Itchy, my spotter. Same terms.'

'Mr Richard Smith?' Chin-Sun said. She smiled. 'Of course, Mr Tan alerted me to the possibility you might want him along.'

There wasn't even a blink from Chin-Sun, and why would there be? Later, when Chin-Sun and Fairchild had left, Silva had googled Jun Tan and discovered he wasn't short of money. He was a Chinese émigré, and back in the nineties he'd started a shipping business and built it into a global brand worth an estimated one billion US dollars. Another twenty thousand was nothing to him.

Silva had called Chin-sun the next day to say she'd take the job, thinking afterwards it all seemed a bit too good to be true. Up to now though, that hadn't been the case. Fairchild had arranged for all the equipment to be purchased and shipped to the Philippines. Chin-Sun had emailed an itinerary and tickets, and a couple of days later a business credit card to use for incidental expenses had arrived by courier. Itchy had said he was 'in' as soon as Silva had mentioned the money, and they'd enjoyed a long but reasonably comfortable flight to Bangkok. So far, what was there not to like?

Silva took one last glance at the city lights and then turned from the balcony and climbed back into bed.

-

Thames House is a stone building on the banks of the Thames a little way down from the Houses of Parliament. While huge, it is also anonymous. It could perhaps be the offices of a large accountancy firm or, more likely, the base for a staid government department. It wouldn't be hard to imagine the building in yesteryear crammed with civil servants pushing pieces of paper back and forth across desks, filing everything in triplicate, a legion of secretaries working in a typing pool, fingers ablur, typewriters clattering. And today there are civil servants in this building, but it's not a boring government department. Thames House is the headquarters of MI5.

Holm often thought the HQ would be better based outside the capital on a leafy campus somewhere in the Home Counties. There'd be room to breathe, staff could come and go with little chance of being observed, and commuting would no longer be a bloody nightmare. Relocation was unlikely though because there was something about political power that required a concentration of the institutions of government. Spread those institutions across the country and you risked weakening the foundations that held the nation together.

After a journey into central London that involved spending twenty minutes stuck on a broken-down tube train, Holm walked along Millbank enjoying the spring sunshine. On the left, just shy of Lambeth Bridge, Thames House was a façade of stone rising from the street, brutal and unattractive. He passed through the extensive security and headed for his office.

Although he'd so far failed to catch Taher, his efforts had been rewarded with a promotion, partly due to his unmasking of a mole deep within MI5's sister organisation, MI6. For years the mole had been passing secrets to terrorists and was one reason why Holm had been thwarted in his attempts to apprehend Taher. Along with promotion had come a bigger office, more staff, and more resources. For how long though, Holm wondered. Today's review would be a crux point. The director general might bring down the axe or she might grant him a reprieve.

As Holm entered his office, Farakh Javed looked up from his laptop. At first glance most people found it hard to see beyond the young man's smile and mop of black hair. Javed was good-looking, charismatic and, Holm often thought, both incredibly engaging and infuriating. Those characteristics said nothing about his intelligence though. He was highly qualified for his role, spoke fluent Arabic, and his knowledge of Islamist terrorism was second to none.

'Morning, boss,' Javed said. 'Good weekend?'

'Went to a gig,' Holm answered. Javed raised an eyebrow, perhaps visualising Holm bopping in the front row to the tune of some indie group. Holm put him right. 'Ronnie Scott's. A mambo band.'

'Mambo? Doesn't sound like your kind of thing.'

'It wasn't. Way too uplifting.' Holm reached into a jacket pocket and pulled out a CD case. 'But I purchased a copy of their latest album so you can decide for yourself.'

Javed gave an exaggerated groan. Holm had brought in an old CD player and speakers and installed the set-up on a shelf on one side of the office. He liked to regale Javed with selections from his extensive collection of jazz.

'I'm surprised you didn't try getting it on wax cylinder,' Javed said, 'I mean you're so up with modern technology, right?'

Holm ignored Javed and sat down at his desk. Turned on his computer. He'd prepared a briefing document for the review and yesterday he'd sent it to Fiona Huxtable and cc'd it to the other participants. Now he read it again just in case there were any glaring errors.

'You're seeing the Spider today, right?' Javed said.

'Yes.' Holm nodded. The Spider was Fiona Huxtable's nickname, given for various reasons including the fact she scared the living daylights out of most of her subordinates. 'In case you'd forgotten, it's the review.'

'And I thought you'd just got out of bed on the wrong side.' Javed tapped his screen. 'By the way, while you're up there could you ask for some extra translators? I'm having a hard time keeping up with these intercepts.'

'The Algerian ones?'

'Yes.'

The Algerian intercepts had been passed to MI5 by the Sécurité Intérieure, a French counter-terrorism security agency. The intercepts comprised hundreds of hours of mobile phone recordings between an Algerian radical and an as yet unidentified man based in the UK. A combination of keywords had been picked up automatically and flagged the conversations worthy of further investigation, but the problem was the participants were talking in Arabic. MI5 had used their own AI – artificial intelligence – to analyse them further but Holm never trusted a computer to be able to understand the subtleties in spoken conversation. An offhand remark or a casual phrase could contain meanings a silicon chip could never properly infer. Hence the need for human translators and analysts, of which there were never enough.

'I'll ask her at the end of the meeting,' Holm said. 'If I survive that long.'

Chapter 3

The eleven-hour flight to Thailand had dragged, even in the relative comfort of business class, but the journey from Bangkok to Manila took three and a half hours. Itchy slept, as he always did, whether on a Hercules transport, a crammed EasyJet flight or this, a luxury, pampered experience. He woke as they touched down at Ninoy Aquino International, missing the dramatic descent over a sea dotted with hundreds of boats and the city spread out to their left.

'Nice,' he said as he opened his eyes, Silva unsure if he was talking about the smooth landing or the view through the window of the squat terminal building.

They gathered their things and were guided from the plane by smiling stewardesses, unaware that they were dealing with a couple of ex-squaddies more used to roughing it than receiving special treatment. After collecting their luggage and passing through immigration, it was Itchy who spotted the neat printed sign with their names on as they entered the arrivals hall.

'Da Silva and Smith,' he said. 'Sounds like a high-class estate agents from back home. Waterside property a speciality. A million and up.'

'Are you looking for a new career?' Silva said as they strode towards the uniformed chauffeur.

'Nah. Doubt there's much opportunity for luxury travel like this. Probably just a company Micra with our names on the side.'

A company Micra their ride was not. The chauffeur led them out to a black Mercedes limo with a glass privacy screen, a blinged-out interior and a well-stocked minibar. After loading the luggage into the boot, he climbed into the front and a speaker buzzed as the man's voice came through on the intercom.

'We'll be driving to the east coast and the port of Mauban, journey time about three hours. From there you'll take a boat out to Mr Tan's island. Please help yourself to refreshments and if there's anything you need please don't hesitate to ask.'

'Sweet,' Itchy said as he reached for a small bottle of bitter lemon, screwed off the top, and settled back in his seat. 'This is the life. Definitely skipping the estate agent thingy, Silvi.'

Silva laughed.

The chauffeur was as good as his word, and a little over three hours later they were at the port boarding a large RIB for what the skipper said would be a short ride up the coast. As they threaded out past the tourist boats, Silva could see a small island ahead, at first a speck and then growing by the minute. The RIB bounced across the waves leaving a foaming wake behind and after twenty minutes or so the island was revealed in all its beauty.

Palms and mangroves fringed a white sandy shore, the water lapping the beach ice-blue in colour and crystal clear. A small harbour, formed in an L shape, jutted into the sea, and a large motor yacht sat moored inside. The helmsman cut the power to the outboard as they glided in, and several shore staff in neat shorts and shirts took lines and made the craft secure. The luggage was unloaded and placed on the back of an electric golf buggy that took them along a narrow road towards some low buildings that clustered round a larger dwelling. From a distance the place looked like some sort of holiday resort, with little thatched chalets dotted in among the palms, the main building something like a Beverly Hills mansion as it pushed up above the surrounding palm trees.

The buggy rolled to a stop beside one of the chalets where Chin-Sun stood waiting. She gave a little bow as Silva and Itchy climbed off the buggy.

'Ms da Silva, Mr Smith.' Chin-Sun bowed. 'Mr Tan says he hopes your trip wasn't too arduous,' she said. 'He offers his apologies that the helicopter wasn't available to shorten the journey from Manila and requests the pleasure of your company later on this evening when you've rested.'

'Blimey, that's a first,' Itchy whispered to Silva. 'I don't think anybody has ever requested the pleasure of my company.'

Chin-Sun gestured into the chalet and held the door as they walked in. Inside the air-conditioned coolness was a welcome change from the heat and humidity. There was a large living area with bedrooms off to one side, both with large en suites. Bifold doors led to a patio area with a plunge pool, a barbecue pit and assorted chairs and recliners. As a porter carried their bags into the rooms, Itchy collapsed into a sofa.

'Seems like we've been travelling for days,' he said.

'We have.' Silva dropped into an armchair opposite.

Later, after unpacking, showers, and a buffet dinner served from a trolley by not one, but three waiters, Chin-Sun was back.

'Mr Tan would like to see you now, if you please.'

There was no buggy this time, only a short stroll to the main house, Chin-Sun making polite conversation as they walked. What was the weather like in England? Did they have an interesting time in Bangkok? Were there any special menu requirements she should know about?

At the main house, steps led up to huge wooden doors adorned with intricate carvings. The doors opened to a vast hall with a marble floor, a curving staircase to the upper levels, candelabras of gold hanging from the ceiling, oriental paintings on the walls, and an overwhelming sense of opulence.

Chin-Sun led them down the hall and into a side room which was smaller and cosier. Wicker furniture round a coffee table. Scatter cushions. A view out to a strand of pure white sand.

'Ah, Ms Da Silva and Mr Smith.' Tan rose from a low sofa to greet them. 'My humblest apologies at not being able to meet you when you arrived. Interludes from business these days are few and far between.'

Tan looked younger than Silva expected. He was fifty-seven, she knew, but obviously kept himself fit. He wore a light jacket with a white shirt, open necked, no tie. Jeans and deck shoes. His hair was dark and luxurious, but whether from good genes or expensive treatments, Silva wasn't sure.

Silva and Itchy shook hands in turn with Tan. He gestured at a couple of wicker chairs and bade them to sit. Chin-Sun appeared to be doubling as a hostess because she was hovering over by a huge mahogany drinks cabinet. Itchy opted for a bottle of Philippine beer, while Silva, thinking she ought to be a little more professional, chose an orange juice.

There were a few minutes of chit-chat, with Mr Tan asking about Silva's competitive shooting career. With a little prompting he modestly drew their attention to a series of photographs over on one wall.

'The individual archery event at the 1992 Barcelona Olympics. In the gold medal match my final arrow had to score ten.' Tan threw his arms up in a self-mocking gesture. Smiled. 'Alas, I fluffed it and could only manage to hit the inner blue for six points. Still, second best in the world is an achievement I am proud of.'

'Do you keep your hand in?' Silva said. She'd spotted a couple of bows hanging on one wall.

'Oh yes, and it's something I've tried to interest my children in, but no.' Tan shook his head, reached for his phone and waved it around. 'My youngest will happily play *Call of Duty* on his Xbox, but if I suggest he goes outside and shoots half a dozen arrows with his old man he'll look at me as if I'm crazy.'

Tan had some more questions about Silva and Itchy's experience in Afghanistan and then he was on to the reason he'd hired them. He hated the media, he explained. They'd done nothing to help him grow his business, only tried to poke their noses into his private affairs. His overriding concern was to make sure his private soirée was just that: private. Guests would be relieved of their phones and there'd be a professional photographer to document the party and provide souvenir pictures.

'And that's where you come in. Various news organisations and some of the more salacious publications have in the past used drones to get shots of me and my family. I want to prevent that.' Tan smiled. 'Or rather I want *you* to prevent that.'

'We'll do our best,' Silva said, trying to appear confident. 'But there are only two of us.'

'True, but your very presence will hopefully deter all but the most persistent. The few that remain you should be able to deal with.' Tan glanced at his watch. Sighed. 'Now, I'm sorry but I have to excuse myself. I have a conference call with London. Please speak to Chin-Sun if there's anything you require for your personal comfort. Tomorrow you'll meet with Paulo Ruiz, my head of security, and plan the mission. I'll be away for a few days, but when I get back we can finalise everything. Until then, goodnight.'

'The mission?' Itchy said when Tan and Chin-Sun had gone. 'We're here to shoot down camera drones, not head into the Mekong Delta.'

'I think Mr Tan might be living in a fantasy world,' Silva said. 'He's getting some kind of vicarious thrill out of hiring us. At least I hope that's it.'

'I guess as long as we get paid it doesn't matter.' Itchy relaxed back in the armchair and took another drink from his glass. 'I mean we can hardly complain about the way we've been treated so far, can we?'

No, Silva thought, there was nothing to complain about. All was good. Very good. Perhaps, even, too good to be true.

–

Holm took the lift so he wouldn't be out of breath when he reached the fifth floor. The doors slid open and he walked down the corridor, paused at the door to the briefing room, checked his watch, and then knocked and entered.

Five pairs of eyes fixed on him. He had a sinking feeling. This already had the look of an inquisition rather than a review.

'Stephen.' Fiona Huxtable smiled from the far end of the table. 'We've all read the document you sent through, so we'll move straight to a summary and then discuss the way forward, OK?'

Despite the smile Huxtable's greeting had a censorious tone to it. Holm glanced at his watch again. He was bang on time. He wondered for a moment if his flies were undone or his tie crooked or whether he'd forgotten to remove a piece of tissue paper from a shaving nick. Then again Huxtable's demeanour could rarely be described as welcoming. He thought of her nickname again. Spider-like was indeed the best way to describe her. Her dark eyes were set into an angular face beneath prematurely greying hair, while the loose clothes she wore hung on a spindly frame. When she moved it was in a slow calculating manner, as if she was getting ready to pounce. *Will you walk into my parlour said the spider to the fly…*

'Stephen?'

'Yes.' He realised he'd paused at the door so he hurriedly entered and took a seat at the end of the table. Huxtable gave him a stare, her gaze following him every step of the way. The others turned their attention to the notepads, tablets and documents on the table in front of them. They wanted to get on with this, get it over.

Holm looked round and made eye contact with everyone. To his right, Helen Kendle, the national security adviser attached to Downing Street. Sharp, efficient, always on top of her brief. Scary. A mini-me to Huxtable. Next to her, James Foster, the deputy director general. Fair-haired, good-looking and overly confident, Foster saw himself as a likely successor to Huxtable's throne even if nobody else did. To Holm's left, Oliver Pelton, another candidate to be the next director general. Pelton was an Eton and Cambridge man and the embodiment of old-school. A high flier in MI5 and world away from Holm's own background but probably his only ally on the panel. To Pelton's left, Simeon Weiss, head of the secretive Special Accounts Unit. The SAU supposedly provided funds for external operations, but in reality it dealt with black ops – deniable operations beyond the knowledge of nearly everyone aside from the director general herself. Weiss was master of his domain and his presence at the meeting suggested some sort of skulduggery might come into play.

Holm cleared his throat for no reason other than to buy a few extra moments to compose himself. He had his own set of papers in front of him but he didn't need to consult them; he knew this stuff by heart.

He began by explaining Taher's background. How the terrorist had been born into poverty in Saudi Arabia, a country outsiders assumed was rolling in wealth, and how Taher's Bedouin family had been wiped out in a missile strike that had been carried out by a British ship. A Tomahawk cruise missile had mistakenly targeted the family's homestead on the Saudi-Iraqi border and it was this strike that had radicalised Taher. He'd found backing from a rich arms broker known as Jawad al Haddad. Haddad, a Saudi with links to the upper echelons of the ruling House of Saud, had been behind a weapons-smuggling operation that had siphoned off a number of AirShield missiles as they'd been exported from the UK to Saudi Arabia, their intended destination various Islamist extremist groups in North Africa.

Holm paused to let the backstory sink in before moving on to more recent events.

'In August of last year, Taher was in Tunisia supervising the shipping of the missiles. Altogether we believe twelve missiles and two launchers were smuggled in. The missiles cannot be fired without the launchers so tracking those down was imperative. MI5, MI6 and the CIA coordinated a continent-wide intelligence operation which resulted in the recovery of one launcher and the destruction of several missiles in a strike from a Predator UAV. Taher, unfortunately, remained at large during this time, and we believe he at some point returned to the UK.'

Holm stopped. Looked round. Continued.

'TGT – Task Group Taher – was set up with the sole purpose of trying to track him down here on home soil. Since September we've had numerous leads and sightings.' Holm picked up a photograph from the spread of documents in front of him. 'One major issue is that we still don't know Taher's true identity, but this image shows him with Jawad al Haddad, the Saudi financier behind the operation to obtain the missiles.'

'I thought Haddad was in Saudi custody?' The question came from Helen Kendle.

'He was.' This from Huxtable. The statement accompanied with a grimace. 'Unfortunately his connections to the royal family gave him an informal pardon. He was allowed to leave the country in return for signing an affidavit confirming he had acted alone and without approval.'

'And had he acted alone?' Kendle again.

'Almost certainly not. There are those inside the Kingdom who back the aims of various Islamist groups. Stopping the flow of cash is almost impossible. Officially

Haddad has been censured, but behind the scenes he has widespread support.'

'And Haddad hasn't been apprehended?'

'He's been in and out of the UK and the US, but no charges have been forthcoming. One reason for that is we'd have to reveal where our evidence came from and this would expose various sources.'

Sure, Holm thought. That was one reason. Another was that the arms trade was worth billions. Annoy the Saudis and they might just decide to purchase their arms from China. Preventing that particular alliance from growing was a major policy priority, and if turning a blind eye to Haddad and other sponsors of terrorism helped to achieve that aim, then so be it.

Holm went on. 'The photograph of Taher and Haddad was taken before the plot to smuggle the missiles was uncovered, but we think the relationship is ongoing. Haddad blames us – that is, the UK – for his fall from grace back home, so his argument may well have moved from the political to the personal. In reality an attack against the UK accomplishes both aims so the motivation for continuing to fund Taher and his group is strong.'

'His group?' This time it was Foster, the deputy director. 'I thought this Taher was a loner?'

'Yes. Very much so. But he knows he can't do every-thing himself.' Holm reached for some more photographs. 'Mohid Latif and Anwan Saabiq. Pictured here during the Tunisian attack last year. We know from sources in Africa that both attended a training camp in the region where Latif received instruction in how to operate the AirShield missile. They were then observed disembarking from a boat in Naples from where they made their way back to the UK. In December we picked up a call Saabiq made to his brother in Manchester. Saabiq implied that the group had managed to recruit some new members and he tried to persuade his brother to join. His brother was having none of it and told Saabiq he was no longer welcome as a family member.'

Foster spoke again. 'So it's possible he has a veritable army at his disposal.'

'Not an army, but several dedicated soldiers.'

'But it begs a question, doesn't it?' Foster scanned the table, looking for support. 'Why have there been no attacks? Taher has had months to set up his operation and yet there's been nothing. We had that nutter rampaging with a knife, the guy who drove a van into a crowd, but neither had any connection to Taher. They were, to use the phrase loved by the media, "lone wolves". Taher, on the other hand, appears to have gone silent, and that begs the question, is he still a significant threat?'

'Yes he is,' Holm said. 'Which is why we need to continue to focus on him. He can't be allowed to fall off the radar because that's exactly the moment he'll strike.'

'You haven't answered my first question. Why have there been no attacks?'

'We believe he's waiting for something.'

'And what's that? Christmas has come and gone and so has Easter. Perhaps he received what he wanted from Santa and went on an egg hunt.' Kendle sniggered and the deputy director continued. 'You've had half a dozen people working on this for six months and the only thing to show for it is a telephone conversation between Saabiq and his brother. You're no closer to catching Taher than a year ago when, to be frank, most people in the intelligence community believed he was a figment of your imagination.'

'Sir, I've met Taher face-to-face. He is quite real and very dangerous.'

'He may be real but perhaps not as dangerous as we've been told.' The deputy director lowered his voice and adopted a more conciliatory tone. 'Look, your work tracking the smuggled missiles and exposing the MI6 mole, Martin Palmer, was exemplary. However, TGT has failed in its primary – no, let me rephrase that – its *only* mission. If Taher is no longer active, then your lack of success is understandable. If he is active then failure must be down to the way TGT has been run.'

A clever trap, Holm thought. He could see the way this was going. His next job would be to write a report detailing the work that had been done to track down Taher. The only way Task Group Taher would come out of this smelling of roses was if Holm exhaustively documented the last few months and could show every step that had been taken, every lead that had been followed, and every piece of evidence that had been considered. If the work was exemplary then he'd be off the hook. However, it depended on Taher not carrying out an attack at any time in the future. And forever was a long time.

'Stephen has done his best in difficult circumstances.' Oliver Pelton smiled benevolently at Holm. Perhaps somebody was going to come to his defence at last. 'I agree that this Taher is a slippery customer, an eel, but I feel we're done. My only comment is *acta est fabula plaudit.*'

Everyone round the table looked blank. Holm didn't know what to say. He did note that Simeon Weiss hadn't said a word. Whatever he thought, he'd kept it to himself. Perhaps, given the man's role as head of Special Accounts, that wasn't surprising.

'So, Stephen.' Huxtable had a pen in her hand. She'd been annotating the document in front of her, and black ink criss-crossed the page. It didn't bode well. 'The over-riding test of whether TGT should continue is one, whether any progress has been made, and two, is Taher still a threat.' Huxtable fixed each person at the table with her gaze for a second or two and then, as she always did, drew her own conclusions. 'I think you have demon-strated that the first test has not been passed. You have accumulated virtually no evidence during the last half a year. And without the evidence the second test is moot. Does everyone agree?'

Murmurs of approval rippled round the table.

'Anything to say, Stephen?'

'Ma'am,' Holm said, fuming inside but trying to remain as calm as he was able. 'Self-evidently if we had made progress we wouldn't be sitting here. Taher would be dead or in custody. However, we never know when we might get a decent lead or a pointer to when and where Taher will make his move. If we wind down the activities of TGT then we have nothing. When Taher strikes – and it's when not if – the absence of TGT will be a gaping hole in our defence to show we tried our very best. Sometimes even the very best isn't good enough, but it's all we have.'

Holm sat back down. He was pretty sure the decision had already been made, and whatever he said would make no difference.

'Thank you, Stephen. Does anyone have further ques-tions?' Huxtable scanned the room. The deputy director squared his papers, mind already made up. The others looked at Huxtable and shook their heads. 'Right. The five of us will discuss this further, Stephen. I'll give you my decision tomorrow.'

There we go then, Holm thought as he walked down the corridor away from the briefing room. Six months of work for nothing more than a pat on the back. Top marks for effort, but must do better in the execution. Much better.

—

The man known to the security services as Taher was in a flat high in a tower block in west London, no more than three miles from Holm's apartment in Ealing. He was standing at a window watching the planes lining up to land at Heathrow. Thinking.

Taher did a lot of thinking. Perhaps too much. But then his life was complicated. Occasionally he wished he was a normal man with a job, a wife, children. Occasionally he wanted to be able to go to the mosque and pray. To socialise and converse and laugh with others. To be considered human.

The problem was few people did consider him human. He'd carried out atrocities across the globe and been responsible for hundreds of deaths. Could such a man have even a scrap of humanity left within his soul?

Sometimes Taher wasn't sure, but if he had no humanity then neither did the Western leaders who'd killed tens of thousands and been responsible for spreading misery among millions. And neither did the people who'd elected those leaders. They were culpable too. Doubly so, since they lived in ignorance. They knew nothing of Taher or understood the reasons for his hatred. Few would be able to place Saudi Arabia – his birth country – on a map, nor would they have a clue where Palestine, Syria, Iraq, the Yemen or half a dozen other Middle Eastern countries were located. They wouldn't know anything about them other than they were places they'd seen on the TV, places where the news always seemed to be bad.

Bad news had followed Taher from the moment his family had been wiped out in a missile-targeting error during the Iraq War back in 2003. His mother and father had been Saudi Bedouins living on the Saudi-Iraqi border. Their modest settlement had been mistaken for an Iraqi military outpost, Taher's brothers and sisters for soldiers, and their goats, sheep and other animals for what exactly?

Taher didn't know, but the moment of their deaths had stayed with him. He only had to close his eyes to recall the flash of light, the searing heat and the roar of the flames. The screams of his siblings. The smell of their burning flesh. For a while, growing up, he'd tried to forget because he felt ashamed that he had survived. More recently he'd steeled himself to remember their passing on a daily basis. Their suffering drove him forward.

His radicalism had been formed thanks, in part, to a benevolent uncle. Three years' study at a UK university had done nothing to change his mind; if anything it had revealed the hypocrisy of the West and its supposed universal values. Do as we say, not as we do, was the message he saw everywhere. We are in the right even when we are wrong. Kneel before the god of modernity and progress or face bombs raining from the sky.

He looked to the sky now, his gaze following a large aircraft on its final approach to the airport, a mirage of heat haze around it. Soon the passengers would be disembarking, ordinary people with boring jobs and mundane lives. He doubted many would have felt the presence of God as they flew through the heavens, because this was a secular country. The Church of England was a religion in name only, and British politicians paid nothing more than lip service to spiritual morality.

The plane disappeared from view and Taher turned from the window. The passengers were safe. For now.

–

The day after the review Huxtable summoned Holm to her office.

'Stephen,' Huxtable said as he entered. The director general was alone. Another worrying sign. No witnesses to the probable carnage. 'Take a seat.'

Holm approached the big leather-topped desk and sat in one of the armchairs. Its high back and sides made him feel tiny and insignificant.

'I know you don't appreciate small talk.' Huxtable gave him one of her acid smiles. 'So I'll get straight to the point. The overwhelming viewpoint of the participants yesterday was that Task Group Taher should be scaled back. The group is consuming too many resources that would be better focused elsewhere. Taher is but one part of a vast network of extremists, not only Islamist but right- and left–wing too, not to mention other non–state actors such as the climate agitators. I've had representations made to me concerning the allocation of personnel and finances. There is, you might say, resentment.'

'So office politics takes precedence over national security?' Holm said, not trying to hide the sarcasm in the question. 'You're keeping people sweet rather than making the tough decisions.'

'Don't go there, Stephen. You're walking a fine line. I gave you a second chance after the Tunisian debacle, and for a while you delivered. Catching the mole in MI6 gained you a lot of credit. However, the reserve is now almost exhausted.'

'I apologise, ma'am.'

'Accepted.' Huxtable glanced at the document in front of her. 'Save for yourself and Farakh Javed, TGT members will be immediately reassigned to other duties. You'll need to reassess your approach and go back to basics. Work in the way you did before you had access to unlimited resources.'

'This isn't good, ma'am. Taher is still out there. He's still dangerous.'

'Absolutely. And that's why you'll be glad to hear there is currently an operation taking place to neutralise the threat he poses. While you've been failing, the Special Accounts Unit has been making progress. They are closing in.'

Holm nodded. Simeon Weiss, the head of the SAU, had been at the review but hadn't spoken. Now it was obvious why he'd been present and perhaps obvious why he'd kept quiet. 'Why didn't you tell me?'

'The SAU operate outside of the normal channels. Information concerning their activities is on a strict need-to-know basis.'

'But I *do* need to know. They may have gathered evidence we can use.'

'Everything has been properly scrutinised and nothing withheld.'

'I don't believe that. Weiss lives in his own bubble of alternative morals. I wouldn't trust him to tell me if Taher had moved in next door.'

'The operation is overseas.'

'Taher's *abroad*?' Holm shook his head. 'That proves my point. This is exactly the sort of information that should have been passed on.'

'I trust Weiss to get results. Sadly that is no longer the case with TGT.'

'I need to know where Taher is, ma'am, it's important.'

Huxtable shook her head. 'No can do. You know the rules.'

'You don't know, do you?' Holm laughed. 'The head of the service hasn't a clue where the SAU is operating.'

'That's why the SAU is called a black ops unit, Stephen. It's how Weiss is able to be successful. You can't deny it worked in Tunisia. Karen Hope was an unacceptable threat to national security. The SAU eliminated her.'

'Hang on, are you telling me this is a *kill* mission?'

'Weiss has been authorised to take whatever action is necessary to protect this country.'

'So it is a kill mission.'

'No comment.'

Holm nodded. He ran through a list of countries in his head and wondered where exactly Taher might be holed up, where Special Accounts could get away with deploying a kill team. He wondered if he'd been wasting his time for the past few months, trailing back and forth across the country, following leads from Southampton to Aberdeen.

'If I'd been fed the information before, TGT may have had more success. In effect we've been working with one hand tied behind our backs.'

'You've been free to develop your own strategy and cultivate your own leads. Your lack of results speak for themselves. QED.'

'That's it, then?'

'We're done here, yes.'

'I mean for me?'

'That's up to you to decide. You're sixty now, Stephen. You'll draw a full pension. You've done your bit, served this country well. There's nothing to gain by hanging on in.'

Nothing to gain. It hit Holm like a hammer blow. Huxtable was trying to push him out the door again.

'I want to stay,' he said. 'At least until we have Taher.'

'Of course.' Huxtable smiled. The expression said it was only a matter of time. 'And thank you, Stephen, for what you've done.'

Holm noted the sentence didn't end with 'so far'. Huxtable's view was obviously that his usefulness was at an end. There was nothing more to come.

He stood, gave her a cursory nod, and turned and left the room. He ambled back along the corridor and took the stairs down to his office.

'How did it go?' Javed said as Holm entered.

'Not good.' Holm dropped into a chair at his computer. He noted there was a new email from Huxtable. She must have had it ready to send the moment he left her office. 'We were like lambs to the slaughter. Never had a chance. Not a fucking chance. Task Group Taher is to be downsized. There are, according to Huxtable, other priorities.'

'Like what?' Javed said.

'She mentioned other Islamist groups and the far left and right.' Holm opened the email. Bullet points detailed yesterday's meeting and the conclusions she'd drawn. That was Huxtable. Efficient. Merciless. 'Them and climate change activists.'

49

'Climate change activists?' Javed shook his head. 'Not exactly in the top ten of security threats, are they?'

'Depends how you define a threat. If you are concerned about national infrastructure and economic activity then they're right up there.'

'What about if you're more worried about innocent citizens being blown to pieces?'

Holm didn't answer. He read through the rest of Huxtable's email. She'd made her choice. Task Group Taher would be all but abandoned. Holm and Javed would carry on working until the next review, but they would have few resources to draw on. It was just like the bad old good old days when Holm had been ploughing a lonely furrow in his pursuit of Taher. Yes, Weiss was out there on a manhunt somewhere, but Holm couldn't tell Javed that. In MI5 secrets weren't to be shared. Even if Holm disagreed with Huxtable's approach, he wasn't going to go against procedure. At least not yet.

'So what now?' Javed said.

Holm stared at his screen for a moment and then clicked the email closed. 'Lunch,' he said.

Chapter 4

After a weekend trying to forget about the axe Huxtable had wielded, Holm was reminded of the brutal reality when he arrived for work on Monday to find Javed the only occupant in the Task Group Taher office. He surveyed the empty desks and shook his head. The six people he'd been able to draw on in the hunt for Taher had been reassigned to new roles. On Friday, one by one, they'd cleared their things, offered parting condolences, and left. It had felt like the end of something larger than the task group.

'We were lucky to keep the room, to be honest,' Holm said to Javed as he took in the depressing scene. 'Although for how long I don't know. Without my little speech I think Huxtable would have closed us down for good.'

'Might have been for the best,' Javed said. 'It's taken me most of the week to get through a tenth of the Algerian intercepts. We're not going to accomplish much with just the two of us. Seems pointless carrying on.'

'If you feel like that, I'm not stopping you from leaving.' Holm looked towards the door. 'I understand this particular assignment may not be furthering your career and I wouldn't want you to end up tired and bitter like me.'

'I didn't mean—'

'Forget it, I understand. You're a bright lad, Farakh. You're going to go far if you keep your head down and play the game. If you don't associate with the likes of the notorious Stephen Holm.'

'You sound like my father. He regularly warns my brothers to stay away from me in case I'm a bad influence. He's worried I might turn them gay.' Javed nodded towards the birthday card with the three oiled men. 'Not that I don't try and explain the advantages.'

Holm said nothing for a moment or two. 'Your choice, but I could do with your help.'

'Do you think it will make any difference? Huxtable's right in the fact we haven't managed to get even a whiff of Taher since Tunisia. I don't feel we're wasting our time but…'

The words were left hanging. Holm thought about Weiss and the Special Accounts Unit.

'All is not lost yet.' Holm gave a wink. 'I hear that something's going down. Fingers crossed.'

He didn't actually hold out much hope that Weiss was going to be able to accomplish in a few short days what Holm had failed to do over a number of years, but he had to give Javed some encouragement.

'In the meantime we're going to carry on, gather evidence, collate the data, work the leads.'

'What leads? We haven't had anything meaningful since Saabiq's phone call to his brother, and all we got from that was that Taher was looking for more recruits.'

The phone call.

Holm had gone over the transcript several times. Anwan Saabiq had spoken to his brother – Tallin – for around twenty-five minutes and for most of the call both voices had been raised. Anwan had been constantly berating Tallin for bringing shame on their family. He'd married a non-Muslim, he no longer went to the mosque, he'd abandoned all pretence of faith. Tallin, for his part, had pleaded with Anwan to give up the hate-filled ideology he'd been following. Back and forth the conversation had gone. As well as the transcript, Holm had listened to the recording. Even though it had been in Arabic, he'd understood the tone. There'd been no hint of compromise in either man's voice, but close to the end of the call, despite the bitterness, Anwan had wished his brother peace. There'd been a twist though as he added a chilling warning: Tallin should avoid flying out of London for the foreseeable future.

Holm had memoed Huxtable the pertinent part of the conversation but she'd dithered about passing the message on up to Number Ten. There were no hard facts to back up any recommendation she might make about increased security. Saabiq's words were a vague threat to do something sometime in the future. Terrorists were always making such threats. There was nothing new.

'I want to speak to Tallin Saabiq,' Holm said to Javed.

'The police interrogated him for a day and half.' Javed swivelled in his chair. 'They concluded that he didn't know anything, nor did he have any sympathy for his brother or his actions.'

'Nevertheless the phone conversation is all we have.' Holm glanced at his computer screen where his email program was open. There was nothing requiring his attention. 'We'll go now. Give him a call and set something up.'

'*Now?* He lives in Manchester.'

'Yes. Got anything better to do?' Holm looked at his watch. 'We'll go back to my place and pick up my car.

Four and a half hours door to door. We can be there early afternoon.'

'We're supposed to take the train, remember?'

There'd been a directive about carbon emissions from on high a couple of months ago: car expenses would only be paid where alternatives were not available.

'We're the Security Service,' Holm said. 'How are we supposed to work on the train? We can't talk shop when we're surrounded by eavesdroppers.'

'Blame those pesky climate change protestors,' Javed said. 'Not so much a threat to national security as an issue for security operatives who prefer the open road.'

Holm insisted on the open road. Or not so open since they ended up in a traffic jam around Stoke-on-Trent, crawling along for over an hour. They eventually arrived in Manchester mid afternoon and nosed into the maze of little streets that comprised Moss Side. Holm had been here once a couple of decades before on a hunt for an IRA cell, and the area seemed much changed. Tallin Saabiq lived on Beresford Street in a long terrace with no front gardens, not even any porches; the front doors opened onto the street, the pavement passing right beneath the living room windows. They found a parking spot close by, got out and walked to the house. Holm pushed the doorbell and stepped back.

The door was opened by a young woman. She was in her mid twenties, blond hair, plenty of make-up. Holm could see why Anwan Saabiq might disapprove of his brother's choice of bride.

'Yes?' The woman said.

'We're here to see Tallin,' Javed said. 'He's expecting us.'

'Right.' The woman glanced over her shoulder for a second. 'There's been a change of plan. He says he'll meet you in the park down the road. Five minutes. OK?'

'Sure,' Holm said as the woman closed the door. He turned to Javed. 'What was that about?'

'Eyes.' Javed began to walk down the street. 'From behind the twitching net curtains. I reckon Tallin may have it hard enough round here being married to a white girl. Two dodgy-looking blokes coming visiting won't make life any easier.'

'Let's hope he hasn't changed his mind about talking to us.' Holm matched Javed's step and fell in beside him. 'I can't face the journey back with nothing.'

The park had a picnic area and a small children's playground at one end. A group of kids were kicking a ball around a patch of grass, while several dogs led their owners on a circuitous route round the edge of the park.

'We're not exactly inconspicuous here,' Javed said. 'We should head for the playground and those trees.'

'We're going undercover as kiddie peepers, are we?'

They strolled across the grass towards the far end of the park. There was a bench beneath a tree. Holm and Javed sat. A young Asian man, dressed in tracksuit bottoms and a hoodie, jogged towards them. He stopped a few metres away and did some stretches. Looked round.

'Mr Holm?' he said.

'Yes.' Holm patted the bench. 'Why don't you sit down, son? You're making me nervous and you're attracting attention.'

Tallin Saabiq walked across. He sat next to Holm. 'Just so you know, I'm not doing this for Anwan. I don't care what happens to him. I'm doing this for me.'

'I understand.'

'No you don't.'

'Fair enough,' Holm said, realising he probably didn't understand the internal conflict involved in reporting a family member to the authorities. 'You have your reasons and they don't matter to me. All I'm trying to do is protect lives. If you can lead me to Anwan, that'll help do that.'

'I've no idea where he is. I told your colleagues that before. I haven't heard from him in months. Since the phone call.'

'We're looking for something else.' Javed stood and walked a couple of paces from the bench. 'Something we may have missed before.'

'I don't know what that is.' Tallin ducked his head as a couple of kids whizzed by on bicycles. 'The police grilled me for over a day. There's nothing I haven't told you.'

'How long have you been married?'

'Hey?'

'Your wife. When did you meet her?'

'About four years ago. We got married last spring.'

'Family approve?'

'Anwan didn't, that's for sure. Said I was marrying a whore. My parents would have preferred a nice Muslim girl, but they've accepted Cheryl now. They're looking forward to the birth of their first grandchild.'

'Your wife is pregnant?' Tallin nodded and Javed smiled. 'Congratulations.'

'Yeah, I've got a good job, a wife with a baby on the way, a foot on the property ladder.' Tallin shook his head. 'If only this stuff with Anwan wasn't hanging over me, life would be sweet.'

'We can help you with that, Tallin,' Holm said. He swivelled on the bench. 'If you can help us find your brother.'

Tallin shook his head. 'I would if I could.'

'Aside from the phone call, when did you last see or have any contact with Anwan?'

'You know that, it's in your records.'

'Go over it again just so we can be sure we haven't missed anything.'

Tallin scuffed his feet on the ground. 'Look,' he said. 'I love Cheryl, but it's difficult being married to a white girl. People talk. My family have accepted her but others haven't. If I give you what you want, will you leave me alone after this?'

Holm nodded. 'We're not the police. All we need is a heads-up. No visit to a station, no interview, nothing on paper. We can even put the information down as coming from an anonymous tip-off.'

Tallin hung his head low so the hoodie top completely covered his face.

'A brief letter arrived from Anwan a month ago,' he whispered. 'He told me he still loved me and once again suggested that I avoided flying out of London.'

'And that was it?'

'Yes.'

'Right.' Holm tried not to sound disappointed. 'It's useful to know Anwan has been in contact, but there's nothing new in this.'

'No, not in the message.' Tallin fumbled in the front pocket of his hoodie. Out came a creased photograph. He turned his head and looked up and down the path and then handed the photo to Holm. 'But there is this.'

Holm moved the picture to his lap. The image showed Anwan Saabiq standing in front of a run-down bungalow. To one side of the dwelling there was a parked car, beyond which were trees and fields. This was somewhere rural.

Holm looked for other signs. The licence plate of the car – a dark-blue Fiesta – was hidden behind a bush. He wondered how many models in that colour were on the roads. He turned his attention back to Anwan. The young man stood posing next to a black flag that had been hung from the sill of one of the windows. White writing squiggled across the top of the flag, while in the centre there was a crooked circle of white with black writing within. This, he knew, was the flag of the Islamic State, known variously as IS, ISIS, ISIL, or Daesh.

He peered down, trying to extract more detail from the photograph, but seemed to have exhausted the clues until Tallin reached out and put a finger on a window to the right of the flag and on the very edge of the picture. There was something there, a figure reflected in the glass.

Holm stood and walked over to Javed. He grasped his arm and wheeled him away, pointing out the reflection in the window.

'It's him,' Holm said. 'Taher.'

–

They'd been in the Philippines now for four days. The first day they'd spent chilling and examining the equipment Fairchild had shipped over for them. There was a stack of drones – brand new and still in their packing – to be used for target practice, binoculars, a spotting scope for Itchy, a sniper rifle for Silva – the L115A3 she'd used in Afghanistan – and plenty of ammunition. At one end of the island Tan had built an archery range and he'd extended it to make it a decent length for rifle shooting. There were plate-metal targets and a variety of shooting positions.

The first job was setting up the rifle and firing it so they could get enough material in the DOPE book. The 'data of previous engagements' book was actually an app Itchy had on his phone. In it he recorded every shot Silva made with the weapon, noting down the temperature, wind, air pressure, distance and numerous other details. The information was used to help perform the complex ballistics calculations they needed to fire the rifle in varying conditions.

After set-up, they divided their time between target practice on the range and attempting to hit drones in the air. Silva found spotting a tiny object in the sky and fixing it in the scope incredibly difficult, but after a while she made progress and Itchy flew the drones higher and further away. The job so far, if it could be called a job, wasn't exactly taxing. There was a covered veranda where they could shelter from the frequent heavy rain showers, food delivered at lunchtime, and even a fridge stocked with cold drinks.

'Get treated like this in the army and they'd have queues round the block at recruitment offices,' Itchy said when he saw the set-up. 'Mind you, must have cost a pretty penny. All the stuff he's bought, flying us out here, the money he's paying us. Simply to stop a few photographers taking pictures at a party.'

When Itchy had said that, Silva once again felt uncomfortable. Things were beginning to not add up. For instance, while Tan and Chin-Sun had talked of a party, there was, as yet, no sign of any preparations. The event was supposed to be happening at the weekend – a couple of days away – but there was no sense of any urgency. When Silva had asked Chin-Sun if the party was still going ahead, she simply said it was and that everything was in hand. Paulo Ruiz, Mr Tan's head of security, was similarly vague.

'Shoot the drones, have some beers,' he said smiling. 'Don't worry.'

Ruiz was a big man with a fair few extra pounds round his middle and a casual good nature that was infectious. He joined them on the range and roared with laughter as they blew apart one thousand-dollar drone after another. When Silva once more enquired about the party he stopped laughing long enough to tell her that Mr Tan was off on business, but he'd be back the next day and wanted to see Silva and Itchy that evening.

The next day, Silva rose early and took a swim before breakfast. A trail led down from their chalet to a beautiful beach where palm trees fringed a stretch of sand. The water was clear and warm and she swam out to where waves broke over a protecting reef. When she arrived back at the chalet, Itchy was polishing off a plate of sausage, bacon and eggs.

'So, I took a chance,' he said, spearing a sausage, 'I ordered a full English and it turned up perfect, even down to the baked beans.'

They had a day's leisurely practice on the range and then returned to the chalet and got ready for their meeting with Mr Tan. Up at the main house they were once more shown into the cosy office area. Tan was waiting, as polite as ever.

'I hope you've been sleeping well,' he said, beckoning Silva and Itchy to take a seat. 'The sound of the sea is very soporific, I find. Refreshing.'

Tan made chit-chat for a few more minutes until it got to the point where Silva wondered if it would be rude to interrupt him. As she was about to, Tan switched topics.

'I have an apology to make.' Tan was standing over by a display housing one of his bows. He looked at the bow for a moment, his brow creasing. 'I have deceived you and brought you here under false pretences.'

Silva cast Itchy a glance before speaking. 'How so, Mr Tan?'

'There is no party. No camera drones, no prying photographers.' Tan smiled. 'And if there had been I'd have got my very capable security team to deal with them.'

'I don't understand.' The uneasiness Silva had been feeling rose again. 'If there isn't a party then why are we here?'

'As I said, under false pretences, but for honourable reasons.' Tan reached out and touched the bow on the wall, almost as if the object held some special significance. 'You probably don't know my history, but your government gave me a home when I was first exiled from China and for that I'm grateful. I owe you.'

'Not me, Mr Tan. You don't owe me anything.'

'No, I mean the UK. Thirty years ago I was given a chance. I started with a one-room office in London and built my business from scratch. In the early 2000s I relocated to the Philippines so as to be at the centre of the fast-growing economies of East Asia. After the move the company grew exponentially and nearly two decades later I find myself here.' Tan made a gesture at the view. 'Rich beyond imagination, beyond anything my parents could have dreamed of.'

'That's capitalism. You're obviously one of the winners.'

'Of course. I don't mean to sound conceited. I understand the way the system works. For every success there is a failure.'

Beside Silva, Itchy shifted in his seat and gave her half a glance.

'But for every winner there are dozens of losers, and those losers are easily beguiled or coerced.'

'Mr Tan,' Silva said. 'I'm not quite sure what your point is?'

'ISIS, Ms da Silva. They've established a foothold here and are growing in influence. In one particular area in the north of the country, they've even been recruiting child soldiers. Their leader up there is a man called Adil Hassani, although he is more commonly known by the moniker "The Butcher". The local population try to resist, but Hassani encourages compliance with his diktats by living up to his nickname. Last month, for instance, he hung a transgressor upside down over a bonfire. The simple fact of the matter is the world would be a lot better place if Hassani was dead.'

'I think I can see where you're going with this, Mr Tan, but if you think that because my mother was killed by terrorists I'm up for fighting them wherever and whenever, then you're mistaken. I'm sorry about the situation here in the Philippines, but it's not my war. I'm just an ordinary young woman, not a superhero or an angel. I'm not some sort of avenging force that can right the wrongs of the world. I'm not brave, either. Itchy and I are just two ex-squaddies. We were moderately good at our jobs, but we don't have a miracle cure that can wipe away injustice.'

'You're being disingenuous, Ms da Silva. You and Richard were more than just good at your jobs. You were at the top of your game. And while I concur that killing Hassani isn't a miracle cure, it can alleviate some of the symptoms and provide a respite for the victims.

'You thought you could get us here and then dump this on us? That we'd just roll over and accept? We're not mercenaries. We came here to do a security job and it didn't involve killing anyone.' Silva turned to Itchy. 'Right?' Itchy nodded, but without much enthusiasm. 'Come on, Itch, we've been conned into coming here and now Mr Tan is trying to pressure us to do his bidding. I'm not going along with it.'

'I'm sorry.' Tan bowed his head in contrition. 'But if you'd been told the full details back in the UK would you have come?'

'Absolutely not.'

'Then I can only apologise fully. I feel shame for my actions. You will still receive your full fee. Your flights are booked for the middle of next week. Please feel free to stay on the island for the rest of the week.' Tan bowed again and then turned and left the room.

'Silvi!' Itchy was aghast. 'He's given us a job and we should bloody well do it. He's paid us twenty K each to boot. Flights and everything.'

'I'm done with killing people for a living, Itch. I thought you were too.'

'Yeah, of course, but this is different. Hassani sounds like a nasty piece of work and we get to save those child soldiers.'

'Tan's not stupid. He brought that up deliberately knowing about my past. He's hoping it would somehow be triggering.'

'Well perhaps Mr Tan is right. You help him out and solve your personal issues as well.'

'Fuck off, I don't have issues.'

'You do, Silvi.'

'Look, I'm never going to forget what happened in Afghanistan, but killing Hassani isn't going to help.'

'Are you quite sure about that?'

'Yes.'

Silva walked from the room and made her way back to the beach chalet. In her room she sat on her bed and gazed through the open shutters. The moon was up, its reflection shimmering in dark water. Paradise, Mr Tan had said, but thanks to him all she could think about now were the hot, dusty streets of Kabul, the crosshairs of her rifle sight alighting on the face of a young boy, the second or two she'd had to make a decision she would regret for the rest of her life.

–

Later, Itchy stumbled back to the chalet. Mr Tan had returned and shared a couple of drinks with him. Perhaps more than a couple.

'He's a Chelsea fan, Silvi,' Itchy said as he fumbled with a bottle at the minibar. 'He's got a box at the Bridge. Says I can join him next time he's in London.'

'It's a bribe, Itch.' Silva went across and found Itchy a bottle opener. 'He's softened you up so you'll try to persuade me to do the job. To be honest, in your state it's going to be a hard sell.'

'Hey?'

'Tan seems like a decent guy, but something's not right. It doesn't matter how rich you are, you don't spend all that money getting us to the Philippines on the off chance we might take the job. Then, once we're here, he tells us the details and when we refuse he gives up without so much as a raised voice, almost as if his heart wasn't in it in the first place.'

'He's a gentleman, Silvi.' Itchy raised the bottle in a 'cheers' gesture and then knocked back a few gulps, suppressing a burp. 'Like Englishmen used to be. You know, before the internet and all that.'

Silva decided that since Itchy was well on the way to being blottoed further conversation was pointless. He, however, was keen to continue. He couldn't see a reason for not doing the job, he said. Hassani was an evil piece of shit. There were kids to save. Put a bullet in the man, collect their payment, fly home. No worries.

The trouble was Silva was worried. The more she thought about the whole set-up, the more she realised something was very, very wrong. Yes, Tan did appear to be honourable, but he was concealing the true nature of what was going on here. What that was, Silva didn't know. She left Itchy conversing with the minibar and went to bed.

Chapter 5

'Worth the journey,' Javed said. 'Well worth it.'

That, Holm thought, was an understatement of huge proportions. They had a photograph of Taher on British soil, possibly at his hideout; they had the make of a car he or Anwan Saabiq might be using; they had Anwan in front of an ISIS flag worryingly looking every inch a potential martyr. Javed had taken a picture of the photo with his phone and emailed it to Claire Evans, the head of MI5's technical unit. In an initial conversation with her, Holm had asked whether there might be the possibility of finding the location of the bungalow by scanning a database of property photos or from identifying the trees or landscape in the background. Evans, disappointingly, hadn't held out much hope of success.

They were in the bar area of the budget hotel where they were staying. They'd promised Tallin that they'd interview his parents in the morning. The visit would provide him with a cover story since he could say the authorities were questioning everybody connected with Anwan. Afterwards they'd return to London and work on the picture.

They sat with their drinks – Holm with a pint of bitter, Javed with a Coke – musing on the possibilities.

'We just need a tiny thread,' Holm said. 'Something we can cross-reference with other evidence.'

In the end the picture might not produce the lead he was hoping for, but it would keep Huxtable sweet for a while, perhaps even persuade her that Taher was still active and very much a threat. It would only delay the inevitable though and before long she'd once more be telling Holm that the Security Service needed to focus on areas that might produce tangible results. He glanced up at the TV in the corner of the bar. Case in point, he thought, as he read the subtitles scrolling at the bottom of the screen beneath a local news bulletin. A far-right group was suspected of a firebombing in a quiet residential area, interracial marriage supposedly the justification for the attack. Holm sighed. Peered down into his beer. What a crap world they were living in.

'Boss?' Javed was studying the TV intently, his face creased into a frown. 'Does that street look familiar?'

Holm returned his attention to the screen. Blue light strobed on a wet road, fire hoses snaking along the front of a terrace of houses, dozens of firefighters milling around their engines. Not much to do now but clear up the mess. The scene cut to earlier footage of the fire. Three properties well ablaze, smoke, flames and an eerie orange glow in the darkness.

'That's…' Holm put his glass down with a clunk and stood up. 'Oh Christ.'

Holm was out of the bar in a couple of seconds, Javed on his heels. For a moment he hesitated in the lobby area – their car was in the underground car park, the keys up in his room, an avoidable delay. He decided to forget the car and instead headed out onto the street where he flagged down a passing minicab. He jumped in the front seat. Javed got in the back.

'Moss Side,' Holm said. 'Beresford Street.'

'Could be tricky,' the cabbie said. 'I heard there's a house fire. Lots of road closures.'

'Just get us as close as you can.'

'Are you journalists? Only you're not from round here, are you?'

'We're from London,' Holm said, 'but we're not journalists. Tell us about these right-wingers. The ones who carried out the attack. Are those sorts of groups prevalent in Manchester?'

'No idea.' The driver pulled out into the traffic. 'Didn't know there were any round here. You got a bit of aggro after the Arena bombing, but nothing organised. That was understandable. I was bloody angry myself, but it's no good blaming a whole religion for the behaviour of a mad zealot. Most people round here pay their taxes and support the police. Nearly everyone loves this city.'

The driver dropped them two streets away, and they walked the rest of the way. A police car was parked across the end of Beresford Street, a couple of officers standing behind some blue and white tape. Dozens of people mingled in the road.

'Sorry, mate.' One of the officers moved across as Holm ducked under the tape. 'No access. Back you go.' Holm pulled out his ID. The officer took it and examined the card. Showed it to his colleague. 'This look genuine?' he said.

'If I could just speak to whoever's in charge,' Holm said.

'DI Harris.' The officer pointed towards the back of a fire engine where a figure stood talking to a firefighter. 'He's your man.'

'Thank you.' The card came back and Holm held up the tape for Javed. They headed for the fire engine.

'Yes?' Harris turned as they approached. 'Are you health and safety? Took your bloody time.'

'No,' Holm said. 'The Security Service.'

Harris looked them up and down. 'Figures, I guess.'

'Number forty-two, right?'

'Yes.'

'Tallin Saabiq?'

'On a watch list, is he?' Harris shook his head. Took a glance at Javed. 'Because it looks like the Nazi thugs have done your work for you. You should have been quicker off the mark. You don't often hear me praising the right wing, but in this case I guess we owe them. Perhaps if you guys had been on the ball a few years ago we'd have—'

'He's not on a watch list.' Holm's gaze followed a fire hose that curled towards the house. 'Where is Mr Saabiq?'

'He's in there,' Harris said. 'Along with his wife and, according to neighbours, an unborn child. Fried to a crisp. It's sad about the woman but I guess that's what you get when you consort with suicide bombers.'

'For fuck's sake, Tallin wasn't a suicide bomber. He was helping us with our enquiries.'

'If you say so.'

'Do you have evidence to prove otherwise?'

'Well, no.' Harris followed Holm's gaze. 'And I guess there won't be anything in there for us now.'

'Any theories as to who did this?'

'Some fascist group, I'd have thought.'

'Your reasoning?'

'There's a swastika spray-painted on the outside back wall.' Harris looked pleased with his powers of deduction. 'Plus a neighbour from a property at the rear has given us some footage from a security camera. Shows the cut that runs along the back of the terrace. I've had a quick gander and there's a white male, shaved head, who climbs over the gate into the backyard with a jerrycan. Five minutes later he's back out, sans can. That tallies because the fire investigator tells me a large quantity of accelerant must have been used for the fire to take hold so quickly. Those upstairs never had a chance.'

'Why Tallin though?'

'Easy target. He married a nice white girl. Polluted the gene pool.' Harris shrugged. 'And these nutters aren't the sharpest thinkers.'

No, Holm thought. And neither are you. He thanked Harris and stepped away.

'Bit of a coincidence,' Javed said as they strolled back up the street. 'We visit Tallin and a few hours later he's dead.'

'Yes.' Holm turned. Smoke drifted into the air. Illuminated by the street lights, it formed an orange cloud overhead. 'But it doesn't sound as if the guy on the CCTV footage is either Taher, Anwan Saabiq or Mohid Latif.'

'Could be he's a hired thug.'

'But if Taher has an operation pending why do anything to draw undue attention? Tallin didn't give us enough to track down Taher.'

'Maybe Taher couldn't take the risk, or perhaps there was more Tallin didn't tell us.'

'Yes, or possibly it's just a coincidence.' They reached the blue and white tape. 'Let's get back to London pronto. We'll request the CCTV footage and run our facial recognition software over it and see if we get some kind of match.'

'What about Tallin's parents?' Javed said.

'Forget them.' Holm turned and looked back down the street where the house stood smouldering. 'Tallin doesn't need the cover story any longer, does he?'

–

Paradise or not, Silva slept badly. The waves, soporific on previous nights, now sounded more like a distant barrage. She imagined shells falling from the sky, heard the retort of IEDs, the staccato of automatic weapons. In her dreams she saw the ruined streets of Kabul and found herself running through them, fleeing from a kid with half his face blown away. He came after her with a manic grin of exposed teeth, a wail of anger pouring from his mouth, the anger taking physical form in a cloud of flies. She stumbled and the flies swooped down on her, laying eggs that hatched instantly, tiny larvae growing to maggots, feasting on her own face until she woke with a start.

Itchy had said she had issues, she thought. But then who wouldn't, given the circumstances?

She rose late, showered, and dressed. Skipped breakfast and had an early lunch. Itchy was still in his room and Silva figured he must have drunk more than she'd thought. After lunch, she walked over to the archery range at the far end of the island and looked at the set-up. Tan had gone to a lot of trouble for no reward. The nagging doubt surfaced again. All was not as it seemed. She took the long route back, circumnavigating the whole island. Chin-Sun was sitting in the living area when Silva returned to the chalet. She rose and gave a little bow.

'There's someone to see you,' she said. 'Down by the guest beach.'

Silva nodded. 'OK.'

Talking to Tan again wasn't going to be easy, but she reasoned he was the one in the wrong. As he'd said, if she'd been told the truth back in London then she'd never have come.

She headed through the palms to the beach. A strip of white sand ran from the villas to a small wooden pier where a couple of sailing dinghies sat tugging at their mooring lines. A man stood on the dock looking at the boats. She walked over the sand and onto the pier, her footsteps causing the man to turn.

'Déjà vu,' he said. The man was mid forties, with oblong rimless glasses, grey hair above. He wore a light-grey suit, complete with waistcoat and jacket, and looked uncomfortable in the heat. 'Or, alternatively, fancy seeing you here.'

Silva flinched, for a second unable to take in the situation. It was almost as bad as her nightmare, a ghost from her past teleporting into an otherwise perfectly delightful scene.

'Weiss,' Silva said as she moved forward. Almost unconsciously she reached out, intending to grasp the lapels of the man's jacket and give him a bloody good shaking. Perhaps push him off the dock into the sea. 'What the fuck are you doing here?'

It was a perfectly good question. Simeon Weiss, head of Special Accounts at MI5, was a very long way from home.

'Manners, Ms da Silva.' Weiss leaned back, away from Silva's clutching hands. He turned his head to the right where one of Tan's security guards stood beneath the palms. 'It's something our guest is very keen on, and I'm sure you wouldn't want to offend him. Especially considering your reaction to his modest proposal. Don't add insult to injury, right?'

'What are you doing here?' Silva dropped her arms and stepped back. 'It's not like this place is easy to get to and it certainly isn't open to holidaymakers.'

'But it is open to Mr Tan's friends.'

'I find it hard to believe you have any of those, Mr Weiss.'

'Jun Tan is a very close friend of the British government. He is, as I'm sure he told you, indebted to us for supporting him in his asylum application and subsequent citizenship approval. All those years ago we were the one country that stepped up and offered him sanctuary. He owes us.'

'This is down to you and Matthew Fairchild, right?' Silva nodded back towards the villas. 'Our invite. The whole party story. I bet that's something the two of you dreamed up.'

'Matthew, for once, is entirely innocent. He was hood-winked by the lovely Ms Chin-Sun as much as you were. The whole thing was rather creative, I thought. Stories leaked to the press, a false guest list, even a mention for you on a couple of the TV channels here in the Philippines. And I'm sure you'll agree Mr Tan and Chin-Sun played their parts very well.' Weiss gestured towards the shore and the palms beyond. 'Shall we walk? I'm getting a little fried in this heat.'

Silva turned and went back along the dock, Weiss following. She strode across the sands to the trees.

'You haven't answered my question.' She stopped in the shade of a palm. 'Which I'll rephrase to what the fuck is going on?'

'An operation, long imagined in my mind, but short on planning.'

'I'm not killing Hassani, especially now I know this scheme was hatched by you.'

'This has got nothing to do with Hassani, at least not directly. Whether he lives or dies is of little consequence to me or the UK government. I know it's a personal issue for Mr Tan, and for the good of humanity dead would be preferable, but it's hardly the issue here.'

'So what is?'

'This.' Weiss reached into his jacket and pulled out a small thumbnail picture. 'I'm sure you'll recognise him.'

Silva took the picture. It was of a young man with a *shemagh* round his head. Dishevelled black hair poking from under the chequered material, a half-smile and strong brown eyes. There was a wisp of hair on his chin, the rest of his face smooth and unblemished.

'Taher.'

'The man who led the attack that killed your mother. He just happens to be coming to the Philippines and will be spending some time as a guest in Hassani's jungle hideout.' Weiss glanced around. 'Although it's not quite on a par with this, to be honest. No breakfast in your own chalet, no clear blue ocean to swim in, and the host isn't our affable Mr Tan, but rather Mr Hassani, and he's not a man to get on the wrong side of. Still, there are benefits. The hideout is in impenetrable jungle for one. Another thing is the number of loyal ISIS fighters at Hassani's disposal, and, while Taher is there, at his disposal too. Finally, it's just under an hour and a quarter's flight time in a helicopter.'

'From where?'

'From here.'

'Mr Weiss, I know you like playing games, but you're not making any sense.'

'Taher has come to the Philippines for a mission. He'll be launching an attack on this island in three days' time. Coincidentally the day my fake party was planned for.'

'He's coming here to kill Mr Tan?'

'No, Rebecca.' Weiss smiled. 'He's coming here to kill you.'

Chapter 6

Holm arrived back in London in the early hours of Tuesday. Having returned to the hotel to grab their stuff, they'd driven south immediately. On the journey, Holm had called DI Harris and asked for the CCTV footage to be made available. After an argument about whether MI5 would keep Greater Manchester Police informed – Holm said he would – Harris promised the material would be sent through first thing in the morning.

'That was a lie, right?' Javed said. 'You're not going to tell him anything.'

'Depends on what we discover.'

After grabbing a few hours' sleep, Holm was back at Thames House by ten. He was soon ensconced in the tech suite reviewing the CCTV material with the help of Claire Evans. Evans was only a few years younger than Holm, but unlike Holm, IT didn't faze her. Recently she'd been in charge of an upgrade of MI5's systems, overseeing a multimillion-pound procurement drive. If an operation needed an analyst familiar with all areas of technology, Evans was the first person most agents turned to. Holm, a man who struggled with anything more complicated than clicking a 'buy now' button, had the utmost respect for her skills. He also felt a moment's guilt in asking her to perform such a menial task.

'Here we go,' Evans said as she loaded up the file sent by Harris. 'Let's see what we've got.'

The video began to run. A fuzzy black and white picture showed part of the alley that ran behind the Beresford Street terrace. The camera was motion activated so what they saw were two separate cuts. The first showed a man climb over the rear gate with a large jerrycan in one hand. He was white, thickset, and had a shaved head. An unlikely recruit to Taher's cause, Holm thought. The man approached the house and spray-painted a swastika on the wall beside the back door. He then moved to the door and opened it.

'Can we see that enhanced?' Holm said.

'Sure.' Evans paused the clip, rewound it a few frames, and zoomed in. She brought up a couple of menus and adjusted some parameters. Clicked 'OK'. A few seconds passed as the image was processed and then it redisplayed with incredible clarity.

'He's using a key,' Holm said.

'Looks like it.'

Evans clicked 'play' and the footage ran on. The man ducked inside, the jerrycan in one hand, and closed the door. The second clip showed him exiting the house, his face momentarily visible as he unbolted the gate and moved away out of shot.

'Any good for facial recognition?' Holm asked, as Evans ran the footage again and froze it.

'Yes,' she said. She pointed at the screen. 'Clear features and front and sideways shots to work with. If he's in the system we'll get a match.'

Holm left Evans to run the search and returned to his office. He told Javed about what he'd seen.

'Whoever it was opened the back door with a key. Now who would you trust enough to give a spare key to?'

'A family member.'

'Just so. My theory is that either Tallin gave his brother a key or perhaps the key was at his parents' house. Somehow this goon gets hold of it, goes in, does the business, and we're none the wiser.'

'Any luck on the identification?'

'Claire's promised a result before lunch.'

In fact Evans delivered within the hour.

'Bingo! We have our man,' she said as she came into the office brandishing a printout. 'Nathan Henson. Goes by the nickname of Thommo. Well known to the Met Police. Last known address was in Gravesend, Kent.'

'A local boy.' Holm took the sheet of paper. There was a photo top right and biographical details below. 'I wonder what he was doing so far from home?'

He scanned through the text. Henson had a string of convictions ranging from burglary to racially aggravated assault. He'd been associated with the neo-Nazi group Combat 18, but in recent years had fallen off the radar. Eighteen months ago he'd re-emerged as a blogger with the handle Thommo. He'd published a number of long rants online, including a manifesto for the 'cleansing' of the UK of non-Christian faiths.

'Where is he now?' Holm said.

'We don't know. After publication of the manifesto, the police interviewed him. A file was handed to the CPS but there was only circumstantial evidence he'd written the piece and not enough to press charges. Police followed up but he'd moved on and there was no forwarding address. After that, nothing.'

'Is there anything else?'

'The file mentions that he used to run a painting and decorating business. The company was registered at the Gravesend address, but it doesn't appear to be in existence any longer. Sorry I couldn't be more helpful.'

Holm thanked Evans and she left.

'What do you think?' he asked Javed. 'Can you see Taher hiring this guy?'

'Don't know, boss.'

'I want everything we can get on Henson,' Holm said. 'Police National Computer, GCHQ, tax files, court proceedings, local government records, information from his time in prison. School reports. If he got a certificate for swimming twenty-five metres when he was eleven years old then I want it.'

'That's—'

'A lot of work, yes.' Holm smiled. 'So we'd best get started, right?'

–

They were back in the villa, sitting round the dining room table, Itchy there too. A maid had brought pineapple juice and some mid-morning snacks and Weiss was eating a sugared roll. Itchy viewed the MI5 man with suspicion, which, on past form, wasn't entirely surprising.

Weiss, it turned out, had been planning this operation for months. Initially the idea had come when he'd picked up rumours that Taher's cell was in contact with an ISIS group in the Philippines. After masterminding the attack in Tunisia, North Africa had become too hot for Taher and his companions, and he appeared to be scouting out locations for future training camps.

'I got a heads–up from the CIA,' Weiss said. 'An ISIS detainee had coughed during interrogation and hinted that Taher and his associates were coming to the Philippines to train local insurgents. I did some digging and discovered several pieces of corroborative evidence. One being that the expenses for the trip were going to be paid by your old friend Jawad al Haddad.'

'He's still around?' Silva said, feeling a surge of anger. Haddad had been instrumental in the death of her mother. When she'd uncovered his arms smuggling operation, he'd hired Taher to deal with her. The end result had been a terrorist atrocity that had killed Silva's mother and several others. When it came to his personal or business agendas, Haddad had no morals and would stop at nothing to get what he wanted.

'Yes. He managed to bribe his way out of Saudi Arabia, and the authorities in the UK and the US are reticent about charging him with anything. If he was ever put in the dock he'd spill the beans on the government corruption endemic in the international arms trade.'

'You promised me he'd face justice. It can't be right he can escape trial.'

'I'm afraid right and wrong don't come into it when you're dealing with billion-dollar trade deals.' Weiss eyed another sugared roll. 'Anyway, when I read the intercept I began to wonder if the Philippines might be the place to take down Taher and whoever was with him. Far away from Europe, out in the jungle, his guard might be down. There'd also be no legal complications. Unfortunately nothing came of the training camp idea and it looked as if my plan might be dead in the water. What I needed was something to lure Taher here on some other pretence.'

'And that was us,' Itchy said. 'We're bait on a fucking hook. How does that work, mate? I mean legally? Setting up British citizens to be popped by a terrorist just so you can spring a trap. Doesn't sound legit to me.'

'It's not.' Weiss smiled. 'But then I don't do legit. That approach is for people who carry warrants and make arrests. I find direct methods produce superior results and using you guys as bait counts as that. You see, you caused Taher and Haddad a lot of trouble in Tunisia. Specifically you ruined Haddad's relationship with the Saudis. There's also the small matter of the killing of his wife.'

'That wasn't me.'

'True, but Haddad thinks it was; understandably considering you were there when it happened and she was shot with your rifle.'

'You know it was one of Matthew Fairchild's men and he was following your orders.'

'Well that's not how Haddad sees it. I thought I could use that.'

'Use us, you mean,' Silva said.

Weiss ignored Silva and continued. 'Mr Tan has been a contact of mine for a long time. Recently he's been grateful to the British for protecting his fleet of merchant vessels from Iranian interference as they pass through the Strait of Hormuz so I decided to call in a favour. He was only too pleased to publicise his fake party and invite you to participate. All I had to do was seed that back to Haddad. Still, while he's a man who allows vengeance to cloud his judgement, Taher is not. For him blind retaliation is a fool's game that too often leads to disaster. However, in this case – either because Haddad has insisted or for some other reason – he's decided to make an exception. Perhaps he even thinks you're still a threat to his cell, that you might be on my team. I've always said you'd be welcome to join; perhaps Taher believes you already have.'

'This time you've gone too far,' Silva said. 'We'd never have agreed to being put in danger like this.'

'Not even to apprehend Taher or one of the others?' Weiss shook his head. 'I don't believe you. I think you'd do anything to avenge the death of your mother.'

'He's got a point, Silvi,' Itchy said. 'You're always telling me how you regret not getting Taher in Tunisia.'

'Shut up, Itch.' Silva stayed silent for a beat. 'Why didn't Taher try to kill us in the UK? Wouldn't that be a whole lot easier than flying out here?'

'A lot easier, but fraught with danger. He doesn't want to jeopardise his plans back home. This is risk free.'

'Not for us.'

'No, I'll give you that, but you've been in these situations before. It's not like you and Mr Smith are ordinary civilians. You're battle-hardened veterans, well used to danger.'

'If you could only hear yourself.'

'I can, Ms da Silva.' Weiss paused. 'I can also hear the tears and anger from the relatives of the victims of Taher's next atrocity. Not an attack on a café like the one that killed your mother, bad enough though that was. The next one will be much worse. In the Security Service we dub it "the big one". We know it's coming and we know Taher has the skills and the resources to carry it out.'

'If you know all this, then why don't you stop him?'

'And so we come full circle.' Weiss wiggled a finger round and round. 'I get you here, that attracts Taher, we take him out.'

'It sounds all too easy.'

'Not easy, but doable. Taher is expecting you to be at the party, that's when he'll strike.'

'But there is no party.'

'No, and that's why we're going to take him at Hassani's camp in the jungle. With the element of total surprise, he'll be a sitting duck.'

'Are you mad? We don't have any experience of fighting in the jungle. We'll probably get lost and wander round in circles for a couple of days before stumbling into one of Hassani's patrols.'

'We have someone up-country. He's ex-special forces, knows the jungle better than the locals, and is one of the best guides around. While I came up with the idea for the op, he – along with Mr Tan and Ruiz – worked up the details into a coherent plan.' Weiss held up his hands. 'Ms da Silva, Mr Smith, I don't have anything else to offer. Either you want to help me eliminate Taher or you don't. If you don't then there'll be a number of ISIS fighters coming round for a quick word in a few days' time. You can scarper, you can stay and fight, or you can take this opportunity to kill the man who murdered your mother. It's your call.'

Weiss was rising then. Walking to the door and not turning back. He headed out of the chalet and Silva watched him through a window as he made his way up to the main house.

Itchy fidgeted and scratched his chin.

'Heavy,' he said.

–

Taher's laptop was open on the table, the screen divided into four sections, each with a man's head and shoulders in the centre. These were his soldiers and they were a mixed bunch. Disparate. A clan united if not by religion or philosophy, then by purpose. Divided by distance at the moment, but not for long.

'Let's go over it again,' he said, trying not to display his exasperation. He'd been giving a briefing, but words had been said and he'd had to give them five to take a breather and calm down. Now he had to start over. 'From the beginning.'

He looked at their faces on the screen in front of him. Little boxes. Windows into their individual worlds.

Top left was Nathan 'Thommo' Henson. Location somewhere in southern England. Henson was white with a shaved head. The blue ink of a small home-made tattoo just below his right ear. A swastika. Thommo hated Muslims like Taher. He hated Pakis, Jews, Chinkies, blacks and Arabs. He didn't care much for *Guardian* readers, *Telegraph* readers, loony lefties, stuck-up toffs, the BBC, or feminists. Politicians were scum, as were the police, and he believed there was a special place in hell reserved for environmentalists and cocksuckers. Mostly he reckoned the last two were one and the same. In fact Taher wasn't sure there was anyone Henson didn't hate aside from himself.

Top right in another window was Anwan Saabiq. He was in London, across town from Taher. A youthful face half covered with a thin beard. Eyes flicking from side to side. Saabiq was a worrier, always nervous, always there with a 'what if' whenever Taher gave him an instruction. His passion and loyalty weren't in question, but as Taher had discovered in the past couple of days, his intelligence was.

The problem had been his brother, Tallin. It turned out that Saabiq had sent him one of the propaganda pictures the group had taken at the bungalow. Taher hadn't taken part and didn't much care for the practice, but Saabiq and the others had been keen, and if it provided them with extra motivation then where was the harm? Well, Taher thought ruefully, there would have been none if Saabiq hadn't been so stupid.

The first Taher had known about it was when Saabiq came to him and said Tallin had been in touch. There'd been a text asking Saabiq to give up the fight, a warning he was seeing security officers later that day. Saabiq was to get back to him immediately with his answer.

Saabiq had at least had the brains to come to Taher before replying. Taher had told Saabiq to ditch his phone, find new digs and lay low. Then he'd given Henson Tallin's address.

Bottom right was Jon Sutherland. His location was rural, a secluded location outside the capital, and he came complete with a soft West Country accent. Sutherland was white like Henson but had a beard like Saabiq and wore his hair long and in dreadlocks. He'd found faith during a long spell in prison, coming to see the same injustices Taher did. Unlike the irrational anger of Henson, Sutherland had a quiet, contemplative nature. And sometimes, Taher thought, the quiet types were the most committed and dangerous.

Finally, in the bottom left window, Mohid Latif. Location currently outside the UK. Latif was Taher's right-hand man. A true soldier, competent with weapons, quick-thinking, single-minded. Taher knew Latif would die – and probably wanted to die – for the cause without a moment's hesitation. That might come in the future, but not now. Latif was essential to Taher's plans because he'd undergone extensive training at a camp in Algeria. He'd learned how to make IEDs and suicide vests, and received tuition in close-combat techniques. Most importantly he'd been schooled in the set-up and use of the AirShield surface-to-air missile.

The system, designed and manufactured by Allied American Armaments, allowed battlefield ground units a high level of protection from enemy aircraft. Firing from a shoulder-launcher, the missile had a range of some ten kilometres and could reach a speed of Mach 4. Laser-guided, it was essentially impervious to countermeasures. Latif was the only one of the group who'd been fully trained to fire the missile, and the fact he was currently abroad made Taher nervous. Without him the whole scheme was in jeopardy.

He picked up a sheet of paper from a pile to his right and turned his attention back to the briefing.

'Step one,' he said. 'Nathan.'

Henson began to talk and Taher kicked back in his chair. Listened. He knew the plan backwards, every section down to its minutest component. He couldn't understand why the others didn't have the same attention to detail. Was it because they didn't believe or weren't as committed as he was? He hoped that wasn't the case. He was relying on them to deliver, but found he was almost expecting them to trip up, for the operation to fail. He was aware he'd grown overly paranoid recently. There was too much information out there for the security services to find. Sure, all the group's communications were encrypted and routed via the dark web, but the downfall of most plots came through what the security services called humint: human intelligence. Humint gathered information from contacts and interrogations, from interpersonal interactions. In the most trivial circumstances this could be mere gossip. More significantly it could take the form of an informant. In a previous mission, Taher had reversed the flow by finding somebody inside the intelligence services who had been happy to turn traitor for a pile of cash. Unfortunately the persistence of one particular MI5 officer had resulted in the traitor being exposed and Taher almost being captured or killed. It had been a close-run thing and was something he was keen to avoid in the future.

A good thing, then, that Stephen Holm was going to play a big part in Taher's ongoing plans.

Chapter 7

After Weiss had gone, they talked it over.

'We thought we were coming here for a bit of a jolly,' Itchy said. 'But we've gone from shooting down some drones to Weiss expecting us to go on a full-scale kill mission into the jungle. And if we fuck up it's not a few pictures of Tan's celebrity guests that end up in the papers, it's a couple of mugshots of you and me and a lurid headline about British tourists dying at the hands of ISIS. I expect you'll get a decent write-up, what with your Olympic success and all; I'll get barely a mention.'

'That's why we're not doing it, Itch,' Silva said. 'I'm fed up with being treated like dirt. It happened when we were kicked out of the army and again the first time we encountered Weiss.'

'I agree that Weiss is a piece of dog shit, but that doesn't change the facts. If we don't kill Taher then he'll come here and shoot up Mr Tan's island and afterwards head back to the UK and wreak havoc.'

'But why place the burden on our shoulders? Weiss could use other agents to take Taher out. He could pick him up when he returns to the UK – there's a hundred and one ways of stopping him.'

'Mr Tan.' Itchy looked up. Tan stood at the doorway holding a small canvas bag. He bowed. Itchy beckoned him in. 'Take a seat, maybe have a beer.'

'Thank you, Richard.' Tan walked in and took a seat. 'I'll have that beer, but I think we're done with the Mr Tan stuff. Call me Jun.'

Itchy got up and went to the minibar. Pulled out three bottles of beer and brought them over. Cracked them open. He passed the bottles round and raised his own. 'Cheers.'

'Yes,' Tan said. 'And once more apologies for the deception, although I feel somewhat deceived myself. Mr Weiss informed me you would be very likely to play ball. He said I only needed to appeal to your better natures and you'd be in. Once in the jungle I was to tell you the truth and explain about Taher.'

'Snipers don't have a better nature, Mr Tan,' Silva said. 'We're assassins, killers, murderers. We carry out executions without trial.'

'You do yourself an injustice.' Tan cocked his head. 'I don't believe for one minute you or Mr Smith can be included in that category. As for executions without trial, well, sometimes a trial isn't necessary. Guilt can be assumed by the target's actions. No need for a jury, no need for a verdict, and only one sentence that meets the demands for justice.'

'Justice or vengeance?'

'You tell me, Ms da Silva.' Tan raised his hands in a mock gesture of resignation. 'But sometimes both are served by a single action. In this case there is no doubt about the guilt of either man. Hassani has a rap sheet that includes murder, rape, extortion, drug smuggling, gunrunning, and more. He has caused misery, ordered the execution of ordinary people who tried to put up a fight, forcibly taken young girls from their families so they could become brides for his men. And your man, this

Taher. From what Weiss tells me his part in the attack that killed your mother and claimed the lives of many others is beyond doubt.'

'Weiss is twisting your arm,' Silva said. 'He sent you here as a final play.'

'Perhaps he did, but this isn't all about Weiss. I'm in the lucky position to be able to try to improve people's lives. I give money to local charities, I provide scholarships for bright young students, I founded an orphanage. However, sometimes simply throwing cash at a problem isn't enough. Hassani has control of various officials so he has nothing to fear from the government. I'm afraid direct action against him is the only option.'

'We're not for hire, Mr Tan. I don't know how many more times I can tell you.'

'I quite understand why you don't want to get involved, but you need to know there are reasons to do this outside of your own personal motives. Here.' Tan opened his canvas bag and pulled out a sheaf of glossy photos. He began to drop the pictures onto the table. 'Sorika, age thirteen, abducted from a school in Tabuk. Jenn, twelve, taken from her family's bakery. Lara, fourteen, went missing from a shopping centre in Manila.' One by one the photos fluttered down. 'Pretty young girls. Half a dozen. A dozen.' Tan paused, his gaze moving from the pile of pictures to Silva. 'Finally, Jani and Luki, both fifteen, kidnapped from the very orphanage I sponsor. So you see I have an interest in this beyond helping Simeon Weiss and the British government. This is personal. I want to stop Hassani and his men committing any more atrocities against children. With your help I can.'

'This isn't fair.' Silva held Tan's gaze.

'Life isn't fair, Ms da Silva. These children found that out and their families live with the fact every day of their lives. So do the others caught up in Hassani's evil. I've watched you on the range and seen how professional both of you are. I can't think of anyone more suitable for the job I have in mind.'

'If this Hassani is killed there'll be somebody to take his place.'

'Perhaps, but without him as a figurehead it's likely the various factions will fall to infighting and destroy them-selves. Certainly without Hassani around many people will feel safer.' Tan shrugged. 'As I see the situation, it's pretty much win–win.'

Silva stood there. She looked down at the pictures on the table. Felt the gaze of Itchy and Tan. She'd been skewered. Put in an impossible situation. Outflanked and outgunned.

'How about it, Silvi?' Itchy had a smile on his face. His mind was obviously made up. Perhaps the offer of an executive box at the next Chelsea game had made the difference. 'We nip into the jungle, pop Taher and this Butcher. Job done and we get a pat on the back from Mr Weiss and the British government.'

'Itchy…'

'Think of your mother, the way she stood up for the vulnerable. It was her whole life, wasn't it? Reporting from war zones, helping get the stories out about the way people suffered, trying to get things changed. Well, here's a chance for you to make a difference too.'

Her mother, of course, *would* have jumped straight in. She wouldn't have cared about the danger. Her only worry would have been for the victims and how she might be able to help. What would she think of Silva's reticence?

Silva shook her head, feeling herself wavering. She looked across at Itchy, wondering for a moment where his words had come from. She'd never heard him speak like this before. Had Tan or Weiss coached him? And yet the way he was staring down at the pictures showed he was plainly moved; Silva felt guilty for suspecting him of not being genuine.

She sighed, hoping she was making the right decision. 'Go on then, show me the details of the mission and I'll think about it.'

'Nice one, Silvi.' Itchy bounded across and patted her on the back. 'I told you she'd come round, Mr Tan, I was sure of it.'

'Well, I wasn't.' Tan smiled at Silva. 'A wise man never presumes anything, that way he is never disappointed.' He bent to his canvas bag and pulled out a sheaf of paper. 'Right then, let's get down to work, shall we?'

–

In recent weeks Holm had read a number of newspaper articles about privacy issues. In parliament there'd been a debate on the amount of information the government held on its citizens. The argument often went that those who had nothing to hide had nothing to fear. Holm usually held that view, but even he was surprised by the sheer volume of data they had managed to gather on Nathan 'Thommo' Henson. Big Brother really was watching.

On Wednesday they began to collate everything and work their way through the material.

'No swimming certificate,' Javed said, looking at the list of document titles he'd printed out. 'But we do have details of his most recent dental appointments, a prescription for athlete's foot, and a list of the eleven vehicles he's owned since he was seventeen.'

'Does any of that help us track him down?'

'He last went to the dentist two years ago, so that's no use. However, his current vehicle is a white Transit. No tax, no MOT, but we can cross-reference with data from number-plate recognition cameras and see if we get a match.'

'It's a start.'

'But only that.' Javed waved the sheets of paper. 'There are hundreds of documents to go through and just the two of us.'

'Well there's nothing better to do, is there?'

Holm turned to his computer. Javed had helpfully created a spreadsheet of the document titles and each was catalogued according to date and, if applicable, location. He'd also given them a relevance rating of one to three: not relevant, relevant, and highly relevant. Holm had soon skimmed through all the material with a three rating and nothing popped out at him. There were many more documents with a two rating, and over a thousand Javed had labelled as not relevant.

'What are we looking for?' Javed said.

'We won't know until we find it. That's why a computer could never do this type of work. It's also why I'm taking your rating scheme with a pinch of salt.'

'Thanks. It was only meant to make our task a little easier.'

'And it does because we can eliminate the obvious at the start, but there could be something buried deep in the minutiae of Henson's mundane existence. Uncovering that is the key.'

The possibility of discovering anything grew increasingly unlikely as the day wore on. By late afternoon, Holm had viewed so many credit card bills, flight tickets, MOT certificates and other assorted digitised documents that he was beginning to lose the will to live. He scrunched his eyes up and then tried to blink away a fierce headache.

He took a break and went to get a couple of coffees. When he returned, Javed was head down over several printouts.

'Got something?' Holm said, putting the coffees down.

'I'm not sure.' Javed handed Holm the top sheet. 'Something came up on the PNC. A couple of weeks ago the van registered to Henson was clocked by a speed camera in the village of Mereworth. That's in Kent, near Maidstone. Kent was where he used to live, right?'

'Obviously with no current address, Henson can get as many tickets as he wants. I don't see how that helps.'

'It's the village name. I spotted it on an invoice Henson submitted to the tax authorities a year or so ago.'

'I'm surprised he paid any tax.'

'Before he disappeared it looks as if he tried to pay as little as possible. Anyway, this invoice was for three grand and itemised as "general labouring".'

Holm smiled to himself. Javed often went off on a circuitous route to get to the point and sometimes Holm had a hard time following the young man's line of thought. 'You're losing me, Farakh. You need to explain where you're going with this.'

'Sure. The client was one Terrance Gaugan.'

'The politician?'

'Ex-politician, yes. He was a member of the European Parliament. He scraped in a few years back thanks to proportional representation. A far-right independent. Lost his seat after one term thanks to a dodgy expense claim.' Javed passed across another piece of paper. 'Take a look at the companies I found registered in his name.'

Holm scanned down the list. There was a haulier's, a services company, and one called BAI Ltd.

'BAI?'

'The letters stand for the British Aryan Insurgency, or alternatively – in a nod to the nomenclature of Combat 18 – Braunau am Inn. If you know your history, you'll understand.'

Holm looked at Javed. 'No, sorry, means nothing to me.'

'Braunau am Inn. Hitler's birthplace in Austria. The BAI appear to be a newish right-wing group that Gaugan has set up.'

'Charming. What do we have on them?'

'There's a database entry detailing the group's philosophy. They're white supremacists spouting the usual garbage about immigrants, conspiracy theories to do with mind control, spiked water supplies, you know the kind of thing. Not much else. According to the record further enquiries are pending the allocation of resources.'

'So much for Huxtable's insistence on the far right being a threat. Doesn't look like we're taking them seriously yet.' Holm looked at the sheet again, noting the company name. 'Limited? Doesn't seem right that you can make a profit out of this kind of stuff.'

'I guess it's unlikely to get charitable status – perhaps a limited company is the next best option for the organisation.' Javed brought up a browser and typed in the postcode. 'The HQ is in woodland near Mereworth. I've checked out the website. Says visitors strictly by appointment only.'

'I bet it does. I doubt they want anyone snooping around when they're marching up and down in their jackboots.'

'I'm sure they don't. The kicker is Henson triggered a speed camera near Mereworth not two weeks ago. I'd say that flags up the place for a visit, right?'

They set off the next day as dusk fell, Tan's motor yacht slicing into the blue water and heading out from the island into a choppy sea. The yacht was 25 metres long and had a full-time crew of three, plus, when the situation required, a chef and a steward.

'I left the steward at home,' Tan said. 'But I figured we could do with a decent meal this evening, so the chef's on board.'

Silva stood on the bridge deck with Tan. He was at the helm watching the wheel flick back and forward as the autopilot made adjustments to the course. Itchy, who got seasick in a rowing boat on a duck pond, had taken advantage of one of the luxury cabins below to crash out. Tan gestured at a large screen that displayed a nautical chart.

'We're here,' Tan pointed. 'And we'll land here on a remote, uninhabited part of the coast.'

He'd gone over everything earlier in the day. Hassani's base was deep in the Sierra Madre mountains, a couple of hundred miles north-east of Manila, and was accessible only by helicopter or a long journey in a four-wheel-drive vehicle. They'd head up the coast from Tan's island, a sea journey of some one hundred and sixty miles, and be dropped off in a remote cove. There they'd meet their guide and drive twenty miles inland in a 4 × 4. Finally, they'd hike another ten miles into virgin forest and make camp a couple of miles from Hassani's base. Weiss's intel suggested Taher would be arriving at the base at some point the following morning. The genius part, Tan had said with a smile, was the hide site.

'There's an old viewing platform that was placed in a tree years ago by the wildlife service. It was to facilitate a study into various birds and primates. The platform's in dense forest but on a ridge overlooking Hassani's encampment. Range about four to five hundred metres. The shot is difficult, but not impossible. I believe it's worth a try. Afterwards you'll abseil down from the tree and make double-quick time back to the camp for dust-off. My helicopter will fly us back here.'

'And if there's a problem with the helicopter?' Silva had asked.

'Then things could get rather interesting, rather fast.' Tan had grinned.

Silva glanced across at Tan as he continued to look at the chart. He was revelling in the situation and she wondered if this wasn't some kind of exciting diversion from the more mundane day-to-day life of running a shipping business.

'Were you in the army, Mr Tan?'

'Briefly. I did national service but I ended up as a quartermaster which, to be honest, helped to develop my business acumen.'

'Please tell me this isn't your chance to play soldiers?'

'No.' Tan gave a wry smile, but quickly became serious. 'I won't say I haven't enjoyed planning this, but helping Mr Weiss and ridding the world of Taher and Hassani is my main aim.'

Was that Weiss's aim too? Silva wasn't sure. He'd come sidling back into the villa once he knew Silva had changed her mind, but he'd let Tan do all the talking. Before they'd boarded the boat he'd revealed he wouldn't be coming with them.

'I'm a civil servant,' he said. 'I push pens and drive a desk. If I came along I'd only be a hindrance. Also, the whole thing needs to be deniable if anything goes wrong. Hence the need for me to absent myself.'

Silva wasn't happy about that. Weiss was the master of the double-cross, of the bluff or feint, and his goal was always a mystery that didn't reveal itself until the very last minute. She wouldn't put it past him not to dump her in some dodgy situation because of an obscure ulterior motive. His failure to come on the mission was too convenient.

She settled back into the bucket seat and watched the waves roll in on the starboard bow. Every now and then a larger one crashed against the boat and spray cascaded into the air.

'It's going to be a rough night,' Tan said. 'We'll eat soon and then I suggest everyone gets their heads down. Tomorrow will be a long day.'

Chapter 8

Holm and Javed spent Thursday morning brushing up on the BAI. It was, unsurprisingly given the name, a particularly unpleasant organisation. Its website was full of tirades against pretty much every ethnic, or minority group you could think of. The most recent diatribe was on the fire in Manchester and came close to justifying the murders of Anwan Saabiq and his wife as an act of legitimate resistance.

In the afternoon, having failed to find anything meaningful beyond the sick prose, Holm and Javed headed for the group's headquarters in Kent.

'This isn't doing much for the global warming directive,' Javed said as they once more drove out of London. 'At this rate Thames House will be living up to its name because the river will be flowing in through the front door.'

Holm didn't say anything. Instead he fumbled with a CD as they stopped at a set of traffic lights. *Time Out*. Brubeck and Desmond.

'Not this again,' Javed said as the distinctive piano notes of the first track began. 'We must have listened—'

'My car, my music,' Holm said.

'You were born thirty years too late.'

'Tell me about it.'

They threaded their way out of the city and headed for Maidstone, turning off the M20 at Wrotham. This was greenbelt countryside, a hotchpotch of fields and woods and golf courses, the area dotted with little villages.

'Mereworth Woods,' Javed said as they sped down a ruler-straight road with mature trees on either side. 'Henson got his speeding ticket in the village further on, but the BAI HQ is up here on the right.'

Holm slowed as they approached a turn-off. A discreet sign on a wooden five-bar gate spelled out the letters B.A.I. with no hint as to what might be beyond. Holm pulled in and Javed got out and opened the gate. Back in the car, he was staring down at his phone.

'Ex-MOD,' he said. 'Bet the members wet their knickers with excitement when they turn up for meetings. They can play just like those real nutters in the US do.'

'You mean survivalists?' Holm said.

'They're the ones. Only I guess they're not allowed firearms here.'

'Thank God.'

The track wound in among the trees, the deciduous woodland giving way to tall conifers pushing skywards, nothing but dead pine needles and gloom beneath the thick canopy. Aside from the low tickover of the engine and the crunch of the tyres on the gravel, there was silence. In the heart of Home Counties England, this was a place removed from reality and perhaps that was the point. A little fantasy white-washed world away from it all. Holm wondered what the BAI members would make of Javed. He berated himself for not thinking of it before. On his return to Thames House the checkbox HR managers would be asking if he'd done a risk assessment as to the effect the trip could have on Javed's mental health; Holm just didn't want to see the lad offended.

Up ahead, a metal pylon loomed over the trees. At the top of the pylon was a wooden platform with a simple roof. There was a figure up there watching their approach through binoculars. For a moment Holm wondered if this lot had really lost it. Building a guard tower seemed a step too far. Then he realised the structure was ancient and rusty.

'Fire-watch hut,' he said. 'I bet it's got a great view. They'd have known we were coming for a while.'

'Forewarned, forearmed.' Javed peered up through the windscreen as they passed close to the tower. 'Let's hope I'm right about the guns.'

The track widened and entered a large clearing. Several low concrete buildings stood at one end, while a huge curving turfed roof marked some kind of hanger or bunker. Barbed wire ran in loops round the perimeter, the track passing through at a checkpoint with a decrepit sentry box and a barrier that was in the up position.

'What kind of military installation did you say this was?' Holm asked.

'I didn't, but the bunker looks like it's from the cold war era. Never mind the guns, let's hope they haven't got hold of a couple of nukes.'

Holm nodded. He pulled the car round and parked next to an old jeep. It had a canvas roof and there was an American star painted on the side. There was also a Land Rover Defender that had seen better days, but the other vehicles were more the sort of thing you'd see on the motorway: a Lexus, a couple of mid-range Mercs, a Tesla. How many sales reps had an interest in the far right? While some men went fishing to get away from their wives, did others attend secret meetings wearing jackboots?

'Boss.' Javed pointed through the windscreen as they were about to get out. To one side of the bunker was a large sandy area. There were targets down one end and close to the bunker a man stood holding a crossbow, while another man alongside the first appeared to be an instructor. Both were dressed in black paramilitary gear, but the one with the bow had long brown hair in a tangle of dreadlocks, a beard in need of a trim. 'I hear banjo music. The guy with the bow is right out of the Appalachians.'

The two men looked towards the car as Holm and Javed got out. The instructor, who Holm recognised as Terrance Gaugan, said something to the man with the crossbow and walked over.

Holm remembered Gaugan from *Question Time* on TV a few years back. He'd been a bit of a firebrand on the show, despite having been shouted down by the audience at every opportunity. In real life he wasn't so impressive. He was in his late forties, prematurely balding, with beady eyes behind round wire-frame glasses. *Inadequate* was the adjective that sprang to mind, although Holm realised he was probably letting his own prejudice show through. Prejudice and maybe a little jealousy too, because Gaugan's appearance hadn't dented his life chances, certainly not with women; his wife was a gorgeous ex-model and Holm recalled reading somewhere that the couple had two young children. Perhaps the devil really did play the best tunes.

'You lost, mate?' Gaugan addressed Holm, barely acknowledging Javed. 'Only this is private property. You'd best turn on around and hightail it out of here.'

'I don't think so.' Holm pulled out his MI5 ID. 'I'm Stephen Holm from the Security Service, this is my colleague Farakh Javed. We've got a few questions. Is there somewhere we can talk?'

Gaugan stood still. He gave a not-so-subtle glance over to the other man before nodding and leading the way to one of the concrete buildings. A short hallway opened to a large conference room. Chairs were set out round a number of trestle tables. To the right, against the wall, there was another table where a couple of dozen cups and saucers had been arranged next to a water boiler. Piles of sandwiches wrapped with clingfilm sat on a number of plates. The set-up looked like a Women's Institute lunch, aside from the huge banner hanging on the rear wall. It was red with a white disc in the middle, a swastika in the centre of the disc. The flag of Nazi Germany.

'That could be construed as an offence under the Public Order Act,' Holm said, pointing at the flag.

'No, mate. We're on private land. Freedom of expression, isn't it?'

'Right.' Holm took a sideways glance at Javed. He gestured at one of the tables. 'Shall we?'

They sat, the man on one side, Holm and Javed on the other. Confrontational, Holm thought, and nothing wrong with that.

'Are you Terrance Gaugan?'

'I'm Tel, yes. You here to arrest me or something?'

'What's going on here, Mr Gaugan?' Holm looked across at the sandwiches. 'A picnic?'

'Refreshments for our recruits. They're out training in the woods at the moment.'

'And what's with the guard tower, the archery, the barbed wire?'

'Precautions, that's all.'

'Against who or what?'

'The government.'

'You mean the police?'

'No I mean people like you and your… mate.'

'You're paranoid.'

'Not really. The fact that you're here proves I'm not.' Gaugan held Holm's gaze. 'Have you heard of Ruby Ridge? Waco? Jonestown? That's what happens when the government tries to stop people living their lives the way they want to.'

'I don't know if you realise, but this is the UK, not the USA.'

'There are other forces at work.' A flick of the eyes towards Javed. 'Londonistan. Know what I mean?'

Holm doubted Gaugan realised the word Londonistan had originated back in the nineties and had come from French intelligence officers frustrated by the UK's failure to apprehend known Islamists in London. Now the word was more often used as a term of abuse by the right wing.

'You're talking about me,' Javed said. 'Muslims.'

'Look, mate, no offence, but I don't want you marrying my sister or my daughter.'

'That's extremely unlikely.' Javed smiled, the inside joke lost on Gaugan. 'And, to be honest, I really wouldn't be happy with someone like you sniffing around within ten miles of my own sister.'

'And that's all there is to it.' Gaugan nodded in agreement. 'We don't want mosques replacing churches. We don't want sharia law. We want to preserve the English way of life.' Gaugan was on a roll. 'See, if I went over to Saudi or one of those countries, and I started behaving like I was still in England, then I'd get the chop, right?

Deservedly so. We're culturally different. All of us. Christians, Muslims, Jews. We don't mix. We don't *want* to mix. That's why you have ghettos. Leicester, for instance. If Muslims wanted to integrate they'd have moved in next door to me instead of colonising whole fucking streets.'

As if Gaugan would have warmly welcomed his new neighbours with open arms, Holm thought. Cup of sugar, jar of coffee, and never mind the swastika flag hanging in the back garden.

'You're the leader of the BAI, right?' Holm said.

'That depends on what we're accused of.' Gaugan chuckled to himself. 'Not in my name and all that. The British Aryan Insurgency gets the blame for a lot of stuff that goes down, but we're a legal organisation. We don't condone violence.'

'Really? What about what happened in Manchester on Monday? Your website has a piece on how the victims had it coming to them, do you agree with that?'

Gaugan shrugged. 'You go into a war zone you're liable to get hurt.'

'A two-up two-down family home in a quiet street isn't a war zone.'

'I'm talking metaphorically. The culture war. Cross over into no man's land and you become a target.'

'And was Tallin Saabiq one of your targets, Mr Gaugan?'

'I told you, we're non-violent.'

'Do you know where Nathan Henson is?'

'Right. I get it.' Gaugan leaned back in his chair and folded his arms. 'You're trying to pin the Manchester thing on him are you?'

'Henson's a right-winger. He even did some work for you. I expect you're still in contact.'

'No I'm not. He hung around here for a while but then decided he wanted a lower profile. He was being targeted by a nasty bunch of antifas. Wouldn't leave him alone.'

'When did you last see him?'

'Thommo?' Gaugan shook his head. Glanced, for some reason, over at the table with the sandwiches. 'Don't know. He hasn't been here for months.'

'You got an address? Contact details?'

'Nah, mate. Like I said, precautions.' Gaugan raised his hand and tapped the side of his nose with his forefinger. 'If I had an address and I gave it to you, within a day it would be in the hands of the lefties. Shortly after, Thommo's place would be torched.'

If Gaugan was being ironic, his expression gave nothing away. Unlike the glance at the lunch table.

'Thanks, Mr Gaugan.' Holm stood. 'You've been very helpful, at least in eliminating the BAI from our enquiries.'

'I have?' Gaugan followed as Holm and Javed walked from the room.

'Yes.' At the entrance Holm stopped. He handed the car keys to Javed. 'Could you bring the car round for me?'

Javed's mouth dropped open, but Holm turned so he was facing away from Gaugan. He winked.

'Sure thing, sir,' Javed said and moved towards the car.

'Tel,' Holm said, nodding after Javed before facing Gaugan. 'Don't get the wrong idea about MI5. There's a lot of us in the establishment who are on your side. We don't like this equality crap any more than you do. We can see where it's leading. Londonistan being a case in point. Keep up the good work, right?'

Holm turned and walked over to where Javed had reversed the car. He got in the passenger side.

'What the fuck was that about?' Javed said.

'I just intimated to Gaugan that I was part of their sad little club.' Holm glanced up at the rear-view mirror as Javed pulled away. 'And I think he might have bought it.'

'Not sure, boss,' Javed said. 'You're not really the type.'

'I'll take that as a compliment.'

'He knows where Nathan Henson is though, right?'

'Yes. If Gaugan is hoping to be part of some right-wing revolution then he's going to need to work on his poker face.'

They drove back through the woods and parked a little way up the road from the entrance to the BAI site.

'We'll wait here,' Holm says. 'My bet is that Gaugan will come tootling out in a bit. If we follow him I think we might find he leads us to Henson.'

'Why doesn't he simply make a call?'

'Paranoia. You heard the man. Ever since I flashed my ID I bet he's been thinking we've got eyes in the skies, bugs under the bunk beds and have tapped the phones of every BAI member. He'll play it safe.'

Sure enough, about ten minutes later, the old jeep turned out from the site and surged down the main road. Javed started the car and followed at a distance. Gaugan drove on for a mile and then turned left onto a country lane that weaved through fields and woodland. Another left at a T-junction onto an even smaller lane. Then left again.

'Fuck,' Holm said. 'He's sold us a dummy.'

They were back on the main road, the entrance to the BAI site about half a mile further on. Gaugan had driven in a circle. He pulled the jeep back onto the track and there was a double beep of the horn as the vehicle disappeared into the woodland.

'Well,' Javed said. 'You can't say his paranoia wasn't justified. Perhaps he's not quite as thick as you'd like to believe.'

Despite the rough sea, Silva slept well. Itchy emerged from his cabin looking fresher than he had the night before and eager for breakfast. As they sat in the saloon eating, a smudge of land was gradually revealing itself through the windscreen. A low grey finger became green as they approached. The featureless terrain grew hills and mountains and the flat line of the coast became indented with bays and coves.

A mile out they gathered on the stern deck where a large RIB hung from a set of davits. Along with Silva, Itchy and Tan, there were two other men. One was a member of the yacht crew – he'd bring the RIB back to the boat after dropping the rest of them off – the other was Paulo Ruiz, Tan's head of security. Ruiz's jovial mood had been left behind on the island, his smile replaced with a grimace.

'We're good to go,' Tan said. He raised a hand and made a circling motion with a finger. One of the yacht crew lifted a panel to one side of the davits and pressed the button to lower the RIB. The inflatable settled in the water, rising and falling with the swell. Another crew member steadied it as Silva and the others clambered down to the stern platform and climbed aboard. She could see a pile of equipment had already been loaded, including the long flight case that held her rifle. Tan was at the central console, the wheel in his hand. The twin outboards fired up and he signalled for the crew to fend them off. As the bow pointed out from the yacht, he gunned the engines.

The RIB shot forward, bouncing over the waves. Now the coast was revealed in even more detail. Cliffs above rocky beaches, dense forest on steep hills behind. In the far distance, the peaks of mountains piercing a bank of cloud.

'Looks wild,' says Itchy. 'Not like anything in a tourist brochure.'

'Beautiful, though,' Silva said. 'And a lot more pleasant than Afghanistan.'

'Not really,' Tan shouted from behind, his voice almost lost in the roar of the engines. 'Once you get in the forest it's like hell. Ninety-five per cent humidity, biting insects, no sense of direction, visibility barely more than a few metres.'

'But no Taliban.'

'No, but instead of the Taliban you have Hassani's foot soldiers. They're well trained and well-armed. They're totally at home here and blend traditional military discipline and techniques with native Indian fieldcraft. It's a unique combination and very effective. Last year a crack squad of Philippine special forces was taken out by just a dozen of them. The incident was so embarrassing that the defence minister had to resign. It explains why for the most part the politicians prefer to take Hassani's bribes. Less risky and more profitable.'

'And we're going up against his men?'

'Hopefully not. We'll do our best to avoid encountering anyone.'

The RIB was nearing the shore and Tan throttled back the engines. He made way at the wheel for the crew member and edged forward. The crew nosed the boat into the white froth of the surf line. When they were a few metres from the beach, Ruiz jumped into the thigh-deep water, grabbed the painter and guided the boat in. Silva, Itchy and Tan clambered out and began ferrying equipment to shore. Silva had the flight case while Itchy, Tan and Ruiz had large Bergens.

A figure appeared at the top of the beach near the treeline. Raised a hand.

'That's our ride.' Tan waved and hefted the rucksack onto his back. 'Come on.'

They trudged up the sandy foreshore as the figure turned and disappeared back into the trees. Twenty metres in there was a battered Land Cruiser, 'National Park' stencilled on one of the doors.

'Meet Sandy Gilsmith,' Tan said. 'The best wildlife guide in the whole of the Philippines.'

'Nice to meet you, folks,' Gilsmith said, holding up a hand in greeting.

Disconcertingly, considering he'd just stepped out of a Philippine jungle, Gilsmith spoke with a strong Yorkshire accent. He was early forties with blond hair and a weathered face that had seen too much sun. He wore a camouflage jacket and trousers. At his waist a holster held an ancient-looking revolver while a large bush knife sat in a scabbard on his right leg. Silva wondered how on earth he'd ended up here. Weiss had said something about 'having someone in-country' – did that mean Gilsmith was an agent? Perhaps he was just another of Weiss's wide network of contacts.

'We'd better get moving,' Gilsmith said. 'There could be thunderstorms later and the road in becomes impassable in heavy rain. Let's mount up.'

'This man knows his stuff.' Tan stepped forward and patted Gilsmith on the shoulder. 'We'd better do as he says.'

Silva sat in the front, sandwiched between Tan and Gilsmith. Itchy and Ruiz were in the back, the equipment crammed in around them. Gilsmith started the engine and steered the vehicle away from the beach. A rutted track threaded into the trees beneath a thick canopy. Silva could see what he meant about the rain. The track was thick with mud, the Land Cruiser lurching through deep pools of water.

While everyone else hung on, Gilsmith appeared relaxed and wanted to talk. Silva's reputation preceded her, he said. Tan had told him that she was a bit of a legend. He turned to Silva for a moment and smiled. Was that true?

'I might have over-egged the pudding,' Tan said, leaning forward. 'But only by a little.'

'Let's hope not.' Gilsmith concentrated on the road for a second. 'Because it's going to be a difficult shot. I wouldn't have a hope in hell at half the distance.'

'You're ex-forces,' Silva said. 'Didn't you get much practice with a rifle?'

'I've always preferred hand-to-hand combat.' Gilsmith grinned. 'Up close and personal. Only way to be sure you've done the job.'

Silva was beginning to get the impression that Gilsmith might be a little gung-ho. Not what was needed on a stealth mission into enemy territory.

Gilsmith shifted into a lower gear as the track began to rise. Every now and then Silva caught a glimpse of vertiginous rock formations through the canopy. A huge escarpment towered above them on their left, and it appeared as if there was no way through. Then the track rounded an outcrop and threaded into a canyon that climbed towards the sky. Gilsmith down shifted again and rammed the vehicle into low ratio. They crept forward, sometimes slipping sideways, the track steepening still further until Silva felt as if they were going to topple over backwards.

No one spoke now. Even Gilsmith had a look of extreme concentration on his face. In the rear of the vehicle Itchy and Ruiz struggled to remain in their seats. The rucksacks and flight case had slipped against the rear door, everything piled in an almighty mess.

Just when all progress seemed to have stopped and Silva thought they weren't going to make it, Gilsmith flicked the wheel and changed gear again and they lurched over a final rise. The track now levelled out.

'That was close,' Gilsmith said. 'If it had rained before we got here, we'd never have made it.'

He changed back into a normal gear and they drove on. In half a mile they came to a T-junction and joined a level fairway.

'It's a logging road.' Gilsmith turned right and headed down the centre of the muddy expanse. 'Loggers come in after certain valuable trees. It helps that they pay Hassani protection money, not that he does anything for it. Still, if you argue with the loggers then you're picking a fight with him.'

The road, although not tarmac, was in far better condition than the track they'd come up. They made good progress and after an hour or so Gilsmith edged left and plunged off into the forest down a byway. He drove on for a few minutes and then pulled to the side and rolled the Land Cruiser behind a dense clump of tangled vegetation.

'We'll stop here.' Gilsmith opened the door and clambered down. 'We'll cover our tracks and hide the vehicle as best we can. It's got no plates and the frame and engine numbers have been erased. Should it be found there's no way of tracing it back to me.'

They hauled the kit out and Gilsmith and Ruiz pulled a camouflage net over the Land Cruiser. Hopefully anyone coming down the track would drive past without spotting the vehicle.

Gilsmith gave a quick briefing. In this part of the world, he said, you shoot first and ask questions later. He bent to a big kitbag he'd brought along. Out came two pistols, one each for Itchy and Tan. Gilsmith had his revolver and Ruiz his own handgun. Things, Silva thought, were getting serious.

She unpacked her rifle from the flight case and secured it to the back of her rucksack. She took the case a few metres into the jungle and hid it behind a tree.

'Ready?' Gilsmith glanced round at the group. When each had nodded, he pointed to a small animal trail that led under the canopy. 'Let's go, then.'

The hike into the camp was exhausting. The animal trail was just that, and if you were a two-legged upright biped progress was excruciatingly slow. Ducking and twisting and crawling was almost impossible with a long rifle and, despite having applied anti-mosquito cream, Silva was bitten to shit. The humidity was almost unbearable and she'd drunk all of the water in her hip flask after the first couple of hours.

Gilsmith was a constant up ahead. He seemed to move with the same speed whatever the terrain. Thick jungle, rock faces scattered with scree, bog or marsh, once a flowing river they had to wade waist-deep down for half a mile. The terrain was precipitous, the hills they had to climb like inverted Vs. Tan had said the hike in was ten miles, but to Silva it felt double that. Finally, as they neared the end of the sixth hour, Gilsmith stopped. He held up a hand.

'We're close to where we'll camp,' he said. 'From now on we only talk in whispers. Make sure your safeties are on, check for anything loose that might bang around. We're still a few miles from Hassani's base, but he has a lot of guards who patrol out to a mile or so and I've heard rumours there are microphones too. If he catches us out here...' Gilsmith let the sentence tail off, but the seriousness on his face suggested it would be wise to heed his advice. 'OK, ten minutes to the camp.'

'Thank fuck,' Itchy whispered. 'I'm about done in.'

'Me too,' Silva said. In the army she'd been fit and since leaving she'd tried to keep up some kind of regime by running regularly, but the march in had made her realise she wasn't as tough as she once was. 'I'm bushed.'

The camp was nothing more than a stand of trees looming above a clearing strewn with large boulders. They strung hammocks between the trees and ate a cold meal as the sun went down. Ruiz drew up a watch rota with Silva being first on. The others climbed into their hammocks and pulled mosquito nets around them while Silva sat on a boulder and listened to the sounds of the forest. Tomorrow she'd see the terrorist who killed her mother through the scope of her rifle. And this time she'd make sure he didn't get away.

Chapter 9

The next stop was Gravesend. Henson's painting and decorating business was registered to an address in Bernard Street, a stone's throw from the river Thames. The drive north from BAI HQ took just under twenty minutes.

'He won't be here,' Javed said. 'Tax records show letters returned to sender for the past six months.'

'Maybe not,' Holm said. 'But the traffic camera doesn't lie. He visited the BAI HQ recently so he could still be in the area. We'll see.'

The satnav took them to a hidden-away backstreet of pebble-dashed terraced houses. Cars parked in the road. Little steps up to the front doors. Anonymous, Holm thought. Like so many others. How many façades in similar streets concealed secrets the authorities should know about? Abuse, illegal drugs, modern slavery, tax fiddles, extremism, neglect.

'There it is,' Javed said as they pulled up a few doors down from number twenty-three. 'What are we going to do? Ask the neighbours?'

They started with twenty-one. The man who answered the door had lived in the house for twelve years, and yet he didn't know anything about a painting and decorating business. He hadn't seen anyone come in and out with materials, although there'd been a white Transit parked on the street a while back, and he did remember a man matching Henson's description.

The occupants of number twenty-five, a young couple with a baby, had only lived there for a few months. As far as they could remember Henson hadn't been living in the house since they'd moved in, but somebody was there now because they'd seen a young man coming and going.

There was no response when they knocked at twenty-three so Holm, much to Javed's impatience, decided they'd wait.

'For how long?' Javed asked.

'For as long as it takes.' Holm returned to the car and settled back in his seat, trying to suppress a smile. Back in his police days he'd spent hours on surveillance duties. Boredom, hunger and thirst went with the territory. You hoped your partner had showered that morning and hadn't been for a curry the previous night. You either sweated or shivered and were nearly always desperate for a piss. And most of the time it was all for nothing.

After an hour, Holm took pity on Javed and sent him off to buy some supplies. He returned with nothing more substantial than two cans of Coke, half a dozen bags of crisps and a couple of muesli bars.

'Sorry, boss,' he said. 'There was only a petrol station.'

'No chocolate?' Holm said as Javed handed over one of the muesli bars and a can of Coke that turned out to be sugar free.

'Yeah, but I thought you'd value the healthy option.'

'Great.'

They sat and watched as people returned to their houses after work. Six o'clock turned into seven o'clock, the early evening into something close to Holm's bedtime.

Windows flashed with the glare of TVs, curtains were drawn as darkness fell.

Holm was dozing when Javed prodded him awake.

'There,' he said as a hunched figure darted along the street, unlocked the front door of number twenty-three, and slipped inside. A light went on in the front room.

Holm, now fully awake, was out of the car in a flash. He went over and rapped on the door. A young man opened up. He was early twenties, white, with short hair and little goatee beard. He recoiled at the sight of Holm and Javed.

'You can't cut me off,' he said. 'I'm a vulnerable person. On the spectrum. Stress might push me over the edge.'

'Really?' Holm caught a waft of something rich and sweet. He flashed his ID and stepped forward, placing his foot in the door. 'Then we'd better go inside so you can take the weight off your feet.'

'You're not from Southern Electric?'

'No. Although I imagine you're using quite a lot of juice, would I be correct?' Holm wrinkled his nose, made a play of sniffing the air. 'I think we'd better take a look at what you've got in there.'

'No way!'

'Yes way,' Javed said. He had his own ID out. 'We're from the Security Service. Just a few questions about your mate Nathan Henson.'

'That fucker? He owes me for the gas and council tax. He's no mate of mine.'

'That's good to hear.' Holm inched forward. 'We're not interested in whatever hydroponic set-up you've got in there. Unless, of course, you choose not to cooperate. Then we'd have to call the regulars in. Shall we?'

Holm gestured inside and after a moment the young man nodded and retreated down a hallway. Holm and

Javed followed. Holm sniffed again as he entered. The smell was stronger now, heavy. No longer sweet, more like boiled vegetables and cat piss.

'Skunk,' he whispered to Javed. 'You stay with matey boy, I'm going to look around.'

The house was a two-up two-down, the kitchen having been enlarged and extended into the rear yard. Upstairs there was a bedroom overlooking the street, but the back room had been converted into a grow space. A harsh light shone from within and there was a wash of heady vapour.

Holm peered into the room. There were a dozen plants sprouting from hydroponic granules. The white light came from special lamps hanging on chains from the ceiling. To one side there was some kind of packing area with little plastic bags and a set of scales. The whole set-up maybe brought in a profit of a few hundred a month, but no more.

When he'd sniffed the air and realised some serious cannabis production was going on, Holm had wondered if this was some part of a terror-financing operation. Now, given the small scale of the enterprise, he wasn't so sure. He went back downstairs to the living room where he found the young man sitting on a grotty sofa while Javed watched over him. There was a jam jar resting precariously on one arm of the sofa, inside the remains of a dozen rollups lying on a bed of ash.

'Says his name is Shaz,' Javed said. 'Claims he hasn't seen Henson in months.'

'Months.' Shaz nodded.

'The plants.' Holm nodded towards the hall. 'Are they yours?'

'Nah, they belong to my housemate. Nothing to do with me. Told him I wasn't happy, but what can you do?'

'Your boyfriend, is he? Seeing as there's only one other bedroom in this place.'

'He does nights. We hot-bed.' Shaz tried for a grin but realised Holm had got the better of him. He shook his head.

'Do you know Taher?'

'You've seen what's here.' Shaz shrugged. 'Like I said, not my stuff.'

'Not what's here, *Taher*.'

'Hey?'

'What about Mohid Latif? Where's he?'

'I don't know who or what the fuck you're talking about.'

'Latif's got a beard like you, but he probably wouldn't touch the stuff upstairs. Plus he prays several times a day.'

'You mean a towelhead?' Shaz turned towards Javed.

'Could be.' Holm didn't comment or elaborate further.

Shaz looked blank. Either he was an astounding actor or he really didn't know anything about Taher or Latif.

'Nathan Henson.' Holm walked over to an armchair with the intention of sitting down. One look at the greasy surface and he changed his mind. 'Tell us about him.'

'Thommo? Not much to tell except that he's a complete nutter. No chill. I hardly saw him but when I did he wouldn't give me the time of day.'

'He lived here?'

'No. Paid rent for the spare room but never used it other than as a place for some stuff he had.'

'Materials for his painting and decorating business?'

'Never saw anything like brushes or nothing. There were some chemicals in twenty-five litre containers.

Might have been paint stripper. Mostly the address was a mail drop. He'd come round and pick up letters once a week or so.'

'When did Henson move out?'

'Around nine months ago. Turned up in a van and removed everything from the room. The mail stopped coming a few days after. Reckon he must have got it redirected.'

'Nine months ago?' Holm look across at Javed. He could see his colleague felt the same disappointment. The trail was cold.

'We should shop him, boss,' Javed said. 'He's not given us anything we didn't already know.'

That was untrue, but Holm could see how Javed was playing it.

'You're right. Guess I'll have to phone the local nick. At least I'll get some Brownie points for doing the right thing.'

'Hang on.' Shaz took a glance at Javed and then Holm. 'I didn't say that was the last time I'd *seen* him.'

'Go on.'

'A few weeks after he moved out he comes round and asks me if I could get a weapon for him.'

'What was your answer?'

'I said I had no idea. I mean me? A weapon? Bloke was off his rocker but he seemed to accept my answer. He told me if I did think of anyone who could help him to get in touch.'

'And did you?'

Shaz didn't say anything. Bit his lip.

'Well?' Holm probed.

'It's not just that lot, is it?' Shaz nodded up at the ceiling. 'If I told you anything about a gun there'd be a firearms charge too.'

'You're not in a position to barter. We can get you for production of a controlled drug, possession with intent to supply, aiding and abetting a known terrorist, and failure to provide information to prevent a terrorist attack.'

'A terrorist? What the hell are you talking about?'

'Henson's a neo-Nazi and it looks to me as if you've been helping him out.'

Shaz bit his lip. Appeared to consider the situation. Nodded. 'A few months ago I had to hide a sawn-off shotgun for someone. There wasn't an option to refuse, if you know what I mean. Anyway, what happens is the guy who gave it to me gets caught over Stratford way. Two guys on a moped trundle up. One gets off and slips a blade in under the ribs. Paramedics turn up, like, fifteen minutes late, but matey bleeds out. Now I've got a bit of a problem. This gun is stuck behind a panel in my wardrobe. I could chuck it, but it's got to be worth a couple of hundred to somebody.'

'Henson.'

'Yeah. He'd given me a number, so I texted him. Said I had what he wanted and named a price. Got a reply within five minutes.'

Holm did what he always did in these situations: clenched his fist in response to a tingle that ran up his arm. Nathan 'Thommo' Henson was close. Very close.

'When was this exactly?' he said.

'Four months. Perhaps more.'

Holm nodded and felt the tingle fade a little. 'Have you got his number?'

'Nah, mate. You see I only keep the same phone and number for six months.' Shaz winked. 'As a canny small business owner I've got to keep ahead of you lot, right?'

'Mate?' Holm shook his head. 'Doesn't sound like you're any mate of mine. You haven't given me anything. Reckon our deal is off.'

'Hang on. I was just getting to the gist of the thing.' Shaz paused. 'You see, when he came to get the gun I thought I needed a little insurance policy, so after he'd paid and left I followed him. He was still driving the white Transit, so he was an easy mark. He took the tunnel under the Thames and drove to Dagenham, ends up at a load of warehouses on an industrial estate by the railway. One end there was a string of lock-up garages backing onto the line. Henson pulls into the estate and parks by one of the garages. When he opens it up I see all those containers of chemicals he'd had in my room.'

Holm waited for more but Shaz just cocked his head. Smiled.

'Is that it?' Holm said.

'Yeah, I guess.'

'Let's go, then.'

'Where?'

'Your choice.' Holm gestured to the door. 'Either we take you to the local police station or you take us to Henson's garage.'

–

It was still dark when Gilsmith roused her. They ate breakfast and then broke camp, making sure there was nothing left behind. Ruiz and Gilsmith double-checked the rendezvous point where they'd meet later, Itchy hovering beside them so he had an idea where they were going.

'Just in case,' he whispered to Silva.

Silva nodded. Itchy was a wizard when it came to navigation. If anything went wrong she trusted him to be able to get them out.

It was time to leave. Tan and Ruiz took the majority of the equipment, leaving Silva, Itchy and Gilsmith to travel light.

'Good luck,' Tan said. He shook Silva's hand, did the same with Itchy. 'Do your best and I'm sure you'll be successful.'

Tan and Ruiz disappeared into the predawn gloom, and Gilsmith led Silva and Itchy in the opposite direction down a small trail. At first the going was similar to the previous day, but soon the forest began to change. The trees became larger and taller, huge trunks rising from the jungle floor, lifting themselves above the low scrub and vaunting overhead. Silva estimated the canopy was some twenty-five metres up, a blanket of green almost entirely blocking out the lightening sky. Birdsong rang out all around and the call from an unseen monkey echoed in the distance.

Gilsmith made a hand signal. A finger to his lips, a gesture at a narrow animal track, and a show of his fingers spread, flashed twice: Silence. Take that path. One hundred metres.

They followed Gilsmith down the trail. Every now and then a stick cracked beneath Silva or Itchy's feet, but Gilsmith moved without a sound. After a few minutes they reached a slight rise where a clump of four large trees grew. A tangle of vines hung down from one tree. Gilsmith stepped across and parted the tangle to reveal several dark-green climbing ropes. He removed his rucksack and lowered it carefully to the ground. He opened the sack and pulled out three harnesses, each paired with two rope ascenders. He looked at Silva and Itchy and cocked his head. The question was unspoken but obvious. Did they know how to use the gear?

Silva nodded. Tan had briefed them that they'd be using climbing equipment but she hadn't used this kind of kit since basic training. She removed the rifle from her back and put on the harness. Gilsmith adjusted it, attached the ascenders to the climbing rope, and helped her sling the rifle back on. He flicked his head, his gaze moving to the canopy above. *Up.*

She put her feet into the foot loops and slid one of the ascenders up the rope. Stepped up. Repeated the process with the other ascender. Stepped up. Slide, step. Slide, step. Slide, step.

It took her several minutes before she neared the platform. A large branch spiralled out from the trunk and a sheet of metal mesh sat on a grid of rusty angle iron atop the branch. Wires came from somewhere above to further support the platform. A camouflage net hung from the wires, making a sort of tent-like arrangement. The platform itself was no bigger than the roof of an average-size family car.

Silva moved the ascenders again and stepped up. Repeated the action a couple more times until she was able to reach across and haul herself onto the platform. Three safety lines hung down from a higher-up branch and she clipped herself on before removing the ascenders from the vertical rope. She gave a couple of sharp tugs on the rope and after a moment or two it tightened. She stowed the rifle to one side, sat back against the huge trunk and tried not to think about how high up she was. Instead she looked outwards and admired the view.

The landscape fell away sharply, the green canopy of the jungle rolling down to a plateau devoid of trees about a third of a mile away. A number of large huts surrounded an imposing wooden stockade with guard towers at each corner. In the centre of the stockade there was another building. Several satellite dishes and an array of aerials sprouted from one end. An assortment of vehicles were parked within the stockade, including a jeep with what looked like a large field machine gun fitted on the rear platform.

Although smoke spun into the air from one of the huts, it was still early and there was no one around save a couple of men in one of the guard towers.

'Bloody hell.' Itchy's face appeared at the side of the platform. 'Yesterday's walk was bad enough, this has just about finished me off.'

Silva reached forward and helped Itchy climb onto the platform. She handed him the safety line and he clipped himself on and sat back against the tree.

'Christ.' Itchy placed his hands flat on the platform either side of him. Spread his fingers into the mesh floor and gripped. 'This is bloody high up.'

'Try not to think about it,' Silva said, trying not to think about it herself. 'Just look out on the level.'

'Sure, but we gotta haul the bags,' he said, nodding across at the second rope. 'Don't mind if you do.'

Silva edged over the platform. She grabbed the other rope and gave two sharp tugs. Two tugs came back so she started to pull. The rope ran up and round a pulley but it was still an effort. Eventually the first rucksack arrived at the platform and Itchy, over his initial vertigo, helped her to swing it in. The second bag was lighter and came more easily, and then a few minutes later Gilsmith arrived at the platform. With three of them up there it was very cosy and Silva was thankful for the safety lines. Gilsmith moved out onto the branch to give them room to set up the rifle and Itchy's spotting scope. Silva's shooting position was sitting with her back against the tree, the rifle supported by a bipod on the barrel that rested on the edge of the platform. It wasn't ideal but it was the best they could do and, as long as she didn't look down, she felt reasonably secure.

Itchy input the distance to the target, the weather, air pressure and other variables into his ballistics app. After looking at the figures for a few minutes and making some notes on a scrap of paper, he gave Silva the numbers to dial into the scope. The craft of being a sniper involved the careful marrying of the science of ballistics with the art of the shooter. Both were required to hit the target. In this case Itchy had measured the distance to the compound as 403 metres. On the range it was an easy shot, but this wasn't the range.

By the time they'd arranged everything the sun was fully up and the camp below them had come to life. A truck chugged in from the jungle and parked beside one of the huts. Men unloaded heavy sacks and a number of jerrycans and carried them into a nearby building.

'There's a shabu lab in there,' Gilsmith said. 'Shabu is what you call crystal meth. The raw ingredients come in concealed as regular supplies, but nobody would dare stop one of Hassani's trucks to check anyway. Corruption is endemic, local officials on the take. In the Philippines there is a war on drugs with state-sponsored assassinations, but in reality it is used to remove the people who get in the way.'

'Crystal meth and ISIS?' Itchy said. 'Sounds like an odd mix.'

'No different from Afghanistan where the Taliban benefit from controlling heroin production. Shabu provides Hassani with much-needed income.'

Away from the truck, armed men patrolled the perimeter, while inside the compound a number of women and girls washed clothes at a well.

'Brides of the fighters.' Gilsmith grimaced. 'Taken from their villages. They work during the day and act as sex slaves in the night. They know if they don't comply their families will suffer.'

'Looks like killing Hassani is a no-brainer,' Itchy said. 'The world will definitely be a better place without him.'

'So where is he?' Silva said. 'And for that matter Taher. He's the one we've come for.'

Gilsmith checked his watch. 'Hassani stays up late and rises late, but he'll be up to meet Taher when he arrives. According to Mr Weiss's source Taher should be here within the next half-hour. If fortune shines on us then the truck will leave around the same time. There'll be some shabu on board with a couple of guards. If we take Taher and Hassani as the truck drives off it will create maximum confusion because they'll believe someone is trying to hijack the drugs.'

'Then we hightail it, right?'

'No rush.' Gilsmith reached into the bag of equipment he'd brought with him and pulled out a couple of shiny circles of aluminium. For a moment a look of consternation crossed his face. 'We radio Tan and Ruiz, abseil down from here and make it back to the drop zone. There is no direct path up to this ridge so it will take them at least fifteen minutes to get here. By the time they do we'll be long gone.'

Silva stared at the two abseil devices in Gilsmith's hand. 'Is there a problem?'

'I thought I double-checked the gear, but it looks as if I've forgotten one of the descenders.' Gilsmith smiled. 'No problem, I'll body-rappel down.'

Silva nodded and then checked over her own kit again. She made an adjustment to the scope and wriggled to get comfortable.

'Something's happening.' Itchy was peering through his spotting scope. 'The guard in the tower is turning so as to cover the track in and there's a man down in the compound talking on a radio.'

'He's coming,' Gilsmith said. 'Taher.'

Sure enough a few minutes later a Nissan 4 × 4 emerged from the forest, sliding on the muddy track before coming to a halt at the compound gates. A guard opened the gates and waved the vehicle through. Three well-armed men came out of the main building.

'A reception committee.' Gilsmith shifted back on the branch, giving Silva and Itchy as much room as possible. He had a radio out ready to call Tan and Ruiz. 'And the man at the rear is Adil Hassani.'

Hassani was a large, stocky man who wouldn't have looked out of place at an illicit bare-knuckle fighting contest. He wore khaki fatigues and desert boots and a handgun was holstered on his right thigh. Silva lowered her head to the scope.

The world was magnified. Hassani, she saw, had a small scar on his right cheek. Bad acne. A thinning patch in the centre of his brown hair. She saw a puff of black smoke come from the rear of the Nissan as the engine was turned off. The driver's hands moved from the steering wheel to the door handle. Silva moved her finger to the trigger and settled the crosshairs on the passenger door.

'Three people in the car,' Itchy said. 'Two in the front, one in the rear.'

The driver and front-seat passenger got out. Neither one was Taher. She shifted her aim towards the rear of the vehicle where the offside door was opening.

'Shit,' Itchy said. He was head down at his spotting scope. 'It's not Taher.'

Chapter 10

Holm could tell Shaz was the kind of person who talked a lot when he was nervous, and right now he was very nervous. Words poured out of the man's mouth, garbled sentences which made little sense. Holm listened for anything useful, but most of it was incoherent. After ten minutes he turned to the back seat.

'Aside from giving us directions, just shut up, would you?' Holm said.

They crossed the river at Dartford and followed it north-west to Dagenham where Shaz guided them off the main road. After a couple of turns right and left they came to a brownfield site. Street lamps provided sparse illumination, but the site itself was dark and unlit. Holm thought back to his days in the police, remembering a bust from decades ago. There'd been a factory here, he was sure of it. Car parts or something. Now there was an expanse of rubble surrounded by plywood fencing. To one side of a chain-link gate a glossy picture had been fixed to the plywood. The headlights from their car lit up an artist's impression of the swanky block of flats that would soon be rising from the rubble.

Javed pulled to the side of the road in front of the gates. Holm opened the glovebox and retrieved the torch he kept for emergencies.

'Where is it then, mate?' Javed said as they got out.

'Inside,' Shaz said. 'The garages are at the far end of the plot. Henson's is the second from the right–hand end.'

'So they're not used any more?'

'Dunno.' Shaz gave a shrug. 'As I said, this was a few months ago.'

Holm looked at the gates. A chain had been looped round them to hold them closed, but there was no lock. Shaz was hopping up and down, casting glances up the road.

'We're done with you,' Holm said. 'Run along home.'

'I can go?'

'Yes, but if it turns out you've been telling porkies, then we'll be back.'

Shaz didn't wait for any further confirmation. He spun on his heels and walked briskly away, passing beneath the glow of a street light and disappearing into the darkness.

'Was that wise?' Javed said. 'If he was lying and is still in contact with Henson, then he'll warn him.'

'He was almost shitting himself. I reckon he was telling the truth.' Holm moved across to the gates and began to uncoil the chain. It clanked free and he swung the gates inwards. 'No way is he going to admit to Henson that he shopped him. Come on.'

'Warrant?'

'No need. A crime is in progress.'

Javed didn't answer. Just followed Holm into the site.

They walked across mud and broken hardcore towards the shadowy outline of the garages. There were twelve in all, grouped in blocks of four. There'd been flats here as well as the factory, Holm remembered, but now the garages stood awaiting demolition, the last remnants of what had been here before.

As they walked across the rubble, Holm wondered if they were too late. Shaz had said he'd been here months ago. Back then the garages had probably still been in use, but now it looked as if the tenants had been kicked out so the whole lot could be flattened.

'Second from the right,' Javed said. He stopped a few paces clear. 'Do you think we should call in CTC?'

CTC. The Met's Counter-Terrorism Command. Once known as Special Branch.

'No,' Holm said.

It was breaking procedure, but Holm liked to do things his own way. With CTC involved there'd be dozens of officers, cars, vans, snipers, CSIs. All that attention would undoubtedly attract the press. There'd need to be a briefing and Henson, wherever he was, would be alerted.

'Here.' Holm pulled out a couple of pairs of latex gloves from his pocket. He handed a pair to Javed. 'Wear these.'

Holm snapped the gloves on and Javed did the same. He flicked on the torch and there was a silver flash from the chrome handle near the bottom of the garage door. Holm reached for it and found it turned easily.

'Not locked.'

He pulled the door and it swung up and slid back into the garage above their heads. He shone the torch into the interior.

'Shit.' Javed stood with his hands on his hips staring into the dark shadows. 'It's empty.'

Holm walked in. Swung the beam round. There were a few oil stains on the concrete. Some leaves. An old broom propped to one side of the door. It looked as if Shaz had been playing them all along.

'We should call in about the growing room,' Javed said. 'Get the cops round there before Shaz has a chance to dismantle everything.'

'Yes.' Holm wasn't really listening. He kicked at some of the leaves. He'd been too eager to believe Shaz's story, but now he was beginning to doubt Henson had ever been within a mile of the garage. Holm pushed his foot through another pile of leaves and bent and picked up a piece of yellow plastic. A handle or grip from something.

'What's that?'

'Dunno. We need to get a forensic team in here to see if they can find any trace of the chemicals. Try to work out what Henson was going to use them for.'

'You're thinking of a bomb?'

'All that talk by Gaugan of Waco and Ruby Ridge makes me think of Timothy McVeigh and the Oklahoma bombing. Know it?'

'Not in detail, no.'

'McVeigh built a home-made bomb using ammonium nitrate and other chemicals. The bomb killed over a hundred and fifty people in a government building.'

'Bloody hell. You think…?'

'Henson could load up that white Transit of his and park it outside a mosque or a synagogue. The devastation and loss of life would be immense.'

'Sir?' Javed had moved over to one side of the garage. He knelt and examined something on the floor. 'Ashes. Looks like from a few sheets of paper.'

'Somebody's been burning evidence?'

'Could be.' Javed had his face right at ground level now, his phone out to give illumination. 'There's a fragment with a couple of characters on: "7 EN". Some kind of formula?'

Holm moved towards Javed, stepping sideways to avoid a clod of soggy mud. Stared down. 'This has fallen off somebody's boot. It's come from the building site outside. Still wet. Someone has been here recently, possibly within the last couple of hours. Gaugan must have tipped Henson or somebody else off. They came here and moved the chemicals.'

'You think?' Javed held up the piece of paper between the thumb and forefinger of his gloved hand.

'Unless we're looking at this the wrong way round.' Holm felt a chill. He visualised Henson's Transit loaded with barrels parked on a busy London street. 'He moved them because something is about to kick off. Something big.'

'Shit,' Javed said. 'You think we'd better call CTC now?'

'Yes,' Holm said. He was still holding the piece of yellow plastic and now he turned it over in his hands. He almost chucked it back on the floor but then he read the word embossed in black on one side: Lock. His hand trembled slightly as he realised what he was holding. 'I might be wrong about the chemicals. They could be the least of our worries. This isn't about Henson at all. This is to do with Taher.'

'*Taher?*'

'Take a look.' Holm passed the plastic to Javed. 'There's something written on one side.'

'Hey?' Javed examined the plastic. '*Lock?* As in key?'

'Yes, sort of.' Holm took the item back and slipped it in a pocket. 'It's a safety device. While it's in place it prevents activation. More accurately it prevents firing.'

For a moment Javed appeared not to understand, but then he got it. 'Fuck, you're joking?'

'No. I think this is a locking device from an AirShield surface-to-air missile.'

At that moment, in almost perfect synchronicity, Holm and Javed tilted their heads. Holm flicked the beam of the torch upwards. The metal frame of the roof supports zigzagged above them, but there was something else up there too. Holm stepped to one side. Now he could see two wooden boards attached to the metal frame, one where they stood, and one a couple of paces away. Three U-shaped cut-outs had been removed from the boards as if to support something long and tubular.

'Shit,' Javed said.

Holm looked at the notches again and blinked, as if in doing so he might be able to unsee reality. Nothing changed. A brief moment of panic came and went and then he pulled out his phone. He tapped a number and after four rings a voice answered.

'This is Senior Analyst Stephen Holm,' he said, surprised at how calm his voice sounded. 'Supernova. I repeat, supernova.'

–

Hassani walked forward and blocked Silva's view. His back filled the rifle's sights as he embraced the man who'd climbed out of the rear of the 4 × 4.

'Who is it?' Silva asked Itchy.

Before Itchy had a chance to answer, Hassani turned and began to walk back to the buildings, the other man alongside him.

'Fuck,' Silva said as the crosshairs slid over a familiar face. A full beard. A thick head of hair. She remembered the man from the photographs she'd been shown by MI5.

He'd been in the group who assaulted the café in Tunisia. Her mother had died in a hail of bullets from the man's Kalashnikov. 'It's Latif.'

'Who?' Gilsmith said.

'Mohid Latif,' Itchy said. 'One of the men who killed Rebecca's mother.'

Silva moved the rifle down slightly so Latif's chest was centred in the crosshairs. She took a breath and slowly exhaled, years of experience telling her exactly when in the cycle to take the shot.

A second went by. Two. Three.

She touched the trigger.

The bullet hit Latif in the midriff and he was flung sideways by the impact. His right hand went to his stomach and then he staggered forward and collapsed behind a low wall.

'Hassani!' Gilsmith said. 'By the truck.'

Silva reloaded and edged the rifle to the left as Hassani moved to the corner of the truck, seeking cover from somebody attacking in the direction of the compound gates. Unfortunately for Hassani the truck provided no cover from Silva's position. She composed herself and fired. Half a second later he reeled back, the tailgate behind him exploding in a mass of wooden splinters.

'Good shot,' Itchy said. 'Neck wound, almost certainly fatal.'

Hassani collapsed at the rear of the truck. Through the scope Silva could see blood flowing into a muddy tyre track, oozing across the pattern and filling the little indentations.

'We have to leave,' Itchy said. Silva looked up from the scope. Someone was at the rear of the truck pointing a machine gun in their direction. A group of men gathered at the entrance to the stockade. 'Now.'

Gilsmith handed one of the abseil devices to Silva. 'Clip this on. Once you're down don't wait at the bottom, head back along the trail and make for the dust-off point. Go.'

'The rifle?'

'Leave the fucking rifle!'

Silva clipped the descender to her harness and moved to the edge of the platform. She held the rope tight and leaned back, allowing the strain to be taken up. Then she began to feed the rope into the descender, lowering herself away from the platform.

Voices echoed in the trees now along with the staccato *phut phut phut* of automatic-weapon fire. In thirty seconds she was at the base of the tree. She gave a couple of sharp tugs on the rope and then stepped back. Despite what Gilsmith had said she was going to wait for Itchy.

He seemed to take ages, halfway down fumbling with the rope because it got tangled in his legs. Eventually he freed it and descended the rest of the way.

'Christ,' he said. 'This takes me back a bit. Remember that time in Kandahar when we—'

'Later, Itchy.' Silva helped him unclip and gave another couple of tugs at the rope. 'Let's go.'

'You waited for me. We should wait for him.'

'No. He can move way quicker than us in this terrain. He needs us to give him a head start or else we'll be slowing him down when he catches us up.'

Itchy nodded and they set off at a jog along the animal trail. After a couple of minutes Silva glanced back, but there was no sign of Gilsmith. Ahead, Itchy slowed to a fast walk.

'He's coming, right?' Itchy stopped, hands on hips. He turned round and pulled out his gun from its holster.

'Don't be stupid,' Silva said. She turned him round and pushed him forward. 'There's dozens of them. Going back would be suicide.'

For a moment she thought he'd protest, but then he ducked his head and lurched on down the trail.

After an arduous ten minutes, which included doubling back as they'd taken a wrong turn, they reached the clearing. Tan and Ruiz were standing to one side by a pile of kit, Ruiz with his pistol raised as they burst into the clearing. He lowered the gun.

'Gilsmith?' he said.

'He's coming.' Silva jerked a thumb back at the jungle. 'But so are Hassani's men. Where's the helicopter?'

'Exfil in five minutes.' Tan had a radio in his hand and he waved it at Silva. 'It'll be touch and go.'

'Shit. Do we wait?'

'For Gilsmith?' Tan shook his head. 'No. If anybody has the ability to evade the enemy in a jungle environment, it's Gilsmith.' Tan lowered the radio. Stared at Silva. 'Did you get them?'

'Yup.' Itchy answered for her. 'Latif took one in the abdomen, Hassani in the neck. He's dead for sure, don't know about Latif.'

Tan nodded. Didn't ask for further explanation. He turned and looked to a patch of sky in the west. A solitary bird cruised above the trees. Silva silently counted the seconds. How long had it been now? Two minutes? Three?

'There.' Tan pointed. The solitary bird turned into a flock rising into the air in alarm. Tan reached down to the ground and cracked off a smoke grenade. Orange mist billowed out and he stepped back to the edge of the clearing. In the distance a white speck became a blur of rotor, and the low whine of an engine grew to a roar.

Silva moved to the edge of the clearing too as the helicopter swooped in, descending like a stone. At the last second the pilot changed angle and the aircraft deftly landed on the ground. Now they all rushed forward, ducking their heads from the rotor wash. Ruiz pulled open the side door and Itchy and Tan chucked the rucksacks in. Silva clambered up and in and so did the others. She threw herself into a seat and buckled the belt. In the front the pilot turned and looked to Tan for permission to take off. Tan glanced to the edge of the clearing as Gilsmith stumbled into view. He hobbled towards the helicopter, limping badly. Then a figure moved in the shadows of the treeline and there was a crack from a high-powered weapon, audible even above the roar of the helicopter's engine. Gilsmith spun round as he was hit in the shoulder, falling backwards as a second shot hit him in the chest. Tan appeared stunned for a moment before he reached to undo his seat belt and moved to leave the helicopter. Ruiz pushed Tan back into his seat with one hand and with the other he gestured towards the pilot.

'Go!' he shouted.

The engine roar increased in intensity and the ground dropped away, the aircraft pitching violently forward as the pilot tried to balance maximum lift with maximum forward velocity. In seconds the clearing had gone and they were skimming over the tops of the trees. Ruiz reached over and slid the door shut. Tan rocked forward in his seat and put his head in his hands. Itchy sat back and stared out of the side window. Silva simply closed her eyes.

Operation Supernova was designed to be a multi-agency response to an imminent catastrophic terrorist threat. It wasn't to be initiated for a lone gunman or a group of knife-wielding attackers, nor for a suicide bomber or even half-a-dozen armed extremists. Catastrophic meant something in the order of a nuclear, biological or chemical weapon; an explosive device threatening hundreds of people; or an attempt to destroy a passenger train, ship or aircraft. Several surface-to-air missiles certainly qualified.

The procedures had been well rehearsed in dozens of training simulations, and Supernova kicked into action within two minutes of Holm's phone call. Huxtable, out with friends at a post-theatre soirée in the West End, was ushered from the venue by a minder and led out to a waiting police car. Armed officers covered the street as the car sped away under blue and twos.

She was back in Thames House within a quarter of an hour. A few minutes later, an unassuming but heavily armoured car pulled up at the rear entrance of Downing Street and the prime minister was hustled into the back. The car slipped out onto Horse Guards' Road and sped away to a secure location. Back at Thames House, the operation now went into overdrive. The terrorist threat level was raised to critical and secretive communiques were sent via designated hotline numbers to the chief constables of the nation's police forces. Counter Terrorism Command mustered specialist response teams that proceeded to the region's five main airports – Heathrow, Gatwick, London City, Stansted and Luton – and followed a pre-set plan designed to bolster the existing security. A little over one hundred miles north-west of the capital, villagers leaving the pub at chucking-out time in Credenhill near Hereford observed unusual late-evening activity at the Stirling Lines army base, the headquarters of the SAS. A small convoy of Land Rovers roared out from the base, each vehicle with four men inside. Initially following the same route, they soon began to disperse, each patrol tasked to proceed to a designated regional airport. Once in situ, they would support local police and be ready for immediate engagement with any terrorists. No second chances were to be taken. No challenges would be issued. The terrorists would be shot on sight.

Within Thames House, a list of names was being finalised and then provided to the Met. Many of the people on the list the Met knew about, but others had been gathered by deep-cover operatives whose identities would be blown the moment police officers went out and made arrests. Years of work had gone into infiltrating various groups of radicals, but now it was time to cash in the investment. Those arrested would be held under special powers and there'd be no lawyers, no trial, no right of appeal. Human lives, those in power had decided, were more important than human rights. At least for the time being.

Informants were being contacted and threatened: spill the beans on anything they knew now or face either exposure or arrest. No matter that it was now after midnight, if an informant failed to respond to a phone call or text message then there'd be a knock at the door, the local police standing there, a shadowy figure behind them wanting information. Neighbours peered out of windows or hurriedly turned off their lights, but the police didn't care who was watching; the time for subtlety was gone.

Holm and Javed waited at the lock-up garage until Counter Terrorism Command officers arrived and then headed for Thames House. The streets were eerily quiet, almost as if Londoners were expecting something to happen.

'Taher and Henson?' Javed said as they drove. 'It doesn't make sense. I can understand Taher hiring Henson, but the two of them in cahoots? They're on different sides.'

'My enemy's enemy is my friend,' Holm said. 'They both hate the government and Western state apparatus, likely they both hold anti-Semitic views, and they are similarly concerned about the mixing of cultures and races and the dilution of what they hold dear. Strange bedfellows perhaps, but Taher is nothing but a pragmatist when it comes to operational matters.'

'But whose operation is this?'

'Taher obtained the missiles and he's the clever one. I would guess Henson is merely a pawn.'

Back at Thames House, they made for the situation room. The place was filling up as people roused from their beds began to arrive. Colleagues who'd previously given Holm a wide berth were now coming over and asking for his opinion on various pieces of intelligence. He was, for now, a hero. Not that he felt like one.

'I failed,' he said to Javed in a quiet moment.

'Not your fault.' Javed put out a hand and patted Holm on the back. 'You did all you could.'

'Did I? I'm supposed to be the Taher expert round here, but I came up with nothing but an empty lock-up.'

Holm cast his gaze towards the bank of screens filling the far wall of the situation room. Twenty-four-hour news channels played on several screens, the media as yet unaware what was going on. Other screens showed

CCTV from sensitive sites around the UK. One showed a live stream from a body-mounted cam as operational support officers smashed their way into a terraced house somewhere in the Midlands. Weapons were drawn as the door caved in, grainy footage flickering as the officer wearing the camera moved into the hall and up the stairs. A bedroom door was flung open, an elderly man and woman appearing startled as officers rushed in. No sound, just mouths opening and closing, the barrel of a Heckler & Koch waving. Holm could only imagine the words.

> Down on the fucking floor! Down on the fucking floor!

If the footage leaked it would be a public relations disaster, but needs must. Better that then hundreds dead. Better a lawsuit and accusations of institutionalised racism than bodies torn apart by one of Taher's missiles.

Only, the way things were going, the latter was still all too possible.

'Nothing,' Holm said to Huxtable later when the results of the sweeps were known. 'No leads, no suspicious activity at the airports, no credible suspects.'

'Interrogation?' Huxtable flexed the fingers of her right hand. Holm wondered what she'd be like holding a knuckle duster. 'We need information and I'm not much concerned how we get it.'

'There's no point interrogating people who don't know anything. We learned that from 9/11, right?'

'They found Bin Laden.'

'It's highly debatable that torturing suspects played any part in tracking him down.'

'Perhaps we scared Taher away or he's gone to ground or fled the country. Perhaps that's why the missiles have disappeared. He's run off to be somebody else's problem.'

Holm had to stifle a laugh. Taher did not get scared off, nor did he flee.

'It's coming,' Holm said. 'All the months of inactivity was a prelude designed to show us how badly prepared we are, how impotent our actions are. Just when we think we're safe, he'll strike. Boom! Terror is at its best when chaos follows serenity. It's the contrast. Our green and pleasant land defiled. Peace destroyed. A deformed abnormality replacing the everyday.'

'Please, Stephen, spare me this crap and swallow your self-pity. And if you can't do that then just go home and get some sleep. Come back tomorrow when you've rested. It's been a very long day.'

'Yes.' He did feel tired now, both physically and emotionally. The energy he'd expended in recent weeks and months hadn't been replaced. There'd been no rewards, nothing to bolster his resolve, and the stress was beginning to tell. Much more and his body and mind would break down. 'I'll do that, ma'am, go home.'

Holm passed by Javed's workstation and the young man looked up, eyes wide and alert. The small hours were early for him. Plenty of time still left to party.

'See you tomorrow,' Holm said, all of a sudden not knowing if even that simple statement was true.

Chapter 11

Huxtable called an emergency meeting the next morning. Holm shared the lift up to the fifth floor with Claire Evans.

'All this time,' she said. 'You were right but nobody listened.'

'I'd have preferred to be wrong.' Holm let Evans exit the lift first and followed her down the corridor to the briefing room.

Inside the atmosphere was tense. Familiar faces stared at Holm as he took his place. Huxtable herself; Helen Kendle, the national security adviser; James Foster, the deputy director; Oliver Pelton. Holm noted that Simeon Weiss, present at the previous meeting, was absent. Evans sat in his place. Huxtable called the meeting to order and invited Holm to speak. There was, Holm noted, no apology, no words of praise.

He stood. He disliked being the centre of attention, disliked even more having to give this kind of presentation where his opinions were under scrutiny. Although he reckoned he knew more about Taher than just about any other person, the others – Claire Evans aside – had always viewed his pronouncements with scepticism. He glanced down briefly at a set of notes he'd made and then picked up a photograph of the AirShield locking device.

'Taher has managed to get hold of at least one AirShield surface-to-air missile. We think it's likely he has more though, probably three in total.'

Holm went on to explain in detail the trail he'd followed from Tallin Saabiq to Nathan 'Thommo' Henson and the British Aryan Insurgency, and from Terrance Gaugan to the lock-up garage and the evidence of the missiles. He finished by mentioning how close he'd been to stopping Taher.

'We were literally an hour too late.' He gave a shrug. 'And so here we are.'

He didn't need to add the obvious: if Task Group Taher hadn't been depleted of staff and resources they wouldn't be facing this threat.

Perhaps as an acknowledgement of their failings there was a moment's silence. Then came a barrage of questions.

Was he one hundred per cent convinced this was Taher?

What were his demands?

What level of confidence did he have in his claim that Taher had several surface-to-air missiles ready to use in the UK?

'Put it this way,' Holm said in answer to the last question, 'I wouldn't want to be flying anywhere in the next few months.'

He'd meant the remark to be flippant, but no one round the table took it that way. There was a collective intake of breath, and people reached for pens and pencils and scribbled hurriedly.

'As for demands, well, he doesn't issue demands. He's out to settle scores and to right what he sees as wrongs.'

'Palestine?' Kendle said. 'The Iraq War?'

'Both probably, but knowing that doesn't get us anywhere.'

'And are we sure about this key thing?' Pelton gestured towards the photograph on the desk in front of Holm. 'That it couldn't be a fake or have somehow fallen into his hands?'

'It's real.' This from Claire Evans. 'I've verified it with the manufacturers.'

Pelton wanted to know more about the weapon. 'Just how dangerous is it? I mean, are we over-egging just what this thing is capable of?'

'AirShield is a highly effective air-defence system,' Evans said. 'The absolute latest piece of kit.'

'OK, understood.' Pelton appeared humbled, but he hadn't given up. 'But surely there must be ways of reducing the risk?'

'Not really.' Evans raised her left hand above the table, angling it up slightly. She held a biro in her right hand. 'My pen is the missile, my hand an aeroplane. The missile is guided by two lasers which project a crosshatch onto the target. Upon launch the missile accelerates to a velocity of Mach 4. That is, for those unfamiliar with the terminology, around 2,800 miles an hour. The take-off speed of a modern passenger jet is around 150 mph, the cruising speed a maximum of 600 mph. Since the missile is laser guided it cannot be jammed and its speed means it cannot be intercepted. As it nears the target the missile launches three submunitions which home in on the target. In addition these darts are able to manoeuvre to meet a target evading at up to 9G. Even for a fighter plane escape is unlikely. For something like a large passenger airliner, it's impossible.'

'You said not much could be done.' Huxtable picked up her own pen now, its point poised over a blank sheet of paper. 'That implies there is something we *can* do.

Perhaps we can isolate airports? We've already got patrols out checking the perimeters. We could seek out possible launch sites. We could use the army and lock down the area for a mile in every direction.'

'Nice try.' Evans shook her head. 'The missile has a range of ten kilometres, that's around six miles. In addition, it's shoulder launched. As long as the operator has sight of planes in the air, they're good to go. They could ready the weapon inside the back of the small van, pull up somewhere, and get out and fire the missile.'

'But with heightened surveillance we might just get lucky.'

'Sure.' Evans smiled. 'But you're talking about serendipity. The chances of catching them like that are remote.'

'Stephen?' Huxtable said. 'Anything to add?'

'Yes. I think if we get to the stage where we are hoping to be able to stop Taher from launching the missile, then we've lost. That's because the measures have to be replicated at every UK airport. An almost impossible task.'

Silence. The reality of the situation sinking in. Huxtable gazed down at her notepad.

'Well then,' Kendle said. 'Since Stephen is the expert, why don't we ask him for his suggestions? After all, I need something to take back to the prime minister.'

'Well Stephen?' Huxtable looked up. 'You, more than anyone, are close to understanding Taher. What do you think his next move is?'

For a moment Holm felt like throwing his hands in the air and shouting that he didn't fucking know. Instead he took a deep breath. Calmed himself.

'Taher will be worried we got so close to finding the missiles, but he's not some rash hothead. He'll be aware of all the extra security and won't want to risk failure. I think he'll go to ground and consolidate his position, double-check his organisational security.'

'How long have we got?' Kendle said, plainly not relishing returning to Downing Street with the news.

'Hard to say. The fact he hasn't tried to use the missiles up to now suggests to me he is either not ready or more likely he is waiting for something. What that is I don't know.'

'And his purpose, Stephen?' Huxtable asked. 'If he doesn't have demands he must have some sort of endgame in mind.'

'Absolutely. He doesn't lead some amateur group who use dummy suicide vests or knives or vehicles. They don't blow themselves up or make bombs which fail to explode. Nor are they religious fanatics whose arguments disappear in a puff of logic. Taher has been working up to this day all his life.' Holm paused. For too long his concerns had been dismissed, Taher seen as nothing more than Holm's personal obsession. He wanted his next words to sink in. 'I believe Taher's intention is nothing less than to bring the United Kingdom to its knees. With the AirShield missiles at his disposal, I suggest he will easily be able to achieve his aim.'

—

After a day to recuperate, Silva and Itchy took a flight to the UK via Abu Dhabi, enjoying the business class hospitality paid for by Tan. Or rather not enjoying it. The mood was sombre. After they'd returned to the island, Tan was philosophical. Gilsmith knew what he was getting himself into, Tan said, he was well aware of the risks. On the upside Hassani was dead and Mohid Latif critically wounded.

'It wasn't our fault,' Silva said to Itchy as a stewardess served them drinks. 'The plan was flawed. Tan, Gilsmith and Ruiz misjudged how long it would take Hassani's men to catch up with us. We had no part in that. Plus Gilsmith fucked up by forgetting his abseil kit. He must have fallen and hurt his leg as he was trying to descend using the rope alone.'

She turned to the window. The aircraft was flying above an expanse of cloud below which, Silva guessed, was India. Somewhere to the north-west lay Afghanistan, a country that had filled her head with memories, most of them bad.

She dozed until a squeal of rubber on tarmac signalled their arrival at Abu Dhabi where they had a three-hour wait for a connecting flight. They strolled inside the garish air-conditioned terminal before finding a place to have a cup of coffee.

'I'll be glad to get back to normality,' Itchy said, slurping the froth off the top of a cappuccino. 'We had unbridled luxury followed by a night with the mozzies in the jungle. All in all I prefer my own place.'

'Me too.' Silva reached for her own coffee. 'Although I'm thinking of buying bigger.'

'Really?' Itchy had been on Silva's little boat and knew how cramped it was. Still, he seemed surprised. 'Thinking of going somewhere?'

'Perhaps.' Silva was about to explain when somebody slipped into the seat next to hers.

'There you are.' Simeon Weiss reached up and adjusted his glasses. 'I've been waiting for you.'

'You.' Silva glared at Weiss. 'I'm sure you've heard what happened?'

'I did, Rebecca. Bad luck.'

'Piss-poor planning,' Itchy said. 'Mr Tan might be a medallist in the noble art of archery, but real war is a little different than shooting at a straw target.'

'The good news is that you got Hassani. Local news media are reporting him as dead. According to my source, Mohid Latif was badly wounded, but as yet I don't have any confirmation of where he is.'

'Never mind Latif, you told us Taher would be there,' Silva said. 'Another one of your lies?'

'No, not this time. Taher was *supposed* to be there. I'm not sure why he sent Latif in his place, but there's a possible explanation.'

'Which is?'

Weiss hunched forward. He pulled out his phone and turned the screen so she and Itchy could see the picture displayed there. 'This.'

Something yellow. Plastic, possibly. A handle or grip. The word 'Lock' embossed on one surface.

'And?' Silva stared at the phone. Couldn't work out what she was seeing.

'It's the locking device from an AirShield missile. A safety catch, if you will. It was found in south-east London yesterday.'

'Are you telling me there are missiles in the UK?'

'There could be. I believe your old friend Stephen Holm is still working on that.'

'Fuck.' Itchy this time. 'Lucky you guys don't get paid on a results basis. You'd be down the food bank, right?'

'We just got a result, Mr Smith. Even though Taher didn't turn up in the Philippines, Latif did. It just so happens Latif is the only one in Taher's cell able to operate the missile. He trained on the AirShield system in Algeria. The group he was with actually fired three of the missiles during practice exercises.'

'Might have been better, mate, if you'd prevented the missiles from getting into Taher's hands in the first place.'

'If you cast your mind back to Tunisia, we tried to, remember?'

'Don't try to blame—'

'Itch, stop, it's pointless,' Silva said. 'He doesn't give a toss. We've put our lives on the line twice to help him out and he's still not happy.'

'What do you mean, Silvi?'

'He's not finished with us yet. He wants more. He won't be satisfied until we've joined his team and he can order us to do whatever the fuck he likes. Isn't that right, Mr Weiss?'

'Rebecca.' Weiss held his hands up. 'All I'm trying to do is protect the citizens of the UK from people like Taher. I use whatever means I have at my disposal and recruit the best people to aid me in my task. Mohid Latif is a case in point. Using unconventional methods I – we – have neutralised the threat he posed. All I'm asking is for your help once we're back home. It's that simple.'

'I can't speak for Itch, but my answer is pretty simple too, Mr Weiss.' Silva stood. Grabbed her bag. 'It's no.'

'Same,' Itchy said. He pulled his own bag from the seat and followed Silva as she walked away. Turning back, he held up his hand and raised a single finger.

–

Operation Supernova didn't go unnoticed on the seventeenth floor of a certain tower block in west London. The fact the mainstream media had been slow to cover the police raids meant that for the general public, to all intents and purposes, nothing of note was happening. Taher knew differently. It had started on Thursday evening with a couple of posts on social media that had built quickly to a flurry. Video began to appear online of police smashing down doors, shady figures dressed in black behind them. On the dark web various accounts talked of widespread arrests. Gossip and rumour were followed by earnest warnings: Shut your ops down, they said. Destroy evidence. Get out while you still can.

Taher had ignored the general sense of panic and gone to bed. He'd slept well. He'd been doing this long enough to know that if the police were on to him he'd already be either in custody or dead. The very fact the net was being cast so widely showed the sheer desperation of the authorities. They were throwing everything into the hunt, understandably so considering they'd found evidence of the missiles. But that didn't matter. In fact it enhanced his position since the panic would undoubtedly lead to mistakes being made. And for every door smashed in, for every room turned upside down, for every young man flung face down to the floor, there was a possible convert to his cause. All Taher had to do was sit tight and wait for the right moment to put his plan into action.

The next day, when the news organisations had caught up and the story that a major antiterrorist operation was in progress was everywhere, a text came in. It was from Saabiq, worried but still managing to keep to the communication protocols they'd agreed: *Are we still going to the game next month?*

Taher replied: *Yes, of course. Praying for a big win. See you there.*

He hoped his optimism wasn't misplaced: away from all the coverage of Operation Supernova, and buried away on the BBC website under 'World News, Asia', he'd spotted a short item reporting the death of Adil Hassani. And, worryingly, as of yet he'd heard nothing from Mohid Latif.

Part Two

Chapter 12

Now...

Captain Brian Hammond is one of the most experienced pilots in the fleet. He's been in a couple of emergencies before, but nothing has prepared him for this.

The plane slams into the lake at 153 knots and the impact throws Hammond and Phillips hard against their restraints. Spray flares up round the nose of the aircraft as it slices into the reservoir. The left wing dips to the water and hits and the drag immediately starts to slew the aircraft round. Hammond fights for control but there's nothing. He reaches forward and kills the engines as a hideous straining sound of metal fills the air. The aluminium creaks and stretches and fractures until the left wing shears away, ripping a section of the main cabin with it. Beside Phillips, one of the side windows pops out and is torn back by the rush of water. They're still travelling in excess of a hundred knots, the nose ploughing into the lake and throwing up a huge bow wave. The plane is in danger of burying itself in the reservoir. Hammond knows that will be too much for the aircraft to take and the fuselage will disintegrate. He glances across at Phillips, wanting a moment's human contact before the end, but the co-pilot has his eyes closed, his lips moving in silent prayer. Perhaps the prayer is working because the bow wave is diminishing and the plane is slowing. Now they are gliding over the water like a speedboat, a fast sailing dinghy, a rowing boat. And then they stop.

Hammond releases his restraints and is out of his seat in a flash. He yanks open the cockpit door and rushes through. There's daylight to his right where the left side of the cabin has been peeled back, but the passengers there appear unharmed and are releasing their seat belts and making for the exits. At the rear of the plane things are very different. The last couple of rows are gone, wiped out by whatever happened back there. Flames are licking round the edges of a gaping hole and Hammond tastes the sharp tang of aviation fuel. A miracle there are so many survivors, but a nightmare if there's a fire now. Then he's moving again, helping the cabin crew and trying to calm the passengers. The exits are all open and he gives thanks for the quick actions of the crew as people move to the doors and tumble onto the inflatable slides. Water is filling the plane, but Hammond reckons there's time to get everyone out. As he walks down the aisle, determined to check for stragglers, he has one eye on the rear where flames are licking round bare aluminium. An explosion, he thinks, recalling similar damage he'd seen when he served in Iraq. Not a structural failure, not a drone, not a small aeroplane.

Not, he realises with a mixture of horror and anger, an accident.

–

Holm slept late and when he woke he was shocked to see the sun was well up, a warm glow slipping round the edge of the curtains. It was nearly three weeks since they'd discovered the lock-up and Operation Supernova had sprung into action. He'd worked the period flat out and today was supposed to be a day off, but he knew thinking of anything but the hunt for Taher would be difficult.

He made himself breakfast, ignoring a blinking light on his phone, and took his bowl of cornflakes and cup of coffee into the living room. He sat on the sofa and munched the cereal, trying to free his mind of the stresses of the past month. He decided he'd head up to Camden. There was a little shop that sold rare jazz CDs. He could spend a happy hour browsing and talking to the proprietor. Then he'd find a café, have some lunch, read a book. Try to put Taher from his mind.

He knew focusing on something else would be beneficial to the investigation. They'd worked all the angles and nothing joined up. There was no sign of the missiles, or the chemicals, or Nathan 'Thommo' Henson. As for Taher, well he was as nebulous a figure as ever.

The round-up of suspected extremists had yielded nothing. After a couple of days the lawyers had swooped and most had been released. The arrests and detentions had led to a palpable feeling of anger within the Muslim community and now leaders were calling for action. Trust built up over years had been wiped away by Supernova in one night.

Holm felt enfeebled. He wanted to scream *he's got a bloody missile, what do you expect us to do?* but that was exactly what Taher would want. More panic, more terror, more conflict. The possibility that a UK-based terrorist cell had a surface-to-air missile had to be kept under wraps, otherwise there'd be mass hysteria.

The one piece of good news had come from an unlikely quarter. Simeon Weiss had returned from a secret overseas mission in the Philippines with the news that Mohid Latif had been seriously wounded. The details, as was typical with Weiss, were sketchy, but a kill team had nearly succeeded in taking out Latif. He was likely critically ill and certainly in no fit state to be able to operate the AirShield system. Holm had to concede that Weiss had produced the goods where Task Group Taher had not.

He shook his head. He'd told himself he wouldn't think about Taher today and he'd managed it for less than ten minutes. He put the bowl of cereal down and took a sip of coffee. He picked up the TV remote and pressed a button. Anything for a distraction. The screen in the corner flickered on and Holm switched to a news channel. A reporter was facing the camera standing in front of a chain-link fence. Through the wire, water. Something large and white half submerged in the centre of a huge lake. The volume was on mute so Holm scanned the ticker at the bottom of the screen as the shot changed to show a crowd of people waiting beneath a huge electronic sign, the word 'cancelled' repeated dozens of times.

'Christ,' Holm said, reaching for his phone. The notification light was still blinking and when the screen came on he could see there was a missed call and a text message from Farakh Javed. Four words.

Turn on the news.

He swivelled back to the screen and picked up the remote in his other hand. Blipped the mute off. Tried to get his mind round what the hell had happened. The voiceover was describing a plane crash near Heathrow and a miraculous escape by two hundred passengers. An aviation commentator had wisely declined to give a definitive cause but said it looked like some sort of avionics failure had led to the pilot deciding to return to the airport. He hadn't been able to do that and had instead ditched in a reservoir, somehow managing to bring the plane down in a relatively controlled fashion. A dozen people were dead, but total disaster had been averted by the heroic actions of the pilot.

Holm watched on. Another expert mentioned the possibility of a bird strike, perhaps collision with a large commercial drone. The Air Accidents Investigation Branch were at the scene and would be making an initial statement later. There was nothing about foul play except a denial repeated on the news ticker: *Crash not thought to be terrorism related…*

Holm dropped the remote and flicked to a contact on his phone. Javed answered within a couple of seconds.

'You watching this?' Javed said.

'Yes,' Holm said. 'They're saying it was a bird strike or a drone.'

'Huxtable put up Claire Evans as an expert. She said that based on the damage, it was highly unlikely to be a bomb, but could have been caused by a large drone hitting the tailfin. At speed, the impact would have been substantial.'

'What about a missile?'

'She wasn't asked about a missile because, quite frankly, that would be crazy, right?'

'Bloody hell.' Holm let his sentence hang for a moment. 'Did we just get very, very lucky?'

'Twelve people are dead. Not so lucky for them.'

'There were over two hundred on the plane. If it hadn't been for the pilot things could have been a lot worse.'

'It could still. As yet flights haven't been grounded. Huxtable appealed to the national security adviser, but apparently the decision has been made to keep calm and carry on.'

'Because this *could* still be an accident, presumably?'

'No, boss, it's definitely not an accident. Counter Terrorism Command have found the launch site.'

'Where?'

'A couple of miles west of the airport. Lord knows why the place was never investigated during Operation Supernova.' There was a pause before Javed spoke again. 'I'm on my way there now. Do you want me to swing by and pick you up?'

–

She was floating in a pool of blue, face down. Shimmering silver fish flashed beneath her as they darted among seaweed-encrusted rocks. Black urchins with needle-like spines lay dotted on the seabed. She raised her face from the sea and bobbed upright, treading water. Hot sun. The bleached white cliffs. A sandy beach stretching up to a ramshackle taverna. A pontoon running from the beach out into the little bay. A yacht moored to the ponton. A bronzed figure on the foredeck of the yacht.

Sean…

Silva kicked out for the yacht, her arms slicing into the water. In a few strokes she reached the stern and pulled herself up the boarding ladder. She stood dripping water for a few moments before making her way forward to where Sean was lying on a towel, one hand trying to shield his phone from the glare of the sun.

'I thought that was banned?' Silva said, dropping to the deck alongside him.

'Just checking in,' Sean said. He frowned, putting the phone to one side. 'You know how it is.'

'Something wrong?'

'No, nothing to worry about. Shall we do lunch?' He nodded towards the beach and the taverna. 'Then a drink or two, another swim or a walk, and after that who knows?'

'Sail down the coast a bit? Find somewhere new?'

'Too much effort.' Sean gave Silva one of his grins. 'We're supposed to be on holiday, right?'

They were.

It was three weeks since Silva and Itchy had left the Philippines. The whole affair was just another bad memory to archive with all the rest. Yes they'd killed Hassani and badly wounded Latif, but that had to be set against the loss of Gilsmith. Back in the UK a phone call from Sean had buoyed her mood; his immediate superior owned a yacht in Turkey and Sean had managed to wangle use of it for two weeks. All they had to do in return was deliver it from its winter base in Fethiye up the coast to Bodrum where his boss wanted it for a summer cruise. Did she want to come along?

Initially she was reluctant, but Sean soon talked her round, and now she was here she didn't regret her change of heart. Sailing up the Turquoise Coast had so far been magical, and her on-off relationship with Sean was very definitely back on. At least for the remainder of the trip.

Sean put on a shirt and Silva dried herself and slipped on a dress. They walked up the hill to the taverna. Lunch was sea bass and salad followed by some rather acidic wine.

Afterwards they wandered round a headland and took in the views over the water to the Greek island of Kos.

'We could do this permanently, you know?' Sean said, gesturing at the sea. 'Sail away over the horizon.'

'That doesn't sound like you,' Silva said. 'You must be getting old.'

'Old, no – jaded, yes.'

'Fed up with the job?'

'I don't seem to be making a difference. Sometimes I think we'd be better off pulling up the drawbridge and letting the rest of the world sort out their own troubles.'

'That definitely doesn't sound like you.'

'You know what I mean, Rebecca, you've been there. Look at what we left behind in Afghanistan. It's almost like the place has gone back to square one.'

'We have to try to make a difference, don't we?' Even as she said the words she wasn't sure if she believed them. Trying had left tens of thousands dead, including the young boy she'd shot. Trying hadn't worked out well for her mother either; she'd died while seeking to right injustices. Later, back on the boat, Sean was looking at his phone again. The 'who knows' he'd been hinting at appeared to be off the cards.

'Something *is* wrong,' Silva said. 'Tell me.'

'I've got to go.' Sean rose from the saloon table and made for the aft cabin. Silva heard him pulling clothes out of lockers.

'Back to Mali?'

'No.' Sean's voice floated out from the cabin. He didn't sound best pleased. 'Washington.'

'But the boat?'

Sean emerged from the cabin. 'Yeah, I'm sorry about that. If we leave at first light tomorrow morning we can motor to Bodrum and be there by midday. The Agency have me booked on a flight to Paris in the afternoon and a late evening departure from there to DC.'

'Why?'

'A plane's come down in London. Supposedly it's an accident, but you never know with these things. They want me back in DC in case the security committee need a face-to-face briefing on the likely threat to our assets in West Africa.' Sean disappeared into the cabin for a moment. He reappeared with a half-packed rucksack and a smile on his face. 'Still, the good news is we can enjoy ourselves tonight.'

Supposedly an accident…

Silva nodded, wondering whether she would be able to enjoy herself. After all, Simeon Weiss had hinted that Taher might have got hold of an AirShield missile, and an aircraft had crashed at Heathrow. It seemed unlikely the two things were unconnected.

–

Javed picked Holm up from his flat and they forged through heavy traffic until they reached the M25. On the other side of the motorway, Javed navigated a winding route to the village of Horton, Holm aware that every couple of minutes planes were passing overhead.

After the village they followed a lane through a small copse. Mature oak towered over slender young ash, the leaves of both bright green in the harsh spring sunlight. It was hard to believe this was just a couple of miles from one of the world's busiest airports.

The road crossed a field and on the far side a police 4 × 4 sat diagonally in the road, the lights on top of the vehicle strobing. Holm slowed the car and stopped when directed by an officer in a fluorescent jacket. Close by, two of his colleagues half raised their Heckler & Koch machine guns. On the edge of the copse black-clad figures stood at the treeline and a laser sight flashed red in the shadows.

'They've missed the boat by hours,' Javed said. 'Taher must be long gone by now.'

Holm muttered in agreement as he lowered his window and showed his ID.

'Park over there,' the officer said.

They parked up and got out. Off to the right there was a white picket fence in need of a coat of paint. A gate sat open and a drive led up past a clump of rhododendrons to an old bungalow. Pebble-dash walls and metal-framed windows. Moss patches on an asbestos-tiled roof.

'It's the house in the photo Tallin gave us,' Javed said. 'Looks as if Taher has been right under our noses all along.'

A string of blue and white tape ran from a small apple tree across to the side of the bungalow and prevented access to the front door. They followed the tape round to the back where a large formal garden led down to another wooded area. Just shy of the trees, two white-suited forensic officers worked round an area of scorched scrub. A third stood behind a tripod atop which was some kind of surveying instrument. She sighted up into the sky and made notes on a tablet.

'Stephen!' The shout came from the rear veranda, a slim man in a PPE suit, a head taller than Holm, dusty hair still not grey despite his age. He strode forth, peeling off a pair of blue gloves and holding out his hand. 'I guess you're back in favour now, right?'

'Bob.' Holm stuck out his hand. 'I never wanted to be the one saying I told you so, but there you go.'

Bob Longworth. An old friend from Holm's days on the Met. Longworth had had the same role for literally decades and Holm wasn't sure if that was due to laziness or dedication. Whichever it was, Longworth's job was a thankless task and over the years had involved having to stay on top of threats ranging from the IRA to Islamist terrorists, from the hard right to the revolutionary left.

'Well, at least you said something.' Longworth gestured over to the blackened shrubs. 'Take a look.'

'Are you sure it's not a barbecue gone wrong or a bonfire out of control?'

'If only.' Longworth drew Holm's attention to a white marker on the grass. 'The operator stood several metres back from that bush. As I understand it the AirShield ejects from the launcher but doesn't ignite until well clear. When it did the resulting heat set the bush alight. I guess they miscalculated the initial trajectory.'

'And the other marker?' Holm pointed to a second white marker close by.

'There are four small holes in the ground, each an inch in diameter, set in a square pattern, a foot and a half between each. We don't know what they are.'

'Farakh? Any idea?'

'Some kind of launch tripod, only with four legs?' Javed shook his head, dismissing his own suggestion. 'Only they'd be too close together to provide any sort of stability.'

'Could that explain why the attack failed?' Longworth turned his head, his gaze following an imaginary flight path from the garden to some point in the distance.

'It hardly failed,' Holm said. 'Without a combination of incredible good fortune and the skills of the pilot, this would have been a catastrophe.'

'I meant that a hit on an engine or the wing would have resulted in the plane dropping out of the sky.' Longworth's gaze lowered and he blinked. 'There'd have been no survivors.'

'You're right there.' Holm shrugged. 'Can we see inside?'

'Sure.' Longworth pointed to a crate over near the veranda. 'Get suited up then you're good to go.'

'Suited up?'

'It's a crime scene. There's an old woman dead in there. Throat slit. She was killed this morning by the looks of things.'

Holm and Javed moved towards the house where, to one side of the door, a plastic crate held an array of PPE in all manner of sizes. Holm, with years of police work behind him, pulled on a suit, bootlets, hairnet and gloves in a couple of minutes. Javed took longer, fiddling with the hairnet, ripping a hole in a glove, and failing to secure one bootlet properly.

'Graduates.' Longworth shook his head. 'One wonders what they're taught these days.'

'He's got a masters in Islamist extremism.' Holm was down on one knee, tucking a leg of the suit into Javed's bootlet. He felt like it was twenty-five years ago and he was helping one of his kids get ready for school. 'Or so he tells me.'

'Well, he can wave it at the bad guys next time we have to do a hard entry. Might save a lot of hassle.'

Holm straightened. 'Lead the way.'

Longworth had donned a fresh pair of gloves and re-secured his hairnet. He pulled his hood up and moved to the veranda.

'She's in here.' He pushed open a door into a large kitchen. 'Keep to the side.'

Holm stepped up onto the porch and followed Longworth. Black and white floor tiles led to ageing kitchen units. There were flowers in a vase on a window sill. A selection of cookery books on a shelf. A round table with four chairs, one chair holding a slumped figure. Grey hair on a head bent forward, below nothing but a husk in a floral dress. On the floor a pool of crimson spread from beneath the chair.

'Irene Caxwell. Seventy-three.' Longworth stepped across towards the body, but gestured for Holm and Javed to stay put. He indicated ropes at the woman's wrists and ankles. He pointed to the table where a large serrated breadknife lay plumb centre. 'They tied her to the chair and slit her throat.'

'No sign of a struggle?' Holm was slipping back into his old detective role. He glanced round for clues, noting that the door didn't seem to have been forced and nothing in the kitchen was out of place.

'No, but they didn't need to surprise her because she knew them.'

'She *knew* them?' This from Javed. 'Seems unlikely given the circumstances.'

'Not at all. There's an annex attached to the side of the bungalow. According to a neighbour, Irene sometimes rented the place out. He thinks there's been a couple of students staying here intermittently.'

'Do we have a description?'

'Not a good one, but hopefully we'll get a better idea from the e-fit. However, we do have two first names, Sabin and Mohid.'

'Mohid? As in Mohid Latif?'

'Could be. The neighbour says Irene talked about them all the time, thought the world of them. They'd helped her clear some scrub in the back garden and one of them had been on the roof to fix the TV aerial.'

Holm stared through the kitchen window to where the forensic team were working. 'Let me guess: one, the scrub was out there where they fired the missile from; two, you can see the runway from the roof.'

'Correct on both counts. At the front of the bungalow there's a footpath with a steady stream of dog walkers passing by throughout the day. I guess they wanted to set up everything out of sight. We're making an appeal for anyone who walked the path in the last couple of months to come forward.'

'There's something on the bottom of the legs of that chair.' Holm dropped to his haunches. The chair opposite Caxwell was positioned oddly, considering how neat the rest of the room was. Its feet were stained with dirt or mud. Holm stood. 'The chair was outside. That's what made those marks in the lawn.'

'Could they have used it as an impromptu table?' Longworth said.

'If that was the case, why bother to bring it back inside afterwards? It can hardly have been a top priority to clear up before leaving.'

'I don't know, then.' Longworth shrugged and led Holm and Javed back outside and round the side of the bungalow to the annex.

'They lived in here.' Longworth pushed on a rickety door. The room was open plan, a couple of beds down one end, a kitchenette to the side, and a living area with a sofa and a TV right where you came in. 'They've not left much though.'

'Forensics?'

'Done. Plenty of hairs from the pillows. Finger-prints everywhere. Whoever these guys were they weren't worried about leaving traces. Another thing, again according to the neighbour, the two of them were away a lot. Always coming and going. Trips abroad to do with their studies.'

'Christ.' Holm shook his head. 'And we missed that during Operation Supernova?'

'Officers did call round, but recorded the old woman as being the only person living here. The neighbour said Irene distrusted the police. It's not beyond the realms of possibility that our suspects tried to heighten her fears.'

No, Holm thought, that would be exactly the way Taher would play it. Terrorism, in essence, was about manipulation, and Taher was the master of that.

Back outside, Holm went over to the white markers. No doubt about it, the chair in the kitchen had made the indentations.

'Why, Taher?' Holm said quietly. 'Why bother to take the chair back inside?'

'Does it matter?' Javed stood alongside.

'If it didn't matter, he wouldn't have done it.'

Holm stared at the ground for a few more seconds and then turned and walked back to their car.

Chapter 13

Things hadn't gone to plan.

Taher and Latif were in the west London flat. The TV was on in the corner of the room, the volume low, but the latest news scrolling on a ticker at the bottom of the screen.

'Twelve dead.' Latif shrugged. He slumped in the armchair, his body language telegraphing his disappointment, the wince he gave as he sat back a sign of the pain he was in. 'Sorry.'

Taher stood by a window, his gaze roving to the southeast where a low haze hung over Heathrow. He couldn't pinpoint the exact location of the airport, but every few minutes he could see an aircraft dipping from the sky. Initially all outbound flights had been suspended and many inbound flights diverted, but now planes were flying in and out almost as if nothing had happened.

He turned back to the TV. The ticker was reporting the cause of the crash of the 787 as unknown. Earlier there'd been a couple of aviation experts giving their viewpoints. One suspected a bird strike or possibly a drone, another suggested metal fatigue within the vertical tail fin. Neither mentioned terrorism, and nobody had considered the possibility that the plane had been struck by an American Armaments AirShield surface-to-air missile.

'Don't worry,' Taher said. 'They got lucky. In the end it won't make any difference. The crash will still have the same effect.'

'But they're saying it's an accident.' Latif nodded at the screen. 'Or a drone.'

'Those who need to know realise what actually happened. What you see on the news is a cover-up. The truth is something the godless have trouble accepting because it would mean the end to their way of life.'

The news channel was repeating an interview with one of the survivors of the crash. The woman was eulogising about Captain Brian Hammond. He was a hero, she said. He deserved a medal. It was a miracle they'd been saved. God, she said, was smiling on all of them.

Not all of them, Taher thought. Not the twelve people who'd been sucked out the back of the aircraft. The woman was typical of people who didn't understand what faith was. Their belief was full of contradictions, unable to stand up to any sort of scrutiny. Pray for this, pray for that, thank God for the good things in life and then bomb the hell out of a distant people.

The picture changed again as the channel went to a news summary. There was video footage taken by another one of the passengers as they landed on the reservoir. It showed dozens of people escaping into the water or climbing out onto the remaining wing. A strange look on some faces. Horror and relief.

Taher nodded to himself. Like Latif, he was angry more people hadn't died, but he didn't want his comrade to see his disappointment. Now, more than ever, he needed to be strong and show leadership. His plans, so carefully constructed in the previous months, were now in danger of unravelling and he wondered whether anything else could go wrong.

The failure to destroy the jet was causing him to question his own judgement. He hadn't trusted Saabiq with the mission to the Philippines, but by relying on Latif both there and in the UK, Taher realised that he'd compromised the whole plan. Latif had returned and insisted he was fit enough to fire the missile when it was now obvious he was not. His long journey back from Asia – by sea, air and land – had clearly taken its toll and compounded his injury. It had been a mistake to allow him to even try to fire the missile, but Saabiq hadn't been keen to take Latif's place, once more causing Taher to doubt the man's courage and commitment.

He looked at the TV again, his mind working overtime. Over the next few hours and days the media would be full of stories of how close to disaster these people had come. The stories would only serve to emphasise the nightmare that would unfold if his demands were not met. He wondered if fortune had in fact smiled on him. He walked forward and stood beside the armchair. Patted Latif on the shoulder.

'It's all good, brother,' he said.

'It is?' Latif didn't seem sure.

'Yes.' Taher turned away. 'Remember, this isn't just about the missiles. A missile kills a few hundred people but in a week or a month the act is forgotten. Our plan is far more sophisticated than mere butchery.'

'Of course. I'm sorry for lacking faith.'

'There is no need to apologise. Now, let's turn the TV off and concentrate on what we need to do. The next phase of the mission starts tonight.'

Back at Thames House, Holm and Javed found the situation room abuzz. Whispered conversations were layered over the sound from the various news channels that were displayed on the big wall of monitors at the back of the room. One large screen showed a map with flight radar data, a myriad of little aeroplane icons converging on or leaving Heathrow airport.

Holm considered the screen for a few seconds. At any moment one of those icons could disappear from the display, signifying the loss of hundreds of lives. It really didn't bear thinking about, but he noticed that every so often someone would glance up from their work and take in the mass of air traffic on the screen. Perhaps, silently, offer a prayer. The problem was Taher was praying too. Which deity would listen? Which deity would answer and in what way? Perhaps, Holm mused, that was why he didn't believe in either prayers or gods.

At three there was news that NATS – the National Air Traffic Service – were tracking an inbound Airbus that had failed to respond to radio messages. The aircraft had originated from Qatar and the passenger list included a man by the name of Mohid Latif. The plane, it seemed, had been hijacked. Fighter jets were scrambled and Number Ten gave instructions that the aircraft was to be intercepted and shot down if it looked as if the pilots were no longer in control. A British 9/11 wouldn't be allowed to happen. A tense few minutes followed until the crew of the aircraft eventually made contact with air traffic control. There was no hijacking and, on landing, waiting police discovered Mohid Latif to be a man in his eighties.

Sightings of Taher began to come in from various police forces. None could be verified and if all were true then Taher appeared to have acquired the ability to teleport instantly at will. One case of mistaken identity concerned a young male – matching Taher's description, but actually a French language-exchange student – outside Buckingham Palace. He was tasered by police as he reached into a carrier bag to take out his lunch.

Holm felt his stomach tighten. Fear, panic, over-reaction. The three things any terrorist attack always produced. Even though the attack on flight 117 hadn't fully succeeded, Taher now had the upper hand.

Huxtable returned from a meeting with Helen Kendle, the national security adviser. She came into the situation room and pulled Holm to one side.

'The story is,' she said, 'that flight 117 hit a commercial drone. The drone failed to recognise the geofence set up in its internal software and wandered off course.'

'Sorry?' Holm didn't have a clue what Huxtable was going on about.

'The long and the short of it is that the prime minister has agreed that a little bending of the facts is acceptable considering the circumstances.'

'What about the Air Accidents Investigation Branch? They'll quickly realise it wasn't a drone.'

'It will be necessary to undertake some suppression of the truth in the coming days, but that can't happen indefinitely. I imagine the AAIB will be encouraged to delay their initial report.'

'So if we're not revealing that the plane was hit by a missile then there'll be no grounding of flights?'

'That would be giving in to Taher. It would be admitting that he's won.'

'Ma'am, he's just brought down a 787 and he likely has several more missiles.' Holm shook his head. 'He may not have won but he certainly holds all the cards. Allowing flights to continue is foolhardy at best. In the worst-case scenario we'll be complicit in mass murder.'

'It wasn't my call, Stephen. All I can do is relay the facts. You told me some weeks ago that Taher could force the country to its knees. Well, the prime minister isn't prepared to allow that.'

'And when Taher does fire another missile and it brings down another aircraft?'

'That's not going to happen because we're going to catch him first, right?'

-

It was after nine in the evening when Holm finally left Thames House and made his way home. It had been a long and frustrating day. Huxtable wanted his best guess as to when and where Taher would next strike so he'd put together a document setting out his views: Taher would try again as soon as possible; however, he'd want to make sure he was successful next time. He'd also want to continue to evade capture. Holm reckoned that meant he'd be targeting a different airport.

'So not London, then?' Huxtable had said.

'Not Heathrow, but possibly another London airport or a regional one.'

That in turn meant Taher would need to spend some time planning. He'd need to find a secure site, work up getaway routes and check airline schedules. Most importantly, he'd be figuring out what went wrong with the missile launch. As to how long that would take, Holm told Huxtable he had no idea. Forced to guess he came up with a figure of seven days.

He sat on the train on the District Line staring at the tube map above the window opposite. The dark blue spur of the Piccadilly Line led south-west down to Heathrow Airport. He shivered as he thought about a well-aimed missile hitting a plane landing from the east or taking off in that direction. The aircraft would come down on some of the most densely populated areas in the UK, wiping out not only the few hundred people on the plane, but many others on the ground. Luckily, flight 117 had been taking off to the west. If it had come down when the missile had hit, it would have crashed into the relatively thinly populated areas of Slough or Bracknell or Windsor.

Windsor? Bloody hell.

Holm pulled out his phone and brought up a map. Centred Heathrow and then slid the airport to the right. Windsor came in from the left of the screen, Windsor Castle no more than five miles from the end of one of the runways and in a direct line. How come he hadn't spotted that before? Holm opened an email and composed a quick note to Huxtable suggesting that members of the royal household should avoid staying at Windsor.

When he emerged from Ealing Broadway station, he stopped to pick up a paper from a kiosk. Captain Brian Hammond and flight 117 was the main story on the front page of the *Evening Standard*. Inside there was a detailed examination of Hammond's heroics as well as some speculation as to what had caused the crash. Initially a catastrophic airframe failure had been suggested, but now, the paper said, experts were pointing to the possibility of the aircraft hitting a large commercial drone. The army were going to provide extra security around the airport perimeter. Other airports would also be seeing increased vigilance.

Holm folded the paper and nodded to himself. The media appeared to have taken the bait. Claire Evans's drone idea had been genius. It provided a justification for the increased military presence at Heathrow while avoiding the outright lie that this had been an accident.

Holm left the main street and strolled down the side road towards his flat. Light shone from the front windows of the homes he passed. Happy families. Friends and lovers. Live music from a low-key band rehearsal taking place in somebody's living room. The music focused Holm's mind on his social life. The mambo gig was the first time he'd been out in months. He couldn't remember his last trip to a cinema. He glanced at his watch, realising he'd be back in his flat for the start of *Newsnight*.

He moved to cross the road, the darkened windows of his first-floor flat just over the way, when a car drew up, blocking his path. The window slipped down.

'Can you tell me how…?'

The man in the passenger seat had a phone out and tilted the screen towards Holm.

'Of course.' Holm smiled and moved closer. 'What was—'

He was aware of somebody behind him, the rear door of the car opening, something jabbing him in the back.

'Get in.' The instruction from behind came with a violent shove. 'Or else.'

Holm half turned, seeing the weapon low down. He ducked his head, got into the car, and was pushed across to the middle seat. The door slammed shut and the car moved off.

'Put your head down!' Holm saw the gun clearly now. 'Fucking down!'

Holm leaned forward, feeling a sack or a hood of some kind being pulled over his head as he did so. The last thing he saw before everything went black was the man's face in a flash of white from a passing street light. Dark hair, light-brown skin, a wisp of beard. Those strange, beguiling eyes. Taher.

–

They drove for a little over sixty minutes before the car slowed and bumped along a rough surface. It had been ten twenty-seven as Holm had made to cross the road to his flat and now, as Taher prodded Holm upright, Holm saw the green glow of the dashboard clock: eleven thirty-one. He blinked in the near dark, trying to get his bearings. The route had been through London streets for the first few minutes, stopping and turning frequently. Then they'd accelerated up to a constant speed. That had been the M4 motorway, Holm had thought. There'd been no talking from Taher or the others, just the person in the front passenger seat coughing. Holm listened to the man hacking up phlegm, hearing the occasional gasp of pain. Terminal cancer? Holm wondered. Possibly the last stages. Worryingly that might make the man a good candidate for a suicide mission.

At some point the car had left the motorway and taken a fast main road, followed by the twisting and turning of a country lane until the last half-mile when the vehicle had juddered down some kind of track. At a rough estimate he reckoned they were somewhere south of Reading.

As the car stopped he was hauled upright and the hood was pulled off. Before the driver killed the headlights, he caught a glimpse of trees and an area of heather. There were a couple of wooden benches next to a sign in dark green with a logo of an oak leaf and an acorn. The National Trust.

'Forget it, old man.' The words came out of the darkness, just Taher's vague silhouette against the car window, outside only the hint of a pale greyness. 'We could be anywhere.'

'Anywhere within an hour of London,' Holm said.

'True, but so what?' A shrug of the shoulders. 'This isn't our base or a training camp. It's a place people come to walk their dogs.'

'So why bring me here?'

'Why do you think?'

'To kill me.' Holm lowered his eyes. Taher held the gun steady. 'Well, if you're going to shoot me just get it over with.'

Holm drew a deep breath. He felt his heart racing. His bravado was entirely for show. Inside his guts were like jelly. He wondered if he'd lose control of his bowels.

'Kill you?' Taher laughed. 'It would be a waste of a bullet. Besides, you're much more useful to me alive.'

'We know you downed the plane. We know you have surface-to-air missiles.'

'Good. Then I needn't convince you my threats are genuine.'

'And you killed the old woman too. Slit her throat. You're nothing but a common thug. If you think I'm going to help you in anyway, you're mistaken.'

Taher jerked his hand and the barrel of the gun struck Holm in the mouth. 'No, you're the thug. Your whole race. Interfering in conflicts you should have no part in.

Causing mayhem and misery and suffering. We're going to put a stop to all that.'

Taher withdrew the gun and Holm reached up and touched his face. A cut had opened up on his lip and he tasted blood. Holm had heard enough proselytising from ardent young men to know they were utterly convinced of their point of view. Trying to reason with them was pointless and he'd only spoken back to rile Taher.

'We have demands,' Taher continued. 'And if they are not carried out there will be consequences. Grave consequences.'

'Right,' Holm said, trying his best to sound neutral. He didn't want to be hit again.

'You've seen what a single missile can do. It was only through good fortune the plane wasn't destroyed. Next time luck won't be on your side.'

'You have more?' Holm, of course, knew they had more, but now he realised he wasn't going to be killed, his number one task was to gather intelligence. He probed. 'Several more?'

'We have enough to accomplish the will of God. Enough to force your government to accede to our demands.'

'They won't comply. That isn't how the government responds to threats. We don't cave in to terrorists.'

'It worked for the IRA, it can work for us.'

'You really believe that?'

'You'll see.'

Silence. A creak from the leather seat in the front as the driver shifted.

'Now what?' Holm had the sense there was a measure of uncertainty, almost as if he was in control of the situation. He wondered if the failure to destroy the aircraft had led to a loss of confidence. The iron will of belief was there, but perhaps the commitment and faith in the actual plan was gone. 'Are you going to tell me what you're up to?'

'There will be a name. A foreign national who is shortly coming to London. You will arrange for this person to be assassinated. We will give you one week's notice to plan the kill.'

'I told you, that isn't how the—'

'Rubbish.' Taher nodded to the front. 'One of MI5's trained assassins just tried to kill my friend, but she narrowly failed. I want you to use her.'

'*Her?*'

'Rebecca da Silva. Don't tell me you don't know who she is, you worked with her in Tunisia. She upset my plans before, now she can help me carry them out.'

'Suppose she won't cooperate?'

'You'd better find a way to ensure she does, because if you do nothing then another plane will be brought down.'

'But—'

'No buts. You will do as we say or your country will descend into the abyss. You won't know when we're going to strike, at what airport, against which flight. Civil aviation will have to be shut down completely. The stock market and the pound will plummet. Citizens will be stranded abroad. All travel will be curtailed and there'll be utter chaos and all-out panic. You will learn what it's like to live in terror, never knowing when a missile might snuff out the lives of hundreds of people.'

'And if, in some crazy world, we do accede to your demands, how do we know you'll stop?'

'I'll give up the missiles. Tell you where they're hidden. You have my word.'

'Your word?' Holm made a snorting noise, something to antagonise Taher, to draw him to reveal something he might regret. 'Why should I trust you?'

'You don't have a choice.'

'What if I refuse to cooperate?'

'Then I'll kill you and find somebody else to carry my message.' The gun came up again, this time prodding Holm in the chest. 'Better do as I say, old man, if you want to live.'

Taher tapped the seat in front of him. It appeared to be some form of signal because the driver opened his door and climbed out. Holm's door was wrenched open and hands grasped at him. He tumbled to the ground. A kick met him in the ribs and then another smashed into his upper thigh. One to the head. Blinding pain seared in his jaw.

'Enough.' Taher was out of the car kneeling beside him. He pushed in the gun once more and twisted the barrel against Holm's temple. 'So, are you going to do what I say?'

Holm groaned. Felt as if he was going to be sick.

'I can't hear you.'

'Yes.'

'Good. Get the girl, get it set up. When I see things are proceeding then I'll be in touch about the target.'

Taher stood. There was a click of his fingers and a vicious kick hit Holm in his midriff. He braced himself and waited for more but there was nothing except the sound of car doors closing and the engine starting. The headlights came on and the car drove away, leaving him in a landscape of blurry grey.

After a minute or so he pushed himself up into a sitting position. He tasted blood from a cut in his gum. Winced as he breathed in. Took another moment before he got to his feet. He put a hand to his jacket pocket, searching for his phone, but then remembered that Taher had patted him down shortly after he'd been bundled into the car. The phone had been chucked out the window as soon as it had been found. Holm stood and listened for some sound of civilisation but there was nothing except a gentle rustling of the wind in the trees. Then he began to walk.

Chapter 14

It was after midnight when Holm stumbled along a country lane into a small village. He passed a couple of houses, their windows dark, before he came to a pub. The car park was empty, but there were lights on in the pub. The door was locked and a rap of the big brass knocker brought the inevitable 'we're closed' from inside. Holm tried again, this time shouting out that he was 'police'. Bolts rattled on the back of the door and it swung open to reveal a red-faced gentleman in a tweed jacket who could have come straight from the pages of an Agatha Christie novel.

'Identification?' The man said.

'I just need to make a phone call,' Holm said.

'Sorry, mate.' The door began to close.

'Please.' Holm stood there, allowing his dishevelled appearance to sink in. 'I was attacked. Robbed.'

For a moment the landlord hesitated, but then he opened the door and beckoned Holm in. Five minutes later Holm was seated at the bar with a glass of single malt in one hand and a phone in the other. He dialled a number from memory, and when somebody from the night desk at MI5 answered he asked to be put through to Farakh Javed in the operations room.

'Boss?' Javed said a few seconds later. 'I thought you'd be in bed by now. What with you needing your beauty sleep and all that.'

Holm raised a hand and touched his left eye, felt the swelling. 'I was hoping you'd still be there.'

–

Some ninety minutes after he'd made the call to the operations room, Bob Longworth turned up with Javed and a team of CSIs in tow.

'He was here?' Javad said, glancing round at the pub, sceptical.

'Not here,' Holm said. 'Out there. In the woods.'

They followed the landlord's directions to the National Trust car park and the CSIs cordoned off the area and got to work searching the ground and making casts of the tyre marks.

'There'll be CCTV and traffic cameras,' Javed said as Holm leaned against Longworth's car. 'Should be able to ID them and the vehicle.'

'It was Taher, Farakh,' Holm said. 'And one of the other men was Mohid Latif. It came to me on the long walk to the pub. He was in a bad way – the result, I suspect, of Weiss's kill mission. While Taher and the other man got out and gave me a kicking, Latif stayed in the front.'

'What kill mission?'

Holm reached up and rubbed his forehead. The landlord at the pub had been generous with the whiskies and Holm was feeling a little fuzzy. 'Forgot. Classified. Tell you about it later.'

'Any idea of the vehicle make?' Longworth said. 'Family car? SUV? Estate?'

'Mercedes,' Holm said. 'The badge on the wheels was the last thing I saw as I lay spitting blood into the mud. Big lump of a thing. Black or dark blue. Luxury interior.'

'Probably stolen, but finding it's got to be our top priority.' Longworth paused. 'Don't suppose you managed to catch the index as it drove off?'

'No I didn't.' Holm nodded across to where the CSIs were working the ground. 'They got anything?'

'Three sets of footprints. One trainer-type tread marks, another more of a boot. The third is plain.'

'That's mine. Only three sets because Latif stayed in the car. Think you can do anything with them?'

'Things have moved on since you were in the force, Stephen. We've got a database of shoe sole patterns. We might just get lucky and find that one of these boys wears distinctive trainers or boots. Could even narrow it down to a handful of stockists. From there we might get credit card details and an address.' Longworth shrugged. 'A long shot, I'll admit, but you never know.'

'What did he want, boss?' Javed said. 'Did he make any demands?'

'Yes. And it's not good. He also said I could expect another message soon.' Holm rubbed his ribs again. 'I just hope he doesn't choose to deliver it in the same way.'

'We'll get you protection,' Longworth said. 'Round-the-clock surveillance.'

'No. None of that. Taher's highly trained and he'll spot if you're involved. I don't want him impeded.'

'And do you think Huxtable will see it in the same way?'

Holm didn't answer the question. Thought she almost certainly wouldn't see it in the same way.

On the journey back to London, Holm gave Javed the rundown on exactly what had happened and what Taher wanted.

'Assassination?' Javed said. 'That's what this is about?'

'Apparently, although I don't buy it.' Holm watched the headlights of the cars on the opposite carriageway speeding towards them. Tried to follow them as they whizzed past. His head ached as his gaze flicked from car to car. 'Simeon Weiss claimed that Latif had been critically injured and from what I saw of him he certainly appeared to be in a bad way. I think he's hurt so badly that he's unable to operate the AirShield launcher. It explains the chair in the garden of Irene Caxwell's cottage. He had to sit down. In such a position he wasn't able to track the aircraft properly. The missile failed to lock on to the laser hatching projected from the launcher.'

'But can't Latif instruct somebody else to fire the missile?'

'I would imagine that's what will happen next time. However, perhaps Taher doesn't want to risk another failure. He's had to adapt to circumstances and that could account for this new idea of his.'

'So who's the target?'

'He didn't say. He just told me to be ready. To get Rebecca da Silva on board.'

'Da Silva?'

'Yes. From what I remember she's not bad with a sniper rifle.'

Holm leaned back in his seat and closed his eyes. Thought back to the time in Tunisia when da Silva had saved his life. That whole operation had been set up by Simeon Weiss and it was Weiss who'd sent out the kill team to take out Latif. Was it possible she was responsible for wounding him? If so then Taher's request for Silva was beginning to look like a personal rather than professional choice. That would be uncharacteristic but it provided Holm with an inkling of hope. The desire for revenge on a personal level had never been part of Taher's plan before. If it was now then it suggested the terrorist was changing the cold, calculating behaviour that had served him well, and instead he was letting himself be guided by short-term aims. There was just a chance that could lead to his downfall.

—

After Sean had left for Washington, Silva had stayed in Bodrum for a few days before catching a flight back to the UK. She flew into Heathrow four days after what was already becoming known as the Queen Mary Miracle. If the crash had been terrorism related – as Sean's rapid departure from Turkey and recall to Washington had suggested – then there was nothing in the news pointing that way.

Back in Plymouth, the contrast between the luxury yacht she'd spent two weeks sailing and the tiny boat she lived on was apparent when she opened the hatch to a damp, milldewy smell. The boat was moored at a small marina on the banks of the river Plym, jostling for space with other craft well away from the expensive yachts and motor boats. It was cramped, cold in the winter, hot in the summer, but it was somewhere to call home. Tan had paid well, and she wondered whether she could upgrade to something slightly larger. Considering her lack of employment and prospects, perhaps that wasn't a good idea.

On the first evening back she unpacked her stuff and cleaned the boat. In the morning, she made herself breakfast while listening to the news on the radio. The bulletin was still full of the plane crash in London. There could be increased restrictions on drones, the report said.

Silva spent most of the rest of the day doing some odd jobs about the boat. Late in the afternoon she strolled into town and headed for the Barbican area of the city. Cobbled streets ran along the quayside, and there were waterside cafés and bars. People sat at outside tables and drank coffees or sipped beers. It all seemed so normal, a world away from her Philippine adventure.

What wasn't a world away from the Philippines was the grey-suited man sitting at a table outside one of the bars.

Simeon Weiss.

Silva thought about just walking on past, but Weiss wasn't the kind of man you ignored.

'Mr Weiss,' she said as she came across. For a moment she stood, but Weiss indicated the chair so she sat. 'Have you ever thought of making an appointment rather than just materialising out of thin air?'

'I find that people tend to avoid keeping them.'

'Perhaps you should work on the reasons for that.'

Weiss nodded across at a waiter who was taking orders. Without asking Silva, he ordered two bottles of lager. 'You heard the news?'

'What news? There's a lot of it about these days.'

'The crash at Heathrow. Captain Brian Hammond. The hero of the hour. Mass fatalities only prevented by the brilliant pilot.' The waiter was back. He placed a couple of bottles of Becks and two glasses on the table. Weiss paid. 'Thank God, I say. Or rather thank *our* god, because the fanatics believe there's a different god and he's very much on their side.'

'So it wasn't an accident.' Silva reached for the bottle of beer. 'I guessed as much.'

'Would I be here if it was? No, it was a missile.' Weiss poured his own beer into a glass. 'Fired from a garden beneath the flight path. And to be brutally honest, if it had been fired correctly the plane would have been destroyed. Captain Hammond or no Captain Hammond. In fact you deserve more credit than Hammond for preventing a tragedy.'

'Mohid Latif.'

'Yes. Unfortunately for Taher's plans Latif is in a bad way. Either he was unable to properly operate the missile himself or the instructions he gave were inadequate. Without somebody aware of the correct procedure to fire the weapon, something went wrong.'

'But it still hit the plane.'

'Yes, but with minimal damage. If Latif had been operating the launcher properly the missile would have locked on to the target and there would have been a direct hit. Hammond would have had no chance. We'd be reading about mass casualties, not his heroics.'

Silva sat back in her chair. She felt light-headed, even though she'd had no more than a mouthful of beer.

'You fucked up,' she said. 'Something like the Philippines operation should be months in the making rather than a cursory back-of-the-envelope plan. If you'd filled me in on the mission earlier we could have prepared properly and I might have been able to take out Latif instead of merely injuring him. Now people are dead and it's only thanks to Captain Hammond that hundreds more didn't die.'

'And, as I said before, you would have told me where to get off.'

Silva looked over towards the quay. A fishing boat was drifting in, a crew on the foredeck throwing a rope to someone on shore who took it and threaded it through a large ring. Weiss rapped on the table with his fingers, bringing her attention back to him.

'OK, I'll come clean with you,' Weiss said. 'Total honesty. Nothing held back.'

'Right. As if I'd believe you.'

'Believe what you want. The truth is that I need your help. *We* need your help. The whole country. Again.'

'Don't be ridiculous.'

'I'm not.' Weiss took another sip from his glass. He glanced around at the early-evening drinkers. 'Taher has several more missiles. He's threatened to fire them if we don't accede to his demands.'

'And what in the world have I got to do with that?'

'He's asked for you by name.'

'*Taher?*'

'Yes. He wants you to carry out a hit.'

'He wants to kill me, we know that.'

'True, but I think there's something else going on as well. With Latif injured and possibly incapable of operating AirShield, Taher has changed his plans. Hence this attempt to force us to assassinate somebody for him.'

'Well I'm not getting involved. I told you that in Abu Dhabi.'

'Of course, I understand your reluctance.' Weiss smiled. 'Especially considering the way I've treated you in the past. However, this time it's different. Just let me explain.'

Silva let out a long breath. 'Fine.'

'Taher has said he's going to give us a target. If we don't kill the target by a certain date he's threatening to bring down another aeroplane. Without Latif that might prove difficult, but we can't take the risk of calling his bluff.'

'So you *are* going along with his demands?'

'No, but we want him to believe we're complying. We'll set up an operation, carry out surveillance, plan the kill mission. All the while this is giving us time to close in on Taher. He'll undoubtedly be watching, and he'll think we're doing as he wants. We lure him in, let him become complacent.'

'Lure him in? You mean I'm the bait again?'

'In the Philippines I told you he wouldn't attempt to kill you on British soil. I can't say I'm still sure about that, but if he *had* wanted to take you out he could have done it in the last few days. Something different is going on here and while I can't explain exactly what Taher is up to, right now his plans aren't working out and things are going wrong. I think that could cause him to become rash and slip up. This could be our best chance to catch him.'

'And suppose that doesn't happen before the deadline? Then you're stuffed because you've failed to comply with his demands.'

'Ah, but that's the clever part. As the deadline approaches we'll redouble our efforts. If, despite that, we still haven't caught him, then we'll set it up so you take a shot at the intended target, but miss. The whole event will be a charade, a performance purely for Taher's benefit. If it seems to him that we tried our best but failed, we believe he may decide not to fire a missile.'

'And who is "we"?'

'Me. If that proves not to be the case then that's not your problem.'

'It's a very dangerous gamble, especially for me.'

'It's a dangerous gamble for all of us. If it goes wrong, then hundreds of people will lose their lives. However, Taher has fired one missile from a limited supply. He won't want to use up the rest of his bargaining chips too soon. There's also the issue of Latif. Perhaps he's recovering and Taher will decide to wait until he's in a fit state to operate the launcher.'

'And if I say no?'

Weiss shrugged. 'I'll have to tell my boss I failed to recruit you. I've no idea what Taher's reaction will be. I guess we'll only know when another aircraft comes down.'

'Shit.' Silva sat back in her seat. She didn't like the kind of pressure that came from having to make decisions. And this was a big decision.

'You can take Richard Smith with you and you'll both get standard SAU rates.'

Silva looked at Weiss. His face was inscrutable. She wondered if he'd brought up the subject of payment to play on her guilt. After all nobody should need payment for doing their duty. If he was serious, then what the heck were 'standard rates' anyway? Did MI5 have a spreadsheet detailing what they would pay for services? Ten pounds to change a light bulb or fit a new washer in a dripping tap, but fifteen thousand for an assassination? For all she knew Weiss might be making it up as he went along.

'I want to see Fiona Huxtable,' Silva said. 'I want the details from the horse's mouth.'

She'd met the head of the Security Service after Weiss's Tunisian mission. Seeing her wouldn't allay all her worries, but Silva was fed up of being played by Weiss; this time she wanted confirmation that what was going on was officially sanctioned. She certainly needed more than the word of Weiss, the head of a dodgy black ops department.

'Considering the circumstances I dare say that can be arranged.' Weiss twisted on his chair and smiled.

Something like a weasel, Silva thought.

—

It had been five days since the early-morning plane crash and Holm's late-night encounter with Taher. Since then he'd barely slept and had drunk way too much caffeine. He realised the two things were related, but if he stopped the caffeine he'd fall asleep, and if he slept he feared he'd wake to more awful news.

At least he and Javed now had extra help and every now and then someone came into his office and he assigned them tasks. Track a suspect. Set up intercepts. Gather footage from CCTV. Collate number plate data and cross-reference. Examine bank accounts. The list of tasks seemed endless.

'Straws though, aren't they?' Javed said. 'As in we're clutching at them.'

'Yes,' Holm said.

'And we're running out of time. We're in Taher's hands now.'

Or, Holm thought, Weiss's hands.

Holm didn't get on with Simeon Weiss so he'd been surprised when the day following the incident with Taher the man had slipped into his office bearing two cups of coffee and some donuts.

'Be wary of people bearing gifts,' Weiss said.

'Sorry?' Holm looked up from his screen.

'Sometimes all is not what it seems.' Weiss put the coffees and donuts down. Pushed a coffee cup across the desk towards Holm. 'But if you want to believe it is easy to do so.'

'Simeon, I'm too tired for your games. Is there something you want?'

'Want, no. Tell, yes.' Weiss pulled over a nearby chair and sat. 'I've heard all about your meeting with Taher, about his demands, about how he wants Rebecca da Silva involved in some kind of hit.'

'Huxtable told you?'

'Yes. I've worked with Silva recently. We're close. I think she could be persuaded.'

'To do what?'

'To take part in Operation Trojan.'

Holm shook his head. He reached for the coffee and took a sip. The caffeine hit made little difference.

'And what exactly is Operation Trojan?' he asked.

Weiss had smiled and explained, and the more Holm had listened the more he'd thought the idea was the most utterly batshit scheme he'd ever come across.

'Boss?' Javed asked. 'I said have we got anything more on Henson?'

'No,' Holm said, snapping back to the present, realising he needed to focus. 'And that's the part of this puzzle I can't understand. Henson's been storing the missiles, plus some chemicals, in a lock-up garage for Taher. It doesn't make sense. The two of them should be sworn enemies, not best buddies.'

'Perhaps he didn't know about the missiles.'

'But the chemicals were his. Shaz said they were at the house on Bernard Street until he moved them. Then there's the hit on Tallin Saabiq. It can't be a coincidence. They must be working together.'

'But what rationale would either of them have to do that?'

'I don't know. We need to go back and examine the Henson material again. All of it. And I want fresh eyes.'

'You don't trust me to do it?'

'I don't trust either of us. We're too deep in this. We can't see the wood for the trees, know what I mean?'

Within an hour Javed had assembled a team to analyse the documentary evidence. Each piece would be examined by three different people. Random thoughts, hunches and sheer guesswork would be encouraged, and the results collated and cross-referenced. While the new team got to work, Holm took himself off for a walk in an attempt to 'blue-sky' something from nothing. He strolled along the banks of the Thames, pausing every now and then to gaze at the swirling mass of water. The tide was ebbing and so was the time they had left. If they couldn't find Taher soon then Weiss would be forced to run his little charade. The whole thing was complete madness.

Back in the office Javed was bouncing from wall to wall.

'Got a result, sir,' he said, reluctantly sitting down when Holm directed him to. 'The lock-up garage where the chemicals and missiles were is on prime development land. The land was purchased a couple of years ago, an old factory was demolished, and plans submitted for a swish new block of flats. The company that bought the land is Sunrise Global Property. It's a shell company incorporated in the Bahamas and doesn't seem to do very much other than own dozens of London brownfield sites and a residential property north of Hampstead Heath. I checked out the main shareholder who owns ninety per cent of the shares. Supposedly it's a man known as Vladimir Kapinsky.'

'Supposedly?'

'He doesn't appear to exist. There's no immigration record in the Border Force database, nothing from a casual search on the web, no tax information, nothing on the PNC or in our own files. If he's an overseas citizen then he's never visited to check on his investments, yet there doesn't seem to be anyone else connected with Sunrise Property. Of course it could be a coincidence this dodgy company is connected via the lock-up to Taher, but I don't think so.'

'No,' Holm said. 'Neither do I.'

Chapter 15

Itchy wasn't at home when Silva called round. The door was answered by Caz, Itchy's girlfriend. She held a finger to her lips.

'Shush,' she said. 'The baby's sleeping upstairs. Thank God the doorbell didn't wake her.'

Caz looked tired, something Silva supposed went with the territory. Not that Silva had made things any easier by taking Itchy on a joyride to the Philippines. And now she was going to ask him to come away with her again.

'You OK?' Silva said. 'Coping?'

'Just about.' Caz put out a hand and touched Silva on the arm. 'And the money comes in very handy, so I want to thank you for thinking of Itchy. Without you we'd be down the food bank. As it is, we're doing more than all right. What Itchy earned last month is a year's salary in a normal job.'

Silva's guilt slipped away. 'Any idea where he is?'

'He's out with his new toy.' Caz gestured down the road to where the green of Central Park filled the end of the street. 'He'll be up near the pitch and putt. You can't miss him.'

Silva thanked Caz then walked down the road to the park. She headed in and climbed through the trees towards the mini-golf course. She couldn't see Itchy having the temperament for golf, but perhaps he wanted a new hobby to spend some of his excess cash on.

As she came out of the trees and onto a large expanse of grass, something flew above the treeline, a black speck in the sky with four rotors and a hideous whine. She ducked her head in an almost involuntary action and as she did a shout sounded across the playing fields.

'Silvi! Saw you coming a mile off!'

Silva looked up. Itchy stood in the middle of the grass, some sort of controller in his hands. The black speck whizzed towards him, dropped from the sky and landed at his feet. She walked over and stared down at the drone.

'Now I know what your new toy is, Itch,' she said. 'And I thought you'd taken up golf.'

'Nah, that's an old man's game.' He grinned. 'After playing with Mr Tan's drones I decided I needed one myself. Got a great camera and a range of several miles. Can scare the hell out of people too.'

'I noticed that. Expensive?'

'Don't ask. You know me, got to go for a top-of-the-range model. Still – flush, ain't I?'

'For how long?'

Itchy shrugged. 'We worked hard, and this is my reward.'

'I've got another job, Itch.' Silva stared down at the drone. 'If you want it.'

'Where?'

'London, so there'd be no leaving the country. We'd have to be away for a week or so though.'

'What kind of job could we do in London?'

Silva ran through what she knew and explained about the dummy operation designed to fool Taher. 'Mr Weiss is coordinating it.'

'Weiss? That worries me, considering the way he tricked us in the Philippines.'

'Me too, but I'm going above his head to get confirmation that it's legal.' Silva looked at the drone again. 'You'll get paid. Not as much as the job for Mr Tan, but enough to buy a whole lot more toys like that should you want.'

'You're sure it's legit?'

'Pretty sure.' Silva paused. 'Look, Itchy, I don't want you to feel pressured. I could do with your help, but I'm taking the job anyway.'

'You don't need the money any more than I do.'

'No.'

'So why do it, then?'

'It's another chance to catch Taher, so I guess it's personal. Not that I expect that to make any difference to you.'

'Well it does make a difference.' Itchy smiled but then made a glum face. 'Mind you, I hope they'll do more than catch him when it comes down to it.'

'They probably will. I can't imagine he's the kind of man to go down without a fight.'

'So when do we leave?'

'Tomorrow. Is that going to be OK with Caz?'

'Sure. As long as I'm earning she doesn't mind.' Itchy bent and picked up the drone. 'It's when I'm spending she gets cross.'

–

Sunrise Global Property had an interest in forty-seven development sites and owned a single residential property. The house was on Sheldon Avenue, a road that ran up from Hampstead Heath and alongside Highgate golf course. It seemed the obvious place to start and, rather than doing further research, Holm opted for an immediate visit. As they coasted down the road past the huge mansions, Javed was on his phone browsing Rightmove. He filled Holm in on the current state of the housing market.

'Ten million and up,' he said. 'Six to eight bedrooms and back gardens that overlook a golf course. Most have pools and cinema rooms, huge kitchens, triple or quadruple garages. Probably pin money to the mysterious Kapinsky. Chicken feed.'

'Expensive chickens.' Holm slowed the car, checking the house numbers. 'Fifty-six. Here we are.'

Fifty-six stood well back from the road, a modern, neo-Georgian brick property with large sash windows either side of an impressive portal. Tall iron railings sat in front of a young leylandii hedge and a set of double gates hung on brick pillars.

'My next pad,' Javed said. 'I just need to marry up.'

Holm drove by and stopped the car a couple of properties down. He wasn't sure how he was going to play this. They didn't know who lived here or whether they were in any way connected to Taher.

'You stay here and keep watch.' Holm took the keys from the ignition and handed them across. 'Be prepared to tail on foot or in the car.'

He got out, closed the door and walked back to the gates. There was a bell push on one of the brick pillars, a speaker grille below. Holm went over and pressed the bell. Thirty seconds later a muffled response came from the grille.

'Yes?'

'Stephen Holm, HM Government,' Holm said. 'I'd like to talk to Mr Kapinsky if at all possible. It's a diplomatic matter.'

'Mr Kapinsky isn't in residence,' the disembodied voice said. 'He's been out of the country for some time.'

'I want to discuss a property he owns. A crime has taken place there. If you don't let me in then I'll have to call the police so we can investigate further.'

Holm stood and waited. He hadn't really thought this through properly. Javed was right earlier, they were clutching at straws.

He was about to press the bell again when the gate lock buzzed and both gates swung inwards. Holm walked across the neat brick-paved driveway and up to the front door. It opened as he approached, a bulky man in a badly fitting suit standing next to a young woman in a black and white maid's outfit.

'He'll see you in the garden,' the maid said. She gestured for Holm to come in. As he did so the security man stepped forward, bearlike hands reaching out. 'You'll be searched first.'

Holm stayed still as the big man patted him down. His phone and wallet were removed from his jacket pocket and placed in a tray on a table by the front door. The man nodded and the girl showed Holm through a hallway and a minimalist kitchen. Sliding full-length glass doors led to a patio area where a set of wicker armchairs edged a large swimming pool. A man of Middle Eastern origin in a casual suit lounged on a sofa, a phone in his hand. He wasn't Russian, and was definitely not the mysterious Mr Kapinsky.

'Mr Haddad,' Holm said as he circuited the pool. 'This is unexpected.'

Jawad al Haddad, the Saudi who'd bankrolled Taher and helped smuggle the AirShield missiles to North Africa, looked up and smiled. He put the phone on a small table next to a newspaper and a pad and pen, and stood as Holm approached.

Holm, ever observant, noted the handwriting on the pad was in English, the ink purple. The pen was fancy, tortoiseshell or something. Knowing Haddad it probably cost thousands.

'Mr Holm,' Haddad said, offering his hand. 'The poor man's James Bond.'

Holm approached and shook Haddad's hand, thinking the situation was quite bizarre. Of course Haddad would know all about him from Martin Palmer, the mole in the intelligence services that Holm had uncovered, but they'd never met. Holm tried not to let the sham familiarity disarm him.

'Bond is with MI6,' Holm said. 'I'm with the Security Service, a different beast altogether. We deal with direct threats to UK security, Bond operates abroad. Plus he's fictional.'

'Of course.' Haddad gestured to an armchair and clicked his fingers at the maid. She scuttled off. 'But you have been known to venture overseas, have you not? Sunny spots bordering the Med?'

So this was to be a game. An 'I know that you know that I know' sort of game. Fair enough. Even though this was the first time they'd met, Holm had formed an opinion of Haddad through the extensive reports he'd read. The man had an arrogance about him born of immense wealth and privilege. For a while, after missile smuggling, it had looked as if he might face some sort of retribution in Saudi Arabia, but his connections had seen him through. Now he would no doubt feel invincible. Holm could use that.

'I'm not at liberty to disclose operational details.' Holm took a seat. Tried to appear relaxed. 'But occasionally, yes.'

'North Africa, right?' Haddad slipped back onto the wicker sofa. 'Poking your nose into other people's affairs.'

'That's what spies do, Mr Haddad. We try to find out secrets.'

'And that's why you're here, to find out my secrets?'

'Is this your house, Mr Haddad?'

'No. I'm simply staying here for a while. I believe the practice is called *renting*.'

Holm ignored the sarcasm. 'Do you know anything about a company called Sunrise Global Property?'

'Of course, I'm renting from Sunrise.' Haddad leaned forward. 'Tell me, Mr Holm, is real estate your new profession? I can see you as a lettings adviser, perhaps not here in London, more in some run-down seaside resort. Bedsits and studios. Basement flats with damp problems and dodgy gas heaters.' Haddad glanced round. 'This, I'm afraid, would be a little out of your league.'

If this was a game, Holm thought, then so far Haddad was definitely one up. He followed Haddad's gaze. Took in the house and immaculate garden. The pool. When he looked back, Haddad had pulled the newspaper over the pad and pen, as if he was trying to shield whatever was written on the pad from Holm's prying eyes.

'Sunrise own a garage over in Dagenham,' Holm said. 'It's connected to a terrorist plot.'

'Flight 117?' Haddad made a sad face, turned his hands over. 'I know nothing of this.'

No, Holm thought, but you've just slipped up. The true cause of the plane crash had not yet been released to the public. The scoreboard ticked over to one-one.

'In the past you've funnelled weapons and money to terror groups across the Middle East.'

'Really?' Haddad shook his head. 'If that was true then wouldn't your government be pressing charges against me? Wouldn't the police be beating a path to my front door?' Haddad waved his arm around. 'I'm living right in the heart of London and, as you have discovered, am quite accessible. I have a couple of security guards, but nothing that any rich person wouldn't consider as prudent. If I've done anything illegal then how come I can do as I please?'

'You can't return to Saudi Arabia because you were kicked out. The government there wanted to show they were clamping down on citizens who provided funding for extremists.'

'So you're holding the Kingdom up as some kind of moral arbiter now, are you?' Haddad leaned forward. 'Look, I had a falling out with the prince and now I have to live abroad. That's all there is to it. I'll be welcomed back there before too long, you'll see.'

'Let's return to the lock-up garage.'

'No, let's not. That's nothing to do with me. Either come to the point or leave.'

'Fine. You're friends with a terrorist known as Taher. His intention is to kill hundreds of innocent civilians using an anti-aircraft missile. One word from you and he could be stopped.'

'Preposterous. Besides, even if I did know this Taher, what makes you think he'd listen to what I have to say?'

'Because you still have influence.'

'Not over Taher. He walks his own path and his route was predestined many years ago.'

'So you admit to knowing him?'

'I have met many people, but I'm not responsible for any of their actions.'

'I'm afraid you're wrong about that. We're very close to catching Taher and when it comes to light that you failed to help us, you'll be in trouble. I will personally see to it that you are deported, preferably back to Saudi. I trust there will be a warm welcome for you there.'

He stood, alarmed to see the security guard striding purposely across the patio area. Haddad said something in Arabic and gestured at Holm. Holm sidestepped towards the pool, intending to dodge past the guard, but big hands clamped round his right arm and spun him round. He struggled as the guard held him firm. Then the grip relaxed and Holm broke free, for a moment teetering on the edge of the pool before a shove from the guard sent him tumbling over. He hit the water and went under, bobbing back up after a moment. A paw of a hand reached down and grabbed him under one arm, hauling him upwards and depositing him on the floor by the pool.

'Take him round the side,' Haddad said in English. 'I don't want any mess in the house.'

Holm spat out a mouthful of chlorinated water. He shrugged off the security guard and followed him to a gate. The guard opened the gate and pushed Holm through. He traipsed to the front and across the driveway where the gates were swinging to the open position. He walked out and paused as they closed. He stood there, dripping.

A moment later the guard appeared at the front door. He had Holm's phone and wallet. He strode a couple of paces across the drive and then lobbed them high into the air so they sailed over the gates and landed in the road. Holm went to retrieve them. The wallet was scuffed and the phone's screen was cracked. He shook his head. He'd only just bought the phone as a replacement for the one Taher had taken. He walked up the road to his car. Ducked down and tapped on the window before realising the car was empty and Javed had gone.

Holm took off his wet jacket and got in the car. The keys were under the front seat and he saw there was a notification from Javed on his phone: *Maid left straight after you went in. Following on foot.* Holm messaged back: *It was Jawad al Haddad in there. He's sent the maid to warn Taher. Keep on her.* A couple of minutes later another text pinged in: *Waiting for tube East Finchley UG.*

It was another hour before Holm knew where the maid had ended up, the destination teased by Javed every few minutes in a series of texts:

Northern line south

Waterloo boarding overground train

Leaving train at Kew Bridge

Walking

Brentford Towers Boulton House

Flat C 12th floor! She stayed 1 min then left

Holm nodded to himself. It was time to call Bob Long-worth.

–

Itchy's idea of rewarding himself after the Philippine trip had been to buy a drone and take his wife out for dinner.

Silva's involved spending a wodge of cash on a Yamaha XTZ trail bike to replace her ageing Honda. She had some kind of fantasy of one day disappearing off over the horizon, but for now made do with a couple of trips riding on Dartmoor.

On Thursday, Weiss was in touch. She needed to come to London for a meeting with the director general of the Security Service, Fiona Huxtable.

'Don't be surreptitious about it,' Weiss said. 'The whole point is that we want Taher to know you're in contact with us. We want him to believe we're going along with his demands.'

Silva rode to her father's house with the intention of spending the night there before heading to London the next morning. She'd barely come through the front door before he wanted to know what she'd been up to.

'Could have done with a hand felling that ash tree by the lake. Hell of a thing to do on my own.'

'I was sailing in Turkey with Sean. I sent you a text.'

'What about last month?'

'I was doing that job in the Philippines, remember?' Silva dropped her bag in the hallway and followed her father through to the kitchen. She wondered if he'd genuinely forgotten or if there was something else. 'Are you OK?'

'I'm fine.' Her father went over to the cooker where a saucepan of soup was bubbling away. He gave it a stir with a wooden spoon. 'What about you?'

'I'm good. Got a new bike.'

'I saw. Must have cost a pretty penny.'

'The Philippines job paid very well.'

'And all for shooting down a few drones, hey?' He went across to a tall cupboard and rummaged inside. 'I'll open an extra tin for supper.'

'Thanks.' Silva watched as her father pulled out a tin, opened it and poured the contents into the pan. He stirred the soup for a minute or so but said nothing. 'You know, don't you?'

'I know you weren't shooting down drones, Rebecca. You didn't answer a couple of texts so I messaged Itchy. He said things had got a bit hairy but that you were both safe. Signed off with a winking face.'

'Shit.'

'Since Matthew Fairchild was the instigator of the job I gave him a ring. He hadn't heard anything but he said he'd check his contacts and get back to me. When he did he told me he'd discovered that an ISIS leader had been killed by unknown forces.' Her father found a couple of bowls and placed them on the table. Crusty bread came from another cupboard and butter and cheese from the fridge. He poured the soup and then looked over to Silva. 'Now those unknown forces wouldn't just happen to be you and Itchy, would they?'

'Mohid Latif was there, Dad. One of the men who killed Mum.'

'And he's dead, too?'

'I wounded him.' Silva took a chair at the table. She could feel her father's gaze on her. 'Sorry I didn't do better.'

'Right.' Her father sat at the table, picked up a spoon and bent to his soup. He took a couple of slurps. 'After the last time, I thought you were done with all that.'

'Simeon Weiss tricked us just like he and Fairchild did before. When Latif turns up in my sights what was I supposed to do? Pardon him?'

'No, never that.' Her father put the spoon down with a clink. 'Initially, when your mother first died, I was all for revenge. I wanted everyone connected dead. If I'd have been there in the Philippines I'm sure I'd have done the same as you, but it's just...' He looked away. 'I worry about you, Rebecca. I couldn't bear the thought of anything happening to you.'

Silva reached out, but her father pushed back his chair and stood.

'That's all,' he said, before walking to the door and leaving the room.

Chapter 16

Silva was touched by her father's show of affection but also angry it had taken him so long to express his feelings. They didn't talk about it again that evening and the next morning she left for London.

Her new bike, great on the open roads of Dartmoor, was a bit more of a handful when weaving through the traffic in the city, but she managed to get to the Embankment unscathed and find a place to park in a side street. A guard at the front entrance viewed her with suspicion before letting her in. Once inside she had to undergo a rigorous security check before being escorted to a meeting room where she found Fiona Huxtable seated at the head of a large table. To one side was Simeon Weiss. To the other side was an older man, balding.

'Rebecca,' Huxtable said. She rose and offered a hand. 'I'm glad you're on board.'

'I wasn't given much choice,' Silva said as she walked forward. She nodded at Weiss. 'I was told in no uncertain terms that people would die if I didn't help.'

'Which is, unfortunately, true.' Huxtable waved at those present. 'Simeon you know. Stephen Holm you've met too, although I don't think you've been introduced formally.'

Holm extended a hand as Silva approached, a warm smile on his face.

'We meet again at last,' he said. 'In Tunisia I never got the time to thank you for saving my life.'

'That's a bit dramatic, Stephen,' Huxtable said.

'Not at all. If it wasn't for Rebecca I wouldn't be here.'

'I'm only sorry I didn't get Taher,' Silva said, taking a seat beside Holm. 'If I had none of this would be happening.'

'Back then you had a choice of shots and I for one am glad you choose the way you did.'

'Let's proceed.' Huxtable had some kind of agenda in front of her and she glanced down for a moment. 'These are quite extraordinary times and extraordinary times demand extraordinary measures.'

'You can cut the PR speak,' Silva said. 'I want to know what I have to do and that I have the authority to do it. You messed me around before, so I need to know where I stand.'

'Right.' Huxtable cut Weiss an acidic glare. 'I believe Simeon has explained the basic outline of the mission. Taher has presented us with an ultimatum: if we don't kill his designated target then he'll bring down another aircraft. Giving in to the demands of terrorists is not something we usually do. However, if we do nothing Taher is almost certain to carry out his threat.'

'And do you think he can, given that Mohid Latif is wounded?'

'We don't know, but Taher has others who can step in.'

'How many of these nutters are there?'

'That's classified,' Huxtable said. 'It's not something you—'

'To be candid, we don't know,' Holm said, ignoring a glare from Huxtable. 'Taher is able to inspire many young men to follow his example, but as to those directly in contact with him, well we're not sure on the numbers.'

'Are you joking?' Silva looked in turn at Holm, Weiss and Huxtable. She couldn't believe these clowns were responsible for national security. 'Your lack of knowledge doesn't exactly fill me with confidence that what you're asking me to do is going to work out.'

'We made a breakthrough yesterday,' Huxtable said. 'Stephen?'

Holm nodded. 'Counter Terrorism Command have got a flat in Brentford under 24/7 surveillance. We think Taher or one of his men could be inside.'

'You *think*?' Silva said. 'Why the hell aren't you smashing your way in there?'

'So far the surveillance hasn't produced enough evidence either way. We've made the decision to delay any raid so as not to scare Taher off should he not be in the flat. If there's no sign of him or his accomplices by Friday, then we'll go in.'

'You see, Rebecca,' Huxtable said. 'We're closing in on Taher, but we need to buy some time. Simeon's plan is the best option to give us that.'

Silva couldn't help but notice the look Holm gave Huxtable when she said they were closing in. It was obvious Taher was at least one step ahead of them.

'The aim,' Huxtable said, 'is to set up a kill operation that from external observation appears perfect in every way. Taher must believe one hundred per cent that we really do intend to carry out his demands. He'll see you and Simeon planning and hopefully he'll be lulled into a false sense of security, giving us time to catch him. If there is even a hint that the whole thing is a ruse then we're sunk.'

'And if you don't catch him?'

Huxtable didn't answer. Instead she nodded to Weiss.

'We carry on with the illusion,' Weiss said. 'When we come down to the actual hit, you'll be in place and right up to the final moment it will look as if you are going to make the kill. Then you'll miss and hit something close to the target. It will be a real shot with live ammunition. We'd thought about rigging special effects or something similar, but the chance of Taher cottoning on is too great. This way every detail is genuine. When the assassination fails it will look to Taher as if we've simply cocked up for some reason. He'll have to accept we tried but failed. Your job is to put on a convincing display so he has no doubt the attempt is genuine. Afterwards we're counting on being able to persuade Taher to hold back on carrying out his threat for a few more days. During that time there'll be some very difficult political and security decisions to be made. Those aren't your concern.' Weiss glanced at his own set of notes. 'It'll be you, Richard Smith, Lona Castle – a Security Service agent you worked with before in Italy and Tunisia – and myself. Once we begin there'll be no contact with anyone except the director general until the mission is over.'

'Any questions?' Huxtable said.

'The obvious one,' Silva said, gesturing at the pile of documents on the table in front of Huxtable. 'Who's the target?'

'We don't know yet. We're waiting to hear from Taher.'

'You don't *know*?' Silva stared at Huxtable. She couldn't believe what she was hearing. 'Taher's in control, isn't he? He's running the show.'

'We're doing all we can,' Huxtable said, her expression pained. 'But at this stage, yes, I have to admit he is.'

Friday had been a long, hard slog. Holm's eyes were tired from staring at his computer monitor, and his body still ached from the beating Taher had given him at the beginning of the week.

The meeting earlier in the day with Huxtable, Weiss and Rebecca da Silva had been surreal. As he'd listened to Weiss sketch out the details of what had now been officially designated Operation Trojan, Holm felt as if he'd been transported to some parallel realm where fiction trumped fact and bad dreams came true.

Set up a dummy op to shoot someone? Yeah, why not? What could possibly go wrong?

It was batshit crazy. It showed Huxtable was desperate, insane, or both.

Would it work, they'd asked him. His answer, saying it might, was based on the hope that the madness would soon be over. He was counting on a result at the tower block in Brentford. The block was now under constant surveillance by Counter Terrorism Command and Holm was hopeful he'd soon get confirmation that Taher was inside. There were technicians on the floor above monitoring activity in the flat below, snipers on the roof of an adjoining block, and undercover officers staking out the whole area. Several streets away, but within one minute's drive, an armed response unit waited for the 'go' signal.

'One thing's for sure,' Longworth had said. 'If he's in there then he's not getting away. The question is, *is* he in there? Personally, I'm not so sure.'

Now, before Holm left for home, he phoned Longworth and asked for the latest news.

'Inconclusive,' Longworth said. 'There's *somebody* in there. My lads can hear a toilet flushing every now and then, a microwave operating, dishes clattering, that sort of thing. The snipers are reporting a figure moving behind the net curtains, but we can't identify him or her.'

'Him or her? That's pretty inconclusive all right,' Holm said, disappointed.

'The flat is rented to a pensioner by the name of Mr Shah; his name's on the council tax record. The problem is some of these flats are unofficially sublet. There could be anyone in there.'

'What about your undercover officers?'

'They can't exactly go asking around, can they? It would be certain to alert Taher that something was amiss. For now it's a watch and wait situation.'

Indeed, Holm thought as he hung up.

He left Thames House with Javed and tried to tempt him into having a drink at the nearby Morpeth Arms. Javed was teetotal, but Holm just wanted somebody to share a few minutes' relaxation with. He'd learned Javed was an Arsenal fan, and while Holm wasn't much interested in football he thought he could sustain a conversation for a few minutes. Anything to take their attention away from work.

'Sorry, boss,' Javed said. 'I'm off home and then to the gym.'

'Right.'

Holm watched Javed jog away and thought he'd grab a pint anyway. He just needed to sit outside and watch the world pass by for a while. He found a table and made his pint of mild last half an hour. Then he left the pub and headed for the underground station.

The rush hour was over, only stragglers on the platform as a rush of warm air signalled the arrival of the train. Holm slipped on and found a seat. A departing passenger had left a copy of the *Telegraph* and he picked it up. The plane crash and Captain Hammond's heroics had moved from the cover to page four. There was an article explaining the danger of drones and something on the government's response. Holm flicked on a couple of pages, looking for something else to read.

'Don't look up or make any sudden moves.' The voice came from a hooded figure who'd dropped into the seat next to Holm. 'Just get off at the next stop.'

Holm recognised the soft but urgent voice. 'Taher.'

'Don't speak again until I tell you to. I'm going to give you written instructions on what to do after you've got off.'

Holm nodded. The page of his newspaper rustled and a Post-it note slipped onto Holm's lap. He looked down.

> *Take a Circle Line train eastbound. Get off at*
> *Blackfriars and catch the next train back west. Stay*
> *on board until instructed.*

'I'll be watching you,' Taher said. 'If you look back or if you speak to anyone or if you hesitate, then I'm gone. If I see anybody following you, I'm gone. If there's anything suspicious, then I'm gone. Finally, if I'm apprehended, a missile will be fired immediately at an inbound plane at an airport somewhere in the UK. Your stop's coming up now. Is everything clear?'

Holm nodded again, aware the dark walls of the tunnel had gone, replaced by the white of the station flashing past. The train was slowing, passengers lurching, the automated voice announcing they'd arrived at Victoria.

He folded the paper and stood. The train stopped and he moved to the doors. As they slid open, he got off.

He dodged the people heading for the exit and crossed platforms to wait for a Circle Line train. He resisted the temptation to look behind him. Taher was there, he was sure of it. He doubted there was anyone from the security services on his tail but just in case there was he screwed up the Post-it and dropped it.

On the platform he stared at the board which displayed the time the next train was due. Two minutes, it said. People drifted around him. No sign of Taher. There was a whistling and a rattle of the train, the rushing of air again, the train hurtling from the tunnel and slowing to a stop. The doors opened and people boarded. Holm did too. He remained close to the doors, reaching up and grabbing on to an overhead strap. He stayed in position as they stopped at two stations, and at Blackfriars he got off and walked across the platform where a train was waiting with its doors open. Holm got on and took a seat. The westbound train was almost empty as the doors closed and it rumbled off. He resisted the temptation to look round and instead stared down at his feet.

At the next station several people got on including somebody in a hoodie, black this time, not red. The man sat down next to Holm and pulled out a newspaper.

'Now we sit here and ride the train,' Taher said, unfolding the paper. 'And we talk.'

'About?'

'About what you lot are going to do to prevent another tragedy.'

'That's in your hands. You don't fire the missile, then there's no tragedy.'

'Don't try and be clever, old man. I hold all the cards. You're going to do exactly as I say or else hundreds are going to die.'

Holm stared ahead. Through the train window the walls of the tunnel were skimming by. He felt hemmed in, a rush of claustrophobia taking over.

'I'm going to give you a target. You will ensure the target is killed within the next ten days. If that happens then I will give up the remaining missiles, if not then we will bring down another aircraft and publicise the fact that we have more missiles and can target planes, trains, even bridges. Mass panic will ensue.'

'I'll repeat the question I asked the other day. What assurance do I have that you'll give up the missiles?'

'None. You'll have to trust me.'

'That's not going to wash with my superiors.'

'Well you'll have to persuade them, because it's not my problem.'

'You'll be killing innocent civilians, people of all religions and nationalities. It's indiscriminate slaughter.'

'It's a shame the British government didn't worry about such things before. If it had then none of this would be necessary.'

'Two wrongs don't make a right.'

'Maybe not, but this wrong can stop future wrongs. Perhaps foreign policy will be formed more carefully in the future.'

'Suppose I can't carry this off?'

Taher shrugged. 'Then people will die.'

'This is madness.'

'As good a definition of war as any.' Taher raised a hand to silence Holm. 'Now tell me you understand precisely what you need to do?'

'Yes.' Holm nodded. 'I'll do my best.'

'Good.' Taher stood as the train coasted into a station. 'Remain on the train for at least three more stops.'

'But the target? You haven't told me who it is yet.'

'It's him.' Taher smiled. His gaze roved across to the far side of the carriage where a string of advertisements plastered the curving roof. 'Fortuitously he is coming to London in just a few days. Just in time to meet my deadline.'

The train lurched to a stop and Taher walked to the doors as they opened. He slipped out onto the platform and walked away. Holm turned his attention to the poster Taher had been looking at. It advised travellers to avoid Kensington, Notting Hill, Bayswater and Edgware Road underground stations on the Circle Line on the next Saturday but one. An event was taking place in Hyde Park and large crowds were expected. Holm blinked, took in the advert's headline: *Travel Advisory – Pope's Visit to London*.

'Oh shit,' he said.

–

Holm did exactly as instructed: he rode the Circle line for three more stops before alighting at Gloucester Road. He exited the station and took a cab back to Thames House. The first thing he did when safely inside was to call Longworth and alert him to the fact that whoever was in the flat at Brentford, it wasn't Taher.

'We still watch and wait?' Longworth asked. 'Because I've got close to forty officers working shifts to cover this thing.'

'Can you keep a minimal presence just in case Taher does turn up there?'

'I'll stand down the response teams and the snipers, leave the surveillance boys in place. That OK?'

Holm said it was, hung up, and went to find Huxtable. She was still in her office and her PA showed him straight through.

'Stephen.' Huxtable raised her head from behind her laptop screen. 'You look as tired as I feel. Take a seat.'

'It's Taher, ma'am,' Holm said as he walked in and sat in one of the two armchairs that faced Huxtable's desk. 'He's made contact.'

'And do we have a target?'

'We do.' Holm shook his head. 'I was hoping it might be somebody we could justifiably say was a threat to national security. A rival terrorist or the leader of a rogue state. Unfortunately the target is none of those.'

'Don't hold me in suspense, who is it?'

'It's the Pope.'

Holm had to give Huxtable credit. She didn't flinch. He wondered if she'd war-gamed something similar earlier in her career, working through various possibilities in all seriousness. Most likely the scenario would have been the kidnapping of a celebrity or the murder of a cabinet minister. He doubted assassinating the leader of a major world religion would have been anywhere on the radar.

'Is he crazy? Surely he can't believe we'd actually carry out such a demand?'

'Taher isn't crazy. I think he's trying to place us in an impossible situation. It's a stress test and he expects us to fail. At the end of the day though, if we don't comply we're fucked.'

Huxtable, usually one to censor the use of bad language, simply nodded. 'I couldn't have put it better myself.' Her gaze dropped to the screen of her laptop and her fingers flittered over the keys. 'The Pope arrives in the UK next Wednesday. Various engagements on

Thursday in the Midlands, a state banquet on Friday, an evening mass in Hyde Park on Saturday. He leaves Saturday evening. By Sunday morning Taher will realise we haven't acceded to his demands. Which means we've got eight days to find and catch him.'

Huxtable flipped the lid of the laptop down. The fact she didn't add anything spoke wonders. Holm had been hunting Taher for years without success. At times he'd had extra resources and still hadn't managed to get anywhere. Eight days was neither here nor there.

'We've come to a dead end with the British Aryan Insurgency,' Holm said. 'And there's little or nothing from the scene of crime at the bungalow.'

'That's not good. What about the flat in Brentford?'

'The surveillance is ongoing, but nothing yet. The question is do we go in now or wait until the last possible moment? The first option might give us valuable evidence, but the second allows for the situation to develop.'

Huxtable glanced at her diary, open on the desk in front of her. 'Go Friday. That still leaves twenty-four hours to work any evidence.'

'Right. I'll tell Longworth.'

Huxtable continued to stare at her diary, her brow creasing. She looked up. 'Now we know the target, what are your views on the viability of Operation Trojan?'

'Surely you're not considering going ahead with it now?'

'What are the alternatives? We can do nothing and rely on catching Taher before Saturday or we can run the op and hope that first, it brings him out into the open, and second, he believes we tried our very best to comply.'

Huxtable paused and let the choices sink in. 'I'd like your opinion as to whether it should proceed.'

Holm for a second felt flattered that Huxtable valued his judgement, but then realised this was her way of spreading the responsibility. It also showed the parlous state the hunt for Taher was in.

'Weiss's plan, if we get that far, involves carrying out a dummy hit, meaning the world will see an attempt on the Pope's life. Have you considered the consequences of that?'

'Stephen, five minutes ago I didn't know who the target was. If we don't do anything Taher fires another missile. That has huge ramifications too.'

'Taher can't really believe we'd go ahead with the assassination and kill the Pope. He must have some ulterior motive. He's playing us.'

'Maybe so, but we can attempt to out-bluff him to gain time. Weiss called it running interference. When the hit doesn't succeed it will look as though we tried to follow Taher's wishes, but that our endeavours failed. It's a long shot, but there's a chance he might delay his retaliation if he thinks we're under his control.'

Holm nodded. His hand went to his chin and rubbed the stubble from a day's unshaved growth. He deliberately turned his head away from Huxtable and stared towards the window. Tried to imagine Taher out there somewhere, imagine his reactions to a bungled attempt on the Pope's life. He could see him cursing. Slamming his fist into his palm. *So close, so close. What to do?*

'It's desperate, ma'am,' Holm said.

'Remember, Taher likely only has two missiles left. He needs all the leverage he can get, and firing another missile will reduce that considerably. Have you got a better suggestion?'

No, Holm thought, he didn't.

'Are we going to get other agencies involved? Counter Terrorism Command, for instance?'

'No. As we discussed at the meeting with Weiss and da Silva, Taher mustn't suspect anything so we need to keep this very tight. I'm going to stay out of the way and leave the details to Weiss.' Huxtable smiled. 'He's good at this sort of thing.'

'He's going to need to be,' Holm said. 'If Taher even gets a hint something is wrong then the whole edifice will come crashing down.'

'And will he buy it?'

'I don't know. He might believe we're just going through the motions to appease him, at least at the beginning. Later if, God forbid, we get to that stage, I can't predict his reaction. However, he's a pragmatist, not an ideologue, so he may feel he has nothing to gain by punishing us for what he believes is a genuine mistake. That's if he does believe it.'

'And that's where Weiss will come in. Although he doesn't know the target yet, I trust him to put on a show that will be utterly compelling.'

Right, Holm thought. If anything went wrong, utterly compelling wouldn't be the half of it.

Chapter 17

On Wednesday, Silva met Itchy at her father's place. Itchy rode up on his motorbike and gazed longingly at Silva's XTZ.

'It's not new, Itch,' Silva said. 'Couldn't afford that.'

'Nice though,' Itchy said. 'Caz says I've got to get rid of mine. She wants a people carrier or a 4 × 4.'

'You having another baby?'

'Not yet, but she thinks my bike's too dangerous.'

'If only she knew what you got up to in the Philippines, hey?'

Weiss had given them directions to a safe house that turned out to be an empty new build set in anonymous arable countryside a dozen miles south of Oxford. A skip sat out front and rolls of turf were stacked by a levelled area of earth. There were no curtains in the windows and when Weiss opened the door to Silva's knock, sound echoed in the bare interior.

'Basic, I'm afraid,' Weiss said as he ushered them in. 'But we've got four bedrooms, a working kitchen and a few pieces of furniture. It'll have to do.'

Silva and Itchy followed Weiss down the hallway and into a living room. There was a glass-topped table and chairs to one side, while to the other a three-piece suite was still adorned with a clear plastic wrapping.

A woman in a short skirt and a top more suited to a night clubber than a security operative stood at the window. She turned as they entered.

'Lona, you know,' Weiss said.

'Rebecca. Richard.' Lona smiled. Auburn hair, vivid red lipstick, eyes that Itchy had once described as of the extreme 'come to bed' variety. 'It's a pleasure to be working with you again.'

Not, Silva thought. Then again, although Lona was cast from the same mould as Weiss in that deception and artifice came naturally to her, she was nothing but professional.

'We'll remain here for the duration,' Weiss said. 'Taher may well be keeping an eye on us and this makes it as easy as possible for him to do that. Remember, we want him to know what we're up to. After I've given you an initial briefing we'll talk as if the operation is genuine. No mention of it being a ruse because he could be watching or even listening.'

'Listening?'

'The worst thing to do would be to underestimate him. He'll use whatever means he can to track what we do.'

After they dumped their stuff in the bedrooms, they reconvened in the living room where Weiss had laid out a series of documents on the table.

'Do you know the target yet?' Silva said.

'Oh yes.' Weiss smiled. 'Coincidentally, considering your last mission, there's an Italian connection.' He pulled out a picture from the pile on the table and slid it across. 'He's coming to London in a few days' time. Here, I think you might recognise him.'

Silva took the photograph. It showed a building with a balcony. Huge stone columns to either side. Latin writing carved into the structure above. On the balcony a figure clad in white with his hands raised to the heavens.

'You're kidding me?' Silva said.

'No joke, I'm afraid.' Weiss's face was stern. 'I'm deadly serious.'

'This is crazy – we're going to try to assassinate the Pope?'

'Try but fail,' Weiss said. 'Unless Mr Smith's ballistic calculations are way out.'

'But even so…'

'Remember, the idea is that Taher is apprehended before we get anywhere near having to take a shot.'

'And if he isn't?' Itchy was staring at the picture of the Pontiff.

'Then we bluff.' Weiss indicated the material he'd prepared. 'The Pope will be saying a mass in Hyde Park on Saturday evening. He leaves the country afterwards so that's the maximum amount of time we can wring from Taher.' Weiss pointed at a large-scale map with Hyde Park at its centre. He moved his finger to a maze of streets south of the park. 'Knightsbridge. We've rented a top-floor penthouse in a block of flats on Ennismore Gardens. The position is high enough to provide a line of sight over the buildings to the park and the stage set-up where the Pontiff will deliver his sermon. We'll go in under the cover of being part of a decorating team. The flats have a below-ground garage with direct lift access to the upper floor. Getting the equipment in and out won't be a problem.'

'And the shot?' Silva was eyeing the map, doing the ballistics maths in her head. 'How is that going to work?'

'We'll go into detail about that later, but for now I'll give you a summary.' Weiss had another picture in his hand, this time a close-up of a stage set-up. 'We'll wait until the Pope arrives. He'll take the stage and there'll be a hymn before he speaks. When the hymn finishes you'll take two shots. The first will hit part of the lighting rig on the right-hand side of the stage well away from the Pope. The intention is for this shot to have a visual impact by causing a bulb to explode and produce some debris. The second will be way off to the left, making sure the bullet lands in the Serpentine. It's this second shot that will appear to hit a security guard close to the Pope. In actual fact the guard will be a plant – one of ours. A small explosive device will cause a minor flesh wound in his leg and will be triggered by us to coincide with your second shot.

'For real?' Itchy said.

'Yes.' Weiss smiled. 'A very brave volunteer.'

'I'll say.'

'Why not make the first shot an effect too?' Silva asked.

'Too difficult to rig without Taher cottoning on. I assumed you wouldn't have any problem with the shot and it's five metres above anyone so perfectly safe.'

'When you're firing live ammunition, nothing is ever perfectly safe, Mr Weiss.'

Weiss shrugged, conceded the point and continued. 'When we've taken both shots we'll pack up the equipment and leave under the same cover as we arrived. Taher will see the attack, either in person if he's close by, or on the TV, and he'll assume we tried to carry out the assassination but failed.'

'And you think he'll delay firing a missile? Because if not then the whole operation is pointless.'

'I hope he'll come up with a new deadline, perhaps even a new target now the Pope will be under much enhanced security. All the while this is buying us more time to track Taher down.'

'It's a risky strategy.'

'Yes.' Weiss gave another one of his pat smiles. 'But it's the only one in town right now.'

The plan took shape over the next few hours. Weiss and Lona had thought of pretty much everything when it came down to the logistics, but they knew nothing about the art of sniping. The first thing to do was to check the line of fire and do the ballistic calculations. It soon became apparent that the clearance over the row of buildings bordering the park was marginal. Weiss had assumed a bullet travelled in a straight line; Itchy put him right.

'By the time the bullet is there,' Itchy put a finger down on the map, 'it will have dropped a metre. That's only half a metre above the roofs of those houses.'

'But it will pass over?'

'Assuming our calculations are correct, it should do. It would be better if we could shoot from the roof.'

'Not possible. We'd be spotted.'

'What about raising the shooting position? Say we make some sort of platform within the flat so Rebecca is lying a metre and a half off the floor. That will give us a little leeway.'

'OK, I'll look into it.'

They moved on to examine the weather conditions. The forecast a week out looked good, but couldn't be relied upon, and the wind and the atmospherics on the day would play a part in determining the trajectory of the bullet as would any precipitation.

They spread out the maps and aerial photographs and measured and double-checked the distance and elevation.

'I'm puzzled,' Weiss said at one point. 'We're not actually hitting the Pope so why all the worries about accuracy?'

'I have to hit *something*, right?' Silva said. 'And if I miss the something then I'll hit something else.'

With the prep for the actual shot done, they worked on what would happen before and after. Lona had drawn up a route from their initial rendezvous point and she laid out several alternative escape routes should things go pear shaped.

'Like in what way?' Silva wanted to know.

'We get stopped on the way in or discovered before we've made the shot. Then there's the possibility the police are in the neighbourhood as we exit the building. There could be orders to check all vehicles or perhaps they'll deploy roadblocks. If Taher's watching he has to see everything as genuine. He'll know Trojan is a clandestine operation, so us being waved through by a smiling police officer wouldn't make sense. That's why we need a way out.'

'I like out,' Itchy said. 'The one thing Silva and me always tried to avoid in Afghanistan was ending up as sitting ducks.'

'Touch wood it won't happen but running might be the only option.'

'But in the end we're legal, right?' Silva said.

'Yes.' Weiss paused. 'But at the moment only a handful of people know about the operation. Better to ensure we aren't around so we don't have any explaining to do.'

They worked on into the evening, only breaking for takeaway pizzas fetched by Weiss. After a late-night coffee, Weiss was satisfied.

'Tomorrow we'll check the equipment, see if there's anything else we need to procure, and go over the plan and refine, refine, refine. Then on Friday there'll be a chance to do some shooting. The Security Service has blocked out one of the ranges on Salisbury Plain for a practice session. It'll be just us. No prying eyes, nobody to see what we're up to.'

Silva had to admit Weiss was nothing if not thorough. It was just a pity the same level of detail hadn't been put into the Philippine mission.

Thursday was spent checking and planning, and on Friday they headed for Salisbury Plain and the sniper ranges. Silva and Itchy had been there several times before but this visit was different since, aside from a range-control officer, the place was deserted. Silva was impressed with the way MI5 could pull strings.

Practice was mundane, but necessary. Weiss had procured another L115A3 sniper rifle and it needed setting up and repeated firing to get enough material in the DOPE book. Of course, since the whole thing was a dummy hit, accuracy didn't matter a whole lot; Silva only had to take out a spotlight on a gantry and the light was metres from anyone who might be hit accidentally. Nevertheless, Silva and Itchy acted as if they meant it. After all, as Weiss kept reminding them, Taher might be watching.

Back at the safe house Weiss was confident.

'I think we're good,' he said. 'We've covered everything. We relax tonight then tomorrow morning we travel up to London and it'll be time to put Trojan into action.'

'Fingers crossed your guys manage to catch Taher first,' Silva said.

Weiss raised his right hand, second finger bent over the first.

'Yes,' he said.

–

'This has always had a sense of inevitability about it, Farakh.' Holm pointed to a diary he had on his desk. A day per page. He'd always liked the old-fashioned way of doing things, even going so far as to transcribe appointments from his online schedule into the diary. He wetted his forefinger and turned from Friday to Saturday. The facing page – Sunday – was blank. The end of history. Nothing beyond. 'One day left. It's as if we've just been marking time.'

The last few days hadn't felt like they'd been marking time. Holm had worked long hours going over all the evidence and trying to find a new lead – with little success. It seemed as if Taher had pulled his usual trick of appearing in an instant and disappearing without a trace.

Over at Brentford, the surveillance team were becoming less and less confident of a result. Nevertheless, on Friday, late in the afternoon, Holm and Javed set off to rendezvous with Longworth. It was time to raid the flat.

They spotted the estate half a mile away as they struggled through the traffic in Hounslow. The block was one of six hunks of concrete pushing into a swirl of cloud. Twenty storeys tall and the perfect place for a hideaway.

The tower disappeared behind other buildings as they got closer. Then they turned a corner and the block loomed over them. Holm doubted the grey concrete had ever been fashionable, but now it looked tired and due for either renovation or demolition. He could imagine the architects thinking this was the way people should live, while themselves residing in some large detached house in the leafy suburbs.

Holm took a side street and pulled up behind a couple of white vans. Longworth sat in the passenger seat of the front van and he opened the door and climbed out as Holm drove up. Holm lowered his window.

'You're ready to go?' Holm said.

'I thought about jumping the gun, but I know about your obsession with this case. You'd kill me if you missed anything.' Longworth paused. 'Not that I think there will be anything. My boys say somebody is lumbering around in there and they now think the occupant could be Mr Shah, the pensioner. Explains why we haven't seen him.'

'Great.'

'Yes.' Longworth smiled. 'We'll do our best not to shoot him.'

Longworth gave an order and Holm watched the officers pile out of the back of the vans. Black clothing and footwear, automatic weapons, handguns, stun and smoke grenades, tasers, one officer holding a sledge hammer, another a battering ram. If the occupant put up a fight there was only going to be one winner.

'Fifteenth floor,' Holm said as he and Javed got out of the car. 'I hope the lifts are working.'

'They are.' Longworth turned and motioned at the officers clustered by the vans. 'I'll send the boys up first and we'll follow once it's safe to do so.'

'I'd like to be there when they go in.'

'Against procedure, Stephen. If anything happened to you my job would be on the line.'

'You think Mr Shah will poke me with his walking stick?'

Longworth hesitated and then gave in. 'OK, but this is how it works. We take the lift to the fourteenth floor and assemble there. My guys go up and we follow but they enter the flat and search and clear before we go in. I don't want somebody jumping out from behind a wardrobe and popping you.'

'Understood.'

The officers lined up and Longworth gave the order to proceed. They moved towards the building where several of the officers spread out close to the base while the others headed for the entrance foyer. Holm and Javed followed.

They reached the block and went inside. In the foyer, three officers made for the stairs while the rest piled into the two lifts. Holm and Javed crammed themselves in, Holm feeling mildly claustrophobic as the doors closed and the interior light dimmed for a moment as the lift surged upwards.

At the fourteenth floor the doors slid open. The officers fanned out into the hallway and made for the stairs. One of the lead officers carried a steel battering ram designed for forced entry. Holm and Javed climbed the stairs, but at the top Longworth gestured at them to remain in the stairwell.

There was a moment's conversation between two of the officers and then the man with the battering ram stepped forward and swung it at the door to flat C. The door crashed open and immediately bounced closed again until an officer stepped forward, pushed the door with his foot and dived inside, his Heckler & Koch machine gun held ready.

'Armed police,' somebody shouted as more officers raced into the flat.

Holm inched onto the landing area as an order came from within.

'Hands on your head and then face down on the floor.' 'HANDS ON YOUR HEAD!'

The screamed order came before a burst of automatic weapon fire echoed out into the hallway. More shouts, officers moving inside.

'CLEAR! CLEAR! CLEAR!'

'Christ,' Holm whispered to Javed. 'Let's hope that wasn't old Mr Shah.'

Longworth stood over near the door for a moment and then turned and walked across to Holm and Javed. 'It's Mohid Latif but he's not going to be much help to you now.'

'He's dead?'

'Yes.' Longworth nodded. 'We're just checking for IEDs and then you can go in.'

Holm and Javed waited for several minutes before they got the OK.

'Fill your boots,' Longworth said.

'Thanks.' Holm moved past Longworth and into the flat. A short corridor led to a living room, a kitchen off that, the door open and an officer visible inside going through cupboards.

'Shit,' Javed said.

Holm turned. The doors to the balcony were open revealing an incredible view across west London. A man lay slumped against the glass panelling of the balcony, a smear of blood on the glass. There was more blood on the man's chest, the white T-shirt stained like a perverse tie-dye garment.

'He was going for the gun.' Longworth stood alongside. He indicated a small folding table that lay on its side. There was a broken flower pot on the floor, brown earth and a large green fern lying next to a grey Glock 19. 'The gun was concealed in the plant, but he fumbled as he went for it. Still, my lad had no choice.'

'And there was no one else?' Holm asked the question, but it was rhetorical. Of course there was nobody else.

'We'll get the CSIs in shortly and see what they can come up with.' Longworth moved away and shouted orders at a couple of officers.

Holm approached the balcony. Latif was contorted in a corner and his shirt had been rucked up as he fell, blood splattered round the chest area. A bandage circled his midriff, a section of it yellowing with seeping pus.

'There's a foil packet of antibiotics on the dining table,' Javed said. 'Could explain why the surveillance team thought he was a sick old man.'

'I figured he was on his way out,' Holm said. 'And now he's dead Taher has nobody who's trained to operate the missile.'

'Isn't it possible Latif taught the others?'

'Yes, but it's not the same as getting hands-on practice. The AirShield is a complicated piece of kit – it's not like a point-and-shoot camera.'

'So we've won?'

Holm stared at Latif's corpse. Taher might mourn his right-hand man but Holm doubted he'd all of a sudden call it a day. He'd lost Latif, but he still had several accomplices. He also had the resources provided by Haddad and other backers and at least two AirShield missiles. And perhaps Latif *had* managed to teach someone else enough to operate AirShield. This wasn't the end or anywhere near it. Holm turned to Javed.

'That would be an extremely foolish assumption to make,' Holm said.

Chapter 18

Silva and Itchy spent Friday finalising a few minor details and then chilling out. In the late afternoon came news that there'd been a raid in west London. Weiss explained that Mohid Latif had been shot dead.

Silva turned to Weiss. 'So the operation is off?'

'Sadly not,' Weiss said, turning his hands palm up in apology. 'We can't be sure Latif is the only one able to operate AirShield. There's evidence he may have given detailed instruction to other cell members.'

Weiss explained a search of the flat had unearthed a manual detailing the operating procedures for the missile system. The manual had been printed on A4 paper and roughly bound together. The forensic team concluded it had been printed on a printer discovered in the flat, but an analysis of Latif's phone and a laptop found no trace of the original document. Neither device contained any other useful information; Taher was obviously hot on cyber security.

Weiss shrugged. 'Which means until I hear different, Trojan proceeds.'

Itchy looked over at Silva and mouthed the word *fuck*.

On Saturday morning, Weiss headed off to meet the security plant and prepare the effects for the dummy shot. Lona also disappeared for a while, returning an hour later in a white van. A magnetic panel had been attached to each side, each bearing the name of a dummy business: Town & Country Interior Design. Weiss had told them that everything about the business checked out. The phone number went through to an answering service. There was a web address and email, and the business was registered at Companies House. After the operation everything would be shut down, leaving nobody any the wiser.

They loaded the equipment into the van: the flight case containing the rifle, spotting scopes, spare ammunition, tools, a couple of handguns.

'What are those for?' Silva asked.

'Just a contingency,' Lona said. 'In case of an unexpected emergency.'

'Like what?'

Lona smiled. 'If we knew that it wouldn't be unexpected, would it?'

They finished loading the van and then they were ready to go. Silva and Itchy would follow on their bikes; they'd swap to the van at a car park at a shopping centre on the outskirts of Slough for the journey into central London. If there was trouble at any point and they had to split up, the car park would be their rendezvous point.

'Why not come back here?' Silva asked.

'In case this place is compromised,' Lona said. 'I'd prefer somewhere nobody but us knows about.'

As the van drove away Silva and Itchy sat astride their bikes.

'Those two make me nervous,' Itchy said just before they pulled their helmets on. 'And we haven't even set off yet. It's like they're anticipating something will go wrong. Let's hope it's not a repeat of the Philippines.'

The operation in the Philippines was quite different from Trojan, Silva thought. There they'd been dealing with a jihadist maniac and his soldiers. The whole thing had been poorly planned and certainly not state sanctioned. At least that's what she tried to tell herself.

They followed Lona at a distance and met at the retail park. Saturday morning and the place was crowded. Parents with screaming children in tow, boy racers with their modded cars outside Halfords, a queue for the Costa, people milling around in front of the cinema. And then there were the three of them: a hit team on their way to central London to assassinate the Pope. Or so they wanted Taher to believe.

As Silva ducked into the back of the van she was aware he or another one of his gang could be watching. They'd better put on a good show.

The journey into central London took an age. Sitting in the back with Itchy she felt transported back to Afghanistan. It was as if they were in the confines of a Foxhound patrol vehicle heading out on a mission. Only this time nobody was going to die.

They pulled up on Ennismore Gardens outside a tall block of flats. Chunky metal letters on a low wall surrounding the building spelled out the name Kingston House. The block was brick-built, twelve storeys high. Lona turned in and took a ramp that led underground. The ramp curled down to the left to a subterranean garage with spaces for perhaps fifty cars. Lona slotted the van into an empty space and they climbed out. At one end of the garage a door gave access to a stairwell and a lift. The lift had a coded touchpad and a card swipe. Lona produced a card and swiped it through the reader.

'If we meet anybody just smile. No one knows their neighbours in this kind of place and we're in London so there's no need to make conversation.'

The lift arrived and they took it to the top floor. As they came out of the lift and into a corridor, Lona pointed to a door at the end.

'In an emergency you can take the stairs,' she said. 'The doors can be opened from the inside without a key.'

'Let's hope there isn't an emergency,' Silva said.

'Hope for the best, but plan for the worst, right?'

They walked down the corridor and Lona stopped at a door. She produced a key, unlocked the door, and they went in.

'All this for about three and a half million.' Lona gestured off to the right and left. 'Three small bedrooms and a kitchen you can't swing a cat in.' She moved forward down a short hallway that opened into a large living area. 'But all we care about are the views.'

Silva and Itchy followed her in. To one side of the living area there was a dining table and chairs, while to the other a sofa faced a large wall-hung TV screen. Beyond the sofa, double doors led to a small balcony. Silva walked across. The flat looked over a range of buildings and in the distance she could see Hyde Park. An expanse of green on the right-hand side of the park was already dotted with hundreds of people. At the far end a huge stage had been erected. It looked like a music festival.

Lona joined Silva at the balcony. 'Déjà vu, hey? Just like in Italy.' Silva nodded. When she'd been on the op in Italy with Lona, they'd set up their equipment just inside the doors to a similar balcony. The shot had been very long range, over a kilometre, the target perhaps not ranked quite up there with this one in terms of status.

'How long have we got?' Itchy said.

'He is due on stage about eight p.m. so there's plenty of time.'

'Right, then.' Itchy pointed across to the kitchen area at one side of the room. 'You get a brew on while we sort out the kit.'

Silva smiled. Felt relaxed. This wasn't like the Italian operation at all. No one was going to die here. The whole exercise was merely a show for Taher. There was still time for the Security Services to catch Taher, but if not there was nothing to worry about. There'd be worldwide news coverage, headlines in all tomorrow's papers, but ultimately the whole thing was a sham. She would go to sleep tonight feeling perhaps a little trepidation, undoubtedly some excitement, but there would be zero guilt.

It took an hour to set up all the gear. They had to move the dining table over to the balcony doors so Silva could lie raised above the floor level in order to be able to shoot over the brick balustrade of the balcony. A foam mat provided some cushioning and stopped her sliding around. Itchy had a spotting scope on a tripod to one side while Silva had a pair of high-powered binoculars close to hand. They used the ballistics app on Itchy's phone to dial in the correct numbers to the scope, but once again Silva reminded herself that pinpoint accuracy was unnecessary. All she had to do was hit one of the lights on the gantry above the stage with her initial shot. A second shot, five seconds later, had to be fired way over to the left where it would splash harmlessly into the Serpentine. It was the second shot that would supposedly hit an MI5 plant standing on the stage. A bullet would be found close by. At some point ballistics experts would work out where the shot might have come from. Houses and flats and offices within range would be checked. Number one hundred and twenty-four Kingston House would be seen as a possibility, especially since the flat was empty. However, forensic officers would find nothing because the place would have been deep-cleaned long before they arrived.

The afternoon dragged on. At some point Lona switched on the TV and they watched live coverage of the build-up to the mass. As the day turned to late afternoon, more and more people began to fill the park. Through the spotting scope Silva could see groups of worshippers sitting on picnic blankets or setting up deckchairs. There'd be blind panic when everything kicked off, but she hoped no one would get hurt.

At six, Lona disappeared for a few minutes and came back with several sandwiches, a selection of muffins, and some cans of drink. They ate the food in silence and watched the crowd grow and grow. At seven thirty the television pictures showed the Popemobile en route. The distinctive white vehicle made its way through the streets towards Hyde Park. It came down the Mall, past Buckingham Palace and along Constitution Hill. It passed through the Wellington Arch and headed for the park. The crowds lining the route thickened, people craning their heads to get a glimpse of the Pontiff.

In the park the vehicle's progress was slowed to walking pace as members of the huge congregation pushed forward to get close. Eventually, the vehicle reached the foot of the stage. The Pope climbed out and waved. The crowd cheered as he climbed the steps to the stage. He was greeted by the Archbishop of Westminster and several other members of the clergy. To one side of the stage was a choir, on the other an orchestra. In the centre was a raised dais. The Pope approached and sat in a gilded throne, a couple of officiants fussing with his robes as he did so.

'We're on,' Itchy said as he moved to the spotting scope. 'Time to rock 'n' roll.'

Which was when Lona picked up her ringing phone and a moment later turned to Silva.

'We've got a problem,' she said.

'He's with Tallin now,' Saabiq said. 'In heaven, with virgins as his reward.'

'Yes.' Taher nodded, as much to shut Saabiq up as to agree with him. The young man's head was full of absurd thoughts, but if believing in some notional promised land helped keep him calm and focused then so be it. And with the death of Latif, calm and focused was definitely needed.

Taher had first become aware of the police presence at the flat on the Friday before as he'd looked out from the balcony of his *own* flat. He'd spotted movement on the top of a distant building and binoculars revealed a sniper nestled behind a low wall. For a second Taher had thought he was the target, but then he realised the sniper was aiming towards Bolton House, the neighbouring block where Latif lived. The cell occasionally met at Latif's, but Taher was careful to never reveal the location of his own place. Such caution had served him well over the years, and now it was paying dividends again.

Taher picked up his phone and called Latif. Like all communications between cell members, he did it over the internet using a VPN so there was no danger of the call being monitored or traced.

'They're here, brother,' he said. 'Stay calm and take the time to prepare yourself. Don't leave the flat.'

Latif had been in no fit state to leave the flat anyway: the man could barely walk.

A day later, after Taher's encounter with Stephen Holm, the snipers disappeared from the rooftop and the vans that had been hiding in an adjoining street drove off. Taher spent the following morning peering from his flat window, picking up several plain clothes officers doing their best to stay hidden. He called Latif again: *they're still here. Stay low and out of sight.*

The police were nothing if not patient, but on the following Friday they'd had enough. He'd watched as a squad of police encircled the building and another group headed for the entrance. Holm, the coward, brought up the rear. Taher reached for his phone once more, but this time there was no answer. A few minutes later he heard shots ring out across the estate and offered a prayer for Latif.

Now he was with Saabiq and Sutherland in a different part of London waiting for the next part of the plan to unfold. Latif, he knew, would have gone out in a blaze of glory. Martyrdom was what he'd wanted all along. Still, Taher regretted Latif wouldn't be here to watch the ensuing chaos.

'Are you ready?' Taher asked, wanting to bring Saabiq back from his spiritual musings to the real world.

'Yes. I'm all set up. What about Nathan?'

'Let me worry about Nathan.'

While Saabiq was a worrier and always fretting, Nathan Henson was a loose cannon. One spark and he exploded. Taher detested having to work with him because he was foul-mouthed and the worst kind of bigot. Those attributes, of course, made him eminently suitable for the role he had to play, and in the hours and days to come

Henson's ability to rouse a crowd was going to prove invaluable.

Taher allowed himself a smile. With the wounding of Latif, his plans had had to change. The missiles were no longer an essential part of what was to follow, but the end result would be the same. In just a few minutes a chain of events would be triggered and the forces unleashed by them would be unstoppable.

'And so it begins,' Taher whispered to himself. 'And so it begins.'

–

After the raid on the flat in Brentford, there'd been some discussion about whether Operation Trojan needed to go ahead. The discussion became moot when Longworth's team discovered the AirShield manual.

'We go on,' Huxtable had said on hearing the news. 'If Latif has been able to instruct any of the others in the use of the missile then the risk remains too great.'

Now Holm, Javed, Huxtable and Foster were in one of the secure briefing rooms. A large screen at one end displayed pictures from the event in Hyde Park. They'd been watching for half an hour or so, but Holm, bored with the coverage, was taking the opportunity to go through some of the Algerian intercepts on his laptop. The remainder had finally been translated and he was skimming through them trying to find any pertinent points. He looked up as Huxtable spoke.

'Ten minutes until the Pope arrives,' she said. 'Let's hope this goes as planned.'

Holm nodded and returned to the intercepts. Most weren't relevant and were filled with fluff or bravado.

There was nothing to do with operational matters. He moved on to another one, this time pausing when he reached a line about a terrorist camp in Algeria. There was something here about Mohid Latif. Holm read on, dismissing the intercept when he realised it was only confirming what they already knew: Mohid Latif had received training in how to operate the AirShield missile.

Holm looked up. The crowd on the screen had grown and people were gathering on the stage. A choir was singing. The Pope was due any minute.

He bent to the laptop again and was about to move on to the next document when he caught sight of another name he recognised: Anwan Saabiq. One of the speakers in the intercepted call claimed to have spoken directly to Saabiq about ongoing plans. Saabiq, he said, had been in Algeria with Latif. He'd received some intensive training for a mission back in the UK. Holm steeled himself. He hoped the next few lines wouldn't specify that the training was to do with AirShield. He read on, but there was nothing specific about what Saabiq had been up to.

Holm felt a little nauseous. Latif's death hadn't signalled the end of Taher's campaign, but at least it had removed the most competent AirShield operator from the equation. If Saabiq was also qualified – and the manual found in the flat suggested somebody had been brushing up on the firing procedure – then they were back to square one.

'Stephen?' Huxtable said. 'Is everything OK?'

Holm filled her in on the details.

Huxtable turned to the screen. The Pope had arrived and was walking from the Popemobile to the stage. 'In that case we'd better hope our little charade convinces Taher, right?'

Holm nodded. Whether Taher believed the act was down to Simeon Weiss and his team. It was out of his hands. For a moment he looked back to his laptop. There was a final intercept in the series, but a glance at the TV told him he didn't have time to read it. He flipped the lid down and sat back to enjoy the show.

Chapter 19

'It's Simeon,' Lona said as she handed the phone to Silva.

'Hello?' Silva said, turning to the TV screen. The Pope was seated, but the mass would begin shortly. There wasn't much time.

'Rebecca, listen carefully.' Weiss sounded out of breath, uncharacteristically nervous. 'We can't get our plant onto the stage with the explosive charge strapped to his leg. There's a couple of sniffer dogs and they're making everyone walk through a full body scanner. We knew about the scanner – the device can pass through that – but we weren't aware the Vatican security unit were going to use dogs. There's no way the explosives can escape detection.'

'So what do I do? Take a couple of shots at the lights?'

'No. I've got the right security clearance to get on stage so I'm going to take the plant's place. You're to shoot me in the lower leg.'

'*What?*' Silva gripped the phone. 'That's impossible, way too risky. Suppose I miss or hit you higher up.'

'There's no alternative. If you miss then we'll be no worse off, as for the latter…' Weiss paused, his words tailing off. 'Look, I picked you for the Karen Hope job because you're the best. Ditto the operation to kill Latif. I'm confident you can make the shot.'

'I didn't kill Latif, remember? If I had then none of this would be happening.'

'Taher still has the ability to fire the missiles, but we're closing in. He needs to be convinced this attack is genuine and a couple of spotlights exploding on the gantry won't wash.'

'But your leg? The bullet will do permanent damage. I—'

'Rebecca, we're running out of time. I'm at the back of the stage and I need to move now if I'm going to get in place. Take the shot. I trust you. Good luck.'

Dead air, Silva's hand shaking as she handed the phone back to Lona.

'He told you?' Lona said.

Silva nodded. Didn't speak. Lona quickly explained to Itchy what had happened.

'Shit.' Itchy looked over to the table where the rifle lay ready. Then he whipped out his phone, fingers moving rapidly over the screen, numbers flicking up on the ballistics app. 'Nothing's changed, Silvi. It's the same shot as before. We're still good to go.'

'It's not the same shot. I could kill Weiss or miss completely and hit somebody else.'

'Then don't miss. Hit Weiss on the ankle or shin. If anyone can make this work it's you.'

Good old Itchy. As confident as ever. The trouble was it took more than just confidence to fire a rifle.

'Weiss is on stage,' Lona said. She was over by the TV screen. 'The Pope is about to start the mass. You need to get ready.'

Silva went to the window. Over the rooftops she could just make out the stage on the other side of the park, the people congregating at the front like tiny stick figures.

On the stage, a figure in white was the Pope. Somewhere near to him would be Simeon Weiss. Just waiting for Silva to shoot him. She'd never liked Weiss: he'd manipulated her, hidden the truth, cajoled her into doing things she didn't want to do. She'd always thought he only existed for himself. Now it appeared she'd been hugely mistaken.

She moved to the table, climbed on and manoeuvred herself into position. She lay down, wriggled to get comfortable, and then placed one hand on the stock and the other on the barrel. She lowered her head, positioning her right eye up against the scope. The stage was in the centre, the Pope a little way from the crosshairs.

'We go after the first hymn, remember?' Lona said. 'At the end of the hymn the Pope will move forward to give a blessing. Fire then.'

'Right,' Silva said. She had about five minutes, time in which she needed to fully relax her body. 'Let me know when there's a minute to go.'

'Wilco.'

Lona had turned the volume on the television up and the Pontiff's introductory remarks sounded as if he was in the same room. Through the scope his lips moved, each syllable a second or two out of sync with the delayed picture from the television. Silva calmed herself. Took slow and steady breaths. The Pope finished speaking and the orchestra began to play the first hymn.

'Silvi?' Itchy was beside her, his voice lowered. 'I suggest you hit Weiss first and then the light so he gets no warning. If it was me that's the way I'd prefer it.'

'Jesus,' she said. 'This is crazy.'

'He ordered you to do it, remember? I'd have thought you'd have welcomed the chance considering the shit he's put us through.'

'Don't joke about it, Itch.' Silva shifted slightly, moving the crosshairs down and left, trying to find Weiss in the scope.

'Approximately one minute to go,' Lona said.

Silva slipped the crosshairs past a couple of priests and found Weiss standing by a speaker stack. He seemed calm, impassive. She wondered what sort of turmoil was taking place in his head.

'Thirty seconds.'

She moved her aim down a little so Weiss's left leg was centred. If the scope was off or she fluffed the shot, Weiss was going to be in serious trouble. She moved her finger toward the trigger. Just a touch would fire the weapon.

'Here we go.'

A crescendo of music rose as the hymn came to an end. The Pope stood, raising his arms. Silva brushed the trigger with her finger and a second later, through the scope, she saw Weiss catapult forward as his left leg was smashed from under him. She kept her eye to the sight as he writhed on the ground, a horrific look of pain on his face.

'Just above the knee,' Itchy said. 'Great shot.'

Silva felt sick, but she concentrated on moving the rifle so a red spotlight on the gantry was lined up in the crosshairs. She touched the trigger again and a moment later came an exploding flash, the electrical short circuit sending sparks showering down on those below. A security guard knelt beside Weiss, not realising what was going on.

'Come on, mate!' Lona said. 'Get with it.'

Through the scope Silva saw Weiss say something and then the guard was standing and wheeling round, shouting and waving his arms.

'About time.' Lona tapped Silva on the back. 'OK, we're done. Let's pack up and get out of here.'

'Wait!' Itchy swore and jumped back from his spotting scope, his face all of a sudden white. He turned and jabbed at the TV. 'Fuck, look!'

The television picture, delayed by a couple of seconds, took a moment to catch up with what Itchy had seen. As Weiss flailed on the floor and the guard moved forward, the Pope jerked back as if pushed in the chest. A burst of crimson flowered on his white robe as he stumbled on the steps to the dais and collapsed. The Archbishop of Westminster, who'd been standing just to the right of the Pope, stepped across but was barged out of the way by another security guard who threw himself over the now prone body of the Pontiff.

'Oh my God!' This from Lona, standing open mouthed to one side of the screen. 'This is…'

Her words tailed into silence. Silva swung herself off the edge of the table as the camera switched to a wide-angled view. Panic had broken out on the stage. Several members of the clergy had rushed over to the Pope, while other people scrambled to the side of the stage, trying to escape.

'I…' Silva was also lost for words. She glanced at the rifle on the table, trying to work out what had happened. 'It wasn't me.'

'I know.' Itchy was back at the spotting scope. 'He was hit several seconds after you fired your second shot. There's somebody else out there.'

On the screen what had been merely panic now turned to pandemonium. The crowd in the park had at first surged forward with concern as the Pope had fallen. Now people were turning from the stage and running, their way blocked by people further back who couldn't see what was happening.

A huddle of bodies now surrounded the Pope, among them two green-clad paramedics. The rest of the stage was emptying fast as stewards guided members of the choir and the orchestra towards the back. The first armed police officers arrived from the wings and moved to the front of the stage. They aimed their weapons into the crowd, searching for the gunman.

'What do we do now?' Itchy said.

'We need to move,' Lona said. 'Get out of here.'

'What do you mean?' Silva turned to the balcony. Even though the edge of the park was some five hundred metres away, screams of terror could be heard above the London traffic. 'I thought the plan was to wait so we wouldn't get caught in the rush?'

'Christ.' Lona shook her head. 'I don't know.'

'We go.' This from Itchy. Calm in a crisis. 'If something went wrong we were to return to the retail park. Well, something's gone wrong.' He picked up the spotting scope and started to fold up its tripod. 'We carry on according to procedure which means we instigate the backup plan. We need to leave. Pronto.'

'Get the rifle and the other stuff packed away,' Lona said, her indecision broken. She began to pick up the debris from their snacks. 'We haven't got enough time to clear up properly but let's remove all the evidence we can.'

For a moment Silva hesitated, but then seeing the frenetic way Lona and Itchy were moving, she grabbed the rifle from the table and carried it over to its case.

As she and Itchy gathered all their equipment together, Lona began wiping down some of the surfaces with a wet cloth. Five minutes later they had the flight case containing the rifle and several bags stacked in the hall.

'Good to go?' Lona said. Silva and Itchy nodded. Lona opened the door to the flat and peered out. Gave an all-clear signal. 'Then let's move.'

–

Holm watched as the hymn ended and the Pontiff stepped forward. A cheer went up from the crowd as he raised his hands. A few paces away, Weiss collapsed to the ground. Then there was a flash of light from the gantry rig above the stage.

'Weiss?' Huxtable said. 'What happened to the plant?'

'I don't know,' Holm said. He peered at the monitor, trying to see what Weiss was doing. 'Perhaps Weiss took over the role.'

'Yes,' Huxtable said. 'That must be it.'

Weiss was certainly convincing as he rolled round on the floor. And for what was supposed to be a minor wound there was a lot of blood. Perhaps there'd been a miscalculation in the amount of explosive in the charge strapped to his leg. Holm didn't have time to think any more about Weiss because the Pope threw his arms up in the air in a gesture that he at first assumed was some sort of exaltation. Then the Pontiff fell backwards clutching his chest, a red patch appearing on the white robes. Holm gripped the edge of the table, hearing a collective gasp from the other people in the room.

'My God,' he said in a whisper.

'Blood. He's shot.' Huxtable's normally calm demeanour was gone as a shaking hand jabbed at the screen. 'The Pope is fucking shot.'

'I...' Holm was lost for words. He couldn't believe what he was seeing on the TV. A mad panic, people running everywhere, police, paramedics, the Archbishop of Westminster crouching down beside the fallen Pontiff.

'Get Weiss on the phone now,' Huxtable said. 'I want a fucking situation report.'

'Weiss is shot too, ma'am,' Holm said. 'This isn't an act.'

'Will somebody tell me what the fuck is going on? Why the hell has the Trojan team just taken out the Pope?'

'Taher.' Holm felt sick as he said the name. 'He's behind this somehow. We've been set up. He must have guessed the operation was a charade. I said he'd see through it.'

'You're joking?' Huxtable's mouth was agape. 'This is your fault. I asked you for your analysis and you said he'd go along with this, that he'd believe the ruse.'

'With respect, I insisted the whole operation was highly dangerous.'

'Yes, but you didn't consider the possibility that he'd somehow recruit Rebecca da Silva to his cause.'

'Silva?' Holm turned away from the screen. 'No, ma'am, I don't think that's happened. She hates Taher. That was her rationale for helping us.'

'Unless he's got to her somehow and managed to turn her through blackmail, bribery or coercion.'

'No.' Holm didn't believe it. He couldn't see Silva siding with the man who'd killed her mother. 'I don't know what's going on, but I do know Taher. He's impossible to second-guess. Remember how last year he managed to get hold of the missiles, to manipulate Karen Hope, to get what he wanted out of the Saudis? I told you this was a risky option.'

'Bleating isn't helping,' Huxtable said. 'What we need now is sensible analysis leading to concrete suggestions.'

'Right.' Holm had just about had enough and he didn't try to disguise the sneer in his voice. 'There is one thing we can do.'

'And what's that, Stephen?' Huxtable said.

Holm glanced over at the screen. Several paramedics now surrounded the Pope. The camera shot had zoomed closer, showing the Archbishop of Westminster kneeling beside the Pontiff, his lips mouthing words as the Pope lay there still and unmoving.

'Pray,' he said.

–

They didn't encounter anyone on their way down to the van. They loaded the gear and drove out of the subterranean garage. Lona headed up Ennismore Gardens until they came to the road that ran along the edge of Hyde Park. People were streaming from one of the gates to the park, police and stewards trying to calm the rush. Lona swung the van left and filtered into the traffic.

'Let's get out of London to start with,' she said. 'We'll go to the retail park and change vehicles. You on your bikes, me in my car, and as far as possible we'll take the back roads, avoiding the cameras.'

'Where to?' Silva said. 'Not back to the safe house?'

'No, that's much too risky.' Lona stared ahead.

'You've no idea, have you? The rendezvous point was the sum total of your emergency planning.'

'Look, nobody could have foreseen the Pope was going to be shot. We never considered that we'd need a place to lie low.'

'Why do we even need to lie low? We should call in and ask for instructions from Huxtable.'

'You're forgetting about Weiss,' Itchy said. 'He's shafted us before. Could be he's playing some game, setting us up?'

'But he asked me to shoot him.'

'Exactly.' Itchy nodded. 'He'll hardly be a suspect in this now, will he?'

'Lona?'

'I can't see it,' Lona said. 'I've been with Special Accounts Unit for five years and in that time Simeon's always done what's right for the security of the nation. I can't see how this fulfils that objective.'

'Neither can I.' Silva paused. Thought about the options. 'But we can't risk it. There's no harm in staying off the radar for a couple of days until we know the truth. The question is, where?'

'Could we go to your dad's?' Itchy said. 'Plenty of room for us there.'

Silva considered Itchy's suggestion for a moment. Her dad had been a soldier too, and after leaving the army he'd worked in the Ministry of Defence. Matthew Fairchild was a good friend and Fairchild had frequent contact with MI5.

'No, that's way too obvious, but there's somebody that Dad knows from his days in the special forces. A guy called Danny. A few years ago he married an eco-warrior princess and they went off into the wilderness to go self-sufficient and make babies. Lives halfway up a mountain in Wales. Off the grid. No electricity, no TV, no internet, no mobile coverage.'

'Toilet paper?' Itchy said.

'Leaves, probably.'

'Home from home.'

'Yes.' Silva remembered the latrines in Afghanistan. Toilet paper had been at a premium. 'I met him loads of times when I was a kid, once a few years ago, and thought he was a complete nutter. I've never been to his place but the location is near perfect.' She turned to Lona. 'Does that sound good?'

'As good as anywhere,' Lona said.

'Itchy?' Silva said. 'Can you work up a route? It's ten miles or so south-east of Barmouth.'

'Sure thing, I'm on it.' Itchy had his phone out. He brought up a map. When they'd been in Afghanistan together Itchy had always been the one to take care of navigation. He had an unerring sense of direction and could plot a way through the most dangerous and inhospitable terrain. Working up a route along a series of B roads through the Home Counties and on to Wales wouldn't be a problem. 'You reckon we'll be safe there?'

'Fuck knows.' Silva looked through the windscreen. On the other side of the road three police cars were racing towards Hyde Park with their lights flashing and sirens blaring. 'But we don't have too many other options, do we?'

Chapter 20

The meeting had broken up and everyone decamped to the situation room. On their way down, Huxtable had reminded them that Operation Trojan was ongoing. Nobody else could know the truth.

Right, Holm thought. Whatever the truth was.

By ten that evening, things were no clearer. An agent had been dispatched to talk to Weiss, but on arrival at the hospital found that after having his leg patched up he'd managed to slip past his police guards and discharge himself. Lona, the agent with Silva, was also uncontactable. The Trojan hit team had vanished from the face of the earth.

It was uncomfortable being in the situation room. Speculation on who'd carried out the attack was being bandied back and forth, and every now and then somebody would ask Holm if, in his opinion, Taher was responsible. He answered each enquiry the same way: he didn't have any specific information to suggest it was Taher.

'This is madness,' Javed whispered at one point. He gestured at the people hunched behind screens. 'How can they be expected to do their job when they don't know the full facts?'

Madness indeed. Holm couldn't see this playing out in a good way. Sooner or later Huxtable was going to have to bring everybody in on Trojan. The issue was highlighted when Holm took a call from Bob Longworth at Counter Terrorism Command. So far the police hadn't been able to identify the sniper's location, but Longworth reckoned it was only a matter of time.

'We've got ballistics experts analysing the various pieces of video footage and we're hoping the Vatican will consent to releasing pictures of the Pope's wound. Put the two together and we should be able to pinpoint the shooter's position.'

'But you haven't identified it yet?'

'No. They're reluctant to give us the pictures. Something about protecting the sanctity of the role. Bloody religion.'

'Let me know when you get something.' Holm hung up, thinking if it wasn't for 'bloody religion' none of this would be happening.

Not for the first time in his life, Holm remained in the situation room for most of the night. At six in the morning he went to his office and bedded down on the floor, his jacket rolled up beneath his head. It took a long time for sleep to come, his mind full of what he'd witnessed. However he tried to play the situation back it made no sense. Why would Rebecca da Silva go rogue? It was unthinkable she'd have agreed to actually shoot the Pope, unless, Holm thought, Weiss had somehow been behind it. Could he have manipulated her into believing that assassinating the Pontiff was the only option to protect British lives? Holm didn't think so. Then again, Weiss had taken a shot in the leg. Had Silva tried to kill him before the attempt on the Pope's life?

The only glimmer of hope was that the Pope, so far, was still alive. He was in intensive care in a London hospital and the last piece of news Holm heard before he went to sleep was that surgeons had removed the bullet from his abdomen and he was stable.

At a little after ten in the morning, Holm was woken by a prod from Javed. The young man loomed over him, the very definition of bright eyed and bushy tailed. It was as if he didn't need sleep.

'We've got a problem.' Javed plonked a laptop down on the desk. Opened the lid. 'A big problem.'

'Hey?' Holm rolled over.

'Al Jazeera have come upon a little exclusive. I think you need to watch it.'

Holm sat up as Javed began to run the piece. A news anchor spoke to camera and explained the story: members of an elite unit under the direct control of the security services had carried out the attack on the Pope. This was in response to threats made by an Islamist extremist group. A blurry video played over the anchor's voice. It showed the kill team entering a property in London close to Hyde Park. Then came some long-range still camera shots of a sniper at a balcony window. A series of graphics and maps showed the exact location and explained about the distance and angles and the difficulty of making the shot. Only a highly skilled sniper – of which there were only a handful in the world – could carry off such a shot.

'How the hell did they get this?'

'No idea, but every other outlet is running the story too. If you know who you're looking at you can see it's Silva and Smith on the CCTV.'

'Shit,' Holm said as he continued to watch. 'This was Taher's game plan all along. We've been set up. Silva hasn't gone rogue at all. There was a second shooter.'

The pictures cut to a reporter standing by a mosque in south London. A crowd was gathering, voices raised, the beginnings of a powder-keg situation. The reporter moved back, the camera panning to show a group of riot police emerging from a couple of vans.

'Are you saying Taher played us?'

'Yes, of course. He knew we wouldn't kill the Pope, but he set us up so it looks like the British state has done a deal with terrorists. It's the consequences he's after.'

'But nobody will believe it. We simply have to reveal the whole operation.'

'Which is what?' Holm jabbed at the screen. 'We pretended to go along with Taher to keep him sweet while we worked to catch him?'

'It's the truth.'

'It's too far-fetched. He's rigged all the evidence and we walked straight into his trap. We thought that by not hiding the operation from him, he'd believe we were going along with his demands. Actually he was learning about the mission so that he could set things up and gather the pictures and video he needed. Whatever we say now it's too late. Look.' Holm waved at the screen again. A bright orange gush of flame had erupted from a petrol bomb lobbed at the mosque, while round a side street came a group of local residents keen to defend their place of worship. They were armed with a variety of improvised weapons. The riot police stood between the two groups. 'It's got to be why he's in league with Nathan Henson and the British Aryan Insurgency. Taher has set the spark and they're going to step forward and fan the flames. This is what he wanted all along.'

'And that is?'

'Nothing less than all-out holy war.'

They'd made it to the retail park in Slough where they removed the magnetic signs from the van so it was anonymous, and switched to the motorbikes and Lona's car. They left the rifle in the van, but took the handguns. Silva and Itchy went to a nearby supermarket and bought two burner phones using the credit card Mr Tan had given her. Then they'd driven west along the motorway and stopped at a services where they parked up, since driving deep into the Welsh countryside late at night in a convoy of a car and two motorbikes didn't seem like a good idea. Instead the three of them kipped in Lona's car and in the morning they grabbed breakfast from the services.

As they prepared to set off again, Lona beckoned them over to her car. The latest news was that photographs and other material had been released that suggested the attack on the Pope had, bewilderingly, been carried out by the security services. A government spokesman strongly denied the accusation and said investigations were continuing.

'We. Are. Toast,' Itchy said. 'Burnt toast.'

'What's going on, Lona?' Silva said. 'How come we've been dumped in it like this?'

Lona could only shrug.

It took them three and a half hours to cross from Swindon to Mid Wales. Eventually, near Aberangell, they turned off the main road and climbed into rolling hills that soon changed to a virtual wilderness of steep, pine-clad slopes. They passed through a tiny hamlet and came to a gate, 'Private' etched on a rough wooden sign. Silva waited for Lona to catch up in her car.

'Let me and Itchy go first,' Silva said. 'Follow after a few minutes. From what I remember of Danny, he's not keen on crowds.'

Beyond the gate, a rutted track headed up a barren hillside populated with a few sheep and hundreds of tall thistles. The track seemed to climb forever, fording several streams and threading through an old quarry. Eventually it cut round a ridge and a house came into view set into the hillside below a small wood. Huge pieces of oak clambered out of the ground like the arms of a living creature and met a grass-covered roof, and floor-to-ceiling glass panels encircled the front of the house in an octagonal pattern. As they rode the last hundred metres, they passed trees with coloured ribbons, wind chimes and glittering spinners.

'I'm guessing this guy doesn't do war,' Itchy said, as they parked up.

'Danny was SAS. Like my dad.'

'Well, he's batting for the other side now, right?' Itchy gestured at a succession of flags which streamed from a halyard attached to a pole on the side of the house. CND. A dove. Rainbows.

'I wouldn't be so sure.' Silva tapped Itchy on the shoulder and pointed. 'That's him.'

Danny stood to one side of the house, edging from behind a stone wall. He was rotund and had a long beard. An over-sized dwarf. Gimli, or perhaps Happy if he was in a good mood. Right now he didn't look so friendly. He held a shotgun in his arms, his head nestled down behind the rear sights.

'If you're with the council you can bugger yourselves,' he bellowed. 'If you're selling something you can piss off, and if I don't know you then I don't like you and I'm inclined to shoot people I don't like. What that all means is you've got ten seconds to fucking turn around and head back the way you came or else I'm going to show you what this beauty can do.'

'Danny!' Silva pulled her helmet off and shook her hair free. 'It's Rebecca! Rebecca da Silva.'

For a moment there was no reaction. The gun remained pointed towards them.

'Rebecca?' Danny raised his head a little and his finger slipped from the trigger. 'Kenneth's girl? The one who got nobbled for doing her job?'

'Yes, that's me.' Silva placed her helmet on the handlebars. 'Dad sends his regards.'

'Well, I don't know what to think about that.' Danny lowered the shotgun, cracked open the barrel and pulled out the two cartridges. 'But I guess I won't be shooting anyone today.'

Silva walked forward and held out her hand. Danny put the gun down. He nodded towards the bikes. 'Who's lover boy over there?'

'He's a friend. Actually, he was my spotter in Afghanistan.'

'His fault then, all of the shit that happened with the kid?'

'Nobody's fault except the fact we were sent to do an impossible job in impossible circumstances.'

'That's modern warfare for you. Not like the good old days. Not like when I was with your dad.'

Itchy came across and Silva introduced him, and then Danny was off on a trip down memory lane, reminiscing about his exploits with Silva's dad in Iraq at the start of the nineties.

'We knew what we were up against back then. Enemy soldiers in uniform. *Bang bang bang*. Slot them before they slot you. We were rather good at it if I remember. I wouldn't be a soldier nowadays though. Not with all that PC bollocks and the legal stuff.'

Silva turned to a little squeal off to her right. A woman walked from the house with a baby on her hip.

'He's not boring you, is he?' the woman said. Long blond hair tied in a plait hung down to her waist, and she wore a wraparound skirt and a lace-up bodice. She could have just stepped off the set of *Game of Thrones*. 'He gets lonely out here, the poor old dear.'

'Greta,' Danny said. 'My better half.' He reached out and took the baby. 'And this little fella is Clover.'

Never mind better half, Silva thought, Greta was half Danny's age. 'Clover?' she said. 'Like the butter?'

'Like a shamrock. Brings us luck, doesn't he, Greta?'

'Luck and love and who needs anything else?' Greta said. 'Now, why don't you invite your friends in, Danny. I was just about to serve lunch.'

'What the fuck?' Danny said as Lona's car lurched over the final rise and stopped by the motorbikes. 'She with you? Because she sure as fuck don't look ex-military.'

'She's a colleague.' Silva made a sign at Lona to come on over. 'We're in a spot of bother. I'll explain in a minute.'

Inside the house, unworked oak beams contorted across a vast living space. A set of stairs spiralled up round a pillar of stone to gallery bedrooms, while in one corner a wood-burning stove radiated fierce heat.

'All our own work,' Danny said, noticing Silva's interest. 'We made it up as we went along, and if that's a metaphor for our life then so be it. Worked out OK though, didn't it, love?'

'Perhaps, perhaps not,' Greta said as she came over with an armful of bowls. 'Because the council want us to tear the whole thing down.'

'Over my dead body.'

'That's what I'm worried about.' Greta gave Danny a look. 'Your dead body and a pile of corpses comprising half a dozen council officials and police officers.'

'You didn't come halfway up a Welsh mountain to hear about our problems,' Danny said. A large saucepan appeared and he ladled broth into the bowls. Greta brought across a basket of bread. 'And this isn't a social call either. Is it your dad? Got himself into a spot of bother has he?'

'Not my dad, no.'

'You, then.'

'Yes.' Silva bent to her bowl and took a spoonful of broth. It was homely and delicious. Comfort food.

'Look, you don't have to tell me if you don't want to. If you're just looking for a place to crash then that's fine. We've a couple of old mess tents we can rig up out the back. Camp beds, sleeping bags, everything you need. This time of year it'll be perfect. You can stay as long as you like, no questions asked.'

'Thanks. You deserve the truth though.'

Danny shrugged. 'Up to you.'

'You heard about the Pope?'

'On the radio, yes. Bunch of nutters from the sound of it. Trying to stir up trouble and by all accounts succeeding. I don't have any truck with extremists no matter which side they're on. Left, right, commies or Nazis. We should put the whole lot of the fuckers on an island somewhere and let them fight it out.'

'It's not quite as simple as that.'

'No, I don't expect it is.' Danny scratched his head. 'More's the pity.'

'We're mixed up in the whole thing. We were on an operation that went wrong and now somebody is out to frame us for the attack.'

'*Somebody?* You mean the government? I've not much truck with them either. Bunch of wankers interfering in people's lives. Politicians, planners, council—'

'Danny.' Greta reached out and touched Danny on the arm. 'Stop rabbiting. Rebecca's going to start thinking you're like a scratched record the way you keep jumping back to the same old subject.'

'You're right. Sorry, Rebecca. Go on.'

'We were working for the security services, only now we don't know who to trust,' Silva said.

'No shit?' Danny looked concerned. 'What are you going to do?'

Silva looked across at Itchy and Lona. Itchy shrugged. Lona shook her head.

'I really don't know.'

–

Early afternoon and Holm took a call from Bob Longworth at Counter Terrorism Command. The video and pictures obtained by Al Jazeera meant they no longer needed to analyse the ballistic data to discover the shooter's position.

'Ennismore Gardens, Knightsbridge,' Longworth said. 'A couple of streets back from the park. You want to take a look?'

Holm could hardly refuse and some thirty minutes later he and Javed were ducking under a line of blue and white tape that had been strung across the road at the bottom of Ennismore Gardens. Uniformed police were going door to door along the adjoining streets, while armed officers enforced a strict cordon.

The weather had changed, as if in response to the attack on the Pope, and the week-long spell of sunshine had given way to strong winds and rain. A bedraggled Longworth stood in the middle of the street waiting for them, his hair plastered to the top of his head and water running from his nose.

'Full on,' Longworth said, sticking out a hand as Holm and Javed approached. 'We've locked down the surrounding area. No one goes in or out until we've confirmed their identities, conducted an interview and done a full search of their property.'

'Belt and braces?' Holm said, hunching against the wind funnelling down the street. 'Or the good old stable-door policy?'

'Bit of both, but you're right, the shooter and their team have long gone. Still, visible policing helps calm the situation.' Longworth looked upwards, blinking against the rain. 'This weather is helping too. One of our analysts, a chap who specialises in crowd control, reckons the damp should cool down passions on both sides. Who knew extremists could be so fickle, hey?'

'Have you ID'd any of the suspects?' Holm had studied the pictures and, although it was obvious to him that the shooter was Rebecca da Silva, he didn't think the images were good enough for an identification.

'Not yet.' Longworth cocked his head to one side. 'Are you going to give me a heads-up on this or do I have to take the *Al Jazeera* report as gospel?'

'You know I can't discuss operational details, Bob, but I'd consider alternatives to the obvious for the answer to this one. This isn't what it seems.'

'Are you saying the security services aren't involved?'

'It's a fluid situation.'

'That's a euphemism for you know fuck all, right? Well, whatever went on, trying to appease terrorists usually produces a strong public reaction. The backlash is going to be considerable. There are already pockets of disturbance breaking out across the country and a big demonstration is planned for central London tomorrow.'

Holm lowered his voice. 'He fooled us again. We were waiting for another missile strike and this happens. He's always one step ahead.'

'This wasn't Taher, Stephen. You can see that from the images. You need to drop your obsession.'

'He was involved.'

'If that was the case then why didn't you warn us?' Longworth fixed Holm with a stare. It was as close to angry as Holm had ever seen him. 'Because of the missile threat, the jam has been spread thinly. Yesterday we had fewer specialist officers on the ground. We had a helicopter and some spotters, but we didn't fully stake out the area. It would have been impossible with the resources I had at my disposal.' Longworth looked to the heavens. Holm wasn't sure if he was looking for a police presence up there or appealing to divine intervention. Possibly he was seeking absolution for his failure to prevent the shooting. Longworth turned, his gaze moving to a nearby block of flats. He shook his head. 'Shall we go up?'

Holm nodded and he and Javed followed Longworth across to the flats and down into a subterranean garage.

'The attackers drove in here in a van and masqueraded as decorators. There's direct lift access to the penthouse flats.' Longworth stopped at the doors to the lift. 'Out of action while we do a full forensic sweep. Let's take the stairs.'

The top floor was twelve storeys up, and by the time they got there Holm was struggling to speak. He took a breather as a scene of crimes officer at the top signed them in and gave them protective suits, gloves and face masks. They donned the PPE and walked along the corridor to the flat. Inside several CSIs worked the room, dusting for prints and looking for samples. Holm, Javed and Longworth stood near the entrance.

'The sniper lay on the table,' Longworth said, pointing to a dining table positioned by windows that opened to a balcony. 'We believe it was to facilitate making the shot over the intervening buildings.'

'It's a fair old way,' Holm said. He could barely make out the stage at the far end of Hyde Park. 'What, half a mile?'

'Something like that. One of my lads said he'd struggle for accuracy at that distance and he's came top of his cohort on the range.'

Holm nodded as a CSI beckoned Longworth over. How long, even without forensic evidence, before Rebecca da Silva came up as a suspect? How long after that would a firm link be made back to MI5?

'I'm having trouble understanding this,' Javed said, his voice lowered so only Holm could hear, his gaze on the sniper's position. 'Are we to believe that Silva actually shot the Pope? And with Lona, one of our agents, present? It doesn't make sense.'

'Of course it doesn't,' Holm said. 'But that's the point. Taher has twisted the whole scenario like a Möbius strip. We've headed off in one direction and come right back to where we started and shafted ourselves in the back.'

Longworth strolled back across the room, a look of frustration on his face.

'Whole thing's buggered,' he said. 'Turns out the CCTV in the lobby and the lift were working but all they recorded was this.' Longworth held up a clear polygrip bag. Inside a couple of curls of black stuck to the plastic. 'Insulation tape had been placed over the lenses. Simple but effective.'

'Since when?'

'The day before yesterday by the looks of it. The footage before that is fine.'

'These cameras weren't monitored, then?'

'No, more's the pity. Pictures went straight to storage to be reviewed if and when necessary.'

'So we know nothing about who these people were or exactly when they were here?'

'One witness says she saw a van drive into the car park some time yesterday morning. She can't remember the make of the van only that there was writing on the side. Says there were two or more people inside, but no description, except there may have been at least one woman in the group. That tallies with the news footage.'

'A woman?' Holm raised an eyebrow, pretending to be surprised.

'I don't know if what we've seen claimed in the media is correct, but they weren't Islamist terrorists, Stephen.' Longworth gestured at the CSIs. 'We'll see what this lot can find. If the sniper team were here for a few hours then there'll be plenty of traces.'

'We'll leave you to it,' Holm said. He stuck out the little finger and thumb of his right hand and raised it to his ear. 'Give me a call, right?'

'Sure thing.'

Outside, Holm stood in the middle of the road and looked back at the block of flats.

'Boss?' Javed stared up at the flats too, shielding his eyes against the rain. 'What are you thinking?'

'Let's suppose the Trojan team didn't go rogue and that Rebecca da Silva didn't shoot the Pope, that somebody else did and we're being set up.'

'The evidence doesn't look great, but OK.'

'If that was the case then there was a second shooter.' Holm's gaze roved across to a sign. Ennismore Gardens. 'So the question is, where did they take the shot from?'

Chapter 21

Holm and Javed were back at Thames House in time for a crisis meeting called by Huxtable for seven p.m. Holm and Javed sat on one side of the table, Helen Kendle on the other. Huxtable was at the head.

'First, a report on the Pope's condition.' Huxtable peered down at a tablet. 'I've been told he is critical, but stable. The bullet punctured his right lung and exited the body causing significant internal damage. It would likely be survivable for a fit, young adult, but the Pope is an old man.' Huxtable gave a pat smile. 'Even with God on his side it's touch and go. I can hardly tell you the consequences if he dies.'

'A holy war,' Holm said. 'It's what Taher wants. It's what he planned for.'

'And what did you plan for, Mr Holm?' Kendle said. 'Fiona tells me your analysis was way off and that's what has landed us in this mess.'

'But—'

'Given the threat of the missiles the prime minister would most likely have given the go-ahead for the initial part of Operation Trojan in order to dupe Taher, but there'd have been no question of allowing live ammunition to be fired.' Kendle cast a glance sideways at Huxtable. 'There was a complete failure in understanding the risk matrix. You didn't allow for the fact that Taher might get to the kill team somehow.'

'I don't think that's happened. Rebecca da—'

'Enough.' Huxtable cut in. 'We need to find a quick way out of the situation. Right-wing agitators are doing their best to stir up trouble across the whole country and there are already reports of rioting everywhere from Glasgow to Brighton, and Norwich to Penzance.'

'Penzance?' Holm said.

'A local pharmacy was torched. A case of mistaken identity – the couple who owned it were second-generation Hindu Bangladeshis.'

'Right.'

'So far, mercifully, and thanks largely to the police, there haven't been any fatalities, but the situation is deteriorating rapidly. Imagine what will happen when we get to the evening and groups of opposing youths start to congregate. Then there are the pronouncements from the far-right groups, specifically the British Aryan Insurgency. They're saying they will defend Christians from attacks by the invading armies. There's to be a new crusade, this time on home shores. Its website says groups will be mobilising in all major cities. Apparently they've been preparing for this for years.'

'Christ.' Holm cast a surreptitious glance across the table at Javed. Huxtable noticed.

'Explain yourself?' she said.

'It's obvious, isn't it?' Holm said. 'Nathan Henson and the BAI are working directly with Taher. This whole thing has been designed to cause as much hatred between religious and ethnic groups as possible. It was a trap we walked straight into. Taher's aim is nothing less than total societal breakdown.'

Silence. Everyone only too able to conjure up a vision of anarchy.

'And he still has the missiles,' Javed said, raising his hands as if to apologise for stating the obvious.

'Quite.' Huxtable gave Javed a stare before turning to Kendle. 'We need a way out and Helen has the workings of a useable plan.'

'We should start work right now on making this whole operation completely deniable.' Kendle glanced down at a pad on the table where she'd made some notes in garish purple ink. 'We have to ditch da Silva and her team immediately and ensure this is seen as a terror attack by rogue forces.'

'You want us to wash our hands of them?' Holm was horrified.

'They shot the fucking *Pope*,' Kendle said. 'Are you expecting Silva to receive a slap across the wrist or an hour on the naughty step?'

'I don't believe the team went rogue, I think there was a second shooter.'

'Spare me, Stephen,' Huxtable said. 'There's always a second shooter. It's a meme common in these situations, but we're dealing with reality here, not social media drivel.'

'Are they releasing the forensics Bob Longworth's asked for? Because that could be interesting.'

'How so?'

'It will show where the shot was fired from. I'm pretty sure ballistic analysis will prove it wasn't our team that fired the shot that hit the Pope.'

'This is pointless.' Kendle dismissed Holm with a wave of her hand. 'The way out of this is total denial. We spin it that Simeon Weiss and Rebecca da Silva were acting without orders. Weiss was mentally ill and prone to delusions and he persuaded Silva and the others to follow him. He concocted a plan he honestly believed would preserve life, but just the opposite happened and mayhem broke out.'

'Are you saying we're giving them up?'

'We're admitting to a threat from Taher. We are not admitting that there was ever an official plan to even so much as point a water pistol in the Pope's direction. Weiss had the best of intentions but he and his team went rogue. They are now on the run, out of control, and highly dangerous. End of story.'

'You *are* giving them up.' Holm stared at Kendle in disbelief and then turned to Huxtable. 'That's just not fair, ma'am. I'm certainly no defender of Weiss but he was given direct authorisation by you. Ms Silva and Mr Smith believed they were serving their country by going along. If you remember, Silva was reluctant to take part unless she had assurances.'

'There's nothing I can do.' Huxtable. Resolute. 'We can try to spin the truth about what happened but you must see how unlikely it is to be believed. The only option is to hunt down the rogue team and bring them to justice.'

'And by doing a runner from the hospital, Weiss has made things easier to believe.' Kendle leaned in. Tapped her fancy pen on her briefing notes. 'Or should I say, a hobble.'

Holm ignored Kendle's joke. 'But they're not going to keep quiet when it comes to trial, are they? They'll want their day in court so they can protest their innocence.' Holm saw the difficulty of Huxtable's position, but was having a hard time agreeing with the tactics or understanding the strategy.

'You can see the problem, Stephen.' Huxtable's tone hardened. 'The complexities and subtleties of this case don't lend themselves to media scrutiny. If we try to go with the truth about the operation there'll be questions asked. Why did we use live ammunition? Why wasn't there adequate supervision? How come we didn't war-game the possible outcomes? Why did we hide the mission from the police and, perhaps more importantly, the Pope?'

'There's an answer to all those questions. We can deal with this if we just come clean and put the full details out there.'

'That's not how the security services work and you know it. Besides, are you suggesting we reveal the fact that Taher shot down the aircraft? That he still has missiles in his possession?' Huxtable shook her head. 'No. We created this mess and we need to get ourselves out of it. The hunt for Weiss and da Silva will begin immediately. We'll be using a special forces team to track them down.'

'And when we find them, what then? Internment? Trial without jury?' Holm felt Javed nudge him. He nodded down at a piece of paper on the desk where Javed had written a solitary letter: X. Holm had it then. 'You're going to *kill* them?'

'The action we take needs to be both swift and decisive. The threat has to be neutralised. You've seen what's happening. Right-wing fascists are mobilising, while Muslim groups are, quite understandably, preparing to defend themselves. The mass of the general public are horrified the state would contrive to assassinate the head of one world religion to appease a terrorist who purports to speak for a different religion. Even if we can avoid some kind of – as you call it – holy war, there'll still be insurrection and mass civil disobedience. To get out of this situation we need three things. First, we need the Pope to survive. Second, we need to satisfy the desire for revenge. That means eliminating Weiss, Silva and the other operatives. Third, we need to apprehend Taher, dead or alive. If we can achieve all that we might, just might, get through this.'

'I can't go along with this, ma'am.' Holm stood. In the murky world of the intelligence services separating right from wrong wasn't always easy, but this time he knew which side he needed to be on. 'Simeon Weiss had your full approval for the mission and Rebecca da Silva and Richard Smith are entirely innocent. I can't be party to their deaths.'

'That's not on,' Huxtable said. 'I need you to lead the hunt for Taher. If you go, you are jeopardising national security. People will die. Many people.'

'I'm sorry, Fiona.' Holm used Huxtable's forename to address her for the first time ever. It was, he thought, an illustration that his time with the Security Service was over. Rank and position no longer meant anything to him. This was personal. 'I won't have anything to do with this.'

'Me neither.' Javed pushed back his chair and stood too. 'If he goes, I go.'

'You can't…' Huxtable's hands went out flat on the desk as if to steady herself. 'I need Task Group Taher.'

'To save your sorry arse.' In for a penny, Holm thought. 'TGT was always a sham – it was designed so you could shift attention away from the abject failure of the security services to get on top of extremism. You were passing the buck and I was stupid enough to run with it. TGT was the scapegoat, Taher a master terrorist who was so clever nobody would blame you for having failed to catch him.'

Huxtable sat open mouthed as Holm gathered his things and slipped them into his briefcase. He turned to Javed and gave a small shake of his head. 'You don't have to do this, Farakh.'

'No, but I am, sir. I'm done here too.'

Holm led the way towards the door.

'Wait!' Huxtable was on her feet now. She slammed her pad of paper down on the desk with a thump. 'Dammit, Stephen!'

Holm half turned. He expected anger, expected Huxtable to rage and vent. Knew that he would simply ignore her and walk away. Never mind his pension, never mind trumped-up charges and a possible court case. Fuck her. He was therefore surprised that when she spoke her voice was soft and low.

'A deal,' she said. 'If you catch Taher alive before the kill team get to Weiss and da Silva then perhaps there's a way out. With Taher in our hands we might be able to explain things. He has to be alive though. If he's dead it's just another layer to add to the conspiracy.'

Holm removed his hand from the door knob. What Huxtable was offering was only a tiny morsel. The chance of catching Taher in the next day or so when they hadn't managed to get anywhere near him in the previous six months was minuscule.

'I need more time,' Holm said. 'Delay the kill team by seventy-two hours. It gives me a chance, da Silva too.'

Huxtable met Holm's gaze. It was as if she was trying to gauge whether she could call his bluff or not. She looked down at the sheaf of documents on the table in front of her. Picked up a piece of paper. The paper shook as she appeared to read for a moment or two.

'Too late,' she said. 'The dogs have already been let loose so you have a choice to make. You can either leave and let Silva and the others die, or you can stay and do your fucking job. It's up to you.'

Holm's hand was back on the door knob. He wasn't going to let Huxtable boss him around. He was out of here.

'Sir?' Javed stood beside him. 'We owe them, remember?'

For a second Holm was back in Tunisia. Kneeling on the floor with a gun barrel jammed in the back of his head. Only seconds to live. His survival entirely down to the sniping skills of Rebecca da Silva.

After a moment he took his hand from the door knob and sighed.

'We'll stay,' he said.

–

Later, they sat outside and watched the sun sink behind a distant mountain. Danny had opened a bottle of home-made elderberry wine and the alcohol had a soporific effect on Silva; for the first time in a long while she felt able to relax.

'Nobody's going to find you here,' Danny said. 'There's no mobile reception and we're off-grid. We don't even have a postal address.'

'That's good to know,' Silva said.

'We can't stay here forever.' Lona stood a little way from the house staring down the track. 'We need to find out what happened to Simeon and whether he can help us.'

'Help us?' Itchy, already tipsy, spluttered out a mouthful of wine. 'He's shafted us, love. We're on our own now.'

Itchy was probably right, Silva thought. They'd heard the news bulletin at six and the story had changed. The government were no longer denying that security service personnel had shot the Pope. However, the line was now that the operatives involved were part of a rogue unit led by someone with mental health problems. For reasons unknown the agents had hatched a plot to assassinate the Pope, somehow believing they were following orders. Tracking down the operatives and neutralising any threat they posed was now the number one priority. As Itchy remarked when the bulletin had finished, they were fucked.

Silva bedded down for the night wondering if she'd see Sean or her father again. She woke some hours later to a voice in the darkness.

'Rebecca!' A hand on her shoulder shook her from a dream about her mother. 'Wake up!'

Silva rolled over, momentarily blinded by the glare of torchlight in her face. 'Danny?'

'I've just had a call from Jack,' Danny said. 'He's the chap who lives at the end of the track.'

'A call, how?' Silva said. 'I thought we were off-grid?'

'Radio.' Danny held up a walkie-talkie.

'And?'

'They're here.'

'Who?'

'The government.' Danny's face was grey, his voice resigned. 'Jack says there's two police cars and an army Land Rover. It's showtime.'

'Shit.'

'Don't worry, Jack's blocked the way up with his tractor and I've got a few surprises up my sleeve. They won't take this place easily.'

'It's not your fight, Danny.'

'No.' It was Lona. At Danny's shoulder. 'But it is mine.'

'We're outgunned, trapped,' Silva said. 'We should give ourselves up rather than go down in a blaze of glory.'

'No arguing.' Danny said as he stepped back from the bed. 'Your girl and I have already talked this over and come up with a plan. Diversion tactics. Smoke and mirrors. We'll give them the runaround while you get away.'

'How are we going to do that? There's only one way into this place, right?'

'Wrong. There's only one track in, but if you think I'd live somewhere where I could be cornered then you're not your father's daughter. Get dressed and get your stuff and I'll show you.'

Five minutes later and Silva was standing outside next to her motorbike. Itchy was looking longingly at his machine: it was a road bike and had struggled to get up the track; no way was it heading up the side of a mountain. He'd have to ride pillion on Silva's Yamaha.

'The tractor will delay them for a few minutes,' Danny said. 'But you'd better get going.'

Silva turned to Lona. 'You know we could—'

'We can't. My car won't make it out and there's not room for three on your bike. You have to get away and try to sort this. Clear all our names. Here.' Lona pressed a folded scrap of paper into her hand. Something hard slipped inside. 'This might help. He's a decent man. I'd trust him.'

Silva shoved the piece of paper in a pocket and sat astride her bike. Itchy climbed on behind her. She kicked the engine into life and blipped the throttle. She turned back to Danny.

'Thanks, Danny. We owe you. Don't do anything stupid.'

'Stupid is exactly what I like doing best,' Danny said smiling. 'Now go!'

He patted Silva on the back and she clicked the bike into gear and dropped the clutch. The bike lurched forward and they roared round the side of the house and across an open field.

'Do you know where we're going?' Silva said. Danny had shown Itchy a map and given him directions but he'd only had a couple of minutes to memorise them. 'Because right now it looks like we're heading into the middle of nowhere.'

'That's the plan,' Itchy said. One hand grasped Silva firmly round the waist, while the other pointed to an open gate. 'Through there and into that wood.'

Beyond the field, a dense pine forest climbed the side of the mountain. Rows of mature firs staggering up towards the skyline where a rocky ridge emerged from the trees. Silva opened the throttle and they shot over the field. A forestry track curled into the pine trees, hair-pinning up a steep slope before levelling out and following the contours round a sharp escarpment.

They ripped up the track in the pre-dawn light and had soon put a couple of miles between themselves and Danny's place. Silva slowed and stopped the bike at a junction. One way led down into the thick firs, while the other headed upwards and out onto the side of the mountain.

'Which way?' Silva said.

'Up.' Itchy waved his hand at the skyline. 'We need to go over the top and down the other side where we can join a road.'

Silva was about to pull away when she heard a dull percussive thudding in the distance. She pulled her helmet off and the noise grew louder. *Chop chop chop chop.*

'What is it?' Itchy cocked his head on one side.

'A bloody helicopter.'

At that moment a dark-green shape arced out above the trees, rotors in a blur. Branches swayed in the downdraft, a metallic voice echoing over the noise.

'Stay where you are. Get off the bike. Lie down on the ground. Do not resist.'

Silva rammed her helmet back on and pointed the bike towards the open mountainside.

'No!' Itchy tapped on the shoulder. 'Down. Into the woodland.'

'I thought you said—'

'Change of plan. Danny told me about another option. Down!'

Silva twisted the handlebars and gunned the bike into the woodland. The trees closed in around them but a dark shape loomed overhead as they roared along the track.

'We can't outrun them,' Silva shouted. 'And they've probably sent the vehicles round and will be waiting for us when we hit the main road.'

'Let's fucking hope so.' Itchy was laughing. 'Take the next left. There!'

Silva stared ahead. A narrow trail branched off to one side, but there was barely room to squeeze the bike through the trees.

'Are you sure?'

'Yes, do it!'

She turned onto the path and ducked her head as the branches closed in above. Somewhere above the trees the helicopter hovered. They'd be guiding the others in on foot. Then there'd be vehicles arriving from further down the valley. With continuing air support the pursuers would be able to catch them as soon as they emerged from the forest. The little trail was good for now, but ultimately they'd had it.

A branch caught her across the face, almost knocking her from the bike.

'This is no good, Itchy.'

'It is, I promise. Next right.'

Ahead the path opened into a small clearing. On the right-hand side the trail dove down into a narrow ravine that looked like a dead end. Water tumbled over slippery rocks. Treacherous. Silva put her feet out to steady the bike.

'There's no way out.'

'Down there!'

The ravine bottomed out in an area of older woodland. A couple of spreading oaks standing next to a looming cliff face. Silva bounced the bike to the bottom and stared. There was an opening in the rock. A square hole carved into the mountainside.

'Get inside,' Itchy said.

Silva turned the bike and steered into the opening. She flicked the headlight on and the beam shone into the blackness, picking out broken slate on the floor and a grey tunnel disappearing into the mountain.

'So, what now?' Silva said, pulling the brake on. 'We hide out in here?' She shook her head. 'They'll find us eventually and then we're cornered. This was a stupid idea.'

'Stupid if we wait for them, yes.' Itchy jabbed a finger down the tunnel. 'But we don't wait. We go on.'

'On?'

'Yes. That's what Danny said. Drive into the mine and keep going. Apparently we'll know when to stop.'

'Fuck.'

Silva eased the clutch up and rode forward. The slate clattered beneath the wheels of the bike and the chugging engine echoed off into the distance. The mine tunnel was almost dead straight, but angled downwards slightly as if the ultimate destination might be some subterranean realm. Gimli, she thought, seeing Danny's long twisting beard.

They rode for some ten minutes, the odometer ticking over a good two miles since they'd entered the tunnel, before she became aware the white of the headlight was merging with a wan greyness. The grey turned paler and became suffused with a warm yellow and then suddenly they emerged into daylight, the early-morning sun just cresting the top of a distant ridge. Silva stopped the bike. They were in a small grassy cwm, a hillside stretching down away from them. A village stood at the bottom of the hill and she could see a milk tanker winding along a country lane towards a farm. Up the valley there was a busier road, a dual carriageway. Cars and lorries speeding in both directions. They could be there in five minutes.

'That Danny,' Itchy said. 'He's played a blinder, right?'

Chapter 22

After another long day, Holm had managed to return home and grab a few hours' sleep in his own bed. He headed back to Thames House on Monday morning where Javed informed him of an overnight development.

'They've caught Lona Castle,' he said. 'Halfway up a Welsh hillside, hiding out with an old hippy friend of Rebecca da Silva's dad.'

'She's alive?' Holm said.

'Yes. There was a mix-up. Turns out this old hippy was ex-SAS. When the kill team, comprised of special forces personnel, discovered he was one of them they changed the rules of engagement. Talked Lona and the guy out instead of going in with extreme prejudice. Now Lona's in custody and a hell of a lot of people know about it including the pregnant wife of the hippy guy. Neutralising all of them would seem to be out of the question. Huxtable's livid.'

Holm smiled. 'I'll bet.'

'Doesn't change things for Silva and Smith though.'

'You don't think the kill team will be sympathetic knowing they're ex-army too?'

'They've been replaced. Huxtable has now tasked the job to police units. She's confident they'll get the job done.'

Get the job done.

Meaning eliminating Weiss and the others. Huxtable certainly wasn't squeamish, but then there was no honour among spooks. The rules of the game were that the rules were there to be broken. Weiss had ignored protocol so many times, he'd hardly be surprised with the end result.

Holm powered up his computer, wondering where the hell to start. A couple of windows opened, one showing the intercepts he'd been working through when the Pope had been shot. They seemed pretty irrelevant now, the whole series a complete waste of time. He was about to close the window when he remembered he hadn't gone through the final transcript. The last but one had detailed unspecified training received by Saabiq. For the sake of completeness, Holm clicked open the document; it would at least clear up whether Saabiq would be able to fire AirShield or not.

The intercept started with some casual talk, nothing more than chit-chat. Saabiq – called Little Lion by the speaker – was mentioned a minute into the conversation.

> You understand the importance of this for Little Lion?
>
> Yes, of course.
>
> And the teacher will be there on Thursday and stay for the week?
>
> Don't worry, everything is arranged. Payment has been made and the teacher will bring the materials for the lessons with him.
>
> Good.
>
> You need to ensure there is a suitable place where Little Lion can be taught. Somewhere with a thousand metres clear line of sight, preferably flat terrain. If there is a building,

several storeys high at one end, then that would be preferable.

I think that can be found.

Is the pupil right- or left-handed, and does he need correction for his vision?

Right. And no, he doesn't wear glasses or contacts.

Does he have any experience whatsoever?

Some. He was on a team when he was a teenager. There was a facility at his school.

Really?

Yes, private schools in the UK often have one.

OK.

The rest of the transcript drifted back to more casual talk. Holm closed the document, mystified. Initially, it sounded as if this could be confirmation about Saabiq and AirShield, but the reference to private schools didn't make sense. No school Holm had every read about taught surface-to-air missile combat.

'Sir?' Javed interrupted his thoughts. He'd printed something out and was waving the document at Holm. 'I think I might have found something.'

Holm took the printout. It had a photo dead centre.

'You might remember this from the lock-up garage,' Javed said.

It was an image of the scrap of paper Javed had found. Singed edges. '7 EN' written on it.

'Yes.' Holm put the printout down on the desk. 'We had no idea what it meant. A chemical symbol or something, but when I asked Claire Evans she didn't know what it was.'

'I think it's an address: Seven Ennismore Gardens. Could be where the second shooter fired from.'

Holm looked at the picture again. Wondered about how Javed's brain was wired. Was it genetic or a result of his expensive education?

'Let's go,' he said.

–

They rode through rural Wales. Soft hills and pine forests and hardly a soul on the roads this early. They passed through Rhayader and headed for Builth Wells, stopping at a roadside burger van for a breakfast of bacon butties and coffee. While Silva got the food, Itchy put SIM cards in the burner phones and set them up.

As they stood by the bike and ate, Itchy nodded towards the south where the mass of the Brecon Beacons rose in a brown-green lump.

'We could go there,' he said. 'Remember that training exercise we went on?'

Silva could hardly forget. Three days and nights of wind and rain followed by a fourth when the rain turned to snow. They'd been in serious danger of freezing to death until they managed to find shelter.

'You're talking about that bivvy hole?' Silva said.

'Yes. Nobody would find us there and at this time of year we could hide out for weeks. Every few days we could go down for supplies and stuff. When everything blows over we can decide what to do and where to go.'

'But it isn't going to blow over, Itch. Not until we're dead or the truth is exposed, and the latter won't happen if we're holed up on some godforsaken Welsh mountainside.'

Itchy looked crestfallen. He balled up the wrapping his bacon butty had come in and lobbed it in a nearby bin. 'So what are we going to do?'

For a moment Silva had no idea. Then she put her hand in one of her jacket pockets. Found the piece of paper Lona had given her just before they'd left Danny's place. There was a scrawl of writing with a name and address. Two keys wrapped in the paper.

'Lona gave me this. Said she'd trust him.'

'Who?'

'Stephen Holm.' Silva read the name. 'Fancy that.'

Silva wondered how Lona had obtained the keys, but then realised that she was Weiss's protégé. His secrets were her secrets. Had the pair of them been keeping tabs on Holm? Searching his flat or planting bugs when he was out? If Lona's words and the keys were genuine then it didn't much matter what they'd been up to.

If.

Itchy wasn't having it. 'But Holm's one of them. He'll turn us over and then they'll either give us the old waterboard treatment until we confess or else there'll be some sort of accident where we end up dead.'

'I saved his life, remember? He owes us. Besides, I don't think he'd stand by while somebody puts a round in the back of our heads. He's a decent guy.'

'I hope you're a good judge of character, Silvi. Else we're fucked.'

Itchy was spot on. If they put themselves in Holm's hands and she turned out to be wrong, then it was all over. And what did she really know about Holm? She'd saved his life in Tunisia and spent a couple of hours with him at the planning meeting at MI5. She might as well place her trust in a complete stranger.

Half an hour later Holm and Javed were parking up on Ennismore Gardens. There was still blue tape strung across the road near the block of flats they'd visited the previous day, but the police presence was reduced.

'No number,' Holm said, looking at the block. 'Just a name. Kingston House.'

Javed turned in the street and scanned the rows of tall buildings. 'There are numbers further down.'

Holm started to walk in the direction of the police roadblock. 'And number seven is outside yesterday's cordon.'

'Are you going to tell Longworth?'

'Not yet.' Holm ducked under the blue and white tape and crossed the road. 'Let's see what's inside number seven first.'

'All these properties are expensive,' Javed said. 'A bit out of Taher's reach, I'd say.'

'Sure, but nothing to Haddad.'

They walked down the street towards Hyde Park and stopped at number seven, a distinctive block of flats but only five storeys tall. Javed was sceptical.

'It's not high enough. You couldn't see over the inter-vening buildings to take a shot. I think I may have been wrong.'

They stood for a minute and then wandered down to the main road where a steady stream of traffic roared past. There were properties here that did overlook the park, but Holm thought it unlikely Taher would have risked such an exposed position. Beside, Javed's hunch was based on the property being number seven.

They retraced their steps, passing a Russian Orthodox church with a tall tower on the left-hand side of the road.

'You'd get a good line of sight from up there,' Javed said.

A little further on there was a narrow side street. Holm eyeballed the name. Ennismore Mews. 'Here,' he said. 'Right name, wrong road.'

The mews ran back from the main street for a few paces before turning south, away from the park. Round the corner it was indeed a mews: tiny little dwellings of no more than two storeys.

'No chance,' said Javed. He looked down the street before turning. 'Completely blocked by that building.'

'Which, it so happens,' Holm said, 'is number seven.'

The property was Victorian, sitting oddly between the mews cottages and the church. Holm gazed up. There were six main storeys and an attic, little windows at the top nestling under dormers. He walked across. An iron gate stood in front of a short tiled pathway, a porch beyond. Holm pushed the gate open. To the right of the front door there was a set of name tags and bell pushes. A to J.

'That many flats, they must be crammed in,' Javed said.

'Still, I doubt fifty years of your salary could buy one.' Holm reached out and pressed the bell for flat A. After thirty seconds or so a tinny voice, a woman's, came from a speaker grille. Holm leaned forward. 'Parcel delivery.'

'One mo,' came the response before, a minute later, there was a figure behind the frosted-glass panel of the door. It swung open, an elderly woman gazing up from a wheelchair. 'Hello?'

'Police.' Holm had his MI5 ID out ready. He waved it casually at the woman. 'Nothing to worry about, we're just conducting a house-to-house search.'

'I saw it on the news,' the woman said. 'Just awful.'

'Yes.' Holm sidled in. 'No need to concern yourself though. I'm sure any danger has passed. We'll start up the top, shall we Farakh?'

'Um, yes,' Javed said, following Holm in and smiling at the woman.

'Are you with them?' the woman asked. 'Only...'

'With whom?' Holm stopped beside the woman. Resisted the temptation to drop to his haunches in the way he would with a child.

'The men in flat J.'

'Why do you say that?'

'Well...'

'There's no need for political correctness here. Can you describe them?'

'There were three of them. Two were of Middle Eastern descent, I'd say, the other was white, scruffy. Looked like an ancient hippy.'

'When was this?'

'They've been coming and going for a couple of weeks. When I met them in the corridor they told me they were moving in.'

Holm cast a glance at Javed. 'If you wouldn't mind going back into your flat. Somebody will be along to question you later.'

He didn't wait for the woman to comply, rather he strode along the corridor to where the entrance to a lift stood alongside a stairwell.

'You take the stairs,' he said to Javed. 'I'll ride the lift. See you up there.'

Holm pressed the button to call the lift. The doors opened immediately and he stepped in, seeing Javed move quickly for the stairs before the doors closed.

The lift clunked upwards, an unseen whirring some-where above Holm's head. He wondered if he should call Longworth now and alert him, but dismissed the thought.

The lift opened onto a narrow corridor, the stairs spiralling up to his right. An arrow on the wall opposite pointed left towards a window at the end. A door stood either side of the window. Javed appeared at the top of the stairs.

'I and J,' he said in something that was a combination of a whisper and a gasp for breath. He nodded along the corridor. 'And J is open.'

Javed was right. The door to flat J stood half open, an Adidas holdall stopping the door from swinging shut. Holm edged forward, waving at Javed to follow down the same side of the corridor. They reached the door and Holm peered in. Just inside, a long flight case with a Fender Guitars logo stood against the wall of a small, square hallway. The sounds of a TV with the volume well up drifted from a room off to the right: *The prime minister has called for calm after the latest revelations concerning the security services…*

'There's someone in there.' Javed was at Holm's shoulder. 'Are you sure this is the right flat?'

'None of the others have the correct vantage point.' Holm stepped into the hallway. The room to the right was a bedroom, the door half open, water running in the en suite, muttered words Holm couldn't make out. He cast his gaze down at the holdall. 'Check that.'

As Javed bent to the bag, Holm slipped across the hallway, walking as quietly as he could, his heart in his mouth. Directly ahead a door led to a large open-plan living area, a dining table to one side, a large L-shaped sofa to the other. He moved into the room. There were two windows, both dormer types, and they looked to the north, the green of Hyde Park clearly visible.

'Pssst.'

Holm turned back to see Javed crouching beside the holdall. He'd unzipped it and now held something wrapped in a towel in his hands. He moved his hands up and down, signalling that whatever was inside was heavy. He placed the towel on the floor and carefully unwrapped the towel to reveal the dull grey of gunmetal. Holm recognised the make and model.

A Glock 19.

He felt a chill run down his spine. The gun was the weapon of choice for Taher. The weapon he'd had when Holm had been kidnapped. All of a sudden he regretted not telling Longworth about their hunch about number seven. He beckoned Javed over and the young man stood and walked across, the gun and towel still in his hands.

'There's more in the bag,' Javed whispered. 'Something like an IED. Wires and stuff leading to a Tupperware container with a timer. And unless Taher has all of a sudden decided to form a rock group, the guitar case must contain the sniper rifle. They left it here yesterday in order to make a quick getaway. They probably just mingled with the crowds coming out from the park.'

Christ. Holm had been out of the police for a decade and a half so why did he continue to act as if he was young and fit and ready to physically take down criminals? He needed to admit to himself he was now a pen pusher. The only thing he should be armed with was a mobile on which he could call for help. Which is what he'd now do. He groped into his jacket pocket and pulled out his phone.

Only the running water had stopped, the newscaster's voice too.

Holm grabbed Javed's arm and led him across the room and through another door into a narrow galley kitchen.

'Give me the gun,' he said. Javed passed the weapon over but even as Holm took it in his hand he knew something was wrong. The weight, heavy as it was, wasn't right. He looked down. There was no clip in the handle. The gun was useless. 'Shit.'

'Here.' Javed slipped by Holm and headed for the sink. He pulled a handle on a drawer to the left. Rummaged inside and brought out a large carving knife. 'This will do.'

'Bloody hell.' Holm stared at the knife. Wondered about shoving the blade between a man's ribs. Shuddered. 'I'll go over to the windows and distract him. You take him by surprise.'

Before Javed could disagree, Holm walked back into the living area. Stood by the right-hand dormer. The view to the park was clear and the window opened to a tiny balcony with an iron railing.

'Who the fuck are you?'

Holm spun round. A man stood at the doorway. White with brown, dreadlocked hair and a full beard. He wore a black T-shirt, jeans and a rucksack was hefted on his right shoulder as if he was about to leave.

'Blake and Jenson Lettings,' Holm said. He glanced back at the window. 'Arthur Blake at your service. Quite an outlook. When did you say the property would be available from?'

'I didn't and it isn't. Would you mind leaving?'

'I'm sorry?' Holm put on his best quizzical expression. 'I'm not sure I follow you.'

'I think there's been a mistake.' The anger had gone from the man's voice. Training had kicked in. 'This property isn't to let, nor is it for sale. Are you sure you have the right address?'

'Flat J?' Holm peered down at his phone, pretending to read something. 'Mr Arkman?'

'Right flat, wrong name.' The man was still by the doorway. No chance of Javed surprising him. He dropped the rucksack, one fist clenching as he did so. 'Perhaps I could show you out and you can check in with your office.'

'Right. You wouldn't by any chance know a Mr Taher, would you?' Holm turned to the window again, keeping his back to the man, trying to encourage him closer. 'Only I was hoping to do business with him.'

'What's this about?' the man said, edging across the room.

'Something important.' Holm paused, almost expected a bullet between his shoulder blades. 'Tell him Stephen Holm is here.'

Silence. A couple of seconds. And then footsteps.

Holm turned to see the man almost upon him. He raised an arm to defend himself but the man lunged in, a fist breaching Holm's defences and catching him on the right side of his face. The punch knocked him backwards and he crashed against the window. Glass broke and wood splintered as Holm fell through the window onto the small balcony. As he struggled to get up, Javed came running across the room, the knife in his hand.

Whether the man heard Javed or followed Holm's gaze, something made him spin round. Javed thrust the knife forward, but the man moved his right arm in a sweeping motion, easily deflecting the blade. Then he pirouetted, a kick snapping up and catching Javed in the stomach. Javed staggered backwards, but managed to hold on to the knife. As the man moved in, he slashed at his face. Again an arm came up, but this time the man grabbed Javed by the wrist. In one fluid movement he twisted Javed's wrist and at the same time punched him in the face, following the punch with another balletic turn that ended with a roundhouse kick. The kick hit Javed in the chest and he fell to the floor, poleaxed.

'You want some, too?' The man whirled about and headed towards the window.

Holm scrabbled upright. The roof sloped down on either side of the dormer and met a substantial stone parapet a metre or so below the balcony. He grasped the railing, climbed over, and lowered himself until his feet touched the stonework. A gulley with a hidden gutter ran behind the ledge, crossing the boundary to the next property. Everything was wet from the recent rain, the surfaces treacherous, but he moved away from the balcony as fast as he dared, leaning into the roof so as not to overbalance. After he'd gone halfway along the gulley, he turned back, half expecting the man to be right behind him, but there was no sign of him. As he turned, he tried not to look down to his right, remembering that he was seven storeys up, but then there was the sound of a vehicle braking hard in the street below. The honk of a horn. He stopped and peered over. A white van was slewed in the road and the man from the flat was racing across to it, the flight case in one hand and the holdall in the other. He wrenched open the side door, threw the luggage in, and climbed up. For a moment the light reflected from the windscreen and obscured the driver, but then the van reversed, turning in the road.

Black hair, a wisp of a beard, and – even at this distance – dark piercing eyes.

'Taher,' Holm said. He began to move back to the balcony, and at the same time he reached for his phone. The phone slipped from his hand and skittered on the roof, bouncing once and disappearing over the stone ledge. Then, as he took another step, the roof to the side of the balcony burst open. The tiles and battens and joists folded outwards as if he was viewing the scene through some kind of giant kaleidoscope. There was a rush of air pushing him backwards and sweeping him across the still intact part of the roof. The flames came next, jetting from where the dormer window had been in a rolling billow of heat. Finally the sound, a concussive thump followed by the clattering of debris.

Holm was blown along the tiles and crashed into a valley where another part of the roof joined. He reached up and wrapped his arms round an ornamental stone balustrade as a cloud of smoke billowed over him. The last thing he saw before everything went black was an empty, gaping hole where the flat had been. *Empty*, he thought as he closed his eyes against the heat. No sign of Farakh Javed.

Chapter 23

Holm found himself sitting in the back of an ambulance as a paramedic checked him over. Quite how he'd got there he wasn't sure. The last thing he remembered with any clarity was a cloud of smoke rushing towards him. Everything after that was a blur. He'd heard sirens at one point, then voices calling out in the fog. Arms wrapped round him. Vertigo as the mist dissolved and he found himself in the bucket of a huge cherry picker as it descended to street level.

'Farakh,' he'd muttered as they helped him to the ambulance. 'Where's Farakh Javed?'

He didn't think they'd understood what he was talking about. Now, as he began to come to his senses, he tried again.

'There was someone with me,' he said to the paramedic. 'Did they get him down?'

The paramedic glanced back through the open doors of the ambulance. The whole building was a vertical column of fire, thick black smoke twisting into the London sky.

'Don't know, mate. I thought you were alone on the roof.'

'Christ.' Holm swallowed, tasting debris from the explosion. 'Could you find out?'

'Supposed to get you off to hospital. You need to be triaged. Maybe have a scan on that arm of yours.'

'Please?'

For a moment it looked as if the paramedic was going to be a jobsworth, but then he softened. 'Guess you'll survive for another few minutes. Be right back.'

He climbed out of the ambulance and walked off in the direction of number seven. There was a cordon thirty metres back, a group of fire officers standing there eyeing two colleagues who were spraying the building with water. Holm thought about fire and explosions and death. Tallin Saabiq and his wife and unborn child in Manchester. The twelve passengers on Flight 117. Farakh Javed and whoever else didn't manage to escape from number seven Ennismore Mews.

Holm lay back and closed his eyes. He was done in. Not the from the physical pain of his headache, the possible fractured arm and the other injuries, but from the mental anguish. The strain had become too much. The responsibility for preserving lives too daunting. He'd failed Tallin Saabiq and the passengers and Farakh. He was going to fail Rebecca da Silva and Richard Smith. At the end of it all Taher would still be at large and sooner or later he'd fire another missile. Hundreds would die this time. Holm decided he couldn't take it any longer. He'd let the paramedic take him to hospital. Stay in overnight. In the morning he'd tell Huxtable he was quitting. He'd done his best but it hadn't been good enough. He opened his eyes as the paramedic climbed back into the ambulance.

'No sign,' he said as he closed the rear doors and gestured for Holm to lie down. 'But the fire chief says they haven't recovered all the bodies yet. Could be three or four residents in there plus a couple more people unaccounted for.'

Holm felt a wave of darkness sweep over him as he lay back. He closed his eyes again as the paramedic spoke to the driver. Heard the blare of a siren as the ambulance pulled away.

Nightmare, he thought. Utter bloody nightmare.

The next couple of hours were a blur of doctors and nurses and endless corridors. He was given an X-ray, a good dose of painkillers and, despite protestations, taken up to a ward where he was placed in a bed. At some point he slept.

He woke to a woman whispering.

'He's asleep, but you can sit here until he wakes. He's walking wounded by rights, but because of his age we decided to keep him in overnight for observation.'

'OK. Thanks.'

Footsteps clicking away. Holm imagined someone like a womanly matron. Or was it a matronly woman? He opened his eyes to see which.

'Boss?' It was Farakh Javed, sitting on a chair by the side of the bed. A bag of apples lay in his lap. He held it up. 'Didn't bring a card but then the nurse told me that you're out of here soon so I'm glad I didn't waste my hard-earned cash.'

'Farakh.' Holm looked around at the rest of the ward. Tried to detect something that might reveal this miracle as nothing more than a drug-induced dream. 'You're alive.'

'Good to see your powers of observation are as sharp as ever.' Javed put the apples down and reached up and touched his right eyebrow. There was a line of stitches. 'Just this gash to show for my heroics.'

'But how?'

Javed shrugged. 'I saw him set the IED and then leg it. I was a little groggy but managed to crawl out and roll down the stairs to the half-landing. Next thing I know the stairs above me had collapsed and there was no way back up. I was a bit worried until they said they'd spotted you on the roof and were bringing one of the big engines with a high-reach capability. I'd have stayed to see you rescued but they packed me off to A & E.'

'I thought you were dead.'

'For a moment back there so did I. Others weren't so lucky. Three people didn't escape from the adjoining flats and others are missing. It's been spun as a gas explosion.'

'*What?*'

'Helen Kendle told Huxtable that the last thing the country needs now is news of another terrorist attack. Luckily the building has been almost totally destroyed by the fire so the cover-up will work for now.'

'Madness,' Holm said.

'Yes.'

'Any sign of Taher and the other guy?'

'Taher?' Javed cocked his head. 'He was there?'

'Last thing I saw was him in the driver's seat of a van in the street below. The other man got in and they drove off. I reckon they came back for the gear.'

'The man in the flat was white but it wasn't Nathan Henson. Makes me think we might have underestimated the number of people Taher has managed to recruit, and one of them must be able to handle a long-range weapon.'

'The sniper is Anwan Saabiq,' Holm said. 'This morning I read something in one of the Algerian transcripts about his training. It said he'd had experience at school. It didn't make sense to me, but Saabiq went to a private school and some posh schools have rifle ranges –

either .22s or air rifles. His training wasn't on AirShield – he was learning how to fire a sniper rifle specifically for the hit on the Pope.'

'Shit.'

'To put it mildly, yes.'

For a moment Holm thought about closing his eyes and going back to sleep. There was too much to worry about. Taher, the missiles, snipers, the British Aryan Insurgency, Rebecca da Silva and Richard Smith, the kill team, Huxtable, keeping Operation Trojan hidden, Jawad al Haddad, the state of the London property market…

Holm blinked, remembering his little act in flat J.

'Property in Knightsbridge,' he said as he pushed himself up. 'Check when number seven was last sold and find out who bought it.'

'Hey?'

'Taher must have been planning this for months so they either bought number seven Ennismore Mews or were renting it. There's got to be a trail there somewhere.'

'You think it can be linked to Haddad?'

'Possibly,' Holm said. 'There's something else too. The guy in the flat, I've seen him before.'

'Where?'

'That's just it, I can't remember.' Holm tried to recall the features of the long-haired man with the beard.

'Great.' Javed had removed one of the apples from the bag and started to eat it. 'Sorry, missed dinner.'

'You're supposed to bring grapes or chocolates for ill people, not apples.' Holm, distracted for a moment, returned to visualising the man in the flat, but Javed's munching was off-putting. He stared at the rapidly vanishing piece of fruit and for some reason heard the theme tune from an old black and white western adventure series he used to watch on TV as a kid. *The Lone Ranger*, that was it. Why on earth would that come to mind now? He was either losing his mind or the painkillers were stronger than he'd thought. He began to hum the theme tune and then remembered it was actually from an opera by Rossini. He had the CD at home. Then he made the connection. The opera was *William Tell*.

'He shot an apple from his head with a crossbow,' Holm said absentmindedly.

'Who?'

'William Tell.'

'Sir, you're not making any sense. You should probably lie back down for a minute or two.'

'No. The man with the crossbow at the BAI headquarters. He was the guy in the flat.'

'Bloody hell.' Javed moved his chair back as Holm leapt out of bed and began to walk down the ward. 'What are you doing?'

'Discharging myself.'

'It's ten o'clock at night. You're supposed to be kept in for observation.'

'Fuck that. You can take me home and we can make a start on working out who the guy with the crossbow is on the way.'

'Sure.' Javed nodded. Pointed at Holm's hospital gown. It was untied, a slit revealing more than Holm's thighs. 'But it might be an idea if you found some clothes first.'

—

They rode south and east, avoiding motorways and opting instead for a succession of B roads that zigzagged across the country towards London, arriving at the outskirts at midnight. As they slipped under the M25 at Uxbridge, Itchy's voice came through Silva's helmet radio.

'We won't be able to escape the cameras now,' he said. 'Not all the way in.'

'We won't worry until we get within a few miles,' Silva said. 'Then we'll take the backstreets for a bit before finding somewhere to park about half an hour's walk away. It's the best we can do.'

Trying to make contact with Holm was risky, but they were out of other options. Lying low forever just wasn't possible.

Itchy guided her through the streets, telling her to take left and right turns seemingly at random. Silva was totally lost and it wasn't until Itchy told her to slow on a quiet road next to a large park and told her they were near Wembley that she got her bearings.

'A mile in that direction,' Itchy said as he got off the bike from behind Silva. 'We'll cross the golf course and follow residential streets south until we get to Ealing. Holm's place is a few minutes' walk from the centre.'

Silva kicked down the stand on the bike and took her helmet off. Further down the road detached houses sat on one side. On the other side there was a long fence of iron railings. Beyond the fence, trees were silhouetted against the night sky.

Itchy crossed the road and climbed over the fence. Silva followed.

A line of poplars fringed a long fairway and there was a raised green area at one end. A flag hanging limply on a pole marked the hole. They moved through the trees and crossed the open grassland beyond. There were more trees and a second fairway and then they were at the southern boundary. After climbing another fence they found themselves on a deserted residential street. Semi-detached houses, the occasional street light, a corner shop sign glowing weakly in the dark.

'Not far now.' Itchy peered down at the screen on his new phone. Pointed to the left. 'Down there, second right. Holm's is number thirty-four, flat B.'

'Let's hope he's in,' Silva said.

They walked down the road and took the second right. Holm's house was in a neat Edwardian terrace where nearly all the properties had been converted into flats.

'If he's being watched then we're done,' Itchy said.

Silva shrugged. Without Holm's help they were going to get caught sooner or later anyway.

Holm's flat was one of three in the house. A short path led up to a tiled front step and a door with a Yale lock. She pulled the keys Lona had given her from a pocket and slipped the first key into the lock.

'Nice,' Itchy whispered as she pushed the door open. He closed the door carefully behind them. There was a short corridor with stairs up one side. 'First floor.'

Silva padded up the stairs, the floorboards creaking as she did so. At the top there was a door to the left, while stairs carried on up to the next floor. She crossed to the door and took out the second key and waited for Itchy.

He came up the stairs and unslung the small backpack he'd been wearing. Opened it and pulled out one of the handguns they'd taken to London on the Trojan mission.

'Christ, Itch,' Silva whispered. 'What the hell are you doing?'

'Can't be too careful,' Itchy said as he checked the weapon. 'I'm not going down without a fight.'

There wasn't much point in arguing.

The lock on the door to the flat was a heavy mortise type but it turned easily. She nodded to Itchy before easing the door open.

Itchy moved quickly into the flat with Silva following. There was a hallway with a kitchen to the right and a living room to the left. As she closed the door, she cut off the light from the outside landing. In the kitchen, a clock on a cooker glowed fluorescent green, while in the living room light from the street lamps seeped round the edge of the curtains. Itchy walked down the hall to where there were two more doors. He glanced left into a bathroom, and then pointed right. The low sound of somebody snoring drifted from behind the half-open door. Itchy held the gun in his hand and entered the room. Silva reached for the light switch and flicked it on.

Holm lay beneath a duvet and he stirred as Silva spoke.

'Stay still,' she said. 'We'll shoot you if you try anything.'

'What the…?' Holm rolled over on his back and pushed himself up. He blinked against the light. 'Rebecca?'

'Yes. Who're you expecting? Taher? We'll talk when you've got dressed. To save your modesty I'll wait in the next room.'

Silva went to the living room and peered out through the curtains. The street was deserted aside from the rows of parked cars. She pulled the curtains shut and turned on a lamp on a low table. Holm came in and Itchy directed him to sit in an armchair.

'If you were going to use me as a bargaining chip you're out of luck. Huxtable doesn't think that much of me.'

'We didn't do it.' Silva sat down in the sofa. 'I took two shots just as we planned. The first hit Weiss, the second part of the lighting rig.'

'Why Weiss?'

'There was supposed to be a stooge with an explosive device strapped to his leg. The device was going to explode and simulate a minor gunshot wound. Problem was the stooge couldn't get through security. Weiss told me to shoot him instead so as to ensure the whole thing was convincing.'

'Seems I might have misjudged Mr Weiss.'

'Yeah, me too. Anyway, that's it. Somebody else shot the Pope. End of story.'

'I know.'

'So why the hell are MI5 trying to kill us?'

'Because the alternative narrative is too difficult to get across. There has to be a fall guy, or in this case fall guys plural.'

'What about Taher? Where the hell is he in all this?'

'Exactly. If we had him we'd be in the clear, but since we don't somebody has to take the rap. Plus the pictures released to the media show three team members and their ethnic origins are very definitely white British. We can't pass this off as anything other than a rogue unit gone bad.'

'What about the evidence? The bullet that hit the Pope didn't come from my rifle.'

'That's true, but we don't have your rifle. You'd have to give it up. Even then I'm not sure it would be convincing enough.'

'This is crap. You were there in the room with me and Huxtable. She authorised the mission. You know the whole thing was a set-up, that we were never going to actually shoot the Pope.'

'A mosque was firebombed in Bradford yesterday, while in Leicester a white kid minding his own business was stabbed to death by unknown assailants. That's just the tip of the iceberg. Trouble is kicking off everywhere, and I'm talking worldwide. The way things are going we've got a full-scale global riot on our hands.'

'You can't blame Itchy and me for that.'

'I don't, but at the moment a rogue group of government agents attempting to kill the Pope looks a lot better than blaming it on unknown Muslim extremists.'

'You walked straight into Taher's trap. He had you every step of the way.'

'Guilty.' Holm held his hands up. 'I warned Huxtable that Taher couldn't be second-guessed, but she thought Weiss's plan was the best choice from a set of lousy options.'

'And Huxtable convinced us to go along with it because we thought we were doing our duty.'

'I'm sorry.'

'Sorry doesn't help, mate.' Itchy waved the gun at Holm. 'What the fuck are we supposed to do now?'

'Put the gun down, Itch. Before we have an accident. I don't think Mr Holm is going to take advantage.'

'I promise I won't,' Holm said. 'Besides, I'd probably blow my head off before I managed to hit you. It's been a long time since my last session on the range.'

Itchy moved over and sat on the sofa alongside Silva. He placed the gun on the coffee table.

'So what do we do, Mr Holm?' Itchy said. 'Silvi seems to think you're our last hope, but if we put ourselves in your hands how do we know you ain't going to turn us in?'

'If handing you over was an option, I'd do it.' Holm grimaced. 'The problem is that for Huxtable's plan to work there can't be anyone around to tell the true story. The dead, as they say, don't talk.'

'So we can't even give ourselves up?' Silva said.

'I doubt you'd get the chance. You've been tagged as extremely dangerous and police units have now taken over from the army. They've been instructed to show extreme prejudice.'

'That's irony for you, Silvi,' Itchy said. 'You reap what you sow, right?'

'I've never been one for ironic humour, Itch. Especially when it's at my own expense.' Silva looked across at Holm. 'Itchy's question bears repeating, what do we do?'

Holm's gaze dropped to the gun on the table, and for a moment Silva thought he might make a lunge for it. Instead he looked up.

'We're going to do what I've been trying to do for what seems like half of my life.' Holm smiled. 'We're going to find Taher and bring him in.'

Chapter 24

Holm left his house early and drove south to Croydon to call on Javed.

Javed lived in a modest apartment in a low block half a mile from the town centre. Holm found a parking space and headed for the entrance lobby. A push of the doorbell soon had Javed's sleepy sounding voice crackling through the speaker grille.

'It's me, son,' Holm said.

'Boss? I thought I was going to meet you at work?'

'Sure, I just thought I'd come and give you a lift in.'

'At half six?'

The lock buzzed open. Holm pushed through the door and went up the stairs to Javed's third-floor flat. He'd only been here once before, picking Javed up for an early-morning surveillance. Members of the security services weren't supposed to socialise. It was too easy for conversations to lapse from casual chit-chat into work-related matters, and that was strictly prohibited.

The door to the flat opened, Javed standing there in a silk dressing gown. 'This is unexpected.'

He showed Holm in. The flat was the sort of thing millennials might have felt at home in, but to Holm it was soulless. It was open plan, with a kitchen off to the right and a living area to the left. The bedroom was high on a mezzanine level and accessed by a ladder. A bathroom was boxed in below.

Javed moved to the kitchen. 'You want coffee?'

'Sure, as long as it isn't instant.'

For a couple of minutes Javed busied himself with a kettle and cafetière, while Holm asked how he was feeling after the explosion. Javed came over to the living area with two cups and set them down on a coffee table.

'Much as I appreciate the sentiment, you didn't come over just to ask after my health. You're not that kind of person.'

'Thanks for the character assassination.'

'Assassination being the operative word. Any news on that or what happened yesterday?'

Holm stood and walked to the window. The vista was of the backstreet where Holm had parked his car. A council worker pushed a dustcart along the pavement, but otherwise the road was devoid of life.

'Rebecca da Silva and Richard Smith have turned up.'

'They're in custody?'

'No, not exactly.' Holm returned to the sofa and sat. 'Do you trust me, Farakh?'

'Sort of.'

'What's that supposed to mean?'

'You're an honest type of guy, so in that respect, yes.' Javed lowered his gaze for a moment. 'But do I trust you to make the right decisions? Not always.'

'I appreciate the first and take the second as constructive criticism.'

'Is this leading somewhere?'

'Silva and Smith are hiding out at my place. They say I'm their last hope.'

'They must be desperate.'

'Self-evidently.' Holm took a sip of the coffee. 'Huxtable's argument is that we need scapegoats to get us out of the situation without further bloodshed. In a strictly utilitarian sense she's correct, but if we lived by those rules we'd execute people for double parking on the street because they slow down emergency response vehicles. Personally, I think the whole thing stinks.'

'Cover-ups usually do.' Javed reached for his own coffee. 'But in our job they're par for the course, right?'

'I've been involved in a fair few myself, but this is different. There are no double agents, no spy games, no exchange of personnel, no enemy state. This is a mire of shit and all our own doing. I advised Huxtable the phoney assassination was a mistake but she went along with Weiss's plan anyway. Silva and Smith shouldn't have to die because of her error.'

'But it's not looking good, is it?'

'No, and if they're found then it's over for them.'

Holm took a gulp of his coffee. Javed was shaking his head. Likely the young lad couldn't fully comprehend the situation. He'd been with Holm in Tunisia when they'd encountered Taher and back then their lives had been in the balance. Had it not been for Rebecca da Silva and Richard Smith, they'd have wound up in an unmarked desert grave. Now the tables were turned. Payback time.

'So what's the plan?'

'If we can find Taher then the focus changes. If Silva and co. can be painted as rogue state operatives, then surely it must be possible to show Taher to be a rogue actor. He's nothing to do with Islam, he endangers the faith and those who follow it, and has no time for peace and cooperation. If we produce Taher and the evidence then Huxtable will be forced to reveal the truth about what really happened.

The scheme is likely to cost Huxtable her job, so if she discovers what we're up to she'll fight us all the way.'

'And can we find Taher?'

'Finding him is still my official job. Nothing's changed in that respect. We need a break though.'

Javed nodded. He took several more sips of coffee then put the cup down.

'Life comes at you fast, doesn't it?' he said. 'Not much time to work out what to do.'

'I've worked out what's best for me,' Holm said. 'I came here to see if you'd come to the same decision. I'll be honest with you, it's our careers, possibly our lives, balanced against doing what is right.'

'I never much wanted to be a hero,' Javed said as he stood. The silk dressing gown looked ridiculously camp, but that was probably the point. 'But if I'm going to be one, then, much like you back at the hospital, I think I'd better get dressed.'

–

'You carry on checking out Sunrise's property portfolio,' Holm said when they got into the office at Thames House. 'You're good at ferreting around for information. I'll get Claire Evans to help me with our mystery crossbowman.'

'Delegation is the art of leadership, right?' Javed said.

'Something like that.'

In the tech suite, Holm found Evans watching a sequence of videos from what looked like a police raid. She was in a sombre mood, her face lacking its usual brightness.

'What's this?' Holm said, taking a seat beside her. 'Footage from Supernova?'

'You haven't heard?'

'No.'

Evans gestured at the screen and then clicked her mouse to restart the footage. 'Watch.'

Holm leaned in. The view was in black and white and taken from a body-mounted infrared camera. It showed a squad of black-clad figures gathering on a deserted street. Holm noted the time code in the top right of the frame: 02.11. The small hours.

'The Met?' Holm said.

'No, special forces, but London, yes.'

One of the figures dashed up some steps to the door of an Edwardian terraced house. The figure knelt by the door for a couple of seconds before sprinting back to street level and crouching low. Ten seconds later there was an explosion and the door blew in.

'Frame charges,' Evans said.

Fuzzy radio comms crackled through the speakers as half a dozen figures rushed into the house, the camera point of view following close behind. Three ran upstairs, while the others fanned out into the ground-floor rooms. The camera followed one figure along a corridor to a kitchen at the back of the house. The figure made for the door to the outside, wrenched it open and moved out into a small walled garden. The infrared camera picked out the glowing eyes of a cat before the creature turned and bounded away, and then the camera focused on a small shed at the bottom of the garden. The door swung open and there was a man standing there with his hands raised in surrender. Oblong glasses and a familiar face.

'No,' Holm said. 'Simeon Weiss.'

For a moment the man with the gun stood in front of the shed before there was another crackle on the radio, the message unintelligible. Then he fired a short burst from the weapon. Four shots, each clearly distinguishable.

Weiss slumped against the side of the shed, clutching his chest before he fell to the ground. Evans clicked her mouse and stopped the footage, Weiss frozen on the screen, dead or dying.

'Christ.' Holm sat back in his chair, unable to take his gaze from Weiss's last moments.

'He'd sneaked home to visit his wife,' Evans said. 'As you can see, he never had a chance. I'll admit I never liked the man but this is wrong. As for mentally ill, well, I just can't believe it.'

'No,' Holm said. 'Neither can I.'

'You know what this means?' Evans whispered. 'Unless you're very careful, you'll be next.'

'Do you know something I don't?'

'No, but I think you know things you shouldn't and that's dangerous.' Evans reached out and touched Holm on the arm. 'But I'm here to give you help if you need it.'

'Thanks.'

Holm tried to get his head round the situation but the death of Weiss had thrown him. He just sat and stared at the bank of monitors, not knowing what to say.

'So, where do we start?' Evans said. She clicked her mouse again and the image of Weiss vanished. 'Assuming you didn't just come down here to see me.'

'We're looking for a second white van in the streets around Knightsbridge,' he said, trying to get his head together. 'This time plain with no signage.'

Evans nodded. She explained that Counter Terrorism Command had gathered a huge amount of material from the various traffic-monitoring and numerous CCTV cameras that covered the area.

'Most of the stuff is from local residences,' Evans said, bringing up a map on the central monitor. 'This shows where each piece of video came from. Security cameras, dashcams, smart doorbells. You'd be surprised how hard it is to keep anything private these days.'

'I specifically want to see activity in the vicinity of Ennismore Mews.'

'Where the gas explosion was?' Evans shook her head. 'All the material was gathered either on the evening of the shooting or the morning after. There's nothing showing the explosion.'

'Doesn't matter. It's the hours before the shooting I'm interested in.'

'Right.' Evans zoomed the map and read from a textbox. 'We've got data from a camera in one of the mews cottages. Says here the householder was worried about his car getting scratched by passing vehicles as they came round the corner.'

'Sounds good.'

It took a few moments for Evans to load up the video and then she was fast-forwarding through the footage, the time stamp in the top-right corner a blur of minutes and hours passing. Vehicles jumped in and out of shot and people rushed down the street at high speed, the motion jerky and disorientating. Evans froze the video as a white van came into view, but a Harrods logo was visible on the side.

'Not that?'

'No,' Holm said. 'The van was definitely unmarked.'

The footage continued to flash by. Cars, people, several more vans that each had to be checked. Then, with the time stamp at three thirty in the afternoon, she paused the video again.

'That's it,' Holm said. He leaned towards the screen. There were two men in the front of the van. The driver was Taher and the passenger was Anwan Saabiq. 'What about the person in the rear?' Holm pointed at Taher. Just behind his shoulder a third man hunched forward between the front seats. 'Can we get a match on him?'

'We can try.' Evans zoomed the image so the man's face filled the screen. Then she cropped it and hit a couple of keys. 'Searching now.'

A result popped up within a minute.

'Ninety per cent certainty,' Evans said. 'One Jon Sutherland.'

Evans clicked for further details. Holm wasn't surprised to see that Sutherland had form. There was a GBH charge from a few years ago. Before that breaking and entering. Taking without consent. Possession with intent to supply. The list went on. Nothing since the long spell inside for the assault though.

'There's a note on his file.' Evans clicked through to see the details. 'Says he may have been radicalised inside prison.'

'Anything else?' Holm asked.

'He's not on any kind of watch list if that's what you mean.'

'Right.' Holm stared at the screen for a moment. 'Have we got an address?'

Evans clicked the mouse a couple of times. 'South of the river. Catford.' She clicked again and a nearby printer began to hum. She reached over, pulled out a sheet of paper and handed it to Holm. 'There you go.'

Holm thanked Evans and returned to his office where he found Javed reading an urgent internal memo.

'They got Weiss,' Javed said. 'They're calling him a rogue agent.'

'I know, but the lie can't stand. The whole thing will unravel if we can get Taher. The good news is that I've identified the man at the BAI HQ and 7 Ennismore Mews as Jon Sutherland. Turns out he's a convert who may have been radicalised in the nick.'

'So more evidence that the BAI are in league with Taher.'

'What he was doing there I don't know, but he seemed pally with Gaugan, didn't he?' Holm showed Javed the address. 'And now we know where he lives.'

'Catford?' Javed tapped his computer screen with a fingernail. 'Wouldn't be in a block of flats off the Bromley Road by any chance? Davenport House?'

Holm double checked the address. Raised an eyebrow. 'Yes.'

'I've been going through Sunrise Property's list of sites. Forty-seven in total, all prime development land. I doubt we're going to find Sutherland at that address.'

'Why not?'

'This is why not.' Javed brought up a browser window and typed the name of the block of flats. The first result was a video clip. Javed clicked 'play'.

The screen showed Davenport House, a low-rise concrete block, council or ex-council. The place was drab and almost derelict, with no glass in the windows and a surrounding fence of plywood shuttering boards. In the top right of the screen a counter ticked off seconds down to zero. Then the bottom floor of the building exploded outwards, and the rest of the structure collapsed in a cloud of dust.

'Shit,' Holm said.

They stayed hidden at Stephen Holm's flat for the whole day, raiding the fridge for what meagre supplies there were within.

'He lives like a monk,' Itchy said as he prepared an evening meal consisting of a bowl of baked beans and some crackers and cheese. 'Remind me not to get old and single.'

'Let's hope we get a chance to grow old,' Silva said. 'And if we do, that will be down to Holm, so don't diss his culinary predilections.'

'Hey?'

Any further discussion was curtailed by the sound of a key in the door to the flat. Itchy stopped buttering the crackers and reached for his gun. The door swung open, Holm standing there with his briefcase in one hand and three pizza boxes balanced in a pile on the other.

Before they ate, Holm told them some bad news. Simeon Weiss was dead.

Silva tried to take the information in. *Weiss? Dead?* All of a sudden reality hit home. If Weiss was dead then she and Itchy were the next in line. And if Weiss had been shot on his own front doorstep then the chance of them surrendering was minimal.

'At least we've got a decent last meal,' Itchy said, as sarcastic as ever as he reached for a pizza box. 'If I'd gone to face the music on half a pack of cream crackers I wouldn't have been a happy man.'

Later, after the pizzas had gone, they talked.

Holm laid out his ten-year-long hunt for Taher in extensive detail, Silva and Itchy listening and occasionally asking questions. Finally, Holm summed up where the investigation was now.

'Basically, a dead end,' he said. 'Especially with what we found out today about Sutherland.' He held his hands up. 'We've no idea where he, Henson, Saabiq or Taher could be.'

'You said something about a number of properties Sunrise own?' Silva asked.

'Yes, but they're all development sites. Aside from Jawad al Haddad's place – and I don't think Haddad would risk harbouring terrorists inside his home – none are residential. Besides, there are forty-seven of them.'

'Can't you get them staked out anyway?'

'I could possibly get Counter Terrorism Command to do that, but it's a big ask and I'm worried about how Huxtable might handle it.'

'Do you have to tell her?'

'If CTC are involved then she'll know.'

Silva nodded. Initially she'd been buoyed when Holm said he'd help them; now she wondered what could be achieved in a few days that Holm hadn't managed to do over many years. He'd had huge resources at his disposal, intel from around the globe, the best minds in the business working on the problem, and still he hadn't manged to get Taher. Perhaps the issue was the approach. How, she thought, would she get the job done?

Well, she wouldn't have allowed bureaucracy and organisational inertia to get in the way, nor would she have been constrained by legality as Holm had been. Simeon Weiss, much as she'd despised the way he'd manipulated her, had produced results. In the end though, even his bravery in the 'fake shot that wasn't a fake shot' set-up hadn't been enough.

'You mentioned that both Henson and Sutherland had been associated with Gaugan and the BAI?'

'Yes. Henson has been involved with the BAI and I saw Sutherland there practising with a crossbow. Gaugan might well know where Sutherland and Henson are, but there's no way he'd tell us.'

'He has a wife and kids, right? I think I read something about them once.'

'Yes.' Holm sounded hesitant. 'What of it?'

'Well, if Gaugan does know where either Sutherland or Henson are then I've got an idea about how to make him tell us.'

'Is it legal?' Holm was looking increasingly sceptical.

'Not exactly,' Silva said. 'But you leave the details to Itchy and me.'

Chapter 25

The rioting hadn't been as pronounced as Taher would have liked. There'd been a few deaths but the backlash he'd hoped for hadn't come. Nor had the ongoing tit-for-tat escalated into an all-out holy war.

Now, as they carried their gear into a derelict house outside London, he asked Henson to take some responsibility for his failure to raise an army of fascist zealots.

'You told me there was a groundswell of opinion,' Taher said. He dropped a bag down on the bare floor and began to unroll a sleeping mat. They were roughing it for a night, camping out. Sutherland had been living here for months, relishing the survivalist vibe, but for Taher it reminded him of Iraq. Messing in bombed-out buildings, the night sky above as you tried to sleep, gear neatly packed, ready to move on at a moment's notice. He finished with the mat and turned to Henson. 'You said the BAI would be in the vanguard, but behind them would be a huge number of disaffected lower-class whites ready to take up arms and fight.'

'We tried,' Henson said, putting his own rucksack down, 'but they're not fucking educated enough. They don't understand the kind of threat you lot represent.'

'Well we certainly gave them something to think about so perhaps the problem is that you failed to persuade them.'

'Listen, mate, we told 'em. I've been setting up groups all over the country, finding willing volunteers to spread the gospel about sharia law and hordes of immigrants and an end to the British way of life. When the time came, my lot went out on the streets and kicked the shit out of anyone who got in our way.' Henson jabbed a finger at Taher. 'The problem, as I see it, is at your end. Where's the uprising you promised, the fight-back? We tried to provoke it but there's little or no response. It takes two sides to start a war, doesn't it?'

Although he hated to admit it, Henson had a point. Taher had thought there was a healthy contingent of angry young Muslim men who'd be ready to take to the streets and meet the BAI in pitched battles. That hadn't happened. The moderate religious leaders had managed to cool the hotheads down and to a large extent prevent widespread retaliation.

'You didn't do enough,' Taher said. 'We set it up so it looked as if the government tried to kill the Pope to appease extremists. That should have been plenty of fuel for your fire.'

'No one believes that shit now. A mentally ill but charismatic intelligence operative went rogue and persuaded others in his unit to go along with his mad plans. That's the way they're spinning it. Your propaganda story worked for the first few hours but not any longer.'

Again, Henson was right. The story had been far too clever and nuanced for the great unwashed British public. Taher realised he'd overthought the whole operation. The appeasement story was supposed to hint at the way the government was increasingly favouring one particular group over another. It was designed to seed resentment and anger and for the anger to boil over into a pogrom organised from the bottom up, the country destroying itself in the process. Now it all seemed a little foolish. He'd overestimated the factionalism. Most of all, he thought wryly, he hadn't allowed for the British weather. The simple fact of the washout on the day following the hit on the Pope had kept all but the most ardent fanatics indoors and off the streets.

Plain bad luck, some might have said, but Taher knew that wasn't true. In the past he'd always ensured each plan had a contingency for all possible outcomes. This time, juggling the various complexities hadn't allowed for that and now it all seemed to be tumbling down around him.

'We go again,' Taher said, trying to sound confident and assertive. 'That's why we're here, right? We prepare another attack and this time we claim responsibility. With hundreds dead that will be enough to push people over the edge. You need to get back to the BAI and set things in motion. We can still do this, right?'

'Wrong, mate.' Henson shook his head. He looked round at the decrepit building. At Taher, Saabiq and Sutherland. Seemed to come to some sort of decision. He picked up his rucksack and hefted it onto one shoulder. 'I'm fucking done with you losers.'

Henson turned and walked away, heading towards the gash in the brick wall that was once the front door. Taher stepped after him, his right hand moving to the Glock in his shoulder holster. He drew the weapon and fired.

'And we're done with you.'

–

On Wednesday morning, Silva and Itchy headed towards Kent and navigated their way to the BAI camp. A five-bar gate marked the way in. Silva pulled the bike off to the side and she and Itchy got off.

Silva kicked down the stand on the bike, took her backpack off and pulled out her gun. Checked the mag. Itchy was doing the same with his. 'Like old times, hey, Itch?'

'Except we can't call in an air strike, or radio for an emergency dust-off, or shout for backup.' Itchy glanced down the track. 'Plus what was legal in Afghanistan is definitely not legal here.'

'The police think we shot the Pope. Nothing else we do can top that. You clear on what you've got to do?'

'Sure.'

'Good. You've got sixty minutes until I worry. Text when you're done or call if there's a problem.'

Itchy nodded and then got back on Silva's bike and rode off.

Silva climbed over the gate and walked down the track. A stand of oaks gave way to smaller deciduous trees and then to dense conifers. She kept close to the side. If somebody came she wanted to be able to get into cover fast.

A few hundred metres into the wood and she stopped. Ahead, she could see the guard tower Holm had told her about. Today it looked unoccupied. She sidestepped carefully into the treeline and sat down with her back against a large trunk. She checked her phone. No messages yet.

Beyond the tower she could see the BAI headquarters. An old jeep sat out front. According to Holm the vehicle belonged to Gaugan. She pulled out a piece of paper Holm had given her with the registration number and double checked. Yes, the jeep was Gaugan's. She settled down to wait.

An hour later her phone buzzed with an incoming message. She glanced at the screen: *In position, ready to go.* She texted a quick reply and then got up and made her way towards the low buildings, keeping beneath the trees. When she reached the clearing she casually strolled across to the jeep and paused and scanned the area. A squirrel foraged over by a large oak tree, while a couple of pigeons pecked their way across a grassy area. Gaugan was almost certainly inside and hopefully he was alone.

An entrance lobby had three doors off. One led to a large meeting room with a stage down one end, one to a kitchen area and the third to a long hallway. Silva moved down the hallway, the gun in her hand. At the far end a door stood open. As she approached she could hear the clattering of a keyboard. She stepped into the doorway.

Gaugan sat behind a desk working furiously at a laptop. He had black hair with a bald patch, thin metal glasses on a round face, and Silva thought he more resembled a university lecturer than the leader of a fascist organisation. He looked up as Silva entered and rocked back in his chair when he saw the gun. A hand went up to his glasses and he fumbled with them for a moment, as if he needed to check what he was seeing.

'You've got a fucking nerve.' Gaugan scraped his chair back and made to stand. 'If my boys catch you here they'll—'

'Where are Jon Sutherland or Nathan Henson?' Silva said. She came into the room and moved away from the door.

'Who?'

'Sutherland. I know he was training here a few weeks ago, so don't try to mess me around.'

'I don't know anybody—'

'Fine. We'll do this the hard way.' Silva took out her phone and made a video call. Placed the phone on the desk in front of Gaugan. 'Watch this.'

'What the…?' Gaugan leaned over and peered at the phone. The screen showed a neat living room. A woman sitting on a sofa with two children: a boy of about six or seven and a girl in her early teens. Their hands were behind their backs. Gaugan's mouth opened, his lips quivering. 'No!'

'Your wife and kids. You have five seconds to tell me where Sutherland is. One.'

'I haven't heard of a—'

'Two.'

'Honestly, I—'

'Three.'

'I don't know where—'

'Four.'

'I can't tell you!'

'Five.'

'For God's sake!'

'Itch?'

Itchy appeared on screen. He dragged the boy from the sofa and pulled him towards the camera. Raised his handgun and placed the barrel of the gun close to the upper part of the boy's right arm. Fired. The boy fell sideways out of shot and the woman and the girl screamed.

'NO!' Gaugan jumped up and shouted. 'You fucking maniac!'

'I'll ask again. Where is Jon Sutherland? One.'

'OK! I'll tell you.' Gaugan slumped back down in the chair. 'Give me a moment.'

'Muck me around and I continue the count.' Silva muted the phone and then gestured at a spiral-bound notepad. 'Write it down.'

Gaugan nodded. He reached for the pad and found a pen. His hand shook as he scribbled a few lines on the pad and tore the top sheet off. Silva took the piece of paper.

'Leith Hill?' she said.

'Yes.'

'Will they be there now?'

'How the fuck do I know?'

'Well you'd better be telling the truth or we won't be so nice next time.'

'Nice? You fucking bitch. You shot—'

'Itchy?' Silva unmuted the phone and held it up so Gaugan could see. His wife was sitting on the sofa, the boy on one side, the girl on the other. They were distressed, but looked unharmed. 'Assuming Mr Gaugan has told us the truth, he'll be back home later. Tell them not to worry. They just need to sit tight until he gets there.'

'Wilco,' Itchy said.

Silva hung up. She held up the piece of paper. 'Now let's find out if you *were* telling the truth.'

She flicked the phone's screen again and called Holm.

-

'Is it on the list?' Holm asked Javed after Silva had called.

'Hang on.' Javed scanned through a couple of sheets of paper. 'Yes. Smither Farm, Leith Hill. You ever been there?'

'Leith Hill? Yes.' Holm remembered long walks with his father round the woods. The area was noted for being the highest point for fifty miles in all directions. 'If I recall there's a viewpoint and a gothic tower.'

'And Sunrise Property own a brownfield site there. According to the Land Registry they bought it eighteen months ago. Planning permission has been submitted to tear down an old house and farm buildings and erect three contemporary properties. Be worth a fortune when completed.'

'Could Henson and Sutherland be hanging out there?'

'Possibly.' Javed had a map on his screen. 'It's on the side of the escarpment and surrounded by private woodland.'

There was no need for further debate so they set off in Holm's car. The persistent rain of the past few days had cleared eastwards, leaving scattered showers, the sun poking out from behind the clouds every now and then. Holm wondered whether Longworth's crowd control expert would be staring at the sky hoping for more rain.

They headed south through Epsom, crossed the M25 at Leatherhead and drove into the countryside. At Dorking they turned off onto a minor road and began to climb through deciduous woodland. The scenic route was busy with cars, motorbikes and cyclists; several times Holm thumped the steering wheel in frustration as they had to wait to pass on the narrow lane. The road twisted and turned, rose and fell, and they passed a car park with an ice cream van.

'Are you sure this is right?' Javed asked. 'Doesn't feel like we're approaching a hotbed of international terrorism to me.'

'If the address is right then this is right,' Holm said.

'It *is* right. Look, we're here.'

There was a gate to the left, a rough track dropping away through bracken and scrub and seedlings. There was a sign on the gate that read 'Sunrise Property: Private. Keep Out.' A heavy chain with two padlocks had been secured round the gate. Holm slowed the car and pulled over a little way further on. He parked on the verge and they got out.

'Now what?' Javed said.

'We go down there and take a look. If either Henson or Sutherland are there then we call it in.'

'And Taher?'

'Don't worry, we call it in whether he's there or not.' Holm smiled. 'I've finally learned from my mistakes.'

The track dived down the side of the hill and entered a patch of woodland. The surface was rough but here and there tracks could be seen in the mud.

'These are recent,' Javed said. 'Chunky tyres. Four-wheel drive I'd say.'

Holm thought back to the BAI HQ. There'd been several four-wheel drive vehicles in the car park. Had one of them belonged to Sutherland? Had Henson also been there when they'd visited?

The woodland ended at a five-bar gate, this time unlocked, and the track curled to the right and ran along the side of the escarpment. Holm looked out to the south. The view was incredible, a patchwork of woodland, corn-fields and meadows all the way to the horizon where the South Downs rose to a sky filled with white clouds. For a moment Holm was back with his father, walking the hills, anticipating a cup of sweet tea from a flask and half a Mars Bar. Simpler times.

'Boss?' Javed was pointing down the track. 'There it is. Smither Farm.'

The track ran across the hill to where a bright-yellow JCB stood motionless in a scar of brown earth. Beyond, the eponymous Smither Farm was revealed to be no more than a dilapidated brick house with a flimsy prefab tacked on the side. Next to the house, two farm buildings lacked roofs. Parked beside one of them was an old Land Rover that Holm recognised from the BAI HQ.

'What the heck are they doing out here?' Javed said. 'This isn't a safe house or a place to store weapons. It doesn't make sense.'

Javed was right, Holm thought. It made no sense at all.

'We need to get closer without being seen,' he said. 'Let's stick to the wood.'

The edge of the wood curved round the hill and a footpath ran just inside the treeline. Instead of going through the gate and down the track, they could make their way along the footpath until they were above the farm. That way they'd remain hidden.

They walked along the path until they reached a point where the buildings were below them. Holm positioned himself behind a clump of bracken while Javed hid behind a nearby tree.

'We should have brought supplies, sir,' Javed said. 'We might be here a while.'

Javed was right. They didn't have food or drink. They didn't have waterproofs or warm clothing. They hadn't brought binoculars or a camera. Once more Holm felt ill prepared. Too much time behind a desk. He hunkered down and tried to make himself comfortable.

Luckily the weather stayed fine, the sun swinging gradually round to the west, bathing Holm in a warm light. He settled back, finding a soft place to lie on his side where he still had a good view.

Sometime later he woke with a start.

'Sir!' Javed prodded him. 'It's Sutherland.'

Holm blinked. The sun was lower now, the air a little chillier. He raised a hand to shield his eyes from the glare.

There was movement down by the Land Rover and Javed was correct: it was Jon Sutherland, the man they'd seen at the BAI headquarters.

'He's loading stuff. I think they might be leaving.'

'*They?*'

Before Javed had a chance to answer Anwan Saabiq appeared at an opening in one of the walls of the farmhouse. He had a large rucksack slung over one shoulder and a supermarket carrier bag in each hand. He walked across to the Land Rover and stowed the rucksack and bags in the rear. Neither he nor Sutherland appeared to be in any sort of hurry.

'What are they doing?' Holm said. 'They obviously don't think the place has been compromised otherwise they'd be moving with more urgency.'

Saabiq returned to the bungalow and remained inside for five minutes or so. When he came out he was with another man. Angelic features, a wispy beard.

It was Taher.

'Bingo,' Javed said. 'We've done it, sir. Congratulations.'

Holm swallowed. Was this really the end? It all seemed too easy. He pulled out his phone to call for backup. Once he'd done that they'd return to the car and block the gate. There was no other way out. Unless they abandoned their vehicles and legged it, the terrorists were trapped.

Taher and Saabiq walked down to the Land Rover where Sutherland was standing with a phone in his hand. He was peering at the screen; when the two men approached he pointed at it and then looked to the south-east.

Holm stared in the same direction but couldn't see what Sutherland was looking at because the corner of the wood blocked the view.

'What's over there?' he said to Javed, even as he spoke feeling a sense of unease. 'Behind the trees?'

'I don't know.' Javed pulled his phone out. 'I'll take a look.'

Holm took a couple of deep breaths. Gazed into the sky where there were a few clouds floating in a haze. Felt the muscles in his stomach tighten when he spotted something else up there. 'Christ, it's—'

'It's Gatwick airport. It's about seven miles away.' Javed shoved his phone back in his pocket. 'Look.'

Holm nodded to where all the men were now looking at a white object in the sky. An aircraft lined up for final approach. 'The wind is from the east. We never realised the airport was there because there's no take-off noise. The clouds hid the incoming planes approaching from the west.'

'And now the clouds are clearing...' Javed left the rest of his thoughts unsaid because Anwan Saabiq had appeared round the side of the Land Rover with a large box-like contraption on his shoulder, a long, thick tube poking through the box.

'Fuck,' Holm said. 'The AirShield launcher.'

Chapter 26

Time stood still for a few seconds. Holm turned his head to the west, trying to make out if there were any more aircraft coming.

'They're definitely tracking something,' Javed said. 'Sutherland is studying his phone. Probably has some sort of plane-spotting app.'

The initial realisation that the airport was so close had made Holm's guts contort. Now he felt real fear, and thought he might vomit.

'Call the hotline,' Holm said, moving to the fence. 'Tell them what's happening.'

'And what are you going to do?'

'I'm going to stop them.'

Holm climbed over the fence and jogged down towards the farm. He raised his arms above his head and began to wave frantically.

'Stop!' he shouted. 'Put the weapon down and step away from the vehicle.' Even as he said the words he realised how ridiculous he sounded.

Saabiq was kneeling now, bracing his left shoulder against the Land Rover. The tube was pointed to the west at a shallow angle, and his head was bent over, looking through some sort of sighting mechanism in the launcher. While Taher stayed next to Saabiq, Sutherland went to the front door of the Land Rover and retrieved something from inside. He turned towards Holm, a pistol in his right hand. He raised the gun and fired in Holm's direction.

Holm sidestepped and ran parallel to the farm and across towards the corner of the field. Sutherland began to give chase, but while Holm was running on the flat, Sutherland had to climb the steep hillside. Another shot whistled past Holm's head as he reached the fence. There was a stile that led back to the wood, a footpath winding into the trees. He jumped up over the stile and ran along the path. He hoped Javed was taking the opportunity to get back to the car unobserved.

The trees thickened, the sky lost to a canopy of leaves overhead. Holm slowed, looking for somewhere to hide. To the left there was a large fallen tree providing good cover. It was an obvious hiding place. To the right, a little further on, there was a low stand of bracken, the green fronds insubstantial, the second-best option. Holm bent to pick up a small fist-sized rock from the path and then made his decision, stepped to the right and dropped to his hands and knees behind the bracken. He crawled forward and then turned round and crouched, trying to keep as still as he could.

Footsteps. Pounding down the path. Slowing.

Holm clutched the rock in his right hand. It was, he realised, fairly insubstantial, but one end was sharp and pointed.

Now Holm could see a figure coming down the path. It was Sutherland, moving cautiously, peering this way and that. As he approached he turned towards the fallen tree. He extended his right hand, the gun aiming towards it. Then he turned back and strode towards the bracken, smiling.

'Jon!' Javed stood a little way back up the path, waving his arms in the air.

Sutherland spun and fired a shot as Javed jumped to the side behind a tree.

Holm leapt up and crashed through the bracken, the rock raised. Sutherland swung round again, but as he did Holm smashed the pointed end of the rock into the man's face. Sutherland fell backwards, stumbling over the fallen tree as the gun went off, the bullet firing harmlessly into the air. Javed sprung from behind the tree and dived for Sutherland, both hands grasping the man's gun hand. As Sutherland writhed and struck out with his free hand at Javed, Holm leapt forward and brought the rock down on the man's head. Once, twice, three—

'Boss!' Javed had let go of Sutherland's arm. He pushed himself up from the ground. 'He's out of it.'

Holm stared at Sutherland's face. His nose was a bloody pulp and his front teeth were gone. Holm nodded, reaching over to free the gun from Sutherland's grip.

'You phoned it in?' Holm weighed the gun in his hand and checked it over.

'Yes. There's procedure for this apparently. Flight controllers will reroute all inbound planes.'

'What do you mean *will*?' Holm started moving back up the path, Javed following. 'This is urgent.'

'There's a chain of command. The authority to make the decision doesn't lie with the Security Service.'

'Shit.' Holm broke into a run, feeling his heart rate rise once again.

They reached the stile and Holm froze. Saabiq was still crouched by the Land Rover, Taher beside him pointing to the sky.

'Shoot him!' Javed shouted. 'He's painting the plane with the laser.'

Holm steadied himself. The stile was a good seventy-five metres from the Land Rover. Hitting anything at this range with a handgun was unlikely, but under fire Saabiq might decide to take cover. The missile relied on the operator sighting the target with a laser grid that it homed in on. If Saabiq had to move he'd almost certainly be unable to aim properly. Holm raised the gun and squeezed the trigger. The recoil surprised him; he hadn't fired a gun for years. What also surprised him was the tuft of grass that flew up some fifteen metres to the right of the Land Rover.

Taher shouted something and at the same moment there was a percussive crack. A missile emerged from the front of the launcher tube, flying almost in slow motion until, a few metres from Saabiq, its rocket fired with a huge whoosh of flame. Then the missile streaked up and away, heading towards the west where Holm could see a speck hovering above the horizon.

Holm took aim and fired again. This time the bullet pinged into the side of the vehicle and, at the sound of the impact, Saabiq half lowered the launcher, stepped back and retreated out of sight. Holm climbed over the stile and began to run down the hill. Seconds later the vehicle lurched forward, Saabiq, Taher and the launcher inside. Holm crouched, braced his arm, and took another shot, once again hitting the side of the Land Rover.

'Sir!' Javed pointed to the sky. The missile was streaking towards the horizon, but the aircraft had banked hard to the right and the missile didn't appear to be compensating. 'You've done it. Saabiq never got a good enough aim with the laser for the system to lock on.'

They watched the missile shoot upwards, its bright yellow flame visible against the dark clouds. After thirty seconds the fuel was gone and the rocket motor shut down. Now all they could see was a wavy vapour trail. Holm looked for an explosion, but there was nothing.

'Let's hope it didn't land on someone,' he said. 'I wouldn't want to get the blame.'

'A small price to pay for saving an aircraft full of people.'

Holm turned his attention to the Land Rover. It reached the bottom of the field and ploughed through a hedge, turning left onto some sort of green lane and disappearing between tall hedgerows.

He tapped Javed on the shoulder. 'We need to get after them.'

'Even if we could smash through the locked gate, we couldn't get down the hill in our car,' Javed said. 'Not in one piece.'

'Right.'

Holm paused for a moment and then turned and began to jog towards the track that led back to the road. After a minute or so he had to stop and walk. Beside him, Javed was talking on his phone, giving garbled instructions to officers who were apparently hurtling along the Surrey lanes attempting to find the Land Rover.

As they approached the gate, a police car pulled up and officers jumped out with weapons drawn. Holm carefully placed the pistol down on the ground and put his hands out to his sides.

'Do as I do, lad,' he said. 'Be a bit stupid to get shot for being heroes, right?'

When Holm and Javed got back to Thames House they found the situation room once more a hive of activity. Large parts of Surrey and Sussex were under total lockdown as the largest manhunt in British history proceeded. Roadblocks had been set up on all major routes and residents were being advised to stay indoors. Every available officer was out looking for Taher and Saabiq and a number of army units had been mobilised. In addition, the SAS kill teams that had previously been guarding regional airports were converging on the south-east. Taher was trapped.

Forensic officers at Smithers Farm discovered the remnants of a terrorist hideout. They also found the body of Nathan Henson, a bullet hole in the back of his head.

'Henson outlived his usefulness,' Holm said. 'Either that or they're falling out and breaking up.'

'You think?' Javed said.

'Yes. Whatever shared objective the group had, the aim is no longer achievable. I'd say we're reaching the endgame.'

And so it appeared, because at a little after four p.m. a garbled report came in. A suspect had been shot dead after a hard stop on the A3 just ten miles from Leith Hill. Clarification came a few minutes later from Bob Longworth at Counter Terrorism Command.

'It's Anwan Saabiq,' Longworth said. 'I'd have preferred to get him alive, but there you go.'

'And Taher?' Holm asked.

'No sign of him, the Land Rover or the missiles. Saabiq was driving a dinky little Fiat hire car and was unarmed. He tried to surrender but the SAS boys wouldn't have it. Took him out with a hail of bullets through the side window. The hire company are going to have a fit when they see the mess inside.'

Holm hung up. Taher's network was no longer in existence: Jon Sutherland was in a critical condition in hospital, and Anwan Saabiq and Nathan Henson were dead. Taher might still be on the run, and he did have one missile left, but it was surely only a matter of time until he too was captured or killed.

Holm headed for the fifth floor and Huxtable's office. He ignored the protestations of Huxtable's PA and pushed open the heavy wooden door to the inner sanctum.

'Rebecca da Silva and Richard Smith are in the clear now, right?' he said as he burst in. 'You need to rescind the shoot-to-kill order.'

Huxtable stirred behind the desk and nodded at the woman sitting to one side in a deep leather armchair.

'I'm sorry about this, Helen,' Huxtable said, a fierce anger in her voice. 'I gave strict instructions we were not to be interrupted.'

It was Kendle, the national security adviser. She leaned round. 'Fiona told me you'd made a deal, Mr Holm? Deliver Taher and the kill team will stand down.'

'Fuck the deal! Farakh and I have just stopped a major air disaster and nearly apprehended Taher. Saabiq, Henson and Latif are dead, and Sutherland out of action. Taher could be in custody within a few hours. There's no need to carry on with the hunt for Silva.'

'Stephen, calm down,' Huxtable said. 'We can work this out. Everything is in hand.'

'That's right.' Kendle smiled. There was a thick wad of documents on her lap; she made an annotation to the top one and then passed it across the desk to Huxtable. 'Things are happening. Soon the whole affair will be over.'

As she passed the document to Huxtable, Holm caught sight of some numbers and letters at the top: 'CAA. Form

CA48'. He stared at the ornate pen in Kendle's hand. A blob of purple ink hung from the gold nib.

'What do you mean?' he said.

'Beyond your pay grade, Stephen.' Huxtable. She fixed Holm with a stare that said: shut up. 'Why don't you clock off and go home? You've been quite the hero again. That should be enough for anyone for one day.'

'It's not enough for me,' Holm said. 'I want assurances that you'll call off the dogs.'

'Unfortunately it's out of my hands.' Huxtable cut Kendle a glance. 'There are other agencies involved now. Different priorities. There's nothing I can do.'

'In that case I'll have to tender my resignation.'

'Fine.' Huxtable's mood changed, any sense of conciliation gone. 'Don't bother to clear your desk. Go straight out and leave your ID at reception.'

'And Mr Holm?' Kendle. 'Please remember you've signed the Official Secrets Act. Don't do anything stupid like going to the press.'

Huxtable had picked up her phone and was talking quietly. Holm only heard a smattering of what she was saying but he got the gist of it. '… to my office… escorted from the building… not to talk to anyone…'

She put the phone down and turned her attention to the document Kendle had given her. There was no goodbye, no thanks for the work he'd done. For a moment he simply stood there while the two women ignored him. Then he left the room.

Security met him before he had a chance to get to the lift. He was taken down to the front desk where he handed in his ID. He stepped out onto the street, crossed the road and lingered by the Thames, wondering what the hell he'd just done.

Out on the river, a tug was towing a barge full of dredged-up sediment, the helmsman carefully manoeuvring the boat between the central piers of Lambeth Bridge. The destination would be somewhere downstream, the mud dumped overboard.

Outmanoeuvred. That was him. Played by Kendle, Huxtable, Weiss and Taher. He'd always tried to do what was best, but at every stage it seemed as if control had been wrested from him. He was nothing more than a speck of sediment that would end up being disgorged into the cold, infinite sea.

'Cheer up, you old bugger,' he said to himself. He pulled out his phone and texted Javed a message about the possessions he'd left in the office. Could they meet in the Morpeth Arms? Javed could bring Holm's things.

Holm turned and walked upstream towards Vauxhall Bridge. The Morpeth Arms overlooked the river, a couple of tables giving a view across to where the MI6 building rose in a series of steps on the far side. He got himself a pint and a packet of crisps and sat watching the traffic hurry past. Thanks to Huxtable and Kendle, hurrying was something he wouldn't have to do any longer. No more setting the alarm, no more commuting, no more office politics. Huxtable would at this very moment be signing off his resignation, perhaps she'd even borrow Kendle's fancy pen to do so. His career would be dismissed by a stroke of purple ink. Huxtable's hand, Kendle's pen; it was as if the two of them were somehow cooperating in his demise.

He sipped his beer and ate the crisps, calmer now, less morose. Retirement wouldn't be so bad. He'd see his daughters more often, go to more gigs, the cinema, join a book club or something. Perhaps he'd even move out of London and make a fresh start.

'Sir?' Javed stood by the table with a couple of cardboard boxes balanced in his arms. 'Got everything apart from the CD player and speakers.'

'Keep them,' Holm said. 'They'd only go to a charity shop otherwise.'

'Er… I don't have any CDs.'

'Of course you don't. Just drop them off at my place sometime, then.' Holm indicated the vacant chair. 'Take a seat, I'll get you a drink.'

'No, I'll get it.' Javed pointed at Holm's near-empty glass. 'You having another one?'

'Why not?'

Javed put the boxes down and disappeared inside. Holm bent to one of the boxes and opened the lid. The box was stuffed with a number of CDs and all his office paraphernalia. He stared down, never before realising just how many pens he'd managed to accumulate over the years. Expensive ones, too. Some gifts, some he'd bought.

Dismissed by a stroke of purple ink…

'There you go.' Javed plonked Holm's beer down on the table and took a chair. 'Be much more of this for you now. Relaxing. Enjoying the sun.'

'Helen Kendle has a pen,' Holm said. 'Tortoiseshell, gold trim. Be worth a few hundred, maybe more. The type of pen you'd treasure. She writes in purple ink.'

'Nice.' Javed sipped his Coke. Gazed at the traffic. 'You're into pens yourself, aren't you? Must be, from the number I found in your drawers.'

'Sure.' Holm took a gulp from the fresh glass of beer. 'But not like hers. Hers is an heirloom or something.'

'This going somewhere, sir, because you're rambling. Of course now you're retired that's your prerogative. You can dribble too if you like.'

'I'm not retired.' Holm put the glass down. 'And I'm not at the dribbling stage either.'

'You're not retired? How so?'

'When I was at Jawad al Haddad's house there was a pen on his table. Tortoiseshell, gold trim, identical to Kendle's. Actually not *identical* – it was the same pen because I noticed the unusual purple writing on a pad he had there. Kendle must have been at Haddad's place at the same time as I was. She hid somewhere inside the house but left the pen on the table.'

'Hey?'

'It means she was in contact with Haddad after the plane crash but before the Pope was shot.'

'Are you saying she gave him a heads-up about Operation Trojan and he told Taher?'

'No. Taher's plans were way too complex to be formed on the spur of the moment.'

'What, then?'

'She was sent by Number Ten to try and negotiate.'

'But the Pope was shot after they'd met and Taher went on to fire another missile. Some deal.'

'Perhaps Kendle hadn't delivered on her side of it back then.'

Holm took another sip of beer. He worked through the possibilities, coming to the conclusion that there were two things Haddad would demand in return for either giving up Taher or calling him off. First, he'd want to be able to return to Saudi Arabia. For that to happen all investigations into his activities would need to be dropped, so something like a juicy new arms deal at favourable terms would soften the Saudi government. That would be a win-win situation for everyone because it would strengthen diplomatic relations, secure British manufacturing jobs and bolster foreign policy aims. Second, Haddad would want revenge for the humiliation he'd suffered and he'd want to avenge the death of his wife. Holm put his beer down and ran through the details with Javed. When he'd finished, Javed cocked his head.

'His wife. You're talking about Lashirah Haddad, the Saudi princess?'

'Yes. She was hit and killed, accidentally, during Weiss's mission to Italy last year. Rebecca da Silva didn't fire the gun, but Haddad blames her anyway. Richard Smith and Lona Castle were there too. In Haddad's eyes they're all culpable. Quite simply, the final part of the deal was for Kendle to make sure all four of them were dead.'

'But she could never deliver on that?'

'No, she couldn't.' Holm considered his statement, more clarity coming as he did so. 'At least not until Taher shot the Pope and set Weiss and the others up. After that it was easy for Kendle to claim the Trojan team had gone rogue and pressurise Huxtable to go along with it. Taher had wrong-footed us, but if Kendle managed to eliminate Silva then Haddad would call off Taher. Taher played us, but Haddad in turn played Taher.'

'I don't know.' Javed gave a half-nod, as if he wasn't fully convinced. 'There's a hell of a lot of speculation in your argument.'

'Perhaps, but have you got a better suggestion as to why Kendle visited Haddad?'

'No.'

'Kendle gave Huxtable a printout. I could only read the heading, but it was some sort of form from the CAA

– the Civil Aviation Authority. The letters CA48 were printed at the top.' Holm smiled. Looked down at his phone. 'While I was waiting for you I googled it. Care to guess what form CA48 is?'

Javed was on his own phone, as if he didn't trust Holm's internet skills. A moment later he looked up, mouth open.

'It's a flight plan,' he said.

Chapter 27

Silva and Itchy returned to Holm's flat and watched the news unfold on the TV. Large parts of Surrey and West Sussex were under lockdown and the public were advised not to travel. Commuters were told to stay at work so as not to clog up the roads and there was talk of a full curfew being imposed from six that evening. The official line was that an extremely dangerous extremist cell had been disturbed while in the process of carrying out a terrorist attack. One member was dead, another in hospital, and an unknown number still on the run.

'Blimey,' Itchy said. 'This could be it.'

Silva nodded. Holm and Javed had certainly flushed Taher and the others from their hiding place. Now all she and Itchy had to do was wait with their fingers crossed.

At half seven, Holm and Javed returned. Javed carried a couple of cardboard boxes up from his car and dumped them in the living room.

Holm smiled. 'I've been sacked.'

'Because of us?' Silva said.

'Because of me.'

'He's not making sense,' Javed said, 'but don't worry about that, we've got a result.'

Javed explained they'd discovered a flight plan filed by Jawad al Haddad. His private Gulfstream jet would be flying from Biggin Hill, the airfield where it was based, to Bristol. From there a second plan showed an onward destination of Dalaman in Turkey.

'After that, who knows?'

'So Haddad's doing a runner?' Silva said.

'We don't think the jet is for Haddad.' Javed glanced at Holm. 'It's for Taher. That's why it's flying from Bristol, away from all the upheaval around the south-east.'

'And they'll be waiting for him at the airport, right? The SAS, the police or even Special Accounts?'

Javed said nothing, just nodded at the TV screen. The sound was muted, but the news report was still running. Only something had changed. The scrolling headline bar at the bottom of the screen claimed that all the terrorists had been accounted for. While a strong police presence would be maintained to reassure the public, army and other units were being stood down.

'I don't understand,' Silva said. 'Have they got Taher or not?'

'They're letting him escape,' Holm said. He turned his palms up. 'Not my idea of a good resolution but then I guess that's why I'm out on my ear.'

Silva couldn't believe what she was hearing. 'How can this be allowed to happen? Taher has to face some kind of justice.'

'It's the least worst option. Taher still has one or more missiles. In return for giving them up, he gets to flee the country. Haddad has managed to persuade both sides they're in a zero-sum game. The best result for both parties is to abandon the game entirely. Neither wins but then neither loses.'

'Bollocks.' Itchy. Characteristically blunt. 'This can't be right. The fucker's going to get away and the victims are the ones who suffer yet again. Once he's safe he'll start over. More people will die. We can't let it happen.'

'I agree.' Holm pulled out a fold of paper from his jacket. 'Which is why Farakh went back to the office and printed off the flight plan details.' Holm looked at his watch. 'Haddad's plane leaves Bristol at ten tomorrow evening so we've got plenty of time.'

'To do what?' Itchy said.

Holm smiled. Turned to Silva.

'To get you into position so you can kill Taher,' he said.

–

When the missile had fizzled out into nothing but a drifting trail of vapour, Taher knew the game was over. They had one missile left, but the launcher had been damaged by a round from Holm's weapon. The lens that focused the laser pointer had shattered and the missile was useless without the launcher.

Saabiq wanted out and Taher couldn't blame him. The young man had never had the passion of Taher and didn't want to die a martyr's death like Latif. Perhaps he'd never had the commitment either and that was why he hadn't been able to operate the missile. And when the bullets had started flying, Saabiq had sought cover rather than stand and fight.

By some miracle they'd managed to take a green lane that avoided the roadblocks and made it to the station car park where they'd left a hire car as a getaway vehicle. As Saabiq ducked in, Taher had patted him on the shoulder and wished him good luck.

Now Taher was in central London. He'd taken a train to Waterloo and then a tube back west because he wanted to return to his flat to pick up a few things. He was certain the place hadn't been compromised and it was as good a place to wait for instructions as anywhere. As he rode the train along the District Line, he'd momentarily thought about staying on all the way to the end. The last station on the route was Ealing Broadway, just a short walk from Stephen Holm's house. It would be the work of moments to slip in and put a round into the MI5 officer. He dismissed the thought as quickly as it had come; Holm was nothing and revenge was for fools. He knew that now. He'd allowed Haddad to persuade him that going after Rebecca da Silva in the Philippines was a good tactical move, but it had instead turned into a strategic disaster. With Latif critically injured, Taher had lost the means to fire AirShield effectively. And with AirShield out of action he'd had to create a new plan on the spur of the moment.

He should have known better.

Once inside his flat he gathered together a few personal items including a small piece of rubble that had come from his parents' house in Saudi Arabia. There was a blackened scorch mark on one edge, a reminder of the flames that had consumed his mother and father and brothers and sisters all those years ago. Back then he'd stood and watched his family burn, utterly powerless to do anything to save them. The same sense of powerlessness overwhelmed him now, as if everything he'd done had accomplished nothing. The feeling was compounded when he switched on the TV news to see pictures of a little white Fiat slung sideways on a dual carriageway, its tyres flattened by a stinger device, the side windows shattered by a fusillade of bullets.

Never one for wasting energy on emotion, he nevertheless felt himself choking up. Poor Anwan Saabiq. Loyal but stupid, always under Taher's feet, asking pointless questions. Like a little brother.

Taher clutched the piece of rubble in his fist, squeezing until the rough edges pressed hard into his palm. Grief was replaced by pain and anger. The chunk of concrete had driven him to do the things he'd done. To kill and maim and terrorise. But anyone who thought that he'd become a terrorist to seek revenge was very wrong.

Taher moved to the window and looked out for the final time. Soon he'd be far away from this godless country, likely never to return. He regretted not being able to carry out his plans, but there were an abundance of targets overseas: British tourists lounging on foreign beaches; British politicians criss-crossing the globe; British soldiers stationed in so-called hotspots. He held the piece of concrete in his hand as he waited for the phone call he knew was coming.

'It was for justice,' he said to himself. 'Nothing more than justice.'

—

Late Thursday morning they picked up the van from where they'd left it at the retail park. The flight case with the rifle and all the other gear was still in the back. They drove west into darkening skies thick with rain clouds.

'A couple of hours to the airport,' Itchy said, looking at his phone, 'and an hour to get into position and set up. No rush.'

'OK.' Silva checked the dash and moderated her speed – senseless to get stopped at this point. 'Have you found a good spot yet?'

'There's a large car park to the south that will prevent us from getting close, but beyond is a wooded area. We'll need to leave the van on a country lane and cross several fields. I've checked the maps and the contours are iffy,' he said. 'Up, down, up, down. I'm not sure there's a clean line of sight, so we might need to do some tree climbing to get the height.'

'Not again.'

They drove in near silence, each with their own thoughts. For once Itchy kept still and didn't fidget; Silva wasn't sure if that was a good thing or not.

Bristol airport sat on a bluff of land south of the city. The runway pointed out to the Bristol Channel, the terrain falling away sharply, the sea grey in the distance. Silva had flown from there many times as a tourist and checked in at the main terminal building. Passengers for private jets boarded at the southern perimeter where there were various aviation companies, an aeroclub and a flight school.

They turned off before the airport and followed a road that ran down round the bottom of the single runway and back up the other side. Despite the rain, at one point several cars were drawn up next to the perimeter fence, a number of guys standing with long lenses aimed at the airfield.

'Plane spotters,' Itchy said. 'We'll stop round the corner out of sight.'

Silva nodded. Getting out of the van with a weapon that was over a metre long needed to be done discreetly.

Halfway along the runway the lane turned to the right, forging downhill away from the airport. Silva found a lay-by and pulled in.

'This will do,' Itchy said. They got out and stood for a moment. A hedge bordered a cornfield and on the other side lay a small copse. 'Beyond the woodland is one of the long-term car parks. It's about five hundred metres to where the jet should be parked.'

'Fingers crossed, then,' Silva said.

Javed had called as they were nearing the airport. Haddad's jet had landed at Bristol an hour ago and a new flight plan confirmed it would leave for Dalaman at ten p.m. that evening. Javed himself was making his own way to the airport and would park in one of the car parks where he'd keep a look out for Taher.

Silva moved to the rear of the van and, after checking no one was coming, she opened the rear doors and hefted out the flight case containing the rifle. Itchy scribbled a note on a piece of paper – 'Broken down, back tomorrow' – and placed it under the windscreen wipers. He clambered over the gate and she passed the case to him and climbed over herself.

Behind the hedge she removed the rifle and checked it over. She inserted one five-shot magazine. Itchy pushed the case into the hedge.

The rain clouds had thickened now and dusk was falling early. Silva took a look around. They had to negotiate their way along a hedge, but in this light nobody would spot them from the lane and the hedge shielded them from the airport. She tapped Itchy on the shoulder and they began to move.

It took them twenty minutes to get to the woodland, and by the time they did night had come. An eerie sodium glow came from the car parks and filtered through the trees. The light made the woodland seem all the more dark and they had to move with increased care. Eventually they reached a point in the woodland where they could clearly see several private jets sitting on a parking apron.

'That's Haddad's jet,' Silva said. 'The Gulfstream.'

The aircraft was the largest there and stood over to one side, closest to the taxiway. Light flared from the cockpit and cabin windows. The main door was hinged down, the steps extended.

'Waiting,' Itchy said. 'That's a good sign.'

'Perhaps too good. We'd better get set up.'

They found a small mound next to an oak tree. Itchy set up a tripod for his spotting scope and Silva fashioned a loop from a piece of cord and slung it over a branch. She'd need to stand to shoot over the boundary hedge, and the cars and the cord would steady the rifle while they waited.

'Four zero three.' Itchy looked up from the scope. 'No height difference.'

Silva dialled in the scope. With time and practice it was an easy shot for her; they had neither. Taher would appear for a few seconds as he walked to the aircraft and climbed the steps. The best moment would either come as he paused at the bottom of the steps or when he ducked at the top to enter. At this angle he'd be sideways on, but a body shot was still the best option. The .338-calibre bullet would cause massive internal damage, so a hit on the upper torso would end up being a killing shot. There were bright lights in the distance so Taher would be silhouetted. That could make it easier, but if she caught one of the lights in the scope she'd lose the night vision she'd built up over the past hour. These thoughts flashed through her head one after another. There was no emotion. This was a situation she'd been through numerous times. It was a process. You took account of the variables, made adjustments and subjected everything to constant re-evaluation. You went to the wire and in the final moment you executed the task.

Executed.

The fact she was killing another human being didn't figure. Certainly not this time. Taher was responsible for the death of her mother and half a dozen others in the attack in Tunisia. He'd brought down the 787 at Heathrow that had left another twelve dead. Given the chance he'd have murdered hundreds more with no qualms. She didn't know what motivated him, nor did she care. He might be convinced he was in the right and she was in the wrong, but she could argue the other way around. The conclusion had to be that there was no just war, only war, and all that mattered was the winner.

'You good?' Itchy said, once more picking up on Silva's thoughts. He had a knack for analysing everything about a long-range shot and that included the state of mind of the person pulling the trigger. 'Because this is it, right? You do this and it's over and done. You miss and there are no second chances.'

Itchy was right. If Taher climbed aboard the plane then he was gone for good. Whisked away by Haddad to Turkey and then onwards to a safe haven. He certainly wouldn't be coming back to the UK.

'I'm good, yes,' Silva said. 'Confident, no. I've got one shot and in this light it's tricky. Taher's going to walk to the plane and up those steps. I really need him to hesitate for a moment, because if he does the whole thing at a jog then the chances of hitting him are fifty-fifty.'

Itchy muttered something in agreement and then went silent. There was nothing to do now but wait and that was something they'd had a lot of practice at. An hour passed and it began to rain. The runway and taxiways glistened and somebody on the Gulfstream closed the hatch. For a moment Silva panicked, but then she saw there was no one in the cockpit.

'That's a good early warning,' she said. 'When the steps go back down we'll know Taher is on his way.'

Airport activity had died right down now, with only the occasional take-off or landing. Silva's phone vibrated in her pocket and she took it out. There was a message from Javed.

'Farakh's made it,' she said. 'He's in the car park and watching the jet from close to. Says he's about a hundred and fifty metres away.'

'Excellent,' Itchy said. 'He can give us a heads-up when he sees Taher.'

'Let's hope so.'

They settled down to wait again, Silva stretching every now and then to keep herself alert. After half an hour or so, Itchy began to fret.

'Where is he? Much longer and we'll have to assume the intel was wrong.'

'The plane, look.' Silva pointed towards the Gulf-stream. The door was opening, swinging down, the steps extending. 'He must be here.'

Itchy bent to his spotting scope and swung right. 'Doesn't appear to be anyone coming from the buildings.'

'Not the buildings, the plane.' Silva bent to the tele-scopic sight. Swallowed. 'It's Haddad. He's been on the plane all this time.'

The Saudi stood at the top of the steps, slightly stooped in the doorway. He appeared to be looking towards the buildings.

'Someone *is* coming,' Itchy said. 'But it's not Taher.'

Silva peered through the scope. A figure walked from the shadows to the foot of the steps, the light from inside the aircraft washing onto the woman's features.

'It's Fiona Huxtable.' Silva felt her heart miss a beat. 'Stephen and Farakh were right.'

Haddad descended the steps and held out a hand to Huxtable. They greeted each other and then stood talking. Huxtable's hand was raised, her finger pointing at Haddad. The Saudi stood impassive aside from a gentle nodding of his head.

'What are they doing, Silvi?' Itchy said.

'I've no idea.'

Silva squinted, as if that would make a difference at this distance. She tried to imagine what Haddad and Huxtable were discussing. Then a figure in a hoodie walked into the light and stood alongside Huxtable. It was Taher. Huxtable turned to him, her expression rigid, as Haddad gestured up at the plane.

'They're off, Silvi. It's now or never.'

Silva steeled herself. She moved the rifle a fraction to position the crosshairs on Taher's chest, but as she did so he turned sideways to say something to Huxtable.

'Don't wait,' Itchy said. 'You might not get a better chance.'

Despite Itchy's plea, she did hesitate, almost as if she needed a second to contemplate the journey she'd made to get to this point in space and time. For a moment the view through the scope blurred and she saw not Taher, but the boy in Afghanistan smiling at her from a dusty street in Kabul. Then a vision of her mother sipping a coffee at a café in Tunis, a smile on her face too. Silva didn't understand what the flash of memory was supposed to show her, and now, with Itchy's voice shouting in her ear – *do it now!* – the chance of searching for any kind of meaning was gone.

She touched the trigger and a blink later Taher slipped to the ground, his hand to his thigh.

'Point five low,' Itchy said as Silva ejected the cartridge and reloaded. 'Compensate.'

On the tarmac there was panic. Huxtable ducked down behind the steps while Haddad bounded up and into the aircraft. A moment later another figure appeared at the plane door. A heavyset man in a suit. He held a pistol in his hand. Huxtable waved at him to get back in the plane as she emerged from behind the steps and moved over to where Taher lay on the ground. She began to help him to his feet.

'If he gets on that jet then we're done for,' Itchy said. 'Take him now.'

For a second Silva considered Huxtable. There was a chance she could be hit. But then she wasn't an innocent bystander. She was part of this.

Silva touched the trigger again.

This time she adjusted for the fact she'd been fifty centimetres out, firing slightly high so it appeared as if the bullet would skim above Taher's torso.

It didn't.

Taher jerked back as he was hit. His arms flew up as he rolled over and Huxtable jumped clear. For a moment it appeared as if Taher would rise as his head lifted from the tarmac, his gaze focused towards Silva's hiding place, almost as if there was an acknowledgement that he'd been beaten. Then he slumped down.

'He's dead,' Itchy said. 'You hit him in the chest area. Massive damage. Good shot.'

Itchy's voice was flat and matter of fact, and he described the situation with no emotion. Silva, on the other hand, prepared herself for a rush of feelings to over-whelm her, as if killing Taher would bring some kind of closure. She blinked, half expecting her vision to blur and reveal her mother's face again, but this time there was nothing.

'Huxtable,' she said, focusing on the present. 'What's she up to?'

The director general, seemingly oblivious to the danger, had moved back to Taher. She looked up and beckoned at the aircraft. Haddad appeared at the top of the steps but then ducked back inside, replaced by the burly figure of the security guard. The guard came down the steps, bent, and hefted Taher upright. He dragged him back up the steps and into the aircraft.

'They're taking him away,' Itchy said. 'He was our passport to freedom. Without him we're as fucked as we ever were.'

The steps slid up and the door swung closed. Huxtable turned and walked away, disappearing into the gloom. In the cockpit, Silva could see the pilots reaching for switches, the lights dimming, the engines powering up.

'We could disable the plane,' Itchy said. 'Shoot the tyres out or something.'

'And then what? Call the police to come and investigate?'

'I see your point.'

The aircraft was moving forward and heading down a taxiway, its tail light blinking. It turned onto the end of the runway and paused.

'Last chance,' Itchy said.

Silva pulled herself up from the ground and shook her head.

'No,' she said. 'We're done.'

Chapter 28

Silva and Itchy waited for Javed at a pub in a small village not far from Bath. They were seated at a table nursing drinks when he came in. He wore a smile from ear to ear as he came across and patted each on the back in turn before going to the bar. He returned with a glass of Coke and pulled up a chair.

'Nice job,' he said. 'Just a few threads to wrap up and then we're sorted.'

'Sorted?' Silva said. 'Too right we're sorted. With Taher buried in an unmarked grave somewhere in rural Turkey, our chance of proving our innocence is gone. Sooner or later the kill team is going to track us down and then...'

'Kaput!' Itchy raised his hand and made a gun shape. 'Game over.'

'Exactly.' Silva reached for her beer at the same time as Itchy did. They clinked glasses. 'Cheers all round.'

'I saw Huxtable,' Javed said. 'Just as we suspected, she was in on Taher escaping.'

'And how does that change anything? Nobody is going to believe our story, and adding in the bit about where she allows one of the world's most wanted terrorists to go free doesn't make the narrative any more believable.'

'Possibly this will.' Javed had his phone out. He touched the screen and then turned the phone to show Silva and Itchy the video clip. 'Huxtable at the foot of the aircraft's steps talking to one of the world's most wanted terrorists. Looks pretty believable to me.'

'Bloody hell.' Silva put out her hand and took the phone. The footage wasn't the highest quality but Huxtable and Taher were readily identifiable. 'You absolute genius!'

'I'm always telling Stephen that, but for some reason he doesn't share your admiration.'

'Well he will now. Have you told him what happened?'

'No. I wanted to make sure we were home free before I started spreading the information around.' Javed took back the phone. 'I'm going to send it to a couple of trusted friends. If anything happens to me they'll share the clip to social media.'

'Can't they stop that by issuing D notices or something?'

'That might work for conventional media, but once this is on the web it will spread like wildfire.'

Silva nodded. She wasn't sure if Javed was right or not, but he seemed confident.

'Let's have another, Silvi.' Itchy was nodding down at their empty glasses. 'My round.'

Before Silva could say no, Itchy was up and across to the bar. He made an order and then disappeared to the toilets while the barman poured the drinks. In a couple of seconds he was back, crouching low at the table.

'The toilet window overlooks the car park to the side,' he said. 'There's a van, guys piling out in full kit. Balaclavas, Heckler & Kochs, the works.'

Silva glanced round. There were three entrances: the main way in, a door to the toilets and the car park, and a door out to the beer garden. They could duck behind the bar and go through to the kitchen, but by the looks of things that was a dead end.

'The garden.' Silva was moving as she said the words, pulling Javed by the arm. 'You too. If they find that phone we're fucked.'

Javed jumped to his feet and followed Silva. Itchy brought up the rear. The door led to a short hall and then to the garden. Solar lights hung in a couple of trees above several tables, but the garden was deserted. At the rear, a tall box hedge marked the boundary. Silva sprinted across to it and pushed herself in through the mass of greenery, the branches scratching her face and hands. Itchy came next, and then Javed, tripping over as he tumbled out on the other side.

They were in a field, its long grass grey in the night, the only illumination from distant street lights back on the road near the pub.

'How did they find us?' Silva said. 'They don't know what vehicle we're using and we've got new phones.'

'They didn't find you,' Javed said. He facepalmed himself. 'My phone was issued by work. They're tracked twenty-four seven. I didn't think.'

'Turn it off now and remove the battery,' Silva said.

Javed nodded and pulled out his phone. Then the three of them began to jog across the field.

'There'll be dogs,' Itchy said. 'We've got to get away from here fast.'

'Can we get back to our van?' Silva said.

'Doubt it. The pub is going to be crawling for hours. We need to find another vehicle.'

'Could be tricky. We're in the middle of nowhere.'

They reached another hedge and ran along it until they came to a gate. There was a lane beyond, the grey surface twisting into the darkness. Left was back towards the village, so they climbed over the gate and began jogging down the lane to the right.

'Won't be long before they get a helicopter up,' Itchy said. 'Thermal imaging.'

'Is he always this optimistic?' Javed said.

'Mate, I'll be optimistic when we're fifty miles from here.'

Silva glanced back over her shoulder. Beams of torch-light cut across the field as ghostly figures advanced towards the gate. She upped her pace, aware Javed was breathing heavily. They needed to find a car.

Ahead, a solitary street lamp marked a cluster of build-ings, a little terrace of post-war council houses. They slowed their pace as they came into the glow of the street lamp.

'Hot wire?' Javed said.

Itchy shook his head. 'We'll need to get a set of keys.' He pulled out his gun. 'Probably best if we forget about subterfuge and just get on with it.'

As they walked up to the first house, headlights cut into the drizzle from down the lane. Silva dashed into the driveway and crouched behind the car parked there. Javed did the same, while Itchy moved so he was shielded by a low brick wall. Silva saw him check his weapon and flick the safety off.

'Easy,' Silva said.

The vehicle cruised into the hamlet at walking pace and stopped. Silva kept low, listening to the engine ticking over, not daring to take a peek. She looked to her right where Itchy sat against the wall, gun at the ready. The car remained idling for what seemed like an age until there was a crunch of gears and it slowly moved off. Silva raised her head and watched the tail lights disappear round a corner.

Javed was on his feet and heading for the front door of the house, when Itchy called out.

'No, we're too late,' he said. He gestured to the lane. Torchlight flickered off the hedges. 'Let's go.'

He ran out of the garden and down the lane in the direction of the car. Silva and Javed followed.

'We could have gone in the house,' Javed said.

'Bad move,' Silva said. 'We'd have been trapped, and sieges never end well.'

After a couple of minutes of running they came to a T-junction. As they paused to decide which direction to go in, Javed put up his hands.

'I'm done in,' he said. He pulled out his phone and handed it to Silva. 'The video will be on the SD card. Take it and make sure it gets into the right hands. They're not looking for me so I'll take my chances with the cops.'

Before Silva could protest, Itchy grabbed her by the shoulder and pushed her to the side. Headlights were coming from the right, another car cruising slowly. He handed her the gun.

'I'll stand in the road with Farakh, you jump the driver.' Itchy moved to the opposite verge, Javed alongside him. He held up his hands to stop the car.

The car came round the corner and stopped a few paces from Itchy. Silva kept low and crept along the verge as Itchy walked to the car. He stood at the bonnet, hands raised. Silva moved to the door, keeping down. She reached up for the handle and in one movement wrenched the door open and shoved the gun forward.

The man in the driver's seat turned and smiled.

'Need a lift?' Stephen Holm said.

They drove along a winding lane back to the main road. Javed sat in the front passenger seat, while Silva lay contorted on the floor in the back; Itchy was beneath the rear parcel shelf. They'd gone about a mile when Javed nodded forward.

'Roadblock,' he said. 'Could be tricky.'

Holm peered ahead. The car's headlights picked out several police cars with their blue lights strobing. A couple of traffic officers in hi–vis jackets were waving down the traffic, while to the side several armed men stood with weapons ready.

'Nonsense. We'll just smile and show them our ID.'

'What ID? You handed yours in when you resigned, remember?'

'Shit.' Holm felt a chill as he slowed the car. 'All up to you then, Farakh.'

'Thanks.' Javed lowered the window as they approached the officers. He flashed his ID as one came across. 'Any sign? Because we'd like to know if we can call it a night.'

The man shrugged and then turned and beckoned at one of the armed officers. He came over.

'Yes?'

'Security Service,' Javed said, showing his ID again. 'Anything doing?'

'Got a developing situation,' the officer said. He turned and gestured down the road. 'They were in the local pub and now we think they could be holed up in a row of houses about a mile away. Just waiting for a "go" from Gold Command.'

'Right.' Javed nodded. He pulled his ID back. 'This pub, wouldn't be food there by any chance? We're famished.'

'There's a forensic team in there at the moment, sir.' The officer looked incredulous. 'Serving food is not exactly a top priority.'

He stepped back and waved them on. Said something to one of the other officers.

'Jesus, was that necessary?' Holm said as he drove off.

'Fooled them though, didn't I?'

Holm eyed the rear-view mirror as the flashing lights faded into the distance.

'I guess you did,' he said.

–

They were back in London in the early hours, Holm swinging into a cul-de-sac in Richmond at a little after four a.m. and parking outside a detached house with a VW Camper on the driveway.

'Wait here,' he said to Javed, Silva and Smith.

He approached the front door and knocked. A minute later the door opened, Bob Longworth standing there in a dressing gown.

'Stephen?'

'I need a favour, Bob. From one old timer to another.'

Longworth glanced at the VW. There was a wooden longboard in the back. Longworth was a surfer, still hanging in there with the youngsters, if not quite as trim as he used to be. 'Less of the old-timer stuff and I might be more inclined to listen.'

'It could take a while. Can I come in?'

It took half an hour to persuade Longworth that an old colleague's mad story might be worth risking his entire career for, but in the end he delivered. Holm went back outside and called the others in. Five minutes later he was driving away alone, hoping he hadn't misjudged his friend.

He headed for rural Berkshire and drove into the type of countryside where you'd find the house of a civil servant running a large governmental organisation. In this case the director general of the Security Service, Fiona Huxtable.

After three wrong turns, Holm finally managed to locate the place. He cruised past. A police car sat in the driveway, two officers visible inside. Holm took the next left into a lane that ran into dense woodland. He found a place to pull off the road and parked. More rain had arrived with the dawn, the daylight subdued. Holm got out of the car and pulled his collar up against the damp. He moved into the woodland, dodging between the trees until he came to a field. The rear of Huxtable's house was visible in the distance, horses grazing close by. Holm remembered that Huxtable had once told him how she owned a couple of horses, how she liked to hack out and feel the wind in her hair. It was just about the only time he'd got a sense that she was anything but robotic. The moment had quickly passed, Huxtable moving on to other matters as if she'd been embarrassed that her emotions had shown through.

He climbed over a post and rail fence and edged across the paddock. One of the horses looked up and gave a whinny before returning its attention to the grass. In the house, there were lights on, somebody moving behind windows in what looked to be a kitchen. Holm continued along the fence until he came to a gate. He climbed over into a garden with a large lawn and neat flower beds. The house itself matched Huxtable to a T. It was clad in red tiles, with ivy crawling up one side bordering leaded windows. There was a chimney either end of the roof and Holm had already pictured the kitchen: there'd be a large farmhouse-style table, expensive handmade units, an Aga at one end.

He moved over to one side of the house where a glass-panelled door led directly to the kitchen. There was, indeed, an Aga, and Huxtable was standing by it cooking drop scones directly on the surface of the hotplate. Holm tapped on the glass. Huxtable turned. Didn't seem surprised. She nodded and beckoned him in.

'Stephen.' She slid a fish slice in under a couple of the drop scones and flipped them over. 'You're just in time for breakfast. Be a dear and put the kettle on, would you?'

For a moment Holm wondered if this was some sort of trap. If Huxtable's cool manner hid the fact that there were sharpshooters behind a hedge ready to take him down in the same way they'd killed Simeon Weiss. He watched as she gathered up the scones and placed them on a plate that she had warming to one side. She looked tired. There was no artifice here, no concealment.

'How do you want to proceed?' she said. She paused long enough for the punchline to work. 'Jam, marmalade, or just butter.'

'Jam, please,' Holm said. He came into the kitchen and shut the door. Moved over to the kettle and filled it at the sink. Took it across and placed it on the Aga. A few drops of water ran down the side of the kettle and hissed as they hit the hotplate.

'You got past the police, then?' She brought the plate over to the table. 'I don't expect it was difficult for a man of your experience.'

'No, it wasn't that difficult. But then I guess you didn't intend it to be.'

'I told them I didn't want any hassle, didn't want them nosing round the place. I assured them I could take care of myself.'

'You're alone?' Holm remembered that Huxtable's husband was something in the city. A CEO of a large financial institution.

'Roger's away on a golfing weekend doing deals with his buddies on the back nine. The green ceiling, feminists call it I think. I've never been much of a feminist, never been much of any type of "ist" to be honest. I've just got on with the job, done my best, what I believed was right at the time.'

'This time it wasn't right, ma'am. Silva and Smith did the job you gave them because *they* believed it was right at the time. They didn't think the government was going to do a deal with Jawad al Haddad and then hunt them down with a kill team.'

'A deal?' Huxtable turned away from Holm to remove the kettle from the Aga. 'I'm not sure I follow you.'

'Ma'am, you're being disingenuous. Helen Kendle visited Haddad to broker some kind of arrangement. He would call off Taher if we helped him re-establish his relationship with the Saudis. In addition he wanted Weiss and the Trojan team dead.'

'Our backs were against the wall, Stephen. Downing Street, via Kendle, was calling the shots, and to be fair to the prime minister and Helen this wasn't about politics. They wanted to save lives. I'm sure you'll agree everyone acted with the best of intentions in what was a critical situation.'

'No, I don't agree. Taher nearly brought down another aircraft. Some deal.'

'Haddad required a lot from us, and even when we gave him what he wanted he still had to convince Taher. In the end he only managed to do that once Taher's options had run out.' Huxtable smiled. 'That, of course, was down to you. Stephen Holm the hero once again. Of course the work of the Security Service has to remain classified, but I'm sure you'll receive some sort of official recognition.'

'Don't patronise me.'

'I'm not. I know your true abilities and they are rather limited. You're good in the field but you'll never get your head around the geopolitical nuances. You see, once this is over, we'll see to it that Haddad will be back in favour with the Saudi government and he'll see to it that they continue to do deals with us rather than with the Chinese. Little by little we'll steer them round to our way of thinking. We press them on human rights and encourage them to make changes. Countless lives are improved, even saved, as we influence the way they develop.'

'Are you sure it isn't the other way round?'

'Enough, Stephen. Face the facts. We decided to sacrifice a handful of lives to save hundreds.'

'Simeon Weiss, Rebecca da Silva, Richard Smith and Lona Castle. Say their names, ma'am.'

'It was the best solution. It appeased the public's desire to see somebody punished for the attack on the Pope, and if it gave Haddad what he wanted at the same time then what difference did it make? I repeat, it was a handful of lives, no more.'

'Taher probably believes in the same rationale. A few bombs, a few dozen innocents and he can prevent future wars costing thousands of lives.'

'Who knows, he could be right.'

'If we go down that route then we've truly lost.'

'The situation was impossible. Taher fooled us all – even you, Stephen. There had to be a quick end, and in the circumstances the rogue team angle was the best we could come up with. We had to stamp on the story that we'd sent agents out to assassinate the Pope before the country descended into anarchy.'

'But Taher is dead now and Haddad is gone. The rogue team story is superfluous. You can call off the dogs.'

'I don't believe we have a body. Taher is still in the wind. Perhaps he was always in the wind, just a whisper on the breeze.'

Holm shook his head. Huxtable was rambling. It was time to play his ace card.

'I came here to give you a chance to bow out gracefully. We have a video showing you with Taher and Haddad at the jet. It's obvious from the footage that you've done some sort of deal with Taher. I want you to stop the hunt for Silva and Smith. The alternative is that we release the footage to the media.'

'I can stop that.'

'I don't think you can. Not this time. Your best bet is to go along with it. Showing Taher shot dead at the foot of the steps is a result, in my book. I can see the headline: *Arch Terrorist Shot Dead by MI5 Hit Squad*. The story is that you lured him out into the open. Works for me. With a little spin the crisis is solved and we can all go back to normal.'

'How do we explain the line we've already put out?'

'It was part of a ploy to catch Taher. Self-evidently it worked.'

Huxtable picked up a drop scone and buttered it. Smeared the surface with jam. She took a bite. Holm could see she was in two minds. She'd always favoured an analytical approach. The percentage game. You worked the numbers and took the appropriate action. Guesswork was out of the question. Relying on emotional input to provide guidance was for lesser people. If the death sentence hanging over Silva was to be lifted it wouldn't be because Huxtable had any sympathy for her predicament. This was no spur-of-the-moment judgement call, this was a computation done in an imaginary spreadsheet somewhere deep in her brain.

Huxtable finished the drop scone, picked up a paper napkin and wiped her mouth. She looked over at the Aga for a moment before turning back to Holm.

'It looks like I'm in a similar situation to the one Taher faced,' she said. 'In other words, out of options.'

'That's right.' Holm waited.

'I'll call Number Ten,' Huxtable said.

Epilogue

At a little after nine the next morning, Helen Kendle held a briefing for a group of lobby journalists. She told them that she was now in a position to reveal the truth behind a complex long-term operation run by the Security Service that had saved hundreds of lives. She revealed that for the previous six months the UK had been under threat from a terrorist group who had obtained a number of surface-to-air missiles. The danger had been so great that extreme – not to say unorthodox – measures, had been adopted by MI5 in the hunt for the group, and a specialised team deserved credit for working in difficult circumstances. Kendle was relieved to say that the hunt was now over and all the terrorists, including their leader, had been neutralised. The prime minister would hold a news conference later and, in an unprecedented move, would be joined by the director general of the Security Service. A full briefing document would be released following the conference.

The news broke half an hour later with the *Sunday Times* website carrying a story by the Insight team that filled in the blanks: The Heathrow crash hadn't been an accident, and the attack on the Pope had been carried out by the terrorists. Far from a number of MI5 operatives going rogue, the actions of the Security Services had almost certainly saved the Pope's life and prevented the downing of several airliners. Mass casualties on the scale of 9/11 had been avoided. A photograph on the website showed the body of a man the *Sunday Times* were calling Taher, lying on the tarmac at Bristol airport. Parts of the picture had been doctored to obscure the identity of a senior MI5 officer present at the scene.

Holm, back at Thames House, asked Javed about the picture.

'You sent them that?' he said.

'Yes, anonymously,' Javed said.

'Well I hope you're getting image rights. When Huxtable finds out you'll be for the high jump.'

'Helen Kendle asked if I had anything she could use, so I guess I'll be OK.'

'Kendle?' Holm shook his head and laughed. 'Very canny. It puts Huxtable right in the thick of it, the message being one of us goes down, we all go down.'

'Neither of them can stay on for long though, can they?'

'I wouldn't put money on it either way. Through a combination of arm twisting, the hinting of skeletons in the closet and sheer bravura, they could well see this crisis out.' Holm cocked a sideways glance at Javed. 'And you, you're learning. Sending the picture to Kendle was a smart move. She owes you one now. Bank that for a rainy day.'

'I will.'

Huxtable breezed into the situation room late morning. She'd come straight from the live press conference with the prime minster and by the look on her face it had gone rather well.

'Tame questions,' one of Holm's colleagues whispered to him as Huxtable did the rounds. 'In a pre-briefing the journalists were reminded that issues of national security were at stake. They were told that, despite the spin, operations were ongoing. Careless or overly critical questions could cost lives.'

After Huxtable had finished pressing the flesh, she came across.

'Stephen,' she said. 'A word.'

Up in her office, Huxtable's demeanour changed. She slumped in the chair behind her desk, looking done in. Holm wasn't sympathetic.

'You've managed to come out of this smelling of roses,' he said. 'Even though in reality you're covered in shit.'

'I take it from your attitude that you don't want your old job back?' Huxtable said.

'Not with you at the helm, no. Your morals are not merely questionable, they're non-existent. You and Kendle did a deal with Haddad and were prepared to see the whole of the Trojan team eliminated to save your bacon. Simeon Weiss paid the ultimate price for his loyalty. He's dead and Haddad continues to live in luxury. Where's the morality in that?'

'Morals? Stephen, we're talking about the Security Service. When you cross the threshold you bag your morals and put them in the bin. If you can't do that then you don't belong here. Weiss knew that more than anyone and had he been in my position he'd have done exactly the same thing. I'm surprised it's taken you so long to realise the truth.'

'Well, at least I have, which is more than can be said for you.'

'Despite what you think, I always tried to do what was right.'

'Really?' Holm gave a sarcastic laugh.

'Which is why, once this affair has blown over, I'll be standing down. It pains me to do it because I love this job, but it's for the good of the Service.' Huxtable bowed her head and swallowed before looking up again. 'What would also be for the good of the service is your continuing participation.'

Holm sat back in his chair. He hadn't expected this. He'd been going to rant and rave and then have the satisfaction of walking out once again, this time for good. Now Huxtable was falling on her sword and offering him an olive branch at the same time. He wasn't going to fall for it.

'Forget it. James Foster is cast from the same mould as you. I can't see things being much different when he takes over.'

'It won't be Foster. My recommendation to the prime minister is Claire Evans.'

'Evans?'

'The Security Service needs somebody with an understanding of the way the world is developing. Technology is playing an ever-increasing role in all our lives and Evans is an expert in that area. She has experience of managing multimillion-pound budgets and isn't scared to innovate. We need a new broom. Myself, Foster and Pelton, we're old school, and the cupboards could do with a clean-out.'

'I'm old school too,' Holm said. 'So perhaps we'd best leave it at that.'

He stood, walked over to the door and opened it. He was going to go straight out, but at the last moment he turned back, his sense of politeness taking over.

'I wish you well, ma'am.'

'You too, Stephen.'

A couple of days later, Holm was at home in his flat sorting out a stack of jazz CDs when the doorbell rang. It was a sunny day and he had the windows wide open so he went across and peered out, half expecting it to be Javed. He was surprised to see Claire Evans down at the front steps. He buzzed her up and showed her through to the living room.

'You've heard?' Evans said.

'Huxtable told me,' Holm said. 'Has it been confirmed?'

'All but officially, yes. I'm feeling a bit overwhelmed to be honest. It's a big step.'

'You'll do fine and you'll have a lot of good people around you.' Holm smiled. 'And if I'm not being too forward, I'd like to put a word in for Farakh Javed. He's a fast learner and has the right head on his shoulders. I'd mark him out for promotion.'

'I already have.' Evans returned the smile. 'But that's not why I'm here.'

'You want coffee?' Holm said realising he hadn't even offered Evans a seat. 'Tea?'

'After you've given me your answer, yes.'

'To what question?'

'To whether you'd consider coming back. You're too valuable to lose.'

'I'm done, Claire. I'm not sure there's any more I can offer.' Holm pointed at the mess of CDs on the floor beside his hi-fi. 'Besides, I've got plenty to do. I think I'm going to just enjoy my retirement in peace.'

'I'm offering you Special Accounts, Stephen. With the loss of Simeon Weiss I need somebody who knows the

Service back to front, who can use the tried and trusted methods when the new-fangled ones won't work. You may have heard talk of new brooms, but Special Accounts operations are always going to be old style. I need somebody who knows about surveillance and message drops, who can turn a foreign agent or interrogate a suspect, who won't mind bending the rules in order to do what is right. How about it?'

Holm moved to an armchair and sat. To say he was shocked was an understatement. He'd expected some kind of approach to lure him back to work, but had already steeled himself to resist. The Service was moving on and he was almost glad to be left behind. He glanced across at the pile of CDs. Tunes from another era.

'But who decides what is right?' he said. 'There's the rub.'

'Up to now Special Accounts has been answerable to nobody but the director general. With you in charge I see no reason to change that.'

For a moment Holm thought of his future life if he retired. There'd be afternoons wandering between cafés, evenings listening to jazz, frequent holidays. There'd be time to read more, do the crossword, watch TV, grow older living a stress-free existence.

In a flash of revelation, he realised he'd be bored out of his mind after a week.

'I'll make that coffee,' he said, pushing himself up from the armchair. 'And then we can talk about my answer.'

–

Silva spent three days winding down at her father's place. Danny had called him to find out how Silva was and her father had got most of the story from him. She explained the rest as best as she was able. He wasn't best pleased that she'd managed to get herself into trouble once more, but he was soon back to his usual self, giving orders as if he was a general and she was a lowly private.

His behaviour signalled a return to normality, but she wondered if that was possible for her. One chapter had been closed with the death of Taher and the others who'd killed her mother. However, Jawad al Haddad had escaped on his private plane and was in Turkey. More than ever he was going to want revenge and she wouldn't be able to sleep easy while he was free. Holm had mentioned something about 'charges forthcoming' and 'extradition', but Silva would believe that when it happened. Too often she'd seen political expediency take precedence over what was morally right; she expected little difference this time.

She headed back to Plymouth and Sean came to visit her a week later. She met him on the Hoe by the red and white lighthouse.

'It's been hectic,' he said as they embraced. 'Full on. This thing with the Pope and the terrorists, Jeez, the amount of analysis I've had to produce. And they got the man who killed your mother, but I guess you know that, right?'

'Yes,' Silva said.

'Exceptional work from your guys, they're getting a lot of praise back home. Being compared to the op that took out Bin Laden. The video of the hit is doing the rounds at the agency. Hell of a shot. Bit of a game changer too, I should think.' Sean paused and then kissed Silva on the lips. 'Anyway, you been up to much?'

'Not a lot,' Silva said.

Sean stayed for the weekend before heading back to West Africa via the US embassy in London. A few days after he'd left, Silva met Itchy down at a bar in the Barbican. They sat outside and made a couple of bottles of beer last an hour, kicking over what had happened and discussing the future.

'I'm thinking of using some of that cash to set up a painting and decorating business,' Itchy said. 'Big demand for it, good rates. Couple of hundred a day, I reckon.'

'Really?' Silva had seen Itchy's decorating skills in action at his place. She wasn't sure anyone was going to pay him two hundred pounds a day to wield a paintbrush.

'You want in? I could do with a partner, especially one with DIY skills like you.'

'Doesn't really sound like my cup of tea.'

'It's not mine either, to be honest.' Itchy stared down at his beer. 'Crap idea.'

'What about boats? Valeting, antifouling, that sort of thing? It's easier money than decorating and we get to mess about on the water.'

Itchy looked about as enthusiastic at Silva's suggestion as she had at his.

'All that excitement, Silvi, and we have to come home to this.' Itchy waved at the surrounding tables. 'I don't mean Plymouth as such, just the routine of having to get a job and earn a crust. I'd even consider going back in the army if they'd have me.'

'They won't.'

'I know.'

When their bottles were empty, they stood. Itchy was heading back to his wife and young kid, Silva off to her boat. As they turned to leave, a man of about sixty, a little overweight and balding, rose from a table close by. It was Stephen Holm.

'Sorry, but I couldn't help overhearing,' Holm said. He smiled and pointed at the broadsheet newspaper. 'I was hiding behind that. Old-school tactics. Never fails.'

'You should have told us you were here,' Silva said. 'You could have bought us a beer.'

'That bad, huh? Well I might have a job for you.'

'Your flat need a lick of paint, does it?' Itchy said.

'It does,' Holm pulled out a couple of business cards and handed them across. 'But that's not quite what I had in mind. This is more long-term. You'll have an under-standing boss, a high level of remuneration and a degree of job satisfaction unparalleled in any other field.'

Silva took the card and read the text.

Stephen Holm. Director Special Accounts. United Kingdom Security Service. London.

'You're serious?' Silva said.

'Yes,' Holm answered. 'Deadly serious.'